THE GREATEST STORIES FROM THE NORTHEAST EVER TOLD

In the same series

The Greatest Bengali Stories Ever Told (ed.) Arunava Sinha

The Greatest Urdu Stories Ever Told (ed.) Muhammad Umar Memon

The Greatest Odia Stories Ever Told (eds.) Leelawati Mohapatra, Paul St-Pierre, and K. K. Mohapatra

The Greatest Hindi Stories Ever Told (ed.) Poonam Saxena

The Greatest Tamil Stories Ever Told (eds.) Sujatha Vijayaraghavan and Mini Krishnan

The Greatest Assamese Stories Ever Told (ed.) Mitra Phukan

The Greatest Gujarati Stories Ever Told (ed.) Rita Kothari

The Greatest Kashmiri Stories Ever Told (ed.) Neerja Mattoo

The Greatest Telugu Stories Ever Told (eds.) Dasu Krishnamoorty and Tamraparni Dasu

The Greatest Marathi Stories Ever Told (ed.) Ashutosh Poddar

The Greatest Indian Stories Ever Told (ed.) Arunava Sinha

The Greatest Punjabi Stories Ever Told (eds.) Renuka Singh and Balbir Madhopuri

The Greatest Malayalam Stories Ever Told (ed.) A. J. Thomas

The Greatest Kannada Stories Ever Told (ed.) Chandan Gowda (forthcoming)

GREATEST STORIES FROM THE NORTHEAST EVER TOLD

Selected and edited by

JOBETH ANN WARJRI

ALEPH

ALEPH BOOK COMPANY
An independent publishing firm
promoted by ***Rupa Publications India***

First published in India in 2025
by Aleph Book Company
161-B/4, Gulmohar House,
Yusuf Sarai Community Centre,
New Delhi 110049

ISBN: 978-93-6523-678-1

1 3 5 7 9 10 8 6 4 2

CONTENTS

INTRODUCTION

This anthology is the result of a long engagement with literature from the Northeast. And yet, it would not have been possible without the many people who helped me, including the writers who generously responded to my call for stories. I have built warm friendships with some of the writers included in this anthology. But I always knew them first as writers. This is important, as we come from tight-knit communities where personal lives often blur the boundaries between friendship and professionalism. Their writing allowed me to see them beyond the notions of fondness and aversion that are usually in place when dealing with personal relationships. No writing is, of course, perfect. But the writers in this anthology have shown unusual courage in putting pen to paper. For many writers from the Northeast, the terror of the blank page also means overcoming many of the stereotypes associated with the literature from the region. In this regard, these stories transgress our current understanding of literature from the Northeast, whether it be in theme, form, or style.

As anyone belonging to the region would say, the stories they grew up with reflected the political, social, and cultural upheavals of their time. A history of strife and political instability has been a key feature of the region and has made its way into the literature. There are writers, however, who are challenging this narrative and they derive inspiration from other lived realities in the region. Conflict, in their narratives, originates from the more immediate effects of social and cultural practices in everyday living. Diasporic experiences and sensibilities, too, have impacted the way writers engage with the Northeast, particularly when such identities are cause for marginalization where belonging and transnational histories are concerned. Literatures from the Northeast have always had transnational moorings, especially in relation to other literatures and literary traditions from Southwest China and upland Southeast Asia. Until very recently, however, the relative isolation of the region from the rest of the country has played a role in the way its literature has been seen as being endemic to its geography—speaking only to Northeastern sensibilities and no other. This is an erroneous assumption which writers from the region have long and vehemently opposed. Writers like Robin Singh Ngangom and Mitra Phukan, for instance, insist that literature from the Northeast is a universal literature.

The stories chosen here include those written by established writers as well as newer voices. As such, these stories represent future possibilities as much as established traditions. Stories by newer writers such as Rishav Kumar Thakur, Ramzauva Chhakchhuak, Mainu Teronpi, Mayookh Barua, Gankhu Sumnyan, Saweini Laloo, and Lede E Miki Pohshna have been included to add fresh perspectives to literature from the region. However, in making these choices, it was ensured the stories complied with the key requirements of what a good short story should be. Like any other short story, the stories here represent an idea in distilled form. They also, as with most short stories, abide by the unity of theme, length (averaging about 2,500 to 3,000 words), and plot. Their infinite stylistic variety and the possibilities they present, however, show how difficult it is to club literatures from the Northeast under one umbrella. Nonetheless, an attempt has to be made to trace the historical evolution of the short story in the region. This is done so that it might enable readers who are unfamiliar with the region's history and its literature to grapple with the wide-ranging themes that are explored in this volume. But first, I shall digress into a short account of the narrative influences in the region's short story, which will provide some insight into the formal characteristics of the stories in this volume.

∽

The short story genre in the Northeast emerged from two interrelated phenomena—the oral traditions in the region and the rise of print culture. The former exerted, and continues to exert, considerable influence on the short story in the region. Storytelling traditions and forms such as the khanatang and puriskam of the Khasis, the gozam colo and cubun' colo of the Bodos, the Mosera Kihir of the Karbis, and the wari leeba of the Meiteis inform the stories of writers from their respective communities in terms of content, form, tone, and register. Relying on memory, community, and generational cultural traditions, oral storytelling often reaffirms group identity as well as everyday lived experience. Oral storytelling traditions also reflect socio-economic realities. With no perceivable authorship, oral stories belong to high and low, rich and poor alike. They encompass proletarian ideals of what the world is and lessons on how it should be. This is especially serviceable to people from working-class lineages and communities who, with limited access to modern education, rely on oral narratives to teach their children the ways of the world.

Print culture in the Northeast emerged from a contested history in relation to the region—colonialism. Colonialism brought about the standardization of languages, the effects of which are still felt today. It also introduced English as a lingua franca in the region. Most of the stories featured in this volume are written in English. As many have observed, the global reach of English is one of the reasons why writers from the Northeast choose to write in the language. The other reason is the entrenchment of colonial education and Christianity, especially in the hills. The proliferation of missionary schools in the nineteenth century meant that several generations of peoples indigenous to the Northeast were educated in English worldviews. As such, the early literature in the Northeast was tinged with an English sensibility. Because of this, many writers from the Northeast do not consider English to be a foreign tongue or a second language. 'I move in and out of both languages quite easily,' remarks Esther Syiem on her linguistic inheritance, that is, Khasi and English. Short stories in English written by writers who belong to the Northeast, however, were slow to make their appearance. The first known collection of modern short stories in the English language, *Stories of a Salesman* by Murli Das Melwani, was only published in 1967. It is in the local languages that the first short stories from the region were printed.

States such as Manipur and Assam have a long tradition of literature in the local languages, from well before the coming of the British. The significance of these literary traditions, however, was only acknowledged with the establishment of universities in the region during the mid- to late-twentieth century. At the time when they were written, these texts were only accessible to a select few such as the priestly class of these societies. With the arrival of the modern printing press in the region, literary works in the local languages became accessible to the civilian population. Local printing presses such as the Ri Khasi Press in Shillong established in 1896, the Molung Printing Press in Molungyimsen in 1884, and magazines like *Jonaki* in Assam were instrumental in taking the short story to the masses. 'Litikai', the first Assamese short story written by Lakshminath Bezbarua, for instance, was serialized in *Jonaki* in 1889. Dictionaries that were published and made available in local languages strengthened their standardization. The complexity of linguistic inheritances makes the translation of such stories into English extremely difficult.

The translatability of Northeastern lifeworlds into English is something that has captivated generations of writers and translators from the region. Like any language in the world, languages in the Northeast carry the cultural and historical legacies of the people who use them. Most writers, like Syiem, include words in their mother tongue when there are no equivalents for the same in English. This seems to be a sound practice where stories written in English are concerned. The inclusion of local terms and phrases along with words in English makes the language in which the stories are written a queer language, trespassing norms of purity, and inclusive of marginalized identities too. How this translates into the acceptance of queerness in day-to-day living, however, remains debatable as three stories in this anthology show. The other, more immediate form of translatability is the direct translation of stories originally written in the local languages into English. This appears to be a more arduous task since something of the original story always gets lost while being translated. That being said, something always gets lost in the translation of stories into print since stories are, by their very nature, selective regarding what about the Northeast is committed to remembrance. The stories in translation included here tend to avoid many of the pitfalls of translated works, such as clichés and archaisms. Even when the narratives are set in a certain time and place that are not of the present, the translators here have avoided hackneyed phrases and archaic language, giving the stories a contemporary flavour. My own inability to read the translated stories in their original language has made me realize the importance of translators who are rarely, if ever, acknowledged. I am grateful to Soibam Haripriya, Aruni Kashyap, Stuti Goswami, Ellerine Diengdoh, and Gayatri Bhattacharyya for bringing the stories from the Northeast to the world through their translations. They have achieved no mean feat.

~

Given the myriad literary influences on the short story from the Northeast, a definitive history of the genre is close to impossible since the short story has had an uneven genesis in the region. The history of the short story in the Northeast is also the history of places. Depending on the social, political, and cultural conditions of a locale, therefore, the short story in print emerged at different times in each of the states and communities. Short stories in Arunachal Pradesh, for instance, emerged around the 1970s, long after the first short stories had taken root elsewhere in the Northeast. Their history is also one that is marked by diverse entities where their production is concerned. Little magazines, newspapers, and independent publishing houses have all played a role in the dissemination of the short story in the Northeast. In this regard, three broad phases are discernible in the evolution of short stories from the Northeast. It must be mentioned, however, that these phases are not definitive but are introduced here merely as scaffolding for a genre that is characterized by diversity, historical and otherwise.

The first phase, starting from the late nineteenth century to the early twentieth century, involved the retelling of oral stories and fables. Premised upon an anthropological agenda, the stories of this period saw British and American missionaries transcribing oral narratives so that the philosophies of the communities in the Northeast could be made available in print and as stories. John Roberts's *Khasi Third Reader,* Mrs John Roberts's *Jaintia Folklore and Legends, and the History of the Khasi Religion,* Mrs Rafy's *Folktales of the Khasis,* and Mrs Eliza Brown's *Reading Book in Assamese* were some of the texts that reflect the proselytizing and anthropological enterprise in the region. Fables carried moral lessons and the stories were also influenced by biblical narratives especially since translations of the Bible were among the first books to be available in local languages. The canonization of folk tales began during this period. Many native writers, spurred by Western education, secularized religious texts. Lakshminath Sarma's 'Siraj', for instance, is a retelling of the Ram-and-Sita narrative within the confines of a dysfunctional marriage.

The second phase of the short story began in the mid- to late-twentieth century. This phase in the development of the short story saw the emergence of narratives from writers native to the Northeastern states. Stalwarts of the short story such as Mamoni Raisom Goswami, S. J. Duncan, and Murli Das Melwani published their writings during this time. The stories were realist in nature and influenced by the work of Western writers such as Anton Chekhov, Guy de Maupassant, and William Somerset Maugham. The horizon for what a short story could be had broadened from a mere transcription of folk tales, myths, and fables to an understanding of its form as a modern genre of literature. Ordinary folk were the subject of the stories and the themes included day-to-day life during periods of civil unrest which had affected most of the states in the Northeast, except for Sikkim. Political and civil unrest coloured the vocabulary and subject matter of the short story at this time. Women writers were especially instrumental in interweaving political turbulence with the intimate spaces of the domestic sphere and personal relationships.

The third phase in the short story from the Northeast began at the turn of the millennium and continues in the present. Published in 2005, Nini Lungalang's 'Child of Fortune' dwelt on the effects of violence on the lives of women and children in Nagaland. Temsula Ao's *These Hills Called Home* and Mamang Dai's *The Legends of Pensam* were also published during this time. Ao's stories combined her deep understanding of the Ao Naga storytelling traditions and modern political upheavals while Dai's *The Legends of Pensam* represented indigenous worldviews as valid storytelling modes in their own right. It was also during this time that a diasporic sensibility crept into the literature of the region. As the number of people who left the Northeast increased, their experiences in other parts of India and abroad also coloured their writing. Writers like Anjum Hasan and Prajwal Parajuly, whose stories are featured in this volume, complicate the idea of home and rootedness that were, until the present, a hallmark of the short story from the region. Concurrently, this phase also coincided with the rediscovery of folk cultures. Flora and fauna, rock and stone were considered to be at par with the human characters who populated the stories. Inspired by indigenous philosophies of the cosmos, nature was treated as an entity that possessed its own consciousness. The imbrication of folk forms and narratives with modern storytelling techniques resulted in writings that were not unlike magical-realism traditions. Unlike the nineteenth century, moreover, the stories were written by authors who are indigenous to the region. Emerging identities, such as stories told from the perspective of queer communities and marginalized ethnic communities, are testaments to the diverse forms and perspectives where literatures from the Northeast are concerned.

The storytelling forms and their historical evolution are discernible in the short stories of the writers in this anthology. The themes, ranging from political violence to friendship and romance, carry over the same concerns that have been there in the short story from previous years. The writers here, however, are also aware of storytelling itself being a theme in their writing. At least four of the stories in this volume are *about* storytelling as a method of communication—these are stories about stories. Kynpham Sing Nongkynrih's 'His Mother's Pork and Why He Is Not a Christian', for instance, is a meta-commentary on the art of storytelling. Ap Jutang, the irreverent protagonist of the story, recounts an experience about his mother's pork and, in the process, reveals the hypocrisy of organized religion. In a similar vein, Linthoi Chanu's 'The Bleeding Flowers' is also a story about storytelling. This time, however, the story is set in a camp for survivors of ethnic violence and civil unrest in Manipur. Both writers treat the storytelling traditions of their communities as self-reflexive narrative genres. Their writing shows that storytelling is essential for the articulation of memory and identity, especially if the memory is traumatic.

Mayookh Barua's 'We All Know Something About China' is a humorous narration of identity politics at the dinner table. Contrary to popular assumptions about wars happening 'out there', Barua shows that political conflicts begin at home. The family and the domestic space become the sites of intense drama for a young person who has just returned home from Delhi. The impact of violence among the communities in the Northeast is recounted in Mainu Teronpi's 'The Aftermath' and Sudhiranjan Moirangthem's 'News of a Beloved Friend'. While Teronpi's story ends with the redemptive power of song, Moirangthem's hints at the possibility of quotidian remembrance for people caught in cycles of violence over which they have no control. The sound of bells in Moirangthem's story heralds the disappearance of Manipuri men and combines the twin themes of memory and forgetting. For the protagonists of Mamang Dai's 'Brothers', however, identity politics is set in the more recent debates surrounding citizenship and the clash between insiders and outsiders in southern Arunachal Pradesh. Political unrest, however, is not unique to the Northeast alone as Saurabh Kumar Chaliha reveals in 'Intermission'. Confronting the idea of the death wish in the streets of Calcutta, the characters of Chaliha's story arrive at a belated understanding of what it means to be alive. Moving between past and present tenses, the story reveals Chaliha's experiment with style in the short story genre.

'The Song', written by Namrata Pathak, confronts mortality and its impact on day-to-day life. Pathak frames her understanding of loss against the idea of misrecognition in intimate relationships. Temsula Ao's

'Laburnum for My Head' is a touching story of an elderly lady wanting to create a lasting memory of her time on earth. Although the laburnum is a symbol of death and the fragility of life, it also points towards the unobtrusive ways in which life carries on in spite of loss. Mortality is also a theme in 'The Madness of Tree Ghosts' by Shalim M Hussain. This time, however, it is the forest that generates fear and death. Hussain's story shows that the land, for the writer from the Northeast, survives in a complicated relationship with the people living in the region. Hussain's story alerts readers to natural experiences that are otherwise absent from travel brochures. A similar sentiment is expressed in 'The Smell of Bamboo Blossoms' by Yeshe Dorjee Thongchi and 'For the Greater Common Good'. Steeped in indigenous lifeworlds, these stories show how marginalized identities contend with natural processes and forces that are beyond the reach of the living. The everyday is interwoven with magic and mystery in worlds where the dead live and, paradoxically, the living die. 'Riang Khangnoh' by Saweini Laloo and 'Black Moon' by Aisu Minam Yirang explore the notion of fear in the everyday through myth and belonging. In Laloo's story, the dream she has about a mythical being becomes the source of horror in the everyday. Yirang's story, on the other hand, looks at modern interventions as fragile buffers against age-old beliefs and practices. Oral narratives, in these stories, are seen as providing an identitarian mooring to the way events are interpreted and experienced by the characters. This is also true of 'Ka Diangtimai' written by Desmond L. Kharmawphlang. Kharmawphlang's reimagining of a Khasi folk tale allows him to examine greed and corruption in contemporary life.

In all of the stories introduced above, the everyday is the locus of horror, conflict, and melodrama. Gankhu Sumnyan's 'The Pay Raise' presents the complex entanglements of a woman who is compelled to interact with her office superiors for a raise. In keeping with the theme of the everyday, 'Dielienuo's Choice' by Avinuo Kire explores class in the Angami Naga society through friendship as a narrative trope. Contrarily, for Lede E Miki Pohshna and Rishav Kumar Thakur, the everyday also obfuscates desires that are unacknowledged in heteronormative settings. Written from queer perspectives, their stories—'The Lover of Stories' and 'Sacred Pool'—are meditations on the notions of sanctity that currently prevail in their respective communities. In contrast to Pohshna and Thakur, Janice Pariat's 'Boats on Land' explores queer experiences as events that occur away from the comforts of home. What is foreign, in her story, paves the way for a discovery of self that home does not provide. Anjum Hasan's 'The Question of Style' explores the limits of belonging through style as a theme of yearning. Clothes and hairstyles, in Hasan's story, are markers of difference. In Prajwal Parajuly's 'Making Amends', the humble Tibetan momo—which is now a ubiquitous snack in India—becomes a source of friction between a Nepalese woman and a twenty-two-year-old British tourist. Ramzauva Chhakchhuak's 'Home' narrates internal migration against the backdrop of the Covid-19 pandemic. His story explores the discrimination that most people from the Northeast, especially in the unorganized sector, face across India.

For the characters in Abdus Samad's 'The Cost of Hunger' and Bhabendra Nath Saikia's 'Rats', dehumanization precedes oppression and 'difference' as the characters are compelled to forsake their identities for ones that are imposed from without. Both stories confront notions of ostracization and what it means to live with dignity when it is a privilege that only a few can afford. 'Values' by Mamoni Raisom Goswami dwells on the incongruities of values that are held by characters who are treated as pariahs. Society, in the story, acts as a moral watchdog, ensuring that the two marginalized characters do not reconcile and remain independent in seeking what they want out of life.

∽

The stories in this anthology mirror the various cultural and historical legacies of peoples who have made the Northeast their home. They are true to the locale in which they are set and from which their characters emerge. Despite their differences, however, there are many ways in which they are also alike. Loss, longing, and migration are recurrent tropes in many of the stories present in this volume. As such, they expose universal undercurrents in their making. In this regard, short stories from the Northeast belong, as they have always belonged, to the world. I hope that the reader finds, as I have, enough pleasure in the stories to give them what they deserve—a place in their bookshelves, a home.

Rats

BHABENDRA NATH SAIKIA

Translated from the Assamese by Gayatri Bhattacharyya

All the women who lived in the huts rushed out. They tried to find out what exactly was happening. They behaved very much like a blind man resting with his cane propped up nearby does when he suddenly hears some commotion. His first reaction is to seek out and grasp his cane, and only then does he try to find out the reason for the turmoil. Normally, these women did not bother to find out where their children were or what they were doing, their attitude being that they would turn up when hungry. So, they did not worry. But today, as soon as they became aware of the tumult and confusion, all the women ran out of their huts, frightened and anxious. They began to rush around, each one screaming out her children's names. One woman could see her son standing nearby but this did not calm her anxiety. She went up to where the boy stood, dragged him out of the crowd of onlookers, and clasped him tightly to her. Only when her son was safe in her arms did she try to find out the details of what had happened. Within two minutes, more of the women had found their children, and the shrill voices that were screaming out their names stopped.

Only the voice of Moti's mother gradually got louder. And louder. Her high-pitched voice could be heard clearly over the tumultuous din created by the crowd. In the beginning, she had called out to her son, Moti, like the other mothers, and had run hither and thither looking for him. But, as time passed and there was no sign of him, she grew more and more panicky. She started running around anxiously, calling out his name in distress.

His companions said that Moti had been with them right there.

'He was here?'

'Then where is he now?'

'Are you sure he was here?'

'Exactly where, where was he exactly?'

She went around asking every boy and every girl the questions in an agitated voice. She was hoping to hear that Moti might have strayed away without their knowing. But the children told her categorically that Moti had been right there with them—in the place that was now full of heavy sacks, two and a half maunds each.

The open place abutted a narrow lane leading to huge warehouses. The narrow road emerged from another slightly wider dirt road. A long wall of corrugated sheets, marking the compound of a soap company, bordered one side of the narrow lane, and on the other side was this open space. A bit further on, this lane split up and spread out among the many large warehouses. These were the storehouses that fed thousands of people in the city. The relationship of these to the city was as vital as the relationship of a handsome youth to the horrible-looking entrails of his stomach. They were ugly, but inevitable and unavoidable. Numerous huge trucks roared into that narrow lane, carrying hundreds of tonnes of produce and food products. These they unloaded into the warehouses. Some of the empty trucks would then load up other consignments from the godowns to transport elsewhere. Most rickshaw drivers found it difficult to turn their small vehicles on this lane. The truck drivers alone knew what they had to conjure up as they manoeuvred their trucks within that cramped space. Sometimes, if one vehicle created chaos by not being driven with the requisite skill, there would be a traffic jam in the lane, and the filthy, stinking environment would be overwhelmed with the riotous shouting of drivers and their assistants.

The appearance and size of the drivers matched the size of their trucks. Indeed, it seemed as though the truck-building companies had taken the measurements of the drivers first, and then fitted the vehicles to suit their bodies! Their eyes were always red, perhaps due to driving through the night, or maybe because of something they had imbibed. As far as possible, these drivers preferred to sit comfortably and quietly in their seats and rest; it was the handymen, their assistants, who created noise and confusion. These handymen would sit on top of their loaded trucks, yelling at each other, trying to find out who was to blame for the roadblock. Sometimes, the traffic jam would continue for hours together. That narrow space would become overcrowded with trucks and vehicles lined up, one after the other, all the way up the main road. No one would agree to shift his own vehicle even a little bit to help break the jam. 'Why should I? Let them do what they like!' each driver would say. Each of them would leave his truck and go to spend his time in the tea shop nearby. Sometimes, the trucks would enter the lane at midnight, heavily loaded, but the warehouses opened their doors only in the morning. On such days, the area would become still more filthy and smelly and sometimes both drivers and handymen would sleep, like babies in their cradles, inside their trucks.

A peculiar thick, slimy green-and-black liquid covered about half of this open space. Originally, this was probably plain rainwater. But over time the liquid had got mixed with green moss, motor oil, and such other substances, and acquired this peculiar colour and consistency. When the small children got dirty playing, they cleaned themselves in this water.

The line of shacks built with bits of bamboo, straw, sacks, packing boxes, and so on, that stood on one side of the open space, had been occupied in the past by a few daily wagers employed to load and unload the trucks. But now the owners of the warehouses employed labourers on a regular basis, and no one from these huts got those jobs. So, they had left. Now, there were women living here with their children. There were no men living here permanently, and the few men seen around, at times, were not the fathers of these children. Most of the women, except a few like Moti's mother, were old. Some of them went out in the morning to beg, two of them worked in the hotels nearby, cleaning rice and grinding spices, and one of them kept herself busy selling snacks of puffed rice mixed with salt, oil, onions, and chillies.

But it was the children who helped the women most in earning their daily bread. They spent almost the entire day on the roadside, armed with woven bamboo baskets of various sizes and shapes. When there was no serious work to be done, they spent their time playing, screaming, and crying. But when the empty trucks returned after unloading their consignments in the warehouses, and when they were held up due to a traffic jam, and were forced to stop right here, then these children immediately jumped onto the trucks. Quickly they swept the floor of the vehicles, put the sweepings into their bamboo baskets, and ran home to their mothers. When these sweepings were carefully cleaned, the women would be able to collect quite an amount of rice, lentils, and other commodities. The drivers and handymen were quite happy to let the children do the sweeping because their vehicles were cleaned in a trice. And the boys and girls were happy when there were traffic jams. If the traffic jams were long-drawn, they were even happier, because they got time to sweep all the trucks, and every child got a chance to share in the spoils.

Each child had managed to obtain an iron rod, one end of which was sharpened. If loaded trucks happened to get held up in a traffic jam, children would jump onto the trucks and pierce the sacks with their rods. They would push their fingers through the holes made by the rods, and take out rice, lentils, sugar, and other such goods. If the handymen saw them and gave chase, they would laugh with great merriment and run away. But, after a little while, they would come scampering back again and fearlessly resume their work.

If the drivers and handymen happened to go to the tea shops, the children had a field day. They, therefore, prayed that there would be many more such jams. Whenever they saw two vehicles approaching from opposite directions, they would clap and shout, 'Come on, come on, get into a traffic jam!'

But today, there was no such big traffic snarl. What had happened was this: a truck, heavily loaded with huge, plump sacks of rice, was coming towards a godown. Another truck belonging to some cooperative store was leaving the godown loaded just as heavily with sacks of rice, lentils, sugar, flour, salt, and other food items. Both drivers were aware of the truck approaching from the opposite side but each hoped that the other would give way, allowing him to proceed. Therefore, neither of them stopped, and ultimately both vehicles came to a standstill facing each other. The two drivers started to quarrel and shout at each other. This went on for some time, and the children started yelling: 'Come on, come on, get into a jam!'

Normally, when only two trucks were involved, the drivers took advantage of the open space, and managed to use their skill to manoeuvre their vehicles past each other and go on their way. And indeed, after arguing for some time, the drivers did start to do just that. But they were both still rather angry, and saw no reason why they should give way to the other driver. After backing up just a little, with a huge roar and emitting a great deal of smoke, both vehicles again advanced. The children, seeing the situation, started screaming out their infernal refrain.

And the trucks did get into a jam. The trucker from the cooperative society did not give as much leeway as he could have, and the trucker carrying the sacks of rice was forced to move to his side of the road more than he would have liked to. The vehicle, loaded very high with heavy sacks, slid off the road and into soft mud. It leaned dangerously to the left—and, in an instant, the tragedy had occurred. As the truck veered to the left, one by one, many of the sacks it was carrying toppled over heavily and fell to the ground. The children ran away in confusion from the scene of the accident. Moti screamed in terror, and tried to run, but a sack fell on top of him and squashed him under it. Then another sack fell on top of that…then another and another….

A large crowd gathered to witness the accident. They started to look for Moti only after his mother had gone almost mad with anxiety and grief. One by one, the sacks were removed. At first, one of Moti's feet appeared. The foot looked quite normal and natural. But after the last sack had been removed, they all looked the other way. The only thing that could be seen was blood, a lot of blood. No one had the heart to even try to remember what the boy had looked like before the accident.

The police came. And for that day, all loading and unloading was stopped in the warehouses. It was getting darker anyway, and the trucks lined up on the main road to wait for daybreak. The women surrounded Moti's mother and consoled her while the police collected the boy's body and took it away to the police hospital.

Gradually, night fell. The two trucks that were involved in the accident were taken to the police station. The sacks of rice lay where they had fallen. A few loaded sacks had fallen from the other truck also, on the opposite side of the road, against the corrugated sheet wall. These were laden with salt and lentils.

Most of the children had become quiet and still, and were sitting despondently in the common courtyard, situated at the centre of their huddle of huts. The older ones occasionally talked quietly with each other. None of them could sleep much that night, and although they went to bed quite late, most of them woke up very early the next morning. Probably they had been awake since before dawn. The older ones came out at daybreak armed with their rods and bamboo baskets, and went up to the fallen sacks. They collected rice, salt, lentils, and sugar. But they were careful not to go near the sack covered with Moti's blood.

Later that morning, some labourers arrived, along with a few well-dressed men, and started removing the sacks under the supervision of the latter. It was not known which of these well-dressed persons took the decision, but it was noticed that two of the labourers took the blood-stained sack to Moti's mother's hut. She, who had spent the night sitting on her string cot, jumped up in distress, and cried out, 'No, no! I don't want it!' She clasped the sack, and started wailing in grief and helplessness. The labourers rested the blood-stained side of the sack against one of the hut's walls. When they let go of the sack, the weak wall trembled under its weight.

For quite a few days, Moti's mother continued to shout, 'Take it out, take it away. I do not want it!' The neighbouring women grieved for her, understanding her sorrow.

This woman had no parents. She had lived in her paternal uncle's house and helped with the cultivation of lentils and gram. A man had said he would marry her and brought her here, but he was not a good man. After Moti was born, hearing of a drug smuggling operation, he had abandoned Moti and his mother and gone away to try to make some money working with drug smugglers. Moti's mother waited for a long time for him to return. The drivers and handymen who came to buy puffed rice snacks at the next hut would say to her, 'Stop hoping he will come back. He will never return. And what sort of woman are you, sitting here thinking of him, when there are so many other men here!' The others would laugh when they heard this, and Moti's mother would get angry.

True, she was a bit scared of living alone. But she was afraid not of other people but of herself. Indeed, sometimes the natural needs and instincts of her body and age troubled her greatly, and threatened to overwhelm her. But she had always been able to overcome these feelings by clasping Moti to her breast. If, somehow, she could manage to pass a few more years like this, she thought she would approach the age of 'beggarhood'. She could then transform herself into a beggar by wearing dirty, torn clothes like the older beggar women. And even if she could not beg, it would not matter, as long as she had Moti with her. A son was a far more important possession than a husband! She just wanted the words 'Ma, Ma' ringing in her ears always; that was all.

But this sudden loss, this loneliness, and the empty hut almost drove her mad. She would sit alone, staring at the heavy, full sack and quietly weep her heart out. As time passed, all she would do was sit still and silent all day, not even weeping. Some neighbour would sometimes bring her a little rice and lentils gathered from the sweepings, or from what they had got from begging. She would cook them, but leave them untouched. Sometimes, she did not even bother to cook. The handyman of the truck from which the sacks had fallen on Moti, often came to visit her. He would bring her a packet of sweets, jalebis, and other sweets, too, from the nearby tea shop. But she would never talk to him.

More time passed. Moti's mother was always hungry. Some days the neighbours would not bring rice and lentils. Gradually, she started becoming tormented by hunger pangs. She had noticed as she lay on her string cot that some rats had started making holes in the sack leaning against the wall, and every morning, the floor near it would be strewn with a few grains of rice. Sometimes, her eyes would become moist as she swept away the grains of rice. One day, after lying for a long time on her cot, hungry and desperate, she slowly got up. She brought a bamboo tray and held it against the sack. Poking her finger through the hole made by the rats, she slowly teased out a little rice. The hole was small, and it took a long time to collect enough for one meal.

The hole in the sack got bigger with the constant poking of her fingers. Or perhaps the rats themselves had made it larger. Whatever the reason, after a few days there was quite a lot of rice strewn on the floor. Moti's mother did not like the idea of rats spoiling the rice, so she folded a piece of torn cloth, and placed it over the sack, and placed her bamboo tray against the sack so that it pressed against the hole. Later, she took to getting up whenever she heard a scraping sound. Maybe the rats had made another hole in the sack?

Sometimes the handyman would come and say to her, 'How can anyone eat only rice? Let me get you some lentils or something.' But she would refuse.

In time, the sack became lighter and thinner. It was becoming difficult to bring out much rice with her fingers, even though the hole had become much wider. After some time, Moti's mother could put her entire hand through the hole. Then, after some more time had passed, she found that she could find no rice even after pushing her arm in, right up to her elbow. Whatever rice was still there had become embedded in the stitching of the sack.

One morning, Moti's mother undid the stitches at the top of the sack, and, holding it upside down on the floor, gave it a few good shakes. She was able to collect sufficient rice for the night meal. She swept up the grains, and putting the rice in her bamboo tray, cleaned it properly. She then put the sack out in the sun. The side of the sack which had been leaning for such a long time against the wall now fell flat on the ground. In the evening, she took the sack, shook it out, and placed it on her cot.

After eating her meal that night, she lay down on the cot. It had become quite chilly, and Moti's mother always felt cold at night. In past winters, Moti used to curl up to her in bed, and she had not felt the chill. Today, too, she did not feel the cold seeping in from below because of the warmth of the piece of sacking. As she lay there feeling warm and comfortable, she felt something gnawing at her. It was as if the rats were biting her. She felt, in that instant, that if the handyman came to her and asked if he could get her 'lentils or something', perhaps she would say, 'Yes. Bring me some.'

If not for herself, at least for the sake of the Moti who would come along in the future.

INTERMISSION

SAURAV KUMAR CHALIHA

Translated from the Assamese by Stuti Goswami

This mindless destruction—wanton smashing of human skulls, setting trams and buses on fire, the sudden eruption of an irate mob, crowd dispersing in confused disarray, the siren of police vans emerging out of the din with batons and tear gas, the click of a bullet, the old man stumbling and falling on his face, the little boy hit by a bullet shrieking in pain on the footpath—why do I return to this place after all? There is no logic or meaning. And yet I return. As it is I am a busy man. Out of nowhere a group of young men bearing red flags attacks my taxi and in no time I find myself surrounded by thousands of sloganeering men—wild and agitated—ruining my day. The tram is forced to a halt. Petrol cans are aimed from one direction, bricks and iron rods from another; everything is transformed in the blink of an eye. The flames of the burning tram leap towards the sky, while amidst the fire and smoke, people are running in all directions. The shop shutters clang as they are hurriedly lowered. Someone suffers bruises on his head, someone else's glass panel shatters. In other words, chaos all over.

'Run, Moshai, run—' someone called out in the popular way gentlemen were addressed in this city. 'What are you waiting for—'

'My umbrella! Where is my umbrella? I think I dropped it somewhere—'

Sheila stopped abruptly and turned around.

'Umbrella? Are you mad?! Come on, let us go from here.'

Sheila held my hand and we almost ran until we found ourselves in front of a pharmacy. 'I know this place,' she said. We stood panting near the entrance. A young man, thin and wearing glasses, had almost closed the collapsible gate of the pharmacy when Sheila cried out, 'Wait! Wait! Just a minute. Please!'

The young man eyed us warily, and then muttered, looking inside, 'A girl and a boy.'

'It's okay, let them in.' A grave-sounding voice answered from within.

He opened the gate an inch wider and stood on one side. I hesitated. Sheila pulled my hand. 'Let's get in. This is no time for bravado.'

I followed Sheila, somehow squeezing through the narrow opening of the gate. As I went in, I shot one last glance at the scene outside: the tram was still burning; there were two other cars—diffident red flames leapt out of them too. The siren could still be heard. The *tong tong* of a bell sounded intermittently, low at times, high at others...the fire brigade...the hosepipes uncoiled. Like magic the wide avenue was deserted in a moment, strewn with stones and bricks and shattered glass... cycle and pushcart, somebody's sandals and somebody else's briefcase left behind in fearful haste. The only people around were the men in khaki and white uniforms patrolling the area. The houses nearby had terror-stricken faces with enquiring looks, peeking from terraces, verandas, and windows. Traffic was stalled. Somewhere someone was blowing a whistle. All other kinds of trouble seemed to have been erased.

Sitting amidst stacks of medicines was a bald man, garbed in dhoti and vest. The man, who apparently was the owner of the pharmacy, offered us a seat, looked at Sheila, and asked, 'Were you in the tram?'

'Yes.'

'Do you have any idea of what happened?'

'No...couldn't make out what it was...just that all of a sudden—'

'It is always like this,' the man replied. 'Nowadays, it is impossible to know who keeps waiting, for whom, and where. It just explodes suddenly! This is happening all the time...all over the country—'

Without wasting another word, he put on his glasses and concentrated on the newspaper. It seemed he had grown accustomed to such events. The thin young man, now seated on a stool, was peering at the goings-on outside through the cracks in the door. Glancing at her reflection on a glass panel which had an advertisement of a cold cream pasted on it, Sheila adjusted her hair and took out a handkerchief to dab the sweat off her face. Something occurred to the man, who was still reading the newspaper; he looked in my direction and said, 'It is widespread, you know—all over the country—this death wish.'

'Death wish?'

I was surprised.

'Absolutely—all at once you find a swarm of people rushing out of streets, bylanes, huts, and kiosks, and like mad men and women, jumping into the thick of fire and explosions, knowing that any moment might lead them to their end. What is this if not a death wish?'

'Oh yes, indeed,' I replied out of courtesy.

'Indeed! In fact, all of us have always had this desire for death—that is what the psychologist says, of course, not I—and yet it seems as if Calcutta offers all amenities for fulfilling such a death wish. Here in this city, none can predict when this wish will be fulfilled. Say you are taking a stroll and as you turn along the bend of a road, a long knife is suddenly thrust into your back, a stout stick hits your head, a bomb explodes beneath your feet—boom! And death wish fulfilled—' Taking off his glasses, the man paused and looked at us. We could not figure out what to say in response. He began folding his newspaper and went on, 'And yet it is essential to modify this theory a little, for this death wish does not relate to one's death alone; it implies a death wish for others too. In other words, if need arises, one would not only give up one's life but would kill you, me, or whosoever he can lay his hands upon. It is what they call the gift of death. You are following what I am trying to say, aren't you? Anyway, how will you go now?'

The young man reported that one or two people could be seen cautiously tracing their steps on the road; there were a few odd cars, too. Once we managed to pass through this area, we could easily find a taxi at Madan Street. We remained seated for another five minutes, after which we thanked the gentleman and the young man and cautiously stepped out. The road was deserted. Across from the pharmacy there stood a lone constable, baton in hand, constantly looking up at the terraces…anxious (who knows from which direction an acid bulb might fly towards him and burst on his head), two cars zoomed past; one had 'PRESS' written on its windscreen; on a piece of paper glued to the other vehicle's glass, somebody had written: 'EMERGENCY!' 'Emergency! Emergency!'—I was annoyed. 'This bloody city of yours is perennially in a state of emergency—what is this emergency for? And why? What do they mean by emergency?'

'Bah! As if you don't know what emergency means; birth, death, marriage…' Sheila said.

'Oh yes! Somewhere another baby is born. That is what you mean, don't you? But this is happening all the time in this country, people spilling over…is this an emergency? Someone is dying. The auspicious moment for someone's marriage has passed. Are these—?'

'Ah! You need not rattle off. Just see how we can safely reach the end of this road.' Sheila sounded a little annoyed. 'It is so tough being with you—honestly—you have no interest in knowing a single street, and yet you are criticizing this city all the time!'

We were now walking fast, keeping ourselves close to the shops with downed shutters. Sheila was out of breath; wiping her sweat constantly with her handkerchief, she went on, 'And if you hate this city so much, why do you return? I have never made you promise that each time you are travelling to or from Delhi you would halt at Calcutta to meet me—you can directly go from Guwahati to Delhi! Till today I have not been able to acquaint you with a single street, let alone a single tram schedule. All the time I have to take you to different places. Why do you keep coming here needlessly? Now I cannot get my work done either.'

Sheila was indeed a busy person. She had to go to Chowringhee to buy tickets for the evening show; after that she had to buy a bottle of perfume from some shop at Park Street (they said this fragrance could not be found elsewhere), and then milkshake at the wonderful shop they had discovered that day....

Later that night, seated in a taxi before the cinema hall, I was clueless as Sheila gave the driver the necessary directions. As the taxi went through an unfamiliar road, leaving the sparkling neon-lit faces of the city behind, I thrust my face out of the taxi window.

'What a fantastic place!'

The car picked up speed as a soothing breeze wafted through the night. It was a smooth, broad avenue, deserted, as though this was not Calcutta after all—no chaos, no rumbling trams or buses, no hawkers' cries, no political sloganeering, no beggar, nor any refugee; just trees on either side...enormous trees shielded behind which were houses with spacious compounds, where well-bred children played and families took group photographs, well-maintained lawns with houses in their midst and cars parked on porches; occasionally a car sped past us immersed in its own rhythm; the streets were clean and empty beneath the tall fluorescent lights; there was such peace, such solitude...it seemed quite a cultured and civilized place! Seated beside me, Sheila turned towards me.

I asked the driver, 'Sardarji, which road is this?'

Sheila chirped in, 'This is probably Aamir Ali Abhinyu—'

The Punjabi driver looked at me for an instant and nodded, saying, 'Should be Syed Aamir Ali Avenue—'

'Aamir Ali Avenue...is this Calcutta for real? Hmm, if I were to stay back then this part of the city won't be too ba—' I casually remarked. 'Really, if I could build a house here—'

For a fleeting moment, Sheila looked at me, and then turned her face away.

'You will build your house here?' Her voice was eager and uncertain.

I smiled. 'Here? Well, well, I stay at a hotel in Surya Street, I travel in overcrowded trains; let me arrange a plot of land in Guwahati first—'

'You will buy land in Guwahati?' Sheila asked.

'Yes, it will happen sometime...who knows?' I replied. 'Life is long after all...I shall live long...there will be enough time.'

Feigning concern, Sheila casually asked, 'What if your death wish overwhelms you suddenly?'

'Death wish?' I looked into her eyes. 'Are you out of your mind!'

Sheila knew this was not the time for psychology—not even in this city. She was probably surprised at my desire to live here. She knew that spending even a single night in Calcutta makes me want to run away—the cruelty, the garbage, the muck, the stench, the sorrow, the poverty, the teeming crowds, the lakhs of people stashed in trams and buses, hanging on for dear life...a dhoti undone, sandals flung away, tempers frayed...no one has time for others. Emergency! Emergency! All the time!

One felt stifled while cutting across overcrowded streets; it was impossible to walk on the pavements during daytime—the beggar, the emaciated, the jobless, the hawker, the ruffian, the sloganeer, and the family of refugees—all perform their daily rites on the pavement. At night, the same pavements are carpeted with thousands of sleeping figures—homeless men, women, and children; there are people teeming all over—cinema, theatre, roads, restaurants, offices, football fields; the deceit that awaits you at every step, the chaos, the confusion, the curses flung, the foreheads creased ceaselessly, the mood that is eternally sour—what a beastly, uncivilized city! I wonder how so many multitudes can spend their lifetimes here...is this a place where humans survive? On my journeys to and from Delhi I have somehow managed to spend a night or two here—as what they call an intermission—and then hastened away—

'Who knew such a place as Aamir Ali Avenue lay hidden amidst this greenery?' I said, immersed in my thoughts.

'Why not?' Sheila replied in a complaining tone. 'You get down at Sealdah and get on board at Howrah, you get down at Howrah and rush to Sealdah—travelling all the while in the dirtiest of places. And then you are complaining all the time. How many times have I told you, stay back for a few days, then I can show you so many places, I know you would love them. I know that—'

Sheila got down in front of the girls' hostel. 'You need not get down,' she said. 'Go back to your hotel in this taxi itself—as it is you don't know these places—'

'Wait—let me get down—'

'No no,' Sheila forbade me. 'It is already late; you need not roam about enquiring whoever you meet about trams and buses—return in this taxi itself—'

'Hey! Who do you think I am?'

I got down from the taxi quickly and tried to peer at the meter.

'Why are you behaving like this?' Sheila asked, suddenly seeming preoccupied. 'Even I am late—I don't know what I will get to hear at the hostel tonight—please go back in this taxi itself, Lakhi dear—'

Sheila bit her tongue.

I was silenced. It was the first time I had heard her say this. In those few minutes of silence, I became aware of a radio playing somewhere inside the hostel, sitar notes wafting *tung tang* in the air; somewhere far off on an empty road a rickshaw passed by, sounding *thung thang* across the night. I looked meekly in her direction, and without a word, got into the taxi.

'Take Saab to Sealdah, okay?' Sheila directed the taxi driver. All this while the driver had remained silent, staring glumly ahead, the car engine running. He nodded and laid his hand on the gear. Suddenly I was broken out of my reverie; I saw the familiar silhouette of the hostel receding into the distance and hurriedly called out, 'I'll come tomorrow.'

'Okay but come after five. I will go with Shipra and the others to Bhawanipur again tomorrow morning. Remember, after five.'

A thin sliver of excitement was now running through my mind. The taxi arrived at the turning of CIT Road, and I said, 'Sardarji, please stop the car.'

I got down, paid the fare, and asked, 'The Number 20 goes to Sealdah right?'

'Yes, sir.'

I jumped onto the tram. There was no specific reason really. It was just that I was happy, ecstatic, perhaps a little obstinate too. What did she think of me? Was I so worthless that I could not find my way to the hotel? Women would always be women! Along with the obstinacy, there was probably an anticipation too...of something that couldn't be seen from a car but could be seen from the tram window.

The seats were bare, the tram nearly empty. I sat near a window; the tram started rolling—*clang clang*. Shops were being closed for the night, the roads were increasingly deserted, occasionally another tram passed by the window. C*lang clang*.

Some shops were immersed in complete darkness while a few others were illuminated. People were streaming out of a cinema hall; I could see bluish sparks emerging from the friction of the tram with the cables... then once again stretches of deserted roads, a neon-lit hoarding twinkling in between...a pond covered in hyacinths; the roads seemed so broad at night! The tram lines, crisscrossing one another, glistened in the night light—these roads seemed a little familiar—*clang*—the tram suddenly jerked to a halt—*trring*—was this a stoppage? No, probably there was something ahead—I put my head out of the window. I knew this place: several days ago I had walked through this area unable to find a taxi; there was a big hoarding of Hamam soap, and just beneath it, written in Gothic fonts, there was S. P. Shaw (P) Ltd. Confectioners and General Order Suppliers. The window of this shop displayed trays of cakes and jam, jelly, butter, paneer; the shutter of that window, though lowered, was still open by a couple of inches and a light glowed inside. I saw a packet of Britannia biscuits on a shelf, sitting all by itself—funny and sad! A few pushcarts were leaning against the veranda (not seen during the day); there were also some labourers, sitting, gossiping, rubbing tobacco on their palms; someone had tied a mosquito net between the pillar of this veranda and the lamp post nearby—I was reminded of (sometimes I had even felt like having) the pakoras and brinjal fritters that a man sells under the blazing sun on a makeshift stall in front of this veranda. Beside him there is usually a man who has lost his legs, who keeps trying to drink water from the nearby hydrant with his cupped hands, and lies level with the ground most of the time. Sometimes a visitor to the brinjal fritters stall will throw something his way. Next to him stands a blind beggar with a baby in her arms and an empty tin can in her hand, the baby's belly absurdly bloated. There is also a coarse-looking man in shorts who sells calendars—sweating in the sweltering heat—shouting all the while in a hoarse voice, the same line every single day, a line that I never managed to comprehend. The earthen stove of the brinjal fritter seller was nowhere to be seen (apparently, he spent his night elsewhere as the veranda now belonged to the cart-pullers) and that packet of biscuits—ah! It was lonely tonight in this shop window, its companions long gone. Who kept an account of its fate? But then different people *had* kept an account of its fate in different registers—the manufacturer, the supplier, the agent, the shopkeeper—had properly noted how each of them would profit till the last penny and tomorrow, probably this packet, too, would no longer be here. Who knew if, having passed through an employee's hands, it would enter some housewife's shopping bag and then adorn a certain plate, on a certain table.... *Tling*...the tram started moving again...*clang clang*...death wish, ha! As though I were a little child who could not reach home on his own.... What did she think of me—light and shadow played on my face...on my face played shadow and light—Lakhi dear—it seemed, if one made an effort, one could probably roam about this horrible city even in high spirits...who knew, spend a lifetime even.... A solitary rickshaw passed by—*thung thung*—Aamir Ali Avinyu...fine road...*clang clang*...Lakhi dear...Lakhi dear.

The next morning, while travelling by bus, I read in the newspaper how the previous day an altercation between the Marxists and the socialists had broken out as they were taking out their respective processions. The altercation led to fisticuffs and soon enough, there emerged those mob-makers who seemed to always prowl the city, and that led to all that violence and destruction, leaving seven injured and three dead due to police firing. The protesting Marxists, Forward Block, and RSP had called for a bandh on the 25th, demanding suspension of all activity across the city in solidarity with their protest. However, political parties like the Congress, Jana Sangh, and the communists and others had opposed this bandh. As a result, fear and anticipation of greater violence hung in the air. Anyway, nothing to worry about, I would be in Delhi at that time—let them kill themselves as they pleased.... On the page in the middle, there was a photograph of a few young thieves who had stolen sugar and rice from train wagons. One of them, a young lad of about fifteen or sixteen, with a shock of unruly hair and wearing a tattered vest, seemed to be their leader. Sparkling eyes, alert, wary, the first flush of youth almost hidden by the grime that layered his face. I watched his face for some time. At Howrah station, I bought a third-class sleeper ticket for Delhi. On the way back, from the upper tier of the bus I was travelling in, I could see ladies' umbrellas hanging at a shop window at Dharamtala. I thought of getting down, but the bus had already started moving, so I remained seated…maybe in the evening.... At Gariahat I got down to meet a friend. I had lunch at his place and while returning, I fortunately got a taxi; it was almost 12.30. The sun was sweltering overhead. Opening the newspaper in my hand I had another look at the photo of the boy, the wagon-breaker. It surprised me that the boy's face was not skinny, nor was it broken, nor hunger-stricken; it was quite rosy and healthy—but why? The thought struck me languidly; it seemed he had no mother or sister to offer him a plateful of food in the peaceful ambience of home. The taxi slowed down suddenly; there was a crowd ahead, heated arguments; we were about to cross S. P. Shaw Confectioners when I sat up straight. The signboard was hanging angularly downwards, the brinjal-fritter man was nowhere to be seen; his stove lay smashed on the ground, the coals scattered; S. P. Shaw and other shops nearby had already downed their iron shutters. Somebody had broken the glass showcases, shards of glass scattered on the ground, and people were running helter-skelter. The blind beggar woman was nowhere to be seen, nor was the man with no legs; the pavement was overflowing with water pouring out of the hydrant; the calendar-seller's hoarse cries were silenced…ran away? Dead? Arrested? There was not a single shoe on the broken showcase of the shoe store. In S. P. Shaw's broken showcase, the wooden trays were mangled; last night's lone packet of biscuits had vanished. The police was trying to push the crowd back. A police jeep and a van; a traffic sergeant on a bike ordered something to my taxi; a sub-inspector attired in khaki shook his finger at the crowd saying something…the taxi driver changed gears, the car picked up speed; he turned around once and said, 'There have been student attacks on this road—this morning, a seven-party students' front was supposed to stage their protest—these fellows are simply having fun at their fathers' expenses—they should be silenced with Section 144—'

But I did not hear the driver…I simply shut my eyes….The strong noon sun seemed to have waned; it was suddenly evening…. In the darkness the taxi sped beside a waterbody (as if we were running away), perhaps a river, or some lake...the lights reflecting on the water were playing on the waves and growing longer and spreading out.

'Where have you brought me now?' I asked.

'You need not know,' Sheila replied. 'Just tell me whether you like it or not—'

Her face could not be seen in the taxi's darkness; there were occasional spots of light from the streetlamps outside, and there was darkness again. And yet, a new, mild perfume emanated from her dress and filled the taxi.

'Yes,' I said. We saw a couple on a scooter, probably Anglo-Indian, their hair and the girl's skirt rustling in the wind.... The image of the biscuit packet in the showcase tried to spring out before my eyes and then melted away. It had unsettled all kinds of records and who knew where it was now—passed through which hands—in some stolen-goods shop on some pavement...who knew, somebody might have already eaten it up, probably wolfed it down; probably it was a new, unfamiliar taste for that person. The scooter disappeared a little ahead and I said, 'Oh yes, it's good—could stay here as well, if there was a nice house, of course.' I paused for a moment, and then blurted out, 'Of course, my choice alone will not do—'

Fortunately, the taxi was swamped in darkness; we could not see each other's faces. I searched for Sheila's hand on the seat, as though by simply touching her hand I could tell whether she was blushing or had turned pale (of course, there was nobody else in the taxi).

'You know, Sheila, since yesterday the words of that pharmacy man have been running in my mind—that death wish he had spoken about. I do not know what the psychologist has scraped out of our souls, but the home that we are talking about, is this merely to die? Who wants to die right now—'

In the darkness Sheila remained silent. I became restless. I could not figure out how to make her understand that the pharmacy man was wrong; he had not understood why, despite all this, people had not been able to overcome their attachment to this city, why the creases on my forehead had suddenly eased out. I became anxious to look for her hand in the darkness; I realized I would not be able to say all this; perhaps, as always, I would end up lecturing her. A cool breeze sailed into the moving taxi, across our faces; right ahead an Ambassador slowed down, its red backlight glowing and fading away. Staring at the sight,

I continued, 'With this chaos, this rioting, this murder, wounds, and bloodshed that take place every moment, one feels as though everyone is hell-bent on dying, on killing others. These meaningless episodes are so widespread that each minute they emerge before our eyes in different forms. At that time it does not occur to us that behind this play of death lurks a fierce desire to live—all the chaos of this city, countless people hanging onto trams and buses and rushing to their workplaces—all around, from morning till night, in roads and streets and lanes and bylanes there is this great outcry of the struggle of life. And yet it does not occur to us that even *that* is an indication of the desire to live. Probably I have rushed into a crowd, knife in hand, bent on killing, but just then the rifle-bearing policemen arrive in hordes, and then it is my life, and maya or the illusion of remaining alive that matters most. And I run like a madman to save my life; I have to loot and rob anything that I get and gobble that up, for I have to live—just as today we cannot think of dying; there is so much for us to do, a strong yearning to live, to eat, to love, to build a home, wishes and desires of so many hues. And yes, this uproar that takes place each day does not imply that one ought to die or kill others; this uproar simply tells us that it is not time yet; there are many things waiting to happen, a lot to be accomplished; it is not time yet, to leave.... Howsoever, one does, in whatever way one does, it is time to be alive...ultimately...it is the time to live....'

VALUES

MAMONI RAISOM GOSWAMI

Translated from the Assamese by Gayatri Bhattacharyya

Pitambor Mahajan, the merchant, sat dejectedly on a tree stump in front of his house. He had still not taken off his muddy shoes. At one time, Pitambor had been a fit and well-built man. Now he was about sixty years old, and although that was not an age that could be said to be old for a man, all kinds of worries and discontentment had taken their toll on him. His face sagged, and he had a haggard look about him. His head always hung low; he could never look directly at the person he was talking to. From the way he held his head, it seemed as though he was scrutinizing the ground, searching intently for something.

A big teak tree had recently been cut down, and Pitambor sat on its stump looking at the children with their improvised fishing rods, trying their luck in the gutters that lined both sides of the road. The incessant rains of the last few days had made the entire village muddy and slushy. The sides of the dirt road had become covered with all kinds of vegetation, both edible and useless, and the frogs were having a great time jumping from one ditch to the other.

Pitambor was looking intently at one particular boy who was trying to untangle his fishing line from an arum plant, when a deep voice suddenly caught his attention. He looked up to see the priest, Krishnakanta, standing near him. 'Pitambor,' said the priest, 'you have been sitting there looking at those children for a long time. You were sitting exactly like this when I passed by some time ago, and you are still sitting in the same place in exactly the same way, staring intently, and with a peculiar longing, at those children. Is it because you do not have any children of your own? "Whose beloved child is being chased to the waters? Call out and bring him back so that I can kiss him!"—is that what you are thinking? By the way, is your wife any better? Is she able to leave her bed and do some work now?'

'No. How can she move about when her hands and feet have

swollen? I have already taken her to the hospital in Guwahati at least twenty times, but she is no better.'

'There seems to be no chance of your ever having any children of your own, then? So, your family will become extinct,' said the mischievous and malicious priest.

Pitambor sighed dejectedly. What else could he do?

Krishnakanta stood there silently for a while. He was dressed in an old knee-length dhoti, a tattered and worn-out kurta, and an equally old endi sador. His cheeks were hollowed out as he had only two front teeth left—all the others had fallen out—so that when he spoke, his face took on an odd and twisted shape. His eyes had a malicious glint and a sly look, and his balding pate only intensified his cunning look. He leaned close to Pitambor and whispered, 'Have you given any thought to what you will do if something happens to your wife? Have you thought about marrying again?'

Pitambor was about to answer when he happened to look up, and his eyes fell on Damayanti. She was the widow of the priest, Shambhu, who had died not too long ago. Everyone knew that she was a dissolute woman, and after her husband died, she had become the centre of attraction for all the young men of the village.

Krishnakanta called out to her, 'Where are you coming from, Damayanti?'

'Where do you think I am coming from?' she replied. 'Don't you see the endi silkworms in my hands?'

'So, you have started hobnobbing with that Marwari businessman, have you?'

Damayanti did not reply and instead started to squeeze out the water from the bottom of her sopping wet mekhela. As she bent down to do so, her blouse rode up exposing her slim, soft, and fair waist. Neither man could resist looking at this attractive spectacle, but the priest quickly averted his gaze. After she had squeezed out the water from her clothes, she calmly walked away, without even bothering to look towards the two men.

'They say that she has no inhibitions and even eats fish and meat,' said Pitambor.

'Yes, I've heard that too,' replied Krishnakanta. 'She has put all the Brahmins to shame. She does and eats whatever she likes and does not care for any traditions or rules. In the beginning, after Shambhu died, when she cooked fish for her two daughters, she used to go down to the river and bathe and then cook separately for herself. But now, I am told, she does not bother and even sits with the girls and eats the fish.'

'Yes,' replied Pitambor. 'I have seen her taking fish from the fishmonger in exchange for paddy.'

'Dear me!' exclaimed Krishnakanta. 'What is the world coming to! A widow buying fish in exchange for some paddy!'

'Softly, Purohit, softly,' said Pitambor. 'You do not need to publicize the fact that a Brahmin widow is eating fish. Such things are common these days, even in orthodox places like Dakhinpaar and Uttarpaar. And I do not really think it is such a sin. These old rules should be abolished.'

Staring at the departing figure, Pitambor asked, 'Bapu, what is the condition of your clients these days? Has it changed at all?'

'What a surprising question, Pitambor! You know everything and yet pretend to not know! Don't you know that it is because of the quarrel between my brother and myself over our clients that I am in this poverty-stricken condition?'

'It is mainly because your brother went around telling everyone that you do not know how to read Sanskrit,' replied Pitambor.

Krishnakanta jumped up in anger. 'Tell me,' he shouted, 'how many priests are there these days who can recite the mantras as clearly and correctly as Narahari Bhagabati? He and I studied at the tol, the school for priests, together. He was the one who got the caning, not me. No, no. The main reason for our poverty-stricken condition is the attitude of the clients—of those people who ask us to go and conduct the pujas for them. We priests, who know how to conduct the rituals and pujas, should not have been in such an impoverished condition. In the olden days, there was no problem getting at least one sacred thread, a pair of dhotis, and some money from each of our clients every month. But nowadays, everything is different. People want to perform the rites and pujas, but are unwilling to pay the priests. Only the other day, instead of utilizing our services, Mahikanta Sarma, one of your oldest clients, took his two sons to the Kamakhya temple for their upanayan, the sacred thread ceremony. One of my clients in Maisanpur, Surja Sarma, held the shradh ceremonies of his mother and father, together on the same day. People are gradually starting to ignore the Nandimukh shradh, the shradh ceremony of nine ancestors which is such an essential part of the wedding ceremony. And, of course, the smaller rituals and pujas like the naming ceremony, Basanti puja, pujas for blessing a house and purifying a house by holding a hom, organizing a purifying and sanctifying holy fire if a vulture happened to roost on the house...these have become things of the past. There was a time when a man had to undergo a purifying ritual if he lost his sacred thread. But how many Brahmin boys today chant the Gayatri Mantra!'

Pitambor had been listening to the priest's rant without saying a word. His mind was still on Damayanti and her lovely, silky-smooth back which had been exposed when she bent down to squeeze the water from her mekhela. He thought that he had never seen such a beautiful woman's waist or back. And it was not as though he had not seen or touched a woman's body. He had married his second wife just two months after his first wife had died, mainly because his first wife had died childless. But this second wife was a sick woman. Soon, she became almost completely bedridden due to acute rheumatism. Pitambor had taken her to doctors in Guwahati many times, but to no avail. Ultimately, the woman had become thin, more like a skeleton than a living woman. She lay in her bed all day, quietly watching her husband's behaviour. The man seemed to have almost lost his mind, longing for a son to carry on his family name. People said that he was waiting impatiently for his sick wife to die. After a few years, he had given up going to the hospitals in Guwahati, and had given up all hope for a son and heir. The priest continued to lament his lot in life, but Pitambor hardly heard him. His wife had signalled to one of the servants to give the priest a mora to sit on, but Pitambor was not even aware of the servant!

'You are so absent-minded, thinking all the time about how you don't have a son and heir. In fact, many people belonging to our satra have started saying that you are becoming unbalanced, that you are on the verge of insanity,' said Krishnakanta. 'There are hundreds of people in the world who do not have children. It is nothing so terrible. And why don't you think of what our gurus have said—that families, sons, and so on are, after all, transitory things, and hence valueless—simply manifestations of maya.'

Pitambor simply lowered his head in dejection. The priest noticed that his hair was greying, that his eyes were circled with small cobweb-like wrinkles. The man had become completely unmindful of how he dressed and his shoes were caked with layers of mud.

Krishnakanta was overwhelmed by a sense of pity and compassion for Pitambor. Just a few years ago, many of the older villagers had called him the 'gora soldier', he was so well-built, fair, and fit. Now, even though there was no dearth of money or means, the poor man had no peace of mind. His granary was full, but there was no one to enjoy it.

Then, Krishnakanta said something quite shocking. Before saying it, he looked all around to ensure that there was no one nearby. But the door of Pitambor's bedroom was wide open, and he could see the skeletal body of Pitambor's wife lying on the bed. Her sharp eyes, he noticed, were shining with a peculiar brightness—as though she was trying to find out what the priest was saying to her husband. Krishnakanta was astonished to see that a single glance, even from a distance, could be so keen and express such heartfelt sadness. Even so, he whispered to Pitambor, 'If you think that you can help me with some money, I, too, will help you get what you so desire.'

'How?' asked Pitambor. 'How will you arrange things?'

'Don't worry about the arrangements. There will be no problems,' said the priest.

'What do you mean?' Pitambor asked curiously.

'What I mean is that I will arrange matters so that when you meet her, there will be no question of her not conceiving. I have found out that she has aborted and buried the results of her illicit and guilty pregnancies four times!' Krishnakanta said with confidence.

Pitambor almost shouted, 'Bapu, are you talking about Damayanti?'

'Yes, yes. I am talking about Damayanti,' replied the priest. 'Our Brahmin girls have started going across the Dhanasri River to marry Shudra boys. Don't you know that the Gosain of Mukteswar Satra's son has gone and married a Muslim girl? It seems that our Gandhi Maharaj has shown this path—that caste and community do not matter. That is why I am thinking about Damayanti for you.'

Pitambor jumped up in excitement. 'What are you talking about?'

'If you so desire, you can make Damayanti your own woman.' Krishnakanta glanced towards the open bedroom door again. The eyes of the woman lying on the bed were wide open, and it seemed as though they were burning with a fierce fire. She was staring at Krishnakanta.

Pitambor got up and tried to clutch the priest's hands, but the latter hastily stepped away. He had just bathed and was on his way to the Adhikaar's house. He had been asked to bathe the image of Murulidhar in the Adhikaar's temple, because the regular priest there had gone to Guwahati. It was a very important duty, and he had to be clean and untouched by any other person, particularly one who was not a Brahmin. But the priest's words had opened an unthinkable world for Pitambor, and he did not know how to thank the man.

'So, Pitambor,' said Krishnakanta, 'it seems that you have been thinking about this for some time.'

A happy smile played over Pitambor's lips. Once again, Krishnakanta glanced towards the bedroom. The woman's eyes were now shut, but it seemed as though she was undergoing some terrible suffering and pain. Touching the priest's feet, Pitambor spoke humbly and pleaded, 'Bapu, do this for me. Everyone knows that she goes out at night to bury the things she aborts. I know it, too. But she is a Brahmin woman and I am a Shudra. If she comes to me, I will place her on a pedestal and worship her.'

A sly smile spread across Krishnakanta's toothless mouth. 'It will not be easy. I will have to negotiate. I will have to get the two girls to agree to it, and for that I will have to bribe them with sweets.'

Pitambor got up hurriedly and went inside. The eyes of the woman lying on the bed flew open. She had probably just shut her eyes and was not asleep. She saw her husband go to the small wooden box that was placed on top of a stool and open it; she also saw him going out to Krishnakanta again after a while.

'You will let me know everything soon, won't you?' he said to the priest.

Taking the twenty rupees from the merchant, the wily priest went away with a mischievous smile....

Seven days passed without any word from Krishnakanta, while Pitambor waited eagerly every day for him. He had seen Damayanti a number of times, making her way to and from the Adhikaar's house to deliver the sacred threads she spun from the finest cotton. It was only now that he had begun to look at her properly that he thought he had never seen a woman as beautiful as her. Her mother, they said, was from the village of Routa situated on the banks of the Dhanasri. After seeing Damayanti now, Pitambor came to the conclusion that the Brahmin girls from near the Dhanasri must be among the most beautiful women in the whole country. Her father, the priest Purnananda, had once lost a couple of his ploughing bullocks. At that time, he had had many clients in comparatively distant places like Maisanpur, Gargora, and so on. Searching for his precious bullocks, Purnananda had gone to the village of Routa by the Dhanasri riverbank. No one seemed to know why he had had to go so far to find his cows. But it was then that he had seen and married the beautiful daughter of Bhagawati of Routa. No priest of the area had ever before married a girl from so far away....

∽

It was the month of June, and the rivers and wetlands were overflowing with water. Both sides of the dirt road were full of shrubs and climbing plants that invariably came with the season. The road running in front of Pitambor's house was now covered with mud and slush. One day, in spite of the muddy road, Pitambor saw Damayanti walking along, plucking the edible greens such as the tasty kolmou or water spinach which grew in abundance on the roadsides during the wet weather. She had lifted her mekhela up to her knees, and was accompanied by her six-year-old daughter, who was completely naked. Damayanti's legs and hands were soft and shiny and healthy, like a new mango plant. Her hair, which cascaded down her back, was a reddish bronze colour, very much like the colour of rusted cannons, he thought. Oh yes, the exact tinge of an old, rusted iron cannon! Pitambor remembered the huge iron cannon that was found when they were digging a well. It was said that the Burmese soldiers had left it behind when they had to retreat. He remembered that a group of students had come after some time and hauled it away.

After looking at her for a while, Pitambor plucked up the courage to speak to her. 'You will get sick if you walk about in this foul weather, on this dirty, muddy road,' he said. She turned and looked at him, her face and eyes expressing a surprised curiosity. But, as earlier, she did not utter a word in reply. 'If you had only asked me, I would have sent my servant to get you all....' But before he could complete his sentence, she turned to look back at him again. Her eyes were blazing. Pitambor felt that her fiery look would burn him to ashes. He rapidly walked away and sat down on his usual seat, the stump of the teak tree. He glanced towards his house and saw that his wife had taken to her bed again. She had tried to get up that morning after a long time. Her wasted limbs creaked with a ghastly sound when she tried to lift herself up, and she felt dizzy, so she had to take to her bed again. Now she lay there staring at her husband. Pitambor gazed at her with a heartless and, at the same time, somewhat embarrassed look. It was time for him to go and give her one of her medicines, and he was quite aware of it. But he did not get up—he simply sat where he was, looking down, contemplating his shoes. There were only four people in their satra who wore shoes—the clerk of the satra office, the two sons of the Adhikaar, and he himself. He bent down and tried to clean his mud-caked shoes with his handkerchief, and then again looked up at the road to see if Krishnakanta had arrived. But there was still no sign of him. As he sat waiting impatiently, a bullock cart came creaking into his compound. His tenant farmers were bringing his share of the paddy they had cultivated. On any other day, Pitambor would have rushed over enthusiastically and counted the baskets of paddy. But today, seeing that his master was absent-minded and indifferent, the servant came and counted the baskets and stored them inside the granary. After some time, having rested and had some refreshments, the tenants came up to Pitambor to take their leave. As always, they had some complaints about Pitambor's tight-fisted attitude. But nothing moved him today; he sat where he was, silent and indifferent.

Glancing towards the bedroom of his house, he saw that his wife was lying with her eyes open. He noticed that someone had replaced a tumbler of water near her, and he remembered that the time for her medicine was past. But he got up anyway and was about to go and give it to her when he heard Krishnakanta's voice. Forgetting about his wife's medicine, he hurried to the gateway where the priest was waiting for him. His wife's eyes, he noticed, seemed to be unusually weak—the fire that normally gleamed in her eyes whenever she looked towards him seemed to be slowly dying out.

'Mahajan,' the priest called out.

'Yes, Bapu. Tell me, have you any news?' asked Pitambor.

'You will have to go to meet her on the coming full-moon night in the dhekal,' he said. 'It's located behind her house.' A dhekal is a room containing the dheki, a wooden instrument used for pounding and cleaning rice. The priest looked furtively all around and continued, 'I have found out that she is not pregnant at the moment. Her daughter told me this after I had bribed her with sweets. It seems that it hasn't even been a month since she terminated her last pregnancy. The girl is too young to understand these things. It seems that she had helped her mother by holding an oil lamp while the woman finished her job. She also told me that on this occasion her mother had used a spade belonging to a Brahmin boy from Chataraguri. This boy used to come cycling from his home to study in the college nearby. He is a boy from a well-to-do family, but of loose character. Instead of going to college, he hid his books inside a basket of rice in Damayanti's hut and spent his time with her. He would spend the money for his college fees buying things for Damayanti. The foetus she buried this time was this Brahmin boy's....

'Listen, Mahajan,' the priest continued, 'I have spoken to her about you. At first, she was quite angry. "That Shudra man," she said. "How dare he even think about such a thing! Does he not know that I am the daughter of a good Brahmin priest?" I replied that everyone knew that she was a Brahmin woman. But now that she had taken the sinful path, there could be no difference between castes. I also told her that no Brahmin would stoop to marry her now. They would simply exploit her body and then cast her aside like the useless husks of sugar cane stalks. I told her that you would marry her with all due rituals as soon as your ailing wife died, and that your wife is even now as good as dead. After you marry her, she would live a good and prosperous life, I told her. Do you know, Mahajan, when she heard all this, she went into her hut and cried her heart out, I do not understand why.... She came out after some time, wiping her tears and said, "I do not keep well these days, and it would be a relief if I could lean on someone's shoulders." I replied that it was not surprising that she did not feel well, after having had no less than five or six abortions within a short time; that if her case happened to come up in a panchayat meeting, no one would even consider going near her, because anyone found to be giving her even a tumbler of water would be fined a sum of twenty rupees!

'"What other option did I have?" she wept. "My daughters were starving. The Adhikaar's wife used to ask me to do small jobs for her in the kitchen. But now she says that I am not fit to work in her kitchen, that whatever I touch will become impure and contaminated. Earlier, I used to be asked to spin and make the laguns—sacred threads. But now the Brahmin families of this area will not allow me to make the laguns. They say that I am corrupted. The tenant farmers know that I am all alone with no one to look after me or my interests. So, they, too, have started behaving like monsters. What do they care that I am a lonely Brahmin widow with two small daughters? How can I fight them? I own some acres of farmland in Satpakhila, but I have not been given my share of five maunds of paddy ever since my husband died. I have not been able to pay the revenue tax for that land for three years, and the land could be auctioned off any day now. What was I to do? I had to think of feeding my two daughters…."'

Pitambor was getting more and more impatient. He almost yelled, 'Yes, yes, I understand all that. But what about me, my case?'

'Yes, I am coming to that,' replied the sly priest.

'She said, "He is a Shudra, belonging to the fourth caste. Having relations with him…." But finally, she told me that she would meet you on the full-moon night in the dhekal behind her house.'

Pitambor could hardly contain his joy. And taking advantage of that, Krishnakanta said, 'But you will have to give me about one hundred rupees…. Damayanti says that she needs a mosquito net, and the two girls will have to be given sweets from Bhola's shop….'

Pitambor hurried into his house and went to his bedroom. He walked up to the small wooden chest he kept in the corner of the room. His sick wife opened her eyes and followed his every move. Suddenly, he shouted at her, 'What are you staring at? One day I will come and pluck your eyes out!'

From where he sat outside the house, Krishnakanta could hear everything that was being said in the bedroom. He was a sly fox. When Pitambor came out and handed him one hundred rupees, he whispered, 'If necessary, give your wife a small pill of opium that night. She lies on that bed listening to everything and understands everything. It is better to be careful.' And laughing meaningfully, the sly Brahmin priest left. The woman on the bed simply shut her eyes.

Moments later, Krishnakanta returned. 'Damayanti is very keen on money. She acts like a tigress where money is concerned…. Never mind, you will be able to hold her hands intimately.'

The Mahajan felt rather guilty, and looked back at his wife. No, she had heard nothing. She was asleep. But her forehead glistened with perspiration.

It was the full-moon night of the monsoon month of Ashaar. Pitambor wore an endi kurta and a fine Santipuri dhoti. Across his shoulders, he had thrown a sador of fine cotton. After a long time he had brought out the mirror with the wooden frame and scrutinized his face. He had shaved that morning, and now out in the sunlight, he could see fine wrinkles covering his face, and he was somewhat disturbed. It seemed to him that the wrinkles were a net, and he was the fish trapped in it.

At the appointed hour, he walked towards Damayanti's house. It was located near the bridge on the Singra River, beyond the forest of teak trees. Very few people of the satra lived here, and it occurred to Pitambor that Damayanti was able to live as she did only because she lived in an almost deserted area. He looked up to see some mushroom-coloured clouds floating in the sky, looking for all the world like cannons. And that round moon! As though it was a deer shorn of its skin. As though someone had come and wrapped her dotted skin around the cannons. A skinned deer—her meat shaking uncontrollably without the skin to bind it in place! Lovely fresh vigorous meat! This skinned deer suddenly transformed into Damayanti. A completely nude Damayanti! There were her lovely breasts—like a pregnant goat's stomach. Her body was the colour of tender bamboo stalks, and her lips? They were soft and lovely like freshly cut mangoes oozing sweet nectar.... Pitambor could not stand there any longer looking up at the sky, weaving fantasies about the woman. It was deathly quiet and completely deserted. It was the night of the annual bhaona performance, and the entire village had gone to see it, which was why she had chosen this night for their first assignation.

He heard some jackals howling from the thorny shrubs nearby, as he walked rapidly to Damayanti's hut. He took off his shoes and sat on the plinth. A heady fragrance of champa flowers floated in the air. Damayanti lay with her younger daughter on a small cot, set between a basket meant to store rice and a heap of ripe jackfruit. The other girl was drowsily writing the letters of the alphabet on a slate in the light of a dirty old lamp with a broken chimney. From where she lay, Damayanti was watching the man. After a while, she beckoned him to come inside, and sit on a mora. A small earthen lamp filled to the brim with mustard oil burned nearby. For some reason, Pitambor was afraid to look at her body in the pale light of the lamp—he had a peculiar feeling that everything might be over if he did.... It was all a land of illusion, he felt. Was this Brahmin widow in front of him a real woman?

'Have you brought any money with you?'

Pitambor was startled into reality. He had not expected her first question to be so materialistic.

'Whatever I have is yours,' he replied and handed her a cotton bag. She took the small bag and put it inside a cane basket that was hanging on one of the posts of her dheki ghar. In the meantime, the girl who was writing the alphabet went and lay down with her sister and instantly fell asleep. There was a very low cot in one of the rooms that was used to store baskets of rice. Damayanti's dead husband, a priest, had been given those baskets during the shradh of the Adhikaar's brother.

Pitambor followed Damayanti and sat down on that cot. After a while, she came to him....

∽

Two months passed by. One day, after Mahajan had left her, Krishnakanta happened to see Damayanti bathing in the river, and made fun of her: 'Why Damayanti, I never saw you coming to the river to bathe after you spent the nights with the Brahmin boys of Dudhnoi Bongora!'

Damayanti did not reply. But the sly priest was not put off. 'I suppose it is because this one is a Shudra...?'

Again, she did not reply, but she suddenly jumped up out of the water and began to vomit violently on the riverside.

For some moments, the priest stood where he was, dumbfounded. Then he said, 'This must be Pitambor Mahajan's child then?'

Again, she was silent. But Krishnakanta continued, 'That is very good news. Poor Pitambor will be very happy; he was almost going mad at not having any children! Then I will go and give him the good news.' After a pause, he said, 'Listen, you must not worry or feel bad. Our Gandhi Maharaj did not believe in all this business of caste. He said that all men are equal and the same. Just you wait and see, Pitambor will marry you with all the proper rituals as soon as his wife is dead. I am sure that you are aware that the villagers were getting fed up of your way of life, and were thinking of having a panchayat meeting about it. I don't think you know that some time back, one of the things you aborted and buried beneath the clump of bamboos, was dragged out by a jackal and deposited in one of the priest's courtyards. Have you any idea how much that poor man had to spend to get himself purified—and for no fault of his own!'

Damayanti started vomiting again.

'Be careful, Damayanti,' warned Krishnakanta. 'Do not do anything this time. Even after knowing all about you and your repeated abortions, Pitambor is willing to accept you. If you do anything this time to damage the child within you, I tell you, you will go straight to hell. No one and nothing can save you.'

Krishnakanta then went to give Mahajan the best news he had ever heard. 'Pitambor, if she does not go and abort this child, you can be sure that she will not be unwilling to marry you.'

As usual, Pitambor was sitting on the stump of his favourite tree. He had not even bothered to take off his mud-caked shoes. Hearing the priest's words he started trembling in sheer excitement. He would be a father! Could it be true? Would he really be a father at long last? But of course, it must be true. The Brahmin priest himself had told him so.

He stood up, deeply agitated, and started walking about aimlessly.

Krishnakanta said, 'What is the matter with you! Why are you walking up and down like a monkey! But, of course, you have more than enough reason to be happy and excited! It is not a small matter to become a father after thirty years of waiting! Great good fortune indeed!'

Suddenly, Pitambor came and knelt down in front of the other man. 'Bapu,' he pleaded, 'please see that she does nothing to frustrate the dearest desire of my life. You well know what kind of men my father and grandfather were. Only a sufferer can understand the despair of a childless man! Besides, she is a Brahmin woman from a priest's family, and now she holds my life in her hands! What will I do, Bapu, what will I do?'

Krishnakanta lifted one hand as if in blessing and said, 'I will keep track of her and what she does, like a vulture keeping track of a corpse. Do not worry. I will also warn the old woman who helps in these dreadful things. But I will need some money to bribe her too.'

This time Pitambor did not have to go to his small box to get the money. That morning, he had sold all the fruits from his seven jackfruit trees, and the proceeds were still in his pocket. He took out the entire bundle of notes and handed it to the priest. Extremely pleased at the way his plans were going, Krishnakanta put his hands on Pitambor's head and blessed him.

Later, when Pitambor went to the bedroom, his eyes met his sick wife's. And, in spite of himself, their sad and desolate expression moved him to compassion. But the next moment, he regained his composure and forced himself to anger. 'Oh, you sick and barren woman! How dare you stare at me like that?' And he yelled out to his servants, 'Come, come! Lift this bed. Take it to the small room next to the dhekal. Come, hurry up!' Along with four of his servants, Pitambor carried the bed with his wife still lying on it, and put it inside a small, dark room without any sort of ventilation, near the room where the paddy and the dheki were placed.

Since his affair with Damayanti, Pitambor seemed to have almost forgotten that his wife needed at least some looking after, and had to be given medicines regularly. She was just skin and bones now, and seeing that their master did not bother about her, the servants, too, had started to neglect her. They were even careless about bringing her food on time, and often did not bother to bring her a glass of water with her meals, let alone give her the required medicines on time. The poor woman's throat would often become parched and dry with thirst, but she would not utter a word of protest. People said that she looked more like a corpse than a living woman. Even now, when her husband brought her to this small, dark room and left her there, she kept quiet. But surprisingly, even in the dank darkness, her eyes shone brightly, and it seemed as though she saw and understood everything that was going on more clearly than if she was out in the open.

The very thought of fathering a child made Pitambor delirious with joy. He lived in a world of joyful imaginings—the child in Damayanti's womb seemed to him to be already a boy, then a young man. In Pitambor's imagination, the boy walked along the banks of the Dhanasri, holding his father's hands! The ever joyous and sparkling golden thread that binds fathers to sons, seemed to stretch happily far into the distant horizon, where all was sheer happiness, where the ties and traditions of family were an unbroken celebration of joy....

Pitambor got a couple of his trusted servants to bring down an old wooden box from its perch, near the roof of his room. When he was sure that he was alone, he opened the box and took out a bundle tied in an old gamosa. In the bundle were a few pieces of ashthi—half-burnt bones—of his long dead father, and entwined in the dried-up bones was a chain of the precious poal or coral beads that were so much a part of the traditions of Assam. Pitambor remembered how his father, as he lay on his deathbed, almost choking with the effort to speak, had said,

'Keep this chain of my poal beads carefully. Your son will wear it, and then his son, and then his son's son, and so on. It will be the living symbol, the everlasting flag of our clan....' The old man died before he could complete the sentence. Pitambor took out this chain now, then wrapped the pieces of ashthi in the gamosa again, and put the bundle back in the old box. Finally, he called his servants and had the box put back in its place on the shelf.

Days turned into weeks, and weeks into months, and Pitambor became more and more impatient to hear some news. He had heard that a foetus that was five months old could not be aborted, and he calculated that it was now three months since Damayanti had conceived. As he waited each day without any news, the tension grew more and more unbearable. Each passing day loomed in front of him like a mountain he had to cross in order to gain access to his happiness and survive.

Almost every moment he seemed to hear the Brahmin woman's footsteps approaching him, and he imagined that she was whispering to him, 'Mahajan, hurry up and prepare for the wedding rituals. I can no longer hide my condition. Do you not see how big my stomach is? Hurry up. Get the wedding preparations ready.' Again: 'All those things about Brahmins and Shudras, about Hindus and Muslims, are just a lot of nonsense. We are all human beings, and you will find that the same red blood flows inside all of us.... Get the rituals for the wedding ready.'

She seemed to walk with ghungroos tied to her ankles and came to him with tinkling feet. He imagined her lovely, fair, and slim legs.... 'Mahajan,' she seemed to whisper, 'nowadays, I do not bother to go and bathe in the river after I sleep with you. Go, get ready for our wedding....'

Three months passed by uneventfully, and Mahajan still dreamt of walking along the Dhanasri riverbank with his hands on the shoulders of a handsome youth—his son!

It was the late monsoon month of Bhadra, and violent storms often lashed the villages. A storm had been steadily gaining force since that afternoon. Going inside to shut the door of his wife's room, he noticed that her eyes today burned more brightly, more malevolently than usual. As the storm raged, the lamps were blown out, and all other sounds were drowned out by its sheer ferocity. Pitambor shouted for his servants, but no one could hear him. The only sounds to be heard were the rumblings and thundering of the storm and of trees being felled, either struck by lightning, or uprooted by fierce winds.

There, another tree had crashed down. Which tree was it, Pitambor wondered. Somewhere in the distance, he saw a streak of lightning that had definitely struck another tree! He could hear the frightening sounds of the tree being split down the middle and crashing to the ground. He went outside to see which tree had fallen and how much damage this terrifying storm had caused.

In a corner of the grounds, the fruits of seven of his coconut trees had been heaped up waiting to be sold. Now he saw his servants running about trying to salvage them and store them inside the dheki ghar. Some of the fruits which were still on the trees thudded to the ground, having been blown down by the wind. No one could hear anyone else, but gradually the storm began to calm down, the rumblings and thunder died down, and heavy rain lashed the village. Lighting a lantern, Pitambor could now see the heavy raindrops; he imagined he could hear the tinkling sounds of Damayanti's anklets as her feet came towards him....

Suddenly amidst the rain, Pitambor heard someone calling him by name. Picking up the lantern, he hurried outside, and saw the priest coming towards him, completely drenched and shivering. Pitambor was frightened. Only some emergency could have prompted the man to come out in this terrible weather. Krishnakanta held an umbrella over his head, but it had so many holes that it afforded no protection whatsoever. His dhoti had been drawn up to his knees, and only a thin sador that was dripping wet, covered his bare body.

Holding up the lantern, Pitambor shouted, 'Bapu! What brings you out in this foul weather, so late in the night?'

Krishnakanta sat down on the plinth of the house. Leaning the torn umbrella against a post, he took off his sador and tried to wring it dry, and wiped his wet face with it. Then, pointing a shaking finger at Pitambor, he said in a choking voice, 'Pitambor, when your first wife died, were there three inauspicious stars in the ascendant, three puhkars? Three or four?'

'I do not remember,' replied the Mahajan. 'Why?'

'When three puhkars are found at the time of death of a person in the house, even the dubari grass dries up and dies. When your first wife died, there were three puhkars. And, as a result, the ill effects are still there. Everything is dead and gone!'

'What has happened, Bapu? What is wrong?'

'She has destroyed it, Mahajan, she has aborted! She refused to carry the seed of a Shudra man! She belongs to the highest Brahmin clan, a woman from the Sandilya gotra! She has spoiled your seed, Pitambor, she has terminated her pregnancy!'

As these words crashed into him, the youth holding Pitambor's hands let go and fell into the depths of the Dhanasri River. Who was it who had fallen? Was it Pitambor, or the young man? Dear God, who was it that tumbled and fell headlong into the deep waters of the river!

∽

Soon after this encounter between the priest and Pitambor, Damayanti heard a sound near her house in the dead of the night. Someone was digging something beneath the clump of bamboos behind her dhekal. She shouted, 'Who is it? Who is there?' and woke her elder daughter. The six-year-old girl and her mother stood near the window, listening. The sounds of digging came from the same place where the two of them had gone in the dead of night two days ago and buried that thing the woman had ruined. Mother and daughter had gone out that night and dug a hole with the spade the Brahmin boy from Chataraguri had given them. The young girl had shivered in fright when she heard the jackals howling nearby. And today, the unmistakable sound of digging came from that very same place. Thud, thud! Thump, thump! Standing near the window, the two of them saw a lantern burning on the spot. In the light of the lantern, they saw the figure of a man, a strong, well-built man digging away at the very spot where Damayanti had dug just two days ago. Indeed, he was digging up the same hole!

Damayanti's entire body and soul trembled at the sight. The man was Pitambor Mahajan. He had hung his lantern on a bamboo pole and was digging away furiously. The man had assumed a terrifying aspect, and he was hacking at the earth like a madman. She trembled in fear and terror. Should she shout? Yes, of course, she must. Such a terrible thing was happening outside her own house—of course, she must shout!

'Mahajan! Mahajan!' she shouted. But there was absolutely no response. He simply kept on digging.

'Mahajan, why are you digging up my ground?'

Pitambor looked up towards the window, but did not utter a word.

Damayanti said in a state of great agitation, 'Yes, I buried it. But what will you find there now? It was just an unformed lump of flesh.'

Pitambor lifted his head and looked at her. 'It was my child! I will at least feel the flesh of my flesh! I will feel my child, my son and heir, with my own two hands!'

LABURNUM FOR MY HEAD

TEMSULA AO

Every May, something extraordinary happens in the new cemetery of the sleepy little town. Standing beyond the southernmost corner of the vast expanse of the old cemetery—dotted with concrete vanities, both ornate and simple—the humble Indian laburnum bush erupts in glory, with its blossoms of yellow mellow beauty. The first time it happened, some years ago, surprised visitors to the concrete memorials assumed that it was an accident of nature. But each year as the bush grew taller and the blossoms more plentiful, the phenomenon stood out as a magnificent incongruity, in the space where man tries to cling to a make-believe permanence wrenched from him by death. His inheritors try to preserve his presence in concrete structures, erected in his homage, vying to outdo each other in size and style. This consecrated ground has thus become choked with the specimens of human conceit. More recently, photographs of the dead have begun to adorn the marble and granite headstones.

But nature has a way of upstaging even the hardest rock and granite edifices fabricated by man. Weeds and obstinate bramble sprout from every inch of soil uncovered by sand and cement. So, every Easter week, the community comes together to spruce up headstones and get rid of the intruding natural growth. The names on individual gravesites are lovingly wiped clean of dust and bird shit by loved ones; occasional strangers read them as incidental pastime.

But the laburnum bush will not or cannot reveal readily who or what lies beneath its drooping branches during its annual show of yellow splendour. That particular spot displays nothing that man has improvised; only nature, who does not possess any script, abides there: she only owns the seasons. And the seasons play out a pantomime of beauty and baldness on the tree standing on the edge of the lifeless opulence spread over the remains of the assorted dead: rich and poor, young and old, and mourned and unmourned. The headstones in the old cemetery bear mute testimony to duties performed by willing and unwilling offspring and relatives. The laburnum tree, on the other hand, is alive and ever unchanging in its seasonal cycles: it is resplendent in May; by summer end, the stalks holding its yellow blossoms turn into brown pods; by winter it begins to look scraggly and shorn. Springtime brings back pale green shoots and by May it is wearing its yellow wreaths again, to outdo all the vainglorious specimens erected in marble and granite.

But the story is running ahead of itself and must be told from the beginning. It all started with a woman named Lentina and her desire to have some laburnum bushes in her garden. She had always admired these yellow flowers for what she thought was their femininity; they were not brazen like the gulmohars with their orange and dark pink blossoms. The way the laburnum flowers hung their heads earthward appealed to her because she attributed humility to the gesture. So, she decided to grow a couple of these trees in her own garden which, though not big, could accommodate them if they were planted in the corners, without affecting the growth and health of the other plants. She purchased saplings from a nursery and had them planted at the edge of her boundary wall. She followed the instructions faithfully and hoped that within two years, as the nursery man assured her, the bushes would flower.

That first year, her new gardener pulled out the small saplings along with the weeds growing around them. After loud recriminations, Lentina bought some more saplings and this time, planted three of them in three corners of the garden. She hoped that at least one of them would survive. But it was not to be. One day she heard loud barking and cows mooing very close to her compound. When she came out to investigate, she found that some stray cows, on being pursued by her neighbour's dogs and finding her gate slightly ajar, had rushed into her garden and were blissfully munching on the plants they found there, including her precious laburnum saplings. She began to wonder about these accidents in her garden ever since she had planted the laburnum saplings. Nevertheless, she did not give up, and the third year too, she planted some more saplings of her favourite flowering tree. Almost miraculously they survived the first few months and began to thrive.

Lentina was thrilled and could not wait to see them bear the magnificent yellow blooms she so admired. But before her wish could come true, another disaster struck. One day, a worker from the health department came while she was out visiting a friend and sprayed a deadly DDT concoction on the edges of the garden. As ill luck would have it, it rained heavily that night, flooding the entire garden. Except the full-grown trees, all her flowers including the laburnums withered and died. Lentina was devastated and began to think that her efforts at bringing the strange beauty into her garden would never be successful. But whenever she saw these flowers in bloom, on highways and in gardens, the intense yearning to have them closer home began to overpower her. Her husband and children were convinced that she was developing an unhealthy fetish for laburnum and began to talk openly about this in close family gatherings. She could not understand their concern and was inwardly hurt by their seeming insensitivity to beauty around them. But she never gave up her hope of having a full-grown laburnum tree in her garden someday.

Lentina did not mention laburnum to any one any more; nor did she attempt to plant the tree she so ardently admired and wished to have in her garden. Meanwhile, her husband began to show signs of a strange disease and before any proper diagnosis could be made, he passed away quietly one night in his sleep. The funeral services were long and elaborate because the deceased was a respected and prominent member of society. On the burial day, while the hearse was about to leave for the cemetery, Lentina surprised everyone, including herself, by announcing that she was going to accompany her husband on his last journey. Usually it is men who take part in the last rites at the gravesite and stay on to supervise the erection of the temporary fence around the fresh grave. But when Lentina saw the group, including her sons and her own brothers, stepping out of the house behind the hearse, some impulse urged her to join them. Her words were met with silence, because no one was prepared to voice dissent at such a moment. So the party departed, and in the graveyard while the last prayers droned on, Lentina stood among the assortment of headstones and began ruminating on man's puny attempts to defy death; as if erecting these memorials would bring the dead back to life.

Lentina decided that she did not want any such attempt at immortality when her time came, and at that thought she experienced an epiphanic sensation: why not have a laburnum tree planted on her grave, one which would live on over her remains instead of a silly headstone? This way, even her lifelong wish to have such a tree close to her would be fulfilled. In spite of the sombre occasion, she began to smile but when a relative saw her, she quickly went back to looking appropriately bereaved. But the sense of elation she felt could not be hidden for long. So she looked around for her driver and gesturing to him to follow her, made her way home.

That night she could not sleep from excitement: it was as if a big problem had solved itself; but how was she going to accomplish it? It was clear that she could not confide in her relatives or children; so she had to find someone who would understand her deep-seated longing for the yellow wonders. She turned her attention to her servants: whom among them could she trust? Not the cook or the gardener; they had families, and secrets in families are never sacrosanct. Suddenly her mind turned to the driver who had been in their employment for more years than she could remember. He was a widower. She decided to make him her confidant. She would take him for a drive the next day to the cemetery and would explain to him what she wanted for a headstone when she died, and why. But there would be one condition: she had to see the tree bloom during her lifetime. The driver's name was Mapu but everyone called him Babu because Lentina's grandson called him by that name, unable to pronounce Mapu at first. The name stuck and Mapu good-naturedly did not object even when the older people began calling him Babu.

The next morning, she sent for Babu and they took the road to the cemetery. This in itself would not appear strange: a widow paying a visit to the grave of her husband. But Lentina's intention was different; she wanted to survey the still-empty sites and to reserve a spot where she would be buried. It had to be a spot which would not be disturbed in a long while and would not pose any problem for others. When they reached the cemetery, instead of heading towards her husband's grave, Lentina marched to the extreme corners of the ground, as if looking for a lost treasure. After what seemed to be an arduous trek, she settled on a spot on the southernmost tip of the cemetery and began to nod her head, as if she had found what she was looking for. Babu was puzzled and was almost beginning to see what his young masters had said about madam losing her mind. When she gestured to him to approach, he went hesitantly. Motioning to him to walk faster, she pointed to the spot where she was standing and said loudly, 'This is my spot, I want to be buried here when my time comes.'

Babu was taken aback and began to protest, 'But, madam, your place is already earmarked beside my master!'

'Nonsense, it can go to whichever son goes first. My place is here and you are going to see that the town committee gives a written commitment on this. But mind you, no one at home is to be told.' She knew that Babu's son-in-law was a petty officer in that office. 'Arrange it with your son-in-law. I'll pay whatever amount it costs. And also swear him to secrecy just as you are going to do now. Will you keep my secret?'

Babu, seeing the fire and intensity in her eyes, answered, 'Yes, madam, I will keep your secret and I will see to it that my son-in-law does the same.' Lentina added, 'He is not to tell even his wife.' Babu nodded and said, 'Yes, madam.' Having made this momentous decision, she stretched her hand to him and with her leaning on him, they made their way to the car parked outside the gate and came home. The old woman looked exhausted and went straight to bed. No one thought it strange, because the funeral activities had taken a lot out of everyone and even the young women of the household were looking forward to an early night. But lying in bed, Lentina was wide awake and planning her next move: she wanted to plant a laburnum tree on her gravesite while she was still alive to ensure that all this trouble of securing the plot and keeping everything quiet had the desired results. She *had* to see the tree bloom before she breathed her last. Even for this task she had to enlist the help of her faithful Babu. But unfortunately, it was almost winter and they had to wait till the next spring.

In the meantime, Babu began the preliminary discussions with his son-in-law about reserving a plot in the cemetery. At first the young man was puzzled; why was his father-in-law talking of such a morbid subject? Was he suffering from some terminal disease that he had kept secret from his own family? But he kept his thoughts to himself. From him Babu learnt that most people wanted the front rows in the cemetery and there was always some dispute or the other about such issues among the more prominent people of the town. Babu's request surprised his son-in-law because it was for the most insignificant plot in the cemetery. He assured his father-in-law that as far as the location went, he could foresee no trouble at all. But, he told him that there had to be an official request; only then could the committee take appropriate action.

Babu informed his mistress about this and once again Lentina was faced with a dilemma. Should she sign on the application form or devise another ploy to keep the identity of the applicant secret? The latter seemed to be a better idea but how was she going to achieve it? As she pondered, she remembered a conversation she had with her husband long ago. They were discussing the prospects of real estate and he had said, 'If you want to gain from investments in land, go for inconspicuous plots, but ones which have future prospects. That way no one will pay attention when you buy it, and when the town expands, your holdings will appreciate in value many times over.'

Taking a cue from this, she abandoned her original idea of buying a plot in the already congested cemetery and went for another visit there the next day. This time she invited Babu to walk with her around the perimeter of the wall, and told him to examine the direction in which the cemetery would expand. Babu at once caught on and, asking her to rest a while, did a quick survey of the surrounding area and came to a conclusion. He helped her to the car and after they were seated comfortably, he said, 'Madam, the land adjoining the southern boundary will be the best, though I do not fully understand why you want to do this when a small plot of land would serve your purpose.' She looked at him with a glint in her eyes and replied, 'Be patient Babu, time will answer your question.' With that enigmatic reply she dismissed him and they drove home in silence.

Once again, Lentina withdrew to her bedroom and began to worry about the prospects of acquiring the adjacent plot of land. The only person she could rely on to accomplish this was Babu; she decided to entrust him with the job. But before she could talk to him, fate intervened and an opportunity presented itself to her in the person of a man from a neighbouring village who was the son of her late husband's friend. The friend himself was dead and the son, named Khalong, had been away at the time of her husband's death. When he heard about it he came to pay his condolences. Lentina noticed a certain dejection in Khalong's demeanour and when she pressed him for a reason he blurted out how bad his financial situation had become as a result of the father's prolonged illness and many hospitalizations outside the state. He sighed. 'If only I could sell our land! But unfortunately, now that the cemetery has expanded, people only laugh at me when I talk of selling our land adjoining it. They even joke about it and say, turn it into another cemetery and charge rent! Aunty, I do not know what is going to happen to us.' The poor man was on the verge of tears but Lentina, instead of sympathizing, appeared to become excited about his outburst.

After what he considered to be a period of rude silence, Lentina turned to him and began to ask for the details of his land. Khalong thought that it was simply her way of expressing concern. But what came next completely floored him. 'Will you sell that piece of land to me?' she asked in an excited manner. He could not answer immediately because he was debating with himself whether it would be right to sell her a piece of unsuitable land just because she felt sorry for him. It would amount to taking advantage of her sympathy and would certainly be unethical. Reading his mind correctly, the old woman said in a gentle voice, 'I know what you are thinking, but let me assure you that it is not merely out of my concern for you that I am doing this. I have a selfish motive. For quite some time now I have been looking for a suitable plot where I want to be buried. And before you say anything, let me add that I do not wish to be buried among the ridiculous stone monuments of the big cemetery. I need a place where there will be nothing but beautiful trees over my grave. So, tell me now, will you sell your land to me?' Khalong was convinced that Lentina meant business and uttered a feeble yes. But the woman was not done yet; she continued in the same serious tone, 'Listen, I will buy the land only on one condition: you are to tell nobody about the transaction yet, not even your wife. If you agree to this condition, tell me how much you want and come tomorrow with the documents and we will finalize the deal.'

Khalong was so overcome by the unexpected turn of fortune that he stated an amount beyond his expectation. He was even more shocked to hear her say, 'Okay, come tomorrow at eleven.' He did not wait for any formal dismissal after she gave her instructions, hurrying out of the house in a daze, still wondering whether all that had transpired was actually real. Lentina knew that had she bargained a bit, the price would have been reduced but she felt that heaven's gifts should be accepted without any murmur, and simply proceeded to put together the amount needed for the next day's transaction. Once again she enlisted the help of Babu, who was to be a witness to the deal. When Babu reminded her about the negotiation with the town committee and that he would have to explain the abrupt halt to his son-in-law, Lentina smiled and told him, 'Let him think that it was a wild scheme thought up by someone going senile.'

As instructed by Lentina, Khalong came with the thumbprint of a relative on a paper where the agreement was inscribed. The deal was accomplished without a hitch and Lentina became the proud owner of a plot of land right next to the south wall of the old cemetery. Lentina ordered Babu to engage some labourers to erect a temporary boundary fence. It was only when the fence was almost complete that her sons came to know about their mother's 'crazy' plan. They remonstrated with her, they sulked at having been left out of the deliberations, and even threatened to move out of the compound if their mother treated them like rank outsiders; they were upset that a mere driver had usurped their rightful place in her schemes. But even then, they were not aware of the full extent of her designs for the new cemetery. She tried to pacify them by saying that she did not want to burden them with tasks which she and Babu were perfectly able to handle. The sons kept quiet but the elder daughter-in-law wanted to assert herself and began to accuse Lentina of putting too much trust in a servant and this, she said, amounted to insulting them. Lentina, smarting from the unfairness of the charge, blurted out something which she had overheard during her husband's funeral and had decided to keep secret. It was an argument between the two daughters-in-law about who was to pay for the funeral expenses. The elder one had said, 'It is not fair that we alone should bear the costs; you and your husband should pay half of it.' To this the younger one had replied, 'How can I say anything? Tell that husband of mine, if you feel like it. But I am not going to give a rupee towards this unnecessary show.' Everyone knew that the younger daughter-in-law had money of her own and that gave her an edge over the other. She continued, 'And if you think that we are going to waste money on some grandiose headstone for the old man, think again. Such pretensions this family has!'

Lentina had kept this knowledge to herself and had resolved that she would never divulge this to anyone. But, being goaded into speech by interference from her family on a matter she thought did not directly involve them, she decided to speak out. She addressed the two ladies, 'Why are you all worked up about such a trivial matter? After all, I have not spent anyone else's money. And another thing: you need not worry about any headstone for me. I want none.' The two ladies were completely taken aback; they had assumed that they were alone in the room when the altercation had taken place. The deft and crafty manipulation of her knowledge helped Lentina put an end to all opposition. When the husbands learnt how their mother 'took care' of their wives, they merely chuckled and muttered, 'That's Mother for you. Hope you've learnt your lesson.'

News about Lentina's acquisition of the plot of land adjacent to the cemetery soon became public knowledge, and she knew that sooner rather than later she would be visited by members of the town committee and the issue of 'ownership' would be raised, because all such grounds were to be only in the custody of either the church or other religious organizations, with due permission from the committee. Anticipating their move, she had already drawn up a legal document with the help of her nephew who had just started practising law in the district court. In the document, she had declared that she would donate the piece of land to the town committee and not to the church if, and only if, they gave a written undertaking that it would be managed according to her terms: The new plot of land could be dedicated as the new cemetery and would be available to all on fulfilling the condition that only flowering trees and not headstones would be erected on the gravesites.

Lentina, as the donor, should be the first to choose a plot for herself.

Plots would be designated by numbers only, and records of names against plot numbers would be maintained in the committee register.

The terms were to be widely publicized and the town committee would ensure that they were adhered to strictly.

As expected, the members came one day and were ushered into the big drawing room where they seated themselves with obvious ceremony, stressing their eminent status in society. Lentina greeted them amiably and expressed surprise at their 'official' visit. The chairman cleared his throat and began first by expressing the committee's collective sympathy for the bereaved family. Lentina replied in a befitting manner and enquired to what she owed the honoured visit. The chairman looked at his colleagues and launched into his rehearsed speech about ownership of sacred grounds and what the town's administrators had to say about it. Gently but firmly, Lentina interrupted him and said, 'Thank you Mr Chairman, I want to assure you that I am aware of your responsibility regarding the matter and I have taken the initiative to seek your cooperation by drawing up this legal document for your consideration. Kindly discuss this with your colleagues and let me know as soon as possible if the terms are acceptable to you.'

The chairman gave her a sharp look but refrained from saying anything, though it was clear to all that he resented being cut off in the middle of his speech. He turned to an elderly member and asked, 'What do you say, brother? Shall we discuss this here or take it back with us and discuss it in the office?' The other read the document and said in a voice more authoritative than that of the chairman, 'We can do it here; it seems the terms are quite simple. I see no harm in accepting them because the town is getting a substantial plot of land, the need for which has long been felt. The kind lady has indeed come to our rescue, she must be congratulated.' After this emphatic endorsement by an important member, there was no need for further discussion of the terms. Through another deed drawn up a few days later, the new cemetery with its unusual stipulations came into the possession of the town committee. On the day the legal formalities were concluded, this time in the presence of her sons and their wives, Lentina said, almost like an afterthought, 'By the way, can I choose my plot now?' Everyone in the room was struck by the ingenuity of this seemingly innocuous request. It was as if she were asking for a candy, and not for a place where she would eventually be buried. The entire transaction was of a somewhat morbid nature but she took the sting out of it by what she added next: 'You see, I want to plant something there.' No one could say anything to this and as the visitors departed, the faint voice of the chairman could be heard: 'After all, she being the donor, it is only right that she should be given the first choice.'

Lentina and Babu made frequent visits to the new ground. Then one day Babu drove up with the gardener carrying laburnum saplings which he planted on the prepared ground. Lentina discontinued her visits to the cemetery because she was beginning to feel a fatigue that comes after a sustained effort and achievement of a long-cherished dream. How that plot of land came into her possession was still a mystery to her when all she had craved for was a spot to be buried where a laburnum tree would bloom every May. Ah, the laburnum tree! Would the saplings survive this time, she speculated. Would they really bloom and would she live long enough to actually see the trees flower? Before one knew it, another May with laburnum blossoms everywhere had come and gone. A small consolation for the frail woman was that her plants out 'there' were doing fine. Babu, the ever-faithful friend, for this is how she thought of him now, brought news about many things including that of her treasured plants.

Once in a while she would tell Babu that she wanted to see them herself, to which he would say, 'Soon, madam, but not today.' Her days were now threatening to blur into dusk. Sometimes they would find her roaming in the garden barefoot and without a shawl. That winter Lentina caught a bad cold and fell seriously ill. Everyone thought that she would not last the winter. Even her doctor, usually a jolly person, began to show signs of strain after every visit to her room. Only Babu remained calm and steadfast during the crisis. When relatives and close friends were allowed brief visits, it was Babu who stood guard outside the door to see that they did not stay too long. Sometimes Lentina would pretend to be sleeping when noisy and nosy relatives came to visit; Babu then had the perfect excuse to shoo them out quickly. During the day, Babu would disappear for some time and when he returned, he would make straight for Lentina's room. He would tiptoe in and she would turn her eyes towards the door and as their eyes met, he would give a faint nod and withdraw. This was a message that he had just visited the trees and that they were doing well. This seemed to provide her with the will to live where food and medicines seemed to have failed.

To everyone's astonishment, Lentina survived the fierce winter and one clear February morning she rang her bell peremptorily. The maid went in to find her searching for her gown and bedroom slippers. She offered to bring her tea to the room but Lentina ordered her to take her to the drawing room. She sat by the fireside where her tea was brought and she sipped the hot brew as though she were tasting it for the first time. From that day on, she began to move about the house and resumed her old routine of supervising the activities in it. When her daughters-in-law visited, she was warm and amiable with them; occasionally she would even give them pieces of jewellery: a ring, ear tops, and necklaces. The sons too, sensing a new spirit in their mother, began to ask for her advice on business and family matters, something which had never happened during their father's lifetime. They were pleasantly surprised to find how sharp her mind still was. They also discovered how uncannily like their father she sounded sometimes! There was a visible easing of tension among them and it became apparent that not only Lentina, but the entire family was heading towards healing that was more than physical.

That year, the year of Lentina's recovery, something happened in the new cemetery that only Babu saw; he kept the knowledge to himself.

Of the two laburnum trees planted on Lentina's plot, one languished and died. But the surviving one had flourished and, wonder of wonders, even produced a tiny sprig bearing a few yellow blossoms. One could not see this from the road because the plant was still small and the flowers sparse. But Babu frequently visited the site and discovered the shy showing one fine May morning. He was tempted to tell Lentina but decided against it because the excitement might have been too much for her. And, if the plant did not develop as hoped, the disappointment might have a devastating effect on his mistress, weakened by her recent illness. He was both happy and afraid: happy because the long-cherished desire of his mistress to see a laburnum bloom had been fulfilled; afraid, because he instinctively knew that as soon as Lentina laid eyes on the blossoms next May, she would conclude that the right moment to leave the world had arrived. Not that she would do anything drastic like taking her own life, but she would let everything slide and simply bow out of life, with a contented sigh.

But, for all his apprehensions about the future, Babu knew that he could not hold back the force of nature that had accomplished the small miracle of the first showing that May. By next year, the bush would be taller and the flowers more plentiful; it would become visible to all who passed by that lonely road to the new cemetery. He had to tell his mistress about this, but when? He thought about it for many nights and finally decided that the best time would be the next season's flowering and hoped that she would be alive to hear the good news from him. If Lentina now thought of him as her friend, Babu was also beginning to reassess his relationship with her. Till the time of her husband's death, though she had treated Babu with civility and kindness, she had always maintained a discreet distance as befitting a master–servant relationship. But she gradually broke down the barriers by showing her dependence on him, first by only extracting 'dutiful service'; then imperceptibly as a friend; and finally, a confidant. Outwardly, the protocol demanded by their positions was never breached or altered, but it soon became apparent to everybody how much Lentina relied on the old driver for things she wanted done. And surprisingly, this was accepted by her sons and their wives—it relieved them from the onerous duty of being on call for their frail and aged mother. A strong-willed woman and her faithful servant were thus drawn into an unusual bond of common humanity, based on trust and loyalty.

By the time the new year came, Lentina showed signs of fatigue brought on by old age. Her family watched her keenly all through the winter months and she was never left alone. When March came and the weather became warmer, she wanted to be taken out in the car. Her wish was at first just ignored but when she refused to eat unless she was taken out for a ride, the family decided to accede. And so a routine was established: twice a week, weather permitting, Lentina would go out in the car accompanied by her maid. Lentina did not object to this arrangement and came back from these outings a much happier person. She ate well and some colour returned to her pale face. But during these jaunts, she sat quietly, without uttering a word, and even when Babu or the maid commented on something new or strange they had seen in the town, she did not respond. On return, she would head straight to her room and remain there until dinner time.

And then another May was upon them and everyone noticed a visible change in Lentina; she wanted to go out more frequently. But the doctor put his foot down and the twice-a-week routine continued. Seeing her agitation, Babu approached her door one day and sought permission to speak. He assured her that he was keeping a close watch on the plants and that he was confident that they would bloom this season. He still did not tell her about what had happened the previous year. He promised to give her reports on the days she was forced to stay indoors. But during the outings now, the first thing she wanted was to drive by the new cemetery, to see if the laburnum trees were showing signs of producing flowers. She had seen other trees in town with their gorgeous display of cascading yellow flowers. Her disappointment was acute and after a few times, she refused to go out at all.

And then one day, late into the month, on his daily excursion to the cemetery, Babu discovered the miracle that they had been praying for: the little laburnum tree was awash with buttery yellow blossoms! The unflappable driver gave a shout of joy and darted away, heading to his mistress with the wonderful news. On his way, he rehearsed how he was going to break the news to her. He cautioned himself that he should do it gently, so that his dear mistress would not get too excited. When he reached the house, he walked slowly to the lady's room and knocked gently. To his surprise, he heard a sharp command, 'Come in Babu, I've been waiting for you.' He entered and started to speak but she cut him off. 'I know what you are going to tell me; I felt it in my bones.' He saw that Lentina was dressed as if for a grand occasion and standing by her side was the maid, also dressed. The old lady fumbled for her walking stick and said impatiently, 'Let's go, what are you waiting for?'

The bewildered driver and the slightly dazed maid followed the old lady who suddenly seemed to have a spring in her step, and proceeded on their apparently routine outing. But only Lentina and Babu knew what this phenomenon signified. Once they reached the site, Lentina withdrew into a more sombre mood, as did Babu; only the maid exclaimed at the sight of the luxuriant blossoms on so small a tree. Lentina gazed at the flowers for a long time and, sighing deeply, told Babu to drive to the park, located about four kilometres from the town—the highest point from where the entire town could be seen. It was a popular picnic spot and was full of people on weekends. When they reached the park, they found that not many people were around because it was a weekday. Choosing a quiet corner, Lentina and the maid sat down to rest. The maid had packed some biscuits and a flask of tea, which the three of them shared. After about half an hour they drove back home. As she entered her room, Lentina turned to her maid and Babu and shook their hands, murmuring, 'Thank you and God bless you.'

Lentina stayed in her room for most of the week. She turned down suggestions of any further outing and busied herself with tidying up her room, even refusing help from the maid. On the fifth day of this self-imposed isolation, she called the maid and asked her to help her with her bath and to dress her in her favourite outfit. Having done that, she ordered the maid to bring her some food as she wanted an early dinner. The maid did as she was told and bade her mistress an early goodnight before retiring to her own quarters.

The next morning when she knocked on Lentina's door with the morning tea, there was no answer. She knocked again but only silence greeted her. She entered the room and found Lentina stretched on the bed; she seemed to be sleeping soundly. Putting the tray on the bedside table, the maid said gently, 'Madam, I've brought tea.' She went and drew the curtains as usual but when she came near the bed, she noticed a certain stiffness in the body and an unusual pallor on the old lady's face. Distinctly alarmed, she went out and urgently called the others, the sons, their wives, and all the servants. They all came rushing, except Babu, who stood near a post, crying like a baby. They entered the room and the elder son bent closer to determine if his mother was breathing. He straightened up with a sharply drawn breath and shook his head. When the doctor came, he pronounced that Lentina, the mistress of the house, had died in her sleep.

So ends the story of the undramatic life of an ordinary woman who cherished one single passionate wish that a humble laburnum tree should bloom once a year on her crown.

And every May, this extraordinary wish is fulfilled when the laburnum tree, planted on her gravesite in the new cemetery of the sleepy little town, bursts forth in all its glory of buttery yellow splendour. And if you can tear your eyes away from this display and survey the rest of the ground, you will notice that in the entire expanse, there is not a single stone monument. Instead, flowering bushes take root, blooming in their own seasons on the little mounds dotting the landscape. Hibiscus, gardenia, bottlebrush, camellia, oleander, and croton bushes of all hues comprise the variety of flowering plants, and at one or two spots you can see some jacaranda trees trying to keep up with the others. A lone banyan and a few ashoka trees standing on the far edges also seem to be doing quite well. And if you observe carefully, you will be amazed to see that in the entire terrain, there is so far, only one laburnum tree bedecked in its seasonal glory, standing tall over all the other plants, flourishing in perfect coexistence, in an environment liberated from all human pretensions to immortality.

So, every May, something extraordinary.

CHILD OF FORTUNE

NINI LUNGALANG

In our village called New Village, though it's not new now, they still talk about the beautiful girl-child, Rokono, Child of Fortune. Grim old women, full of years and wisdom, shake their heads and admonish young mothers; they say, 'Never give your children names too heavy for them to carry. Remember Rokono, Child of Fortune,' and a silence follows the name.

Rokono, Child of Fortune, was born that terrible year when the soldiers first came to New Village. It was new then, with only eleven houses, but growing. The soil was rich and dark, if a little heavy, and anything planted grew. More importantly, there was plenty of land for everyone in the valley. The small noisy stream that ran down from the cliff had water clear and cold, and never dried up even in winter.

The forest abounded with good things if one knew how to find them, or hunt. The only trouble, a slight one to be sure, was that New Village was difficult to access: a whole day's march from the Old Village in the dry season, two in the wet, for one had to go round, under the cliff. The cliff leaned over New Village like an upright hand, so high that if one stood at the highest point, they said, and hurled a stone, it seemed to come back in a wide curve, to drop in silence below. Only young fools climb it to chase wild goats, and they talk of the wind there that seems strong enough to pull off one's hair. A wild goat chased off the cliff is never found below except as scraps of bones that hunting dogs sniff at in disdain.

It was just before the planting time, and they were preparing the terraces to receive the rice seedlings. Wild peaches were beginning to bloom as the terraces were being flooded. Then one day the soldiers came: hundreds, it seemed. No one knew why they had come, but they came like a swarm of hornets. Three of the men, brave and foolish, rushed out with spears, and were cut down at once in a hail of bullets. Then the other men were tied and herded away to be beaten with butts of rifles. The women were stripped and raped, even the old crones, while the soldiers laughed and cheered. They spared her only, and that because she was huge and pregnant; but they had stripped her too, and laughed. The soldiers set fire to every house. They killed every pig with bayonets. The dogs, clever beasts, had run off early in the commotion. The wild-eyed children saw everything.

It was by chance that on that day, six of the young men had set off to hunt an old wily mountain goat. They vanished into the mist....

At last, their dead they buried, the wounded they nursed as best as they could. Mothers collected their children whimpering with fear and hunger. But the food was gone, for the granaries were burnt. Painfully, the women salvaged some charred rice from the smoking mounds, and this was scrupulously divided. It was decreed that they must all hide by day and come out only at night, for it was known that soldiers do not venture out at night. No fires were to be lit, lest the smoke reveal their presence; if anyone found something edible, it was to be eaten raw. They must watch and wait.

So they scattered into the forest. The women, as women will, found a rocky hollow at the foot of the cliff and gathered there with the children. All spoke in whispers. And it was there that she was overwhelmed with bitterness and shame, for she alone among the women, was not raped. And was she not a stranger, brought as a bride from the East, by her impetuous young husband against the wishes of his father and hers? And the women had hated her, for she was very beautiful, long-limbed and slender, unlike the women of these parts, who were short and squat. Her great eyes, when she raised the eyelids, were black as ripe berries, and her hair lay smooth and shining over her ears, rolled in a large loop at the back of her neck. Yet she was a willing worker, deft and quick. Her mother-in-law had defended her and accepted her wholly. When the two sons were born to her, she felt less a stranger.

But now, the women slid cruel looks at her. Why did they not rape you? they hissed; have the beautiful women of the East some talisman to keep them pure? Or were the soldiers afraid of the big black eyes that beguiled our brother, that he preferred you above his own kind? He, alas, was always a bragging fool, they said. Do not speak of my husband, she whispered at last, is he not among the dead and his flesh not yet melded into the soil? But she would not weep. She silently busied herself with her little sons, teaching them to chew the grains of rice slowly, and to suck the sap from tender twigs she had gathered for them. She spoke not at all of the babe that lay in her vitals, now sluggish and resting before the crisis of birth. And she remained silent, for she knew that the women needled her to assuage their greater shame.

On an evening as she sat in enforced idleness, she saw the new moon low in the sky holding the old moon in the circle of her horns. Pale she was, the moon, and fragile as the fingernail of a newborn. As she gazed, she felt the first stab of birthing pain. An omen, she thought, and smiled her secret smile; it will be a woman, she thought exultantly. She will be my joy. But as suddenly as the thought was born, it died, for, in her mind's eye, her husband's face swung down from the sky, ruddy, reckless and laughing, and her heart twisted with the grief she would not show.

As the pains increased, she moved around, restless but silent, hoping that none would notice. But women do, and to her amazement they crowded round her, murmuring softly. Their work-rough hands were strangely tender as they stroked and soothed her, and they strove with her, united in the sisterhood of pain. You will have a strong son, they crooned, and he will defend you and avenge his father's death. No! she gasped as she twisted with pain. It will be a woman, as beautiful and constant as the moon that always returns. And it was a woman.

And she named the child Rokono, Child of Fortune, for she must reverse the disaster that had befallen them, she said. There was a murmur of approval from the young women, but the old ones muttered darkly. Surely the name is too heavy, they said. In the face of calamity, one must be cautious, they said. As for the moon, what is more inconstant? they said; the moon is ever-changing, and so fickle that she even gets eaten by the dark shadows in eclipses, bringing sorrow to the children of men, as even now! But everyone needed to hope, so the name stayed.

Soon after her birth, people began to move back into the village, though no word was actually given. It may have been the need to belong to a place, however devastated, or it may have been the rain that came down in a kind, warm downpour. People needed to grow things. So they went back to their fields, and with their labour they were cleansed of fear and bitterness. It was as if her birth had made them whole again.

She had always yearned for a girl, but now in the secret nights, as the child suckled, she was filled with dread and shame. A girl without a father? she would think, and brothers but children themselves? and the mother, a stranger? a cursed one! She'd sigh, clutching the child closer.

She did not know whether she meant the babe or herself.

But the children of the village, lean and dusty, grew as children will. In secret, they played again and again the Visit of the Soldiers. Always in secret, for if their mothers saw or suspected their game, they were cursed and thrashed. And the mothers of the six youths who had melted into the cliff said not a word, but they grew ever more gaunt and sere. But there was a hidden pride in their eyes.

It was a wonder that while the whole village nearly starved, there was always enough milk for the child. She is well named, the women would say to the mother. Indeed, hers was a beautiful babe, with huge black eyes and thick black hair and a round face as succulent as a ripe peach. Her limbs were straight and plump as young cucumbers, and she sucked heartily at the ever-full breast offered to her. The mother's pleasure in her child, however, was always mixed with grief and guilt. O you greedy little cannibal, she would whisper, would you eat your mother's flesh and your father's soul? For she would see again how they had killed her husband by striking his head again and again with the end of a gun. There was not even a new shawl in which to bury him, for everything was gone.

The child was a quiet, placid baby. Too quiet, said the older mothers, for she cried only when she was hungry: a strange, hoarse, low wail, so unlike the high angry shrieks of a hungry infant. And she never smiled. While other babies born after her cooed and gurgled and laughed when tickled, this one was silent and still. If she moved at all, her movements were slow and jerky, and all the time, she would stare out of those great black eyes that seemed to see everything—or nothing at all.

It is well that your little one is so good, the other women would say, you can work without being disturbed. And it was so. The mother would lay the baby on a pile of dry moss in a shawl while she hoed or weeded, planted or plucked the beans, the gourds, and the chilli. And the little one would wave her tiny fists or kick slowly and jerkily, until some dim instinct would compel it to cry that strange, hoarse, low wail.

Sometimes, a kindly woman would offer to take care of the baby, but the mother would always thank her and decline the offer. The small one is no trouble, she would say, and strapping the child to her bosom, she would go forth, even to the forest below the cliff, to gather fuel or herbs, her basket swinging behind her.

The two boys, now over five years and seven, helped to hoe the vegetable patch and weed the rice terraces. She would give them small cane creels to catch fish, and they would always bring something for the pot, for they had learnt even to grope for snails in the soft warm mud. They were good boys, never complaining about food. They rarely fought, for they were so different: the elder, thick-set and ruddy like his father, noisy and impulsive, warm-hearted and hasty; the younger, slight, pale, and slender-limbed, secretive and sharp-witted. These boys, living as they did without a father, were perhaps too precocious; they often spoke out of turn, they sometimes failed to show proper respect to elders. Some elderly man would rebuke them, and a younger one would cuff them. It is well, thought the mother, they must learn. She herself said little to them, for she had no wish to have sons who were either loose-tongued braggarts or useless cowards. So, she rarely praised or berated them. At most, if the food seemed insufficient, she would say, this food must be shared by us all.

As for Rokono, now a toddler, there was little to say. She was slow in everything, but seemed to be always content to be where she was put, silent and staring out of her great black eyes. Sometimes, the mother would worry, but there was little time for that, for there was always work and more work. She was, therefore, thankful that her children were healthy and undemanding. The boys cheerfully minded their sister: if some food was put to her mouth, she would open her little red lips and swallow. So they would strap her on their backs by turns, and go about their boys' business, though she was quite heavy now. One day, the younger boy dropped her, but all she uttered was that strange, harsh wail. The mother ran to snatch her up and looked her over; there was a huge bruise down the whole length of her, but the child only moaned hoarsely, though another would have screamed with pain.

And the baby kept growing: she was a joy to behold, with her great unblinking eyes, her lips red as pomegranate petals, and face, round, flushed, and firm as a peach just ripe. But she never smiled, never cooed or cried. Her gaze, solemn and unflinching, unsettled everyone. Yet everyone had affection for this child. She is well named, they said, for after her birth, we have never had misfortunes. And it was true. No crop had failed, or woman miscarried; no epidemic occurred or livestock lost, after the birth of Child of Fortune.

Yet the mother was uneasy, unwilling now to leave the child with her brothers. One day at evening, the older boy in his impetuous way said, 'My mother, our friends say that our sister is dumb, an idiot. Why can't you teach her to talk? They say that her breath will make other babies into idiots!'

The mother tried. Bitterly she tried, as she carried the child strapped to her bosom as they went to gather fuel—but the child remained silent.

Four years to the month, after the soldiers had come to the village, they returned. Like a swarm of hornets they returned, roaring and shooting into the air. The young men, swift as deer, vanished as they were told. The oldest man and his blind wife, the soldiers tied and questioned. Through an interpreter they learned that two of the six youths who earlier had disappeared, had been caught. They had killed many soldiers and stolen their guns. Where were the others? Had they ever returned? Will they return? And where are all the young men of the village today? Answer, or we will kill you all.

Again, the men were tied and beaten. Again, the women raped. Again, the houses and granaries burnt. Again, the children saw everything. But, this time, many more young men had melted into the forest, and in their mothers' eyes the pride was now open and unbidden.

By mere chance, the mother of Child of Fortune had taken her up the cliff side that day at dawn, to gather mushrooms that grow on the mast of leaves. From the great height she heard the roar of gunfire. She heard the shrill shrieks of the women. She saw the smoke rising, black and thick as rain-heavy clouds. Why am I spared yet again? she mused. She remembered now, how in the old days, her people would offer sacrifice to appease offended spirits. She decided quickly.

Neatly she wrapped the mushrooms in plantain leaves. Quickly she loosened her necklaces of carnelian beads and placed them in her basket. Strapping her child firmly to her bosom, she said, we are going home. She began to climb, after laying aside her basket.

The boys are good boys, she thought, any home will be proud to have them, for they are handy and willing. The rocky slope was steep, and the cold wind rushed and snatched at her hair. We're going home, she told her quiet child. Then she reached the top. The wind snatched and tore at her. We're going home, she said, and clutching her child, she leaped into the howling wind.

THE SMELL OF BAMBOO BLOSSOMS

YESHE DORJEE THONGCHI

Translated from the Assamese by Aruni Kashyap

Instead of fish, rats are swarming the Kameng River—an unprecedented phenomenon! These days, as soon as the sun sets behind the Rang Hills, lakhs of rats come out from the thick bamboo forests that sprawl on both banks of the river. The rats are not only destroying crops and marching around inside houses, chewing everything they encounter, but they are also swimming across the Kameng River despite its strong currents. Maybe they are trying to breed or are searching for food.

Along with the rats, people hunting rats has become a regular sight. As soon as hundreds and thousands of rats run towards the river at dusk to swim across it, the riverbanks are flooded with people trying to hunt them. Every rat-hunter holds two lathis and a torch—it's all they will need for the hunting expedition. The Kameng is a broad and deep river with such a strong current that it is impossible for people to swim across it even during winter when the water level is lower. But these little rats are so strong! They swim across the surging monsoon river from one bank to another, and then back again, so easily. When they are about to reach the bank, the wet and exhausted rats require some kind of support to crawl up. The people waiting on the banks hold their lathis out. The rats crawl onto those lathis. The hunters hold their torches between their teeth, and with another lathi, they hit the rats hard on their little heads. In this way, they create a hillock of rat carcasses on the bank by dawn. In a single night, they gather several bags of rats, and that's how the villagers living near the Kameng River and in Seppa town earn some quick money. They skewer four rats with a small piece of bamboo after cleaning and hollowing out the intestines, smoke them for three–four days, and process them into tasty meat. Four cleaned and smoked rats fetch them twenty rupees in cities such as Itanagar or in the markets of Naharlagun. In places like Along in West Siang district and Pasighat in East Siang district, they can sell them at even higher prices. That's why the people living on the banks of the Kameng are happy with the bamboo blossoms.

Tarak Dadao went to the riverbank every day to kill rats. Saddled with debt incurred to pay for his wedding, this was a golden opportunity for him to earn some money. He was the one who discovered the bamboo blossoms deep inside the forest one day. He had carefully chosen the bamboo plants before felling them. With great effort, he had dragged them out, heaped them together with their leaves and twigs on the ground, and it was then, when he had started to clean the twigs and leaves and branchlets, that he noticed clusters of round seeds hanging from the bamboo—dark green and thick-skinned. He was surprised. Bamboo had been an intimate part of his life since his birth, but he had never known bamboo to produce seeds. This was a nabhuta nashruta incident—never before seen, never before heard. He plucked a seed and smelled it. It smelled exactly like raw bamboo, no difference. Inside the thick green skin of the seed, there was something that looked like wheat grain. He chewed one grain, and it tasted like bamboo shoot. He thought it could be used for food. He fished out his cane naara and filled it to the brim with bamboo seeds, after which he cleaned the bamboo plants, made a raft out of them, and floated the raft on the Kameng towards Seppa. From the raft, he saw that bamboos on both banks of the river were bearing flowers and seeds, like soft, green, new paddy.

A few suns later, as they say here, Tarak reached Seppa. He brought the raft to the bank, tethered it to a tree trunk with a rope and walked home. Though he was tired, he was happy. He would be able to give Medak a gift today. She loved to eat bamboo shoots and he was sure she would love bamboo seeds as well.

When he reached his tin-roofed house, everything was silent. He pushed open the door made of broken tins, making a ker-ker-ker sound and entered the house. When Medak realized her husband was home, she climbed down from the bamboo bed.

'What happened, why is it so dark?' He felt a bit annoyed.

'There's no light today,' Medak replied.

'That doesn't mean you should sleep in the dark. Please light the fire.'

Medak said nothing. She walked towards the hearth in a corner of the room and started to make a fire.

What had happened to Medak, who, on other days, would wait for him impatiently at the gate of the compound? Something must be wrong, he thought.

Though he was exhausted and hungry, he found himself overflowing with love for her despite her odd behaviour. After all, she was still with him after overcoming many hurdles, fights with her parents, brothers, and the community. He still felt as if the life he led with Medak was a dream from which, one day, he might wake up.

'I am starving, is there anything to eat?'

'There's some rice, but no curry. That old man Matung Burha ate everything before leaving. What would you like to have it with?' She started to cough.

'Is your cough worsening?' He came closer to Medak and put his hand on her forehead. 'I think you have a fever.'

'I haven't been feeling well. The cough is getting worse. Tomorrow I will go to the doctor again,' Medak said.

'I will come along and talk to the doctor properly.'

'There's no need. How long can we continue living like this in Matung Burha's house? We need to finish building our own house soon. Should I make some warm fried rice for you?'

'Okay. But tell the doctor everything, make sure he does a proper check-up. One more thing; look at what I've brought home for you from the forest.' Tarak fished out a bunch of bamboo flowers from his naara.

'What are these?' Medak asked, feeling the seeds with her fingers after she put the rice into the heated oil.

'These are bamboo seeds. I think they will be very tasty. We should peel off the green skin and try boiling them.'

'How can bamboo bear seeds like paddy?' Medak laughed.

'I don't know, but I plucked these myself.'

'Before we boil them, we should show these to Grandpa Matung. I have never heard of bamboos bearing seeds. What if something goes wrong after we eat them?'

Tarak thought it was a good suggestion. He finished his hot fried rice cooked with methun chilli powder, and set off to Matung Burha's house

Matung Burha owned the house in which Tarak and Medak lived. Burha was a lonely man with no one to call his own. People said he was around a hundred years old but he didn't look like it. There weren't any contemporaries of the old man alive in the region. But even though he was old, he was quite strong. He lived in a modest house of cane and bamboo, did odd jobs, and depended on the generosity of others for his meals. When Medak eloped with Tarak from Chingi village and came to the town of Seppa, Matung Burha had provided them shelter in his small house which was fit for one person. After Tarak and Medak moved in, Burha went to live in Chama's house.

According to the customs of the Nyishi tribe, Medak was married to Tero Chingi, the man who paid the costly bride-price. But as soon as she had reached her new husband's house, she ran away to Tarak's village, Jejudada, while the guests were busy dancing and singing. It was only after Medak was dressed in her bridal clothes and sent to Chingi that she realized whom she really wanted to spend her life with. On her way to Chingi, she had imagined Tarak beckoning her. By the time the people of Chingi realized that Medak was missing, she had already covered a long distance. They didn't know where to look. The villagers asked people in the neighbouring villages, and when no one offered any helpful information, they concluded that she had been kidnapped by ghosts.

When Tarak heard about Medak's mysterious disappearance from Tero Chingi's house, he was surprised. Though Medak had never loved him, he had been in love with her for a long time. So, when she married someone else, he was heartbroken and then when he heard that she had vanished from her groom's house, he was worried.

Medak couldn't gather the courage to go and meet Tarak when she arrived in Jejudada. She knew he loved her but she had never given him any encouragement. She had left Chingi and her husband on an impulse. She took shelter in the forest near Tarak's village and lived off wild fruits for several days. She would watch the village people come and go. One day, she saw Tarak entering the forest to cut bamboo. They travelled to Seppa together and hid in Matung Burha's house for many days. When people learnt of this, it led to a fierce argument between the Chingi and Dada tribes. But since the Dadas—the tribe Tarak belonged to—were large in number, the minority Chingis were forced to settle and agreed to leave Medak alone on the condition that Tarak paid double the bride-price.

When Yaro saw Medak and Tarak coming, he offered them two wooden stools from the hearth to sit on.

'We are here to show something to Grandpa Matung. Only he will be able to tell us whether it is edible or not.'

Tarak took out the seeds from his naara and placed them on Matung

Burha's palms. 'Grandpa, please tell us what these are.'

The old man picked one seed up and examined it, held it close to his eyes, smelled it, chewed it. Suddenly, the old man looked horrified. He screamed, 'Where did you get these seeds from?'

Before Tarak could answer, Matung Burha spoke in a frenzy, 'The bamboos are flowering again! These seeds are a bad omen! Now rats will rule over people. They will devour the paddy, the maize, the wheat, everything! People will die without food. Village after village will be destroyed. Oh, Doni Polo, did you keep me alive this long just to show me this? Just kill me, please kill me.'

'Why are you so upset? Please tell us what happens when bamboos flower,' Yaro said, trying to calm the old man.

'I haven't spoken about those times to anyone. One day, I will tell you.'

Soon, from Siyang Taju to Bhalukpung, the bamboos started to flower on both banks of the Kameng. Well, not exactly flowers—they were large, green seeds that sprouted in bunches. Rats fed on the seeds and that led to an exponential increase in their ability to breed. As soon as dusk fell, thousands of rats would emerge from every corner and swim across the river. The rats didn't let the paddy ripen—they attacked the fields and destroyed the entire crop. They didn't differentiate between the forest and the farmlands: wherever they saw any fruit or seeds, they ate them all. But still, there were no signs of famine or plague as Matung Burha had predicted. The government was quite quick to act. To prevent people from starving, they distributed large quantities of food.

Tarak was happy that the rodent population had increased. Medak had developed a chest pain and chronic cough in the forest. The doctor said she had tuberculosis. To raise money for the medicine and injections, they processed and sold rat meat. At dusk, Tarak would go with Chomar to the riverbank to kill rats, and they would return at dawn with a bunch of dead rats. Medak and Yaro would then sit down together, hollow the rats by pulling out their intestines, pierce four cleaned rats with a slim bamboo stick, and then smoke them. At first, this made Medak queasy. Burning rat fur produced a terrible smell that nearly choked her. After the fur was burned off, the naked rats would swell up, looking like little roasted piglets. The melting fat, smelling like rotten potatoes, dripped from the rats' bodies into the fire, making a serek-serek sound.

'Chi! What a dirty job!' Medak had said.

'Why don't you eat a little; it's so tasty!' Tarak had exclaimed.

'I can't eat rat meat! I will throw up!'

~

Amidst all this strife, the good news was that Tarak and Medak finally built a house for themselves. They had expanded Matung Burha's house, building rooms for themselves and for him. They had noticed a change in Matung Burha after the bamboos flowered. Fear, anxiety, and hatred oozed from his face. He would keep scolding Tarak. 'How many more rats are you going to kill? Stop this! These are inauspicious rats that have eaten bamboo blossoms!'

'What is so inauspicious? I have earned about nine thousand rupees just by selling rat meat. That's the price of a mithun! Why should I stop killing rats? You should join me.'

'I don't need money! If you kill too many rats, I won't let you stay with me. I will throw you out of my house!'

Matung Burha didn't have much to do except leave the house in the morning and return with a bundle of firewood for the day. Then he would just roam around Seppa for the rest of the day or he would sit and sharpen his machete by rubbing it against a stone, a machete that was already sharp. As he sharpened it, he would say to Medak, 'You are suffering from Rat Disease! You will not survive! No one survives this Rat Disease!'

'I am not suffering from Rat Disease. The doctor says I have TB.'

'Your doctor is lying to you. I know you have contracted Rat Disease. Cough, fever—these are all symptoms of the disease.'

'It was you who said that the bamboo blossoms would lead to a famine, people would starve to death, hundreds of people would die of disease, but see, nothing has happened.' She made fun of the old man.

'It will happen! People will die; entire villages will perish. It hasn't been long since the bamboo started to flower. You wait and see, it will happen.'

'No, Grandpa, no. Nothing like that will happen. This is the age of the harangs. The age of bangni simpletons from the hills are over. That's why, when the bamboos bloom, famines and epidemics don't take place. On the contrary, this is the age to become rich!' The old man would grumble, unable to argue any further. But Medak would usually steer clear of Matung Burha. Sometimes she was afraid of the old man.

Since she did not know about his past life, she was suspicious of him. Who knew, he might have been a killer in his past! On other days, she would placate him by cooking beef or pork with rice, straining a mug of apong beer whenever he wanted one.

∽

A year passed since the blossoming of the bamboo. As soon as the bamboo seeds started to ripen, the bamboo leaves turned yellow and started to fall. After the leaves fell off, the naked trees remained standing for a few days, turning red and then slowly black, before drying up completely to the roots. Both banks of the Kameng River that usually had lush green forests, now looked ugly with the dying, blackened bamboo.

As soon as the bamboo began drying up, the rats too started dying. In forests, thickets, and on the riverbank, there were only rat carcasses. The air had become heavy with the smell of rotting rats. The same rats that used to quickly cross the speedy river drowned or were carried away by the current.

Once the Kameng entered Assam, it was called Jiya Bhoroli, and when the people in Tezpur and Balipura saw the bodies of hundreds and thousands of rats on the banks of Jiya Bhoroli, they were horrified. At the same time, in faraway Gujarat, in a city called Surat, a plague epidemic broke out. The government took quick measures to prevent the outbreak of plague in Arunachal and Assam. They first banned the consumption of rat meat. After the announcement was made through a loudspeaker, Matung Burha lit a large fire and burnt all the skewered and smoked rats.

On the second day, the government officials again made announcements over the loudspeaker: 'Anyone suffering from fever and cough, please avoid contact with other people and report to the nearest Plague Prevention Committee without delay.'

On the evening this announcement was made, the three of them were eating dinner. When Matung Burha heard it, he went into the house swiftly, and brought out his gleaming machete. Medak was so frightened she felt as if her soul was about to leave her body through her head. She thought he had been looking for a pretext to kill her, and that was why he had been sharpening his machete so meticulously. Matung Burha held the machete up in the air and started to sing and perform the traditional Boyo dance. When people in the neighbourhood heard the old man's song, they came out of their houses.Chama, Yaro, and others joined him in the dance. They made a circle.

Matung Burha danced and sang: 'This beautiful girl, Medak, is a fool.' The chorus agreed, 'Yes, what a fool.' 'I sheltered her in my house,' he sang, 'yet she couldn't fathom who I am.' The chorus supported him: 'Hun, hun, couldn't fathom who you are!' He sang again, 'Today, through this Boyo dance, I will tell her who I am, will tell my life story. All of you now listen with full attention.'

He continued singing, while others either repeated parts of his lines or just hummed along. 'Medak's father, Rakap, was my son—a secret that Rakap's mother, Yani, and I kept until today. Yani was my lover. Old Tali seized her from me by paying a large number of mithuns as bride-price. When she was married to Tali, as his seventh wife, she carried my child in her womb. Rakap should have inherited my title, Jomoh, but he was known as Kinoo. In my mind, the flower of sadness bloomed, but in the forests the talamdarak had blossomed from the bamboo. Rats devoured entire crops and people starved to death. Listen, listen, during those days, there were no harang people from the plains like today. The entire hills only had bangni people. When the famine ended, there came the Rat Disease. To get rid of it, we started to burn houses. With these hands, I burnt many people to death, many houses, and many villages. Villages became empty. The hills became empty. The disease was conquered and only I lived till this old age. I didn't marry. I didn't raise a family. Rakap's daughter, Medak, doesn't know that I am her grandfather. Tarak didn't even give me one piece of meat as her bride-price. Now, she has the Rat Disease and I will have to burn her alive along with the house to prevent the disease from spreading. This thought burns my heart. This is my Boyo song.'

The old man stopped dancing and singing. When the villagers heard that Medak was suffering from Rat Disease, they fled.

Medak started to cry, and Tarak hugged her close to his chest and stroked her head. She wept. 'I think it is true that I have the Rat Disease. I will not survive. I will leave you alone in this world and die.'

Tarak wanted to comfort her but he, too, couldn't stop crying. 'The old man is lying. If you die, I won't be able to live. Let the old man burn us alive together.'

Matung Burha watched the couple. They were drowning in a sea of sorrow. Finally, he entered his own room and locked the door.

The next morning, Chama told Tarak that the Plague Prevention Committee's office was hiring. They needed people to burn down the dried-up bamboo and also set fire to the rat carcasses. But Tarak didn't go looking for work. Instead, he took Medak to the doctors again. By then, several well-known doctors had gathered in Seppa. They examined Medak carefully and confirmed that she had nothing but tuberculosis and that she was doing much better.

On their way back, they decided that they wouldn't stay with Matung Burha any more. They would leave their house to him and rent a place in Seppa where Medak could undergo treatment since she was still unwell. Later, they would return to Tarak's village, Jejudada.

When they reached home, they saw that all their belongings were heaped far from the house. The old man had put their clothes and kitchenware outside the house and locked himself in. Everything they owned was thrown in the heap. Along with their belongings, the old man had also kept his own large tin trunk. Medak tried to pick it up. It was impossibly heavy, as if weighed down by a large stone.

'Medak!'

Medak was startled.

'Open that trunk!'

She looked around to locate the source of the old man's voice.

'Open that trunk!' the old man ordered once again.

Scared, she did as he asked. She was shocked to see that it was filled with precious gems, with tadak and chongre. Matung Burha spoke again. 'These jewels have been preserved for you. They belonged to your great-grandmother, my mother. She died of the Rat Disease, and along with her, my sisters too. When I heard that Rakap had a daughter, I was happy to know that a rightful heir had been born. Even though I have been terribly hungry, I never sold a single gem from this trunk. I am now giving these to you. Take them and go away from here.'

'Grandpa, I am not suffering from Rat Disease. All those big doctors have examined me and assured me I'm not,' Medak said.

'I know, I know everything. People who have Rat Disease die after four or five days. You don't have that disease but I have it. I have had a fever since morning and have been coughing too. Don't come near me! Now go away from here, go away, there's no time, go away!'

'We will go and get a doctor. You will be fine,' Tarak shouted.

By then, a group of people had gathered around the house.

The old man screamed from inside the house, 'There is no point going to the doctor! When someone gets this disease, they have to be burnt alive inside the house. Otherwise, it spreads. I have killed many such patients along with their houses! I have burnt my mother, father, brothers, and sisters alive because they had Rat Disease! Let this house burn down completely, otherwise this disease will spread to others and the hills will be empty of people once again.'

The house started to burn.

Matung Burha had set it on fire. Within seconds, flames engulfed the house. On both banks of Kameng River massive flames began spreading. It was the fire that would overpower the smell of bamboo blossoms to welcome orchids. It was the fire of creation.

BROTHERS

MAMANG DAI

They were walking quietly in the moonlight—one with an easy, fluid gait like a shadow gliding on the narrow path, the other almost skipping, lunging along with a swinging movement of his arms.

'Remember,' said the taller of the two, looking sideways at the younger boy who was his brother, 'we don't want to be rash. Stay calm. Try not to show your face too much.'

They were approaching a dense patch of forest. Beyond this, in an hour's time, they would be in Itanagar. His brother didn't say anything. A strip of moonlight glowed on his cheek as if it was plastered there. His narrow face looked ghostly.

'And to think he was the pet of the house,' thought the elder boy, remembering his brother's fat, wobbly legs as a child.

'He will grow up into a strong man!' Their mother had crooned. Back in the village, that was—back then.

At night, the capital city looked different. The mountains appeared sinister, as if they had been pushed away roughly by some unfriendly hand, and they were sulking, towering over the foggy smear of lights—watching, waiting to see what he would do, what anyone would do.

'I'll do good,' he thought. It was so cold. 'I am young and strong. Just watch.'

He shivered. The cold stone gleamed. What did it mean—? Martyr, Ma-ti-r-r? He was a brave fellow, oh yes, sure he was—his brother, lying dead under that stone. Everyone had congratulated him and praised his brother when they had gathered to lay him down.

'His memory will live on. We will build a martyr's monument here. He will never be forgotten. No, no, never!'

He dozed off. The long night moaned in his ears. Rustling, rustling. His brother and he were hunting in the forest. The leaves were whirling down. Cough, cough. It was his brother coughing. Shush, shush. Don't make a sound. He was carrying a gun. Ah—that wonderful piece of metal, borrowed for one night. Tonight! He fired and saw a deer leap sideways and disappear with a crash into the undergrowth. Quick! Let's find him. His brother was staring at him, his eyes popping out. They could see the deer's antlers sticking out above the tangle of fern. His brother jumped up high. There was a sharp crack. His brother screamed. A stream of blood gushed out of his mouth and smeared his face like red rain.

'Aaaah....' He woke up with a start.

The wind was choking him. It was raining and the trees were swaying left and right spraying raindrops on him. Another lousy day. Look, look there—how great are we? He looked about him. No one was around at this godforsaken time, the weary hour between night and this soggy, grey daybreak. He wanted that gun. He had seen it in his dream, just now, and that must mean something.

He wedged himself into the narrow space between the hut and the trees, settling into a cross-legged position with his arms dangling. He was comfortable here, in the shadowy half-light, alone and undetected. He could stay here like this forever. So what! Who could move him? The hut was but a rough shack of thatch, raised on four poles built over the grave of his brother to protect it from the elements. A group of volunteers had laid out a slab of brick and mortar, but they had been unable to roll away the big stone that now half-hid the burial site. They would finish the work later.

'It may take time, but be sure, we will complete it,' they told him.

The capital was a place of memorials honouring martyred young men who had lost their lives in agitations against all manner of social ills and threats to the territory and integrity of the state. He grimaced and squinted up at the sky. He saw an old man with grey hair, like his father before he staggered to his deathbed with his blind eyes streaming slow, sticky tears. Something stuck in his throat. If only I could have a gun! The wind was straining to lift up the sky. It was hammering in his chest and howling in his blood, pounding and pushing him to tear at that grey-faced old man and wipe that grey sky leering at him from the face of the earth.

'Haa—aa-h—' He drew in a lungful of air and pressed his mouth tight.

'There is a way, there is a way,' his uncle had shouted. 'We will leave this village. In the city we will claim our due. Everyone is living there—who is here in the village today? Look! Look! Are we not stupid fools? We have no dignity! Birds build nests and wild animals have a warm place to sleep at night. We will find our dwelling place. We will build our houses in the city. My brothers! If it is war, so be it! We know how to fight! Come on!'

He remembered it had been raining then, and his uncle's face was jubilant with the rain pouring down on his head. Everyone had cheered him on with a mighty roar. 'We know how to fight! We are not afraid of anyone. We will fight for dignity!'

Uncle had a reputation. When he was a young man, a teenager—no older than he was now—Uncle had bumped into a relative near a bridge. They had been partners in a supply business. Uncle had done all the leg work, and he felt he had not received his due share of payment.

'What about my money, eh?' he had asked.

The older man had glared at him. 'What money, I have no money, ha hah!'

He was reeking of liquor and had made a great show of emptying his pockets.

'That was it,' he had said. 'There's nothing more, here—look, here, here!'

Uncle had looked, and there, standing by the bridge he had pulled out a gun and shot the man dead. Then he told the police that he had fired in self-defence. The dead man, as everyone knew, was a drunken thug, the black sheep of a family who had threatened to kill his own family many times, and had now shouted revenge and murder against his. An unknown benefactor had paid a large sum of money to hush up anyone who might make trouble and there the matter had been dropped. Nothing more had been said about the gun.

Since then, Uncle had grown in stature. Everyone bowed to his rallying cry, 'Brothers, come with me!'

And everything that happened had happened as if he and his brother were caught in a dream that tore them from their hut in the village and pushed them into the maze of dark stairways into a building with windows like dirty holes peeping out of the sodden, concrete walls where they were told to watch and wait. His uncle was a city man.

'There are more of us,' he told them. 'They are here in the city, and there are more across rivers and hills. We have called all our brothers to join the rally and now there is no space in the capital, ha-ha!'

His uncle's breath was on his face, the betel-stained mouth laughing, and black eyes glinting—that suppressed, eager look of a hunter waiting in ambush for prey. Such easy, stupid prey. Voices echoed, shadows flitted in and out of the building. Ten migrant settlers had been shot dead by unknown assailants in the middle of the night in a village on the Assam border. The situation was tense. The state governments on both sides of the border were investigating the matter, but it was well known that neither side welcomed unwanted settlers. Still, some action had to be taken.

'They are retaliating with an economic blockade against us,' shouted his uncle.

He looked dangerous. His uncle was a member of an organization. The boy knew little of organizations—but he knew his uncle. He shuddered when his uncle appeared with a gun.

'We are an organization of leaders; people who have ideas.... I am working for our undisputed leader, do you understand?' his uncle said, glaring around at the boys assembled in the dank building.

They were all young men from remote villages present in the capital city for the first time, rounded up on trucks that had carried them like cargo, half-awake, half-asleep, in the middle of the night to dump them in this dark grey place. They were fed platefuls of bland rice and potatoes diced so small it was as if the cook was trying to feed twenty people with five rotten potatoes. They gobbled up their food and moved out in different directions, to guard the entry and exit points of the city.

'Don't worry, you will know which vehicles to allow entry.' His uncle had waved them out of the building.

The idea was to provoke a capital bandh by setting up roadblocks with logs and boulders in selected sites. All the shops had downed their shutters and the government offices were empty. It was to be a show of solidarity that everyone was united on the matter of illegal settlers who wanted to encroach into the state. Who had put these poor families in the middle of Reserve Forest land? Who were the perpetrators of this heinous act—who could say, but the settlers should have known what they were in for, trespassing on land that was claimed by both the states. The boy and his brother were in a group manning the Gohpur road entry to the capital. A stream of cars with identical stickers whirled around them with people waving banners, tooting horns, and calling out to each other. Everyone was smiling, and they hailed the boys giving them the thumbs up. They were all going to the rally. The boys stared at the shiny vehicles and felt a tug of mounting anticipation. They would join the rally in a few hours—they would join the crowd and how they would shout and raise their voices for unity and dignity! They had done all that they had been told to do. He remembered the fumes of burning tyres. Burn them! Burn them! Suddenly he saw the face of a young girl from his village appearing like a ghost before him.

'Come, sit here,' he had called out loudly, pointing to a discarded tractor tyre that he had taken possession of.

It was a swing, a boat, a wheel admired by everyone in his village. Now it was burning, exploding in flames. The face of the girl moved away, her hair streaming in the rain. He followed, pulling her back by the hand. Soft girl's hands. She was smiling with her head bent down. He tried to lift her face so that he could look into her eyes but she murmured something shaking droplets of rain from her hair.

'No...no.... Don't listen to these people—'

Maybe it was his imagination playing tricks. Why should a girl say such words when the whole world was fighting for dignity and their rightful place in society?

'What *place*?' The thought jumped out at him like a mean-faced dog.

'A place where we can live like leaders—eat, drink, enjoy ourselves, get married, ha-ha....' his younger brother had laughed like a maniac, rubbing his hands together—that idiot. It wasn't a wife he wanted. He remembered his mother's face. His father was set on taking a second wife. She was young and shameless, that second woman. He had caught her looking at him as if she could give him some fun, hah! He could give her something, that he could, hurt her and make her cry. What would his father do then, the old man?

He felt perspiration trickling down from his brow. It was hot. The rain had been a teaser. It had come and gone. Women, he thought—nothing but trouble. Desire, to hell with it. It was his brother's nonsense, all that desire. His brother had been like the old man, acting on instinct, strutting around to be the hero and then picking up speed like a tornado with the long blade of his dao held high, screaming, running straight at a man in a brown shirt—another mean-faced cat with wild eyes who had moved his hands up and fired a gun. It's the police! The field was swaying and thudding with people running amok but one thing was clear—the rally did not disperse. Nothing could break their resolve. No one ran away from the police. In fact, his brother had charged straight at the policemen and appeared to be still laughing when he fell, crashing into his arms with his gaping, round moon-face. That's why he was a martyr. There was nothing else to it. His brother had killed himself and a statue would be raised in his honour. They had shaken the government to the core, right here in the centre of the city. Brothers, together! The rampage of smashed glass, burning tyres and chairs, and torched vehicles was evidence enough. No need to say anything now. He did not want to meet his uncle or anyone else. He scoffed at the idea of brothers. Who wanted to work here, or work at all, scratching around for dignity and status, finding food and eating together with all the other mean-faced idiots? He could claw his way through, anyway, if he wanted to *go up*. He was cleverer than Uncle. He could be a better hunter, marksman, organizer, and leader. What did he want most in this world? All he had ever wanted was a gun. He felt his heart about to explode as he glared around. He looked at the fresh mound of earth. Nothing here too. Who wanted to be a grey statue standing all alone when you could be buried in your own place? Right there in the village where everyone could greet you when they walked past your grave on their way to the fields. He stood up. Something was pressing down on his head and he lifted his arm and began rubbing the crown of his head gently. Aa aah—his right hand hung limp and inert, then slowly bent at the elbow as his fingers clenched into a fist. He wanted that gun.

KA DIANGTIMAI

DESMOND L. KHARMAWPHLANG

Translated from the Khasi by Ellerine Diengdoh

Nestled amidst our rugged hills, we Khasis possess a wealth of words, each crafted to capture the very essence of rain. Here in Sohra, our astute locals effortlessly summon eight or nine distinct names, tailored to the rain's myriad manifestations. Whether encountered amid the enchanting depths of our lush forests or upon the rugged slopes of our majestic hills, or even within the intimate sanctuaries of our homes, each and every rain bears a name inscribed in the intensity of its downpour.

Ah yes, the roofs once thatched and singing with rustic melody, are now suffocated by the cold embrace of tin, cement, and plastic—a poignant reminder of the changing tides of time.

Diangtimai Swer, a lone figure in the shadows of Nongsawlia, awaited the bewitching hour, her sanctuary a mere stone's throw from the imposing Irrigation Office where she toiled. As 4.30 approached, the sky unleashed its fury.

While she waited, anticipation brewed like a storm within her, mingling with the awe-inspiring spectacle unfolding outside her window. The rain lashed with an unapologetic rage, as if nature was unleashing its wrath upon the earth. The heavens echoed with the bellowing of thunder followed by an assault of lightning, a silver sword tearing the very fabric of the sky.

Four moons had quietly passed since her departure from Sonapahar, where she had devoted two years of her life. It marked a significant transition, bidding farewell to familiar walls and a comforting routine. Before Sonapahar, Lyngngam had been her sanctuary for two and a half years, its embrace now a distant memory fading into the shadows of her past.

As a solitary woman, Diangtimai embraced a vibrant life, undeterred by the distance from her family although she treasured her monthly visits home. Her role as a UDA bloomed with purpose, surrounded by kindred spirits from her workplace and gentle souls from the church.

Generous visitors to her office gifted her vibrant pumpkins, wild vegetables, and yams, inspiring her to explore their flavours. She also discovered that the wild varieties surpassed the mundane market produce, infusing her dishes with authentic and tantalizing tastes with flavours that danced upon her tongue like whispered secrets.

The sudden arrival of a Bolero outside her veranda shattered the tranquillity of her thoughts, its presence an unwelcome intrusion into her sanctuary. Pherbak, a contractor with ties to Nongjadu, swept into her space with an urgency that hinted at concealed intentions.

This man of means, with a home to call his own and three children pursuing education in distant Shillong, often graced her office with his presence. His small talk masked a deeper agenda while his 'gifts' veiled a hidden motive. Diangtimai, however, stood firm, gracefully declining his offerings of umbrellas, handbags, shawls, and fruits, refusing to be entangled in his web of deceit.

In the span of four months in Nongjadu, his presence loomed like a recurring nightmare, haunting her sanctum with each of his ten visits. His persistent desire to accompany her on journeys to Shillong or Sohra spoke volumes of his intentions.

On this fateful day, Bah Pherbak descended from his vehicle with an air of determination, his footsteps echoing with the weight of unspoken threats. As he invaded the main office room before intruding upon her sanctuary, a chilling sense of foreboding settled over her like a shroud.

'Kong Diang,' he murmured, his voice dripping with false concern. 'The rain shows no mercy. Allow me to escort you home.'

'It's unnecessary,' she countered, her tone resolute. 'The storm has passed, and I am adequately prepared.'

'Why do you persist in rejecting my kindness?' he implored, his facade crumbling to reveal the venomous truth beneath. 'Do you not see me as human, deserving of your compassion?'

'Bah Pherbak,' she retorted, her words laced with steel, 'you know precisely the boundaries I have set. I want no part in your charade, and that is final.'

'You dare to spurn me like an animal!' he erupted, his rage igniting like a blaze. 'Mark my words, you will regret the day you crossed me!' With that, he stormed away, leaving behind a trail of malevolence in his wake.

In a flurry of emotions, Diangtimai departed from her workplace, her steps heavy with unresolved tension. The echoes of her exchanges with Pherbak reverberated in her mind, filling her soul with despair and helplessness.

Returning to the solitude of her dwelling, she sought solace in the familiar routines of domesticity. Yet even as she cooked and cleaned, the spectre of Pherbak loomed large, casting a shadow over her every action.

With the night settling like a heavy blanket, she reached out to her mother in a desperate bid for comfort. Their conversation, though soothing, offered only temporary respite from the turmoil within.

After the weight of the day had settled upon her weary shoulders, Diangtimai sought refuge in the sanctuary of her bed. The darkness enveloped her like a shroud as she lay upon her linens, her mind swirling with tumultuous thoughts. Slowly, she succumbed to the gentle embrace of sleep, her consciousness drifting away into a sea of restless dreams.

∽

'How dare you intrude upon my sanctum, Bah Pherbak?' Diangtimai's voice trembled with a mixture of shock and indignation as she confronted the unwelcome visitor lurking in the shadows of her doorway.

Pherbak's response was a chilling whisper that slithered through the air like a serpent's hiss. 'You think I'm an animal, do you not? Then let me show you the extent of my savagery.'

Diangtimai awoke from her fitful slumber, her heart racing with fear. The first light of dawn filtered through her window, casting long shadows across her room as she struggled to compose herself.

Summoning every ounce of courage she possessed, Diangtimai rose from her bed and stepped into the cold light of morning. And there, on the steps leading up to her home, her gaze fell upon a sight that froze her blood in its veins…wrapped around a crimson wildflower like a sinister embrace, lay the skin of a serpent!

HIS MOTHER'S PORK AND WHY HE IS NOT A CHRISTIAN

KYNPHAM SING NONGKYNRIH

Ap Jutang was asked, as a man well versed in Khasi religion or Niam Khasi, to speak to members of Seng Tynrai, an organization acting as the guardian of Khasi religion and culture, who were gathering at the organization's lecture hall in the locality of Nongthymmai, in the city of Shillong.

Standing at the podium, he began: 'You have asked me to speak about the causes that make so many of us abandon our own religion and join the innumerable Christian sects, including the BBC. That is what I intend to do. But in the process, I will also explain why I'm not a Christian.... This will shed some light on the subject at hand.'

'BBC, Bah Ap?' many voices asked.

Ap Jutang, 'Keeper of the Covenant', was, in accordance with Khasi custom, called Bah Ap by everyone who knew him. It means 'elder brother Ap', or simply, 'Mr Ap'.

'Bible Believing Church,' he replied. 'It's there at Keatinge Road.... The great British philosopher, Bertrand Russell, wrote a magnificent essay titled "Why I Am Not a Christian". But apart from the title, let me hasten to add, there's nothing in common between what he had to say and the story I'm going to tell you. While his rejection of Christianity was based on certain considerations, including his belief in the non-existence of God, mine was because of a deeply personal incident involving my mother's pork.'

'Pork, did you say?' Almost everyone clamoured at once.

'Pork, yes!' he replied. 'But I will tell you the story by and by. Let me begin now with the topic on which I have been asked to speak.

'According to Russell's 1927 lecture, Christianity in the times of St Augustine and St Thomas Aquinas meant an acceptance of "a whole collection of creeds which were set out with great precision, and every single syllable of those creeds you believed with the whole strength of your convictions". A belief in Christianity, therefore, Russell said, also means "a belief in God and immortality"; a belief that "Christ was, if not divine, at least the best and wisest of men"; a belief "in hell"; and additionally, a belief "in eternal punishment" for those who do not believe in Christ.

'In the Khasi Hills, Christianity is all of this and more, for it is practised with missionary zeal. "The unploughed fields of the Lord are still vast" and "the seas are still teeming with fishes" are commonly heard statements. These statements, of course, refer to the fact that about 15 per cent of the Khasi population are still Khasi-Khasis, that's us, although many of us are already asking ourselves, for how long, when we keep having our khun langbrot, our "baby sheep", snatched by our Christian, and even Muslim, brethren at the rate of a few heads per year.'

Some of the men and women in the audience were heard tittering, but the chairman, Bahdeng Kwar, hushed them sternly, saying, 'This is a serious matter.'

At that moment, Bahdeng (that is his nickname because he is the middle brother in his family) looked quite dignified. His lean brown face seemed to glow against a dark blue suit, set off by a white shirt and a red tie. But, he managed to look quite traditional despite his clothing, for he had on his head an embroidered golden silk turban while across his shoulders was a ryndia, a satiny white eri shawl folded neatly and worn like a sash. In stark contrast to him, Ap Jutang was in his trademark corduroy jeans and blue-and-white checked shirt. His only concession to tradition was a ryndia shawl dangling from his neck.

'In actual fact,' Ap Jutang resumed, 'Niam Khasi Niam Tre, as you all know, is a beautiful and attractive creed. It believes in one supreme God, U Blei—whose form man cannot even begin to imagine, for that is forbidden—who is universal, the same for everyone, no matter which ethnic or religious group we belong to. Only the manner of worship is different. The God of the Khasis is thus also the God of Hindus, Muslims, Buddhists, Jews, and Christians. This also explains why there is a complete absence of missionary tendency in the Khasi religion. Isn't this beautiful? If you believe in it, where is the need for conversion? Where is the need for fanaticism?

'And what's more, Niam Khasi believes in the Three Commandments, the Divine Laws, of "ka tip briew tip Blei", "ka tip kur tip kha", and "ka kamai ïa ka hok" (the knowledge of man, the knowledge of God; the knowledge of one's maternal and paternal relations; and the earning of virtue) whose significance is so profound and whose application is so wide-ranging that they embrace all aspects of life without exception.

'But most attractive of all, it does not believe in hell. The Khasi universe is only two-tier—heaven and earth. Words that denote hell are all borrowed concepts: dujok from the Persian dozkh; nurok from the Hindi narak; ka myngkoi u Jom from Hindu mythology about the country of Yama, the god of death; and ki khyndai pateng ñiamra, "the nine stories of Hades", obviously from Greek mythology.

'The only punishment for a person who has committed serious acts of commission and omission is a condemnation of his soul to an earthly existence as a ghost or demon. But even this is not permanent, for if his relatives perform the necessary rites, pleading with God for forgiveness, his soul, too, would be allowed to "Leit bam kwai ha Iing U Blei", or "Go and eat betel nut in the House of God". Eating betel nuts has great cultural significance among us, but that is another story.

'Now, this is not as bad as being burnt eternally in the fires of hell, is it? And yet, why then did so many of us desert our own? The reason lies partly in this often-heard statement, "Because we have been left orphaned, we no longer know much about our own faith; hence, we have no option but to convert." Ignorance is not only the cause of conversion but also scorn. A Khasi who practises his own religion, as you are well aware, is despised as u bym pat long niam—a person who has not embraced any religion, as if his religion is not a religion; or as u bym pat tip Blei—a person who has not come to know God, as if his God is not God; or even u riew pyrthei—a person of the world, as if everybody else is no longer of this world.

'Even among us, there are many who do not really understand our own religion, like those of you who have been so easily misled by borrowed concepts about hell and Hindu gods. As a result, our faith is weak and fragile, and most of us have become the sacrificial goats of love, docilely trailing behind our beloved, not caring where they lead us. If we marry a Christian, we become Christian; if we marry a Hindu, we become Hindu; and if we marry a Muslim, we become Muslim. If we consider the issue of conversion carefully, we will discover that one of the primary reasons for it is the degree of BL, Bachelor of Love, or in Khasi, Bud Lok—following the spouse.'

I don't have to tell you that at that moment the house erupted in thunderous laughter. After Bahdeng had hushed them again, Ap Jutang continued: 'But a person who has an intimate knowledge, who clearly understands the great source, the origin and the foundation of his faith, as well as its teachings, will never easily fall prey to BL. He is like a full-grown tree whose roots have deeply penetrated the flesh and bones of the earth, and such a person cannot be uprooted or shaken this way and that by the winds of conversion. It is time, therefore, that all of us familiarize ourselves with the chief tenets of our creed so that our conviction becomes strong and secure. It may be a good idea for all Khasis to do so, for an understanding of our forefathers' faith, to which we all originally belonged, may encourage us to respect one another and bring about a change of attitude, so that the fact of being Khasi is more important than belonging to this or that religion.'

This serious statement made many heads nod in agreement. But Ap Jutang suddenly changed his tone: 'Let me make a small confession to you, let me tell you briefly the story of my love life.... I, too, nearly fell victim to BL!'

Amidst loud laughter, calls of 'Tell us, tell us!' could be heard.

∽

Obligingly, Ap Jutang began, 'When I was a young man—I'm not old even now, of course, I'm still a bachelor—I was deeply in love with a beautiful Christian girl! I wrote a whole collection of poems dedicated to her, eulogizing her dusky beauty and her charming simplicity. But our different faiths often made us argue with each other till one day she said to me: "How can I love you who have not even come to know God, U Blei?"

'In my youthful anger, I retorted, "Look here! U Blei is ours! Yours is Yahweh or Jehovah! How can you say I haven't come to know my own God, U Blei?"

'In response to this, she said: "You haven't come to know Jesus Christ!"

'I concurred. "That, of course, is true." And in my fear that I might lose her, I added, "Why don't you give me time to get to know him well.... Perhaps a time will come when I shall."

'But instead of giving me time, she gave me an ultimatum: "No! If you truly love me, you must follow me!"

'That peremptory demand made me contemplate things very carefully indeed. How could I accept the idea that a particular community is far above all of us, as the chosen people? I loved that girl so very much, and yet I simply could not convert because it felt like betraying my ancestors and glorifying another community's culture, history, myths, and geography at the expense of my own people's. Isn't this contemptuous attitude towards our own the reason why many of our sacred places are being occupied, and thereby desecrated, by the defence forces? I was reminded of the stag in Aesop's fable, who admired his magnificent antlers but derided his legs because they were slender and thin, although he had escaped the hounds with their help. The antlers of other faiths might be magnificent, but it was the skinny legs of Khasi culture that had carried me thus far.

'But more powerful than all these thoughts was the image of my mother's pork, which floated into my mind off and on. So finally, I pleaded with her to give me some time, hoping that when we were truly engrossed in our love, we would forget all our differences.

'However, my beloved was firm in her resolve and gave me another ultimatum: "Either follow me or forget about me!"

'Forget her I could not; follow her I could not. So, I was left dangling like that for a long, long time. But when the pain was particularly tormenting, I consoled myself with this gnomic phawar, a song meant to mark a special occasion:

Lama u khun Khasi
Ba kaweh halor u sieij,
Ban duh ïa la riti,
Lah ba duh ïa i baieit.

(Flag of the Khasi people
Waving from a pole,
Rather than lose your culture,
Better to lose your sweetheart.)'

Here Ap Jutang had to pause for another round of laughter. After a while, he continued: 'When I now and then think back to that incident, I realize that my belief in everything Khasi was exceptionally strong since childhood. And it was all because of my mother's pork.

'My mother was a strong believer in the Khasi religion, but at the same time, she was quite a liberal soul. She never was one to impose her belief on others. When two sisters who taught at a Christian school in Laitlyngkot (although I was born and brought up in Sohra, I spent two years in Laitlyngkot when I was in Classes V and VI) came to ask me to attend church every Sunday, my mother did not object. She simply asked me, "Do you want to go?" At my tender age (I was about twelve), I was attracted by the sight of other children dressed stylishly and attending church every Sunday. I happily agreed. Soon, I became an ardent churchgoer and was reading both Testaments of the Bible diligently. I came to know many of the stories intimately.

'That enthusiasm rapidly became an obsession, and I started participating actively in evangelical gatherings held at various places in the Khasi Hills. One day, the two teachers invited me to a gathering at a place called Laitjem, some kilometres away from Laitlyngkot, on the road towards Dawki and the Indo-Bangladesh border. Because we had to leave very early, my mother worked all night to prepare my jasong—lunch packed in the tough and resilient betel nut leaf. She cut the potatoes into small square pieces and fried them together with pieces of pork in a mixture of onion, turmeric, and bay leaf. For the chutney, she grilled some tungtap, a type of fermented fish, and ground them together with onions, chillies, and ginger. The combination of tungtap, fried potatoes, and pork, together with boiled rice was a very popular dish for the people of Sohra, prepared especially when they went to eat out in the hills. That was the fare my mother organized for me and just the thought of it made my mouth water.

'Especially exciting was the fact that she had packed several pieces of pork in the jasong, a veritable feast for me, who was never allowed more than one piece of meat when eating at home. This was part of our policy of frugal living, for we were quite hard-up, my mother being what they now call "a single mom". Sometimes we were even asked to "just smell the meat" because there was not enough to pass around. But this time, because it was an outing with neighbours, she had packed quite a lot of pork, and it was, therefore, with a feeling of pleasure and anticipation that I left home.

'The gathering was a huge and exciting one, marked by fervent prayers, rousing hymns, and fiery speeches from well-known and excellent speakers, who spoke about the intentions of the Lord with remarkable confidence. We listened to them with rapt attention.

'When it was lunchtime, the teachers took us to a small hill so we could eat in privacy. There were six of us in the group, counting the teachers' two nieces and a nephew. I was very hungry, for it was past my usual lunchtime. And, of course, the thought of the fried pork waiting just for me made me feel as if I could eat up a hill or two, as the saying goes. All of us brought out our own jasongs and opened them. But before I could eat, one of the teachers began to say grace and launched into a long prayer, asking God to bless the food we were about to eat, to give us all a healthy body, to cleanse our souls and purify our minds, to protect us from the seven deadly sins by reminding us of the Ten Commandments, and to generally make us good Christians.

'When the prayer was done, my right hand immediately went to the nicely browned-and-yellowed pork, for I was determined to begin my lunch with a piece of juicy meat and not with a handful of rice as I used to do at home. Both the teachers, however, shouted, "Wait!" ("Arre!" I said to myself. "Why should I wait when the prayer is done? What now?") They then pulled my jasong towards themselves and looked greedily at my pork: "Your mother must love you very much to prepare this nice jasong for you," they said. I looked at theirs and found that they all contained only some boiled vegetables and a small piece of dried fish. Mine was definitely the better fare. Initially, I was rather pleased with myself until suspicion struck me: why were they inspecting my jasong like that?

'At that moment one of the teachers said, "A small boy like you shouldn't be eating so many pieces of pork!" And with that, she commenced to take my pork and distribute it among the group, giving two pieces each to her nieces and nephew and three to herself and her sister. She also took away quite a bit of my fried potato and tungtap. When she had carried out the distribution, she pushed my jasong towards me. When I looked at it, I found that I was left with only *one* piece of pork!

'All sorts of nasty thoughts passed through my head, and I called them all sorts of names. I felt like crying and telling them to return my pieces of pork, that otherwise I would tell my mother when I got home. But what was the use, they were already tearing at them.

'I didn't feel like eating any more. They had taken my pork without my consent and did not even give me anything in return. Instead, they had said, "We have only boiled vegetables and dried fish; there's no use giving you any of these." What kind of people are these? They had only just prayed to God to protect and liberate them from the seven deadly sins, and now they were behaving like this! Did the seven deadly sins not include "greed...lust, envy, and gluttony?" Did not one of the

Commandments tell us, "Thou shalt not covet" anything that belongs to your neighbour? Did not another say, "Thou shalt not steal"? So why were these people coveting my pork and stealing all those pieces from my jasong?

'Of course, they stole! Isn't taking something that belongs to another without asking and without permission an act of stealing? And I was but a child! My mother had packed several pieces of pork for me, and now I had only this single piece! That, too, the smallest! These people were frauds! They prayed with the right; they stole with the left! Their prayer was a mere façade, a deception to mislead others into thinking them virtuous. Is it because of this that people say, "Khristan ka nam?" Christian in name only?

'All these thoughts passed through my mind as I ate my jasong mechanically, without enjoyment. Obviously when I grew older, I discovered that not all Christians were like those two. I came across many (my relatives included) who were truly simple and virtuous; some have even become lifelong friends. But by then, it was already too late: I had become disillusioned. And at that moment, when my pork was being purloined, I could only think: so, you would steal a boy's pork! So, this is the kind of people you are! If becoming a Christian is becoming like you, then there is no point in becoming one at all. Religion cannot make a person better than he is; it is all pretension. And from that very moment, because they had stolen my mother's pork, I decided never to leave my very own Niam Khasi and convert to any other religion. My mother's teachings are much better, I told myself. My mother used to tell me, "Wherever you are, remember your fellow man; remember God; behave conscientiously. That is enough." And that is true. The pieces of fried pork had led me to this realization.'

That was how Ap Jutang concluded his talk, and when he stopped, the entire house erupted in loud applause, and many went up to congratulate him on what they thought was a marvellous speech.

THE COST OF HUNGER

ABDUS SAMAD

Translated from the Assamese by Aruni Kashyap

Often branded as foreigners or 'illegal immigrants', and forced to prove their nationality, Muslim families originating from Bengal are among the worst victims of the volatile floods in the plains of Assam. In the last few decades, thousands of villages have been eroded by almost all of Assam's fifty-five rivers, creating a huge population of internally displaced people, who are often lower-caste, tribals, and migrant Muslims.

He has been hesitating to make a decision for a long time, but today, after Sultan leaves for work, Romzan Ali caresses the long beard that reaches his chest, sighs, and takes a final decision.

Romzan stands up slowly. As he gets up, to support himself, he places his hands on both his knees and then puts pressure. Then he takes slow steps towards the barber's shop, with some sadness. He has the expression of a man who is about to lose something.

'Ahok, bohok.' Sibpujan starts bustling about as soon as Romzan enters the hair-cutting salon. The first customer of the day after all! His face brightens. 'You want a haircut?'

Romzan doesn't answer Sibpujan's questions. He hesitantly sits down on a chair. He doesn't want to be here. There is a large mirror in front of him.... He is startled. Is this really his reflection in the mirror? Romzan Ali's? Is this the image of Sikandar Maulavi's eldest son, Romzan Ali?

He can't believe what he is seeing. This is a man with a broken body.

His hair stands up on his head, branching in all directions like calendula herbs, and most of his beard is grey. His hair looks quite dirty and messy, and his eyes are those of a person who has been suffering from a prolonged illness. Is this really his reflection in the mirror?

For a moment, he is terrified. But still, he accepts that the image belongs to him; the man in the mirror is him. Right, the man in the mirror is him.

He was sad before coming here, but he is even sadder now.

When was the last time he stood in front of such a huge mirror?

How many years ago? Three?

Yes, about that much.

It has been three years since he last visited a barber. Until around three years ago, he used to visit a barber's shop similar to this one and get a haircut and his beard trimmed, and watch himself in the mirror, transfixed. A young man with deep, dark black hair and beard.

'Are you going to get a haircut?' Sibpujan repeats. He has taken out a large, white silk barber-cape to wrap around his customer. He takes out the scissors and combs, bringing them close to his forehead. He silently prays for good business for the day, and, with great enthusiasm, stands next to Romzan's chair.

'No.'

'Then?'

'Beard. I want to shave off my beard.'

'Ha?!' Sibpujan is surprised. What is this man saying! Does he really want to shave off his beard?

He shouldn't have been surprised. This is his profession. Every day he shaves and trims the facial hair of numerous people, Hindus and Muslims, alike. But now, when Romzan asks him to shave off his beard, Sibpujan feels sad. He doesn't feel this way when other customers ask him to do the same. He realizes that no one has come to his salon to shave off such a long beard that reaches up to the chest.

Whenever Sibpujan thinks about the beard of a Muslim man, he starts to think about his own tuft of hair, at the back of his head. He doesn't know the religious or cultural significance of the beard. What he knows for sure is this: the way his religious sentiments are attached to his own little tuft of hair, the beard, too, has some religious significance. He hasn't tried to figure it out though.

Now, he touches his tuft and asks himself: wouldn't it be awkward to shave it off, and wouldn't it feel the same to shave off the beard of this man? He tries to understand what Romzan is thinking. Perhaps, this person won't feel awkward. Perhaps, this man is really comfortable with the idea of shaving his beard off. Otherwise, why would he come here?

Sibpujan leaves Romzan and goes to the drawer on the other side of the room. He puts aside the barber-cape and takes out a towel that he spreads across the chest of the customers when shaving their beards. When he wraps it around Romzan's neck, he notices the length of his beard. It's a really long beard! This beard has been grown and taken care of for a long time—it actually falls to his chest and lower.

Sibpujan, who can hold a strand of hair on a person's head and predict how long ago it was trimmed, tells himself: this beard is from the man's youth.

But why does he want to shave it off? It is quite healthy. The man also looks handsome with a long beard. Yes, it hasn't been oiled and combed regularly, but still, it looks naturally healthy. At his age, a long beard enhances the man's personality and looks. But why should Sibpujan bother? He should just do his job. Still, he can't stop himself from giving a compliment: 'Your beard was beautiful once upon a time, dei.'

'Era!' Romzan sighs silently. This isn't the first time someone has complimented him on his beard. He has been complimented by numerous people, but from today, no more such compliments.

~

'Don't shave your beard any more, o'. You look good with it and not everyone is lucky to have such a rich growth of beard, you know?' his friend Kadir says.

His beard is new. He has shaved only a few times in his life so far. They are both young men. New blades, new facial hair. He shaves in the morning, and by late afternoon, a thin shadow covers his face just like the ahu paddy that grows quickly after the weeds around its stems are shaved. Romzan's skin is bright. The thick black facial hair against his light, clear, bright skin creates a beautiful contrast.

Kadir is the first one to compliment him on his beard, but he won't be the last.

Idris supports him. 'Hoy de, you should keep it. You will look good.'

That night, Romzan admires his face in a small, round hand-held mirror. The flame of the kerosene lamp barely lights up the room. He observes his face, his beard, and agrees with Idris and Kadir. He decides to grow a beard. To make his resolve stronger, he pulls out the shaving blade stored in the cracks of the wall of fermented jute and throws it into the garbage dump. What if he feels like shaving off his beard if the blade is readily available?

In a few days, the beard covers his face beautifully, and then, slowly, like the tip of the flowers of kans grass, it continues to grow, going past his chest. His father, a maulvi, watches him closely. Perhaps he likes it because one day he encourages Romzan, saying, 'Son, don't shave your beard any more. It looks good on you. It is a good deed to grow a long beard.'

The way gold starts to glitter after a polish, similarly beauty is now accompanied by complimentary blessings. Romzan doesn't think about shaving his beard any more.

But it is not that his beard is universally loved. One day, not so long after their wedding, when Rohima's body still smells of fresh turmeric and lentil paste—ingredients that a bride is bathed with—she tells him, 'You are a young man, why would you choose this appearance? Makes you look like an old man! Shave it off!'

He wriggles out of their embrace in an instant, jumps out of bed, and looks at her with fire in his eyes. 'Khobordar! Don't you say such a thing ever again. Things will get worse at home, I am warning you!'

Rohima is startled. Perhaps she isn't prepared for such a display of anger. She didn't think this would infuriate him so much. As the years go by, Romzan's beard becomes a part of his identity, part of his body, like his legs and hands and other organs. There ceases to be any difference between shaving his beard and chopping off one of his legs.

∽

When Sibpujan presses his razor on the side of his cheeks and pulls downwards, Romzan is shocked. He shuts his eyes.

Romzan Ali, who has trouble watching when the mullah presses the sharp knife against the neck of a cow during Eidul-Zuha, is unable to watch the razor work on his face.

No, he can't watch such heartbreaking scenes.

Three years ago, in the month of Shaon, when the Brahmaputra River had suddenly lost its sanity and eroded away the entire village of Birinabari, he wasn't able to watch that scene too.

It was an unbelievable sight.

In the face of the wild river, the riverbank and the massive village, where they had lived for generations, seemed to be made of dry straw! As the water crashed against the riverbank, huge chunks of earth fell into the river and then eventually swept away the land on which the village stood. The inhabitants of Birinabari watched this horrifying scene. People from neighbouring villages, too, watched as the village was consumed by the river.

Kadir's father, Jabar Burha, began to slap his forehead before crying out in a loud voice. Pointing to the unstable, vanishing riverbank on which the village stood, he shouted, 'Look, look, all of you, how the village is being destroyed! This is not the current of the Brahmaputra! This is like a sharp knife—slicing away our land and the entire village, just as a sharp knife slices the juicy bottle gourd!

Nine days. In just nine days the village was swallowed by the river—the village that belonged to Jabar Burha, Kadir, Idris, and Romzan. After losing everything, the people in the village moved to the top of the long embankment.

Now, when Romzan recalls those nine harrowing days, the sorrow in his heart is so intense that his chest feels like a balloon about to burst due to excess air. Those nine days changed the entire world of Romzan and the other villagers. They had so much in that past life: fourteen bighas of farmland, two pairs of cows, four houses made of bamboo, straw, and mud on that plot of one and a half bighas of land where his father, a maulvi; his wife Rohima; and his three children lived.

In those four mud houses and one and a half bighas of land, Romzan and his family had found peace and happiness. They sometimes faced hardships; his mother died when he was young. But those are now just memories.

∽

Romzan sighs.

He is sitting next to the entrance of a hut made of torn polythene and old gunny bags. The hut is built on the embankment. Previously, when the village was still standing on the riverbank, there was occasional misery, but now all he sees is absence, sorrow, and hunger. Inside the hut, his toddler son cries. He hasn't found a job and the day is coming to an end. The child is hungry because he doesn't have money to buy ration.

What if he does not find work and earn money tomorrow too? How will he buy food for the kids? No, he shouldn't think any further. He doesn't want to go there. Two months ago, his father died of starvation in this hut built on the embankment. No, actually, he had consumed some wild yams after staying hungry for two whole days and they didn't go down well. The stomach and the wild yams immediately got into a war. His stomach made gurum-garam sounds the whole night. With a pot in his hand, he had climbed down the embankment towards the river waters. After that, everything was over.

The boy is weeping again, asking for food.

From a little further down the path, a song floats towards him, 'Mukkala muqabala laila ho laila!' This is Sultan's voice. He is the one who imports these terrible uncultured songs from Guwahati. He came the day before yesterday and he is leaving for Guwahati again the day after. It has been a year or so; he works with a mason as a helper. His family is doing all right.

'Khura,' Sultan asked him the night before, 'would you like to go with me to Guwahati? I will make sure you get a job.'

'No, Bopa, I am not going anywhere. I would rather die here of starvation,' Romzan says.

But…that was last night.

Now Romzan stands up and like a person under a spell, moves towards the source of the song, Sultan.

'Muqabala subhanallah laila ho laila.'

It has been six days since Romzan has come to Guwahati. He lives in Sijubari, along with Sultan and his friends. Every morning, he eats some food and walks out with them to Hatigaon Chariali. At around seven-thirty or eight, thousands of people like Sultan and Romzan crowd the location. The way in which cows are sold and bought in a trading market, bargains and deals are made at this spot for the rest of the day.

Romzan finds work on the day he arrives. The contractor, Bora, asks him to get up on the truck along with Sultan but another contractor looks at him with disrespect and mockery before announcing, 'Hey, don't take this guy—will he work or manage his beard?'

Romzan, who is about to climb onto the truck with the help of Sultan, steps back.

Hurt, he goes back to Sultan's room. In that small room, the child's voice bothers him and makes him even more sad. For the first time, he feels disquiet about the long, beautiful beard he has been so proud of.

Romzan doesn't find work the next day either. When Sultan is about to leave with Saikia, the contractor, he takes Sultan aside and speaks in a low voice. 'Don't ask this person to come to work with us. It doesn't feel good to make someone who has such a long beard work with us.'

This doesn't escape Romzan's ears.

∽

When Sibpujan's razor slows down, Romzan opens his eyes and is surprised: who is this person in front of him?

Is this his reflection?

When he is able to recognize the reflection, he lets out another sigh.

THE QUESTION OF STYLE

ANJUM HASAN

The word for it was 'stylish'. Stylish girls had Lady Diana haircuts, wore low-wedge heels from Bata, and chocolate-corduroy bell-bottoms. Some wore midis and some wore maxis and some wore minis. Ribbed skivvies in single colours were in. Flared, high-waisted jeans and Keds. Or tight churidars with lots of churis around the calf, matching kurtas in pink satin that reached just above the knees, and chunnis wound around the throat but not covering the breasts. Dark leather moccasins with coloured beadwork on the front. Chunky sweaters. Chiffon saris patterned with gardens.

The stylish were a tribe of their own—they either had cascades of hair, sometimes plaited, such as the gorgeous dungaree-wearing pop star, Nazia Hassan's, or that layered, feathery bob copied from the Princess of Wales. She had just gotten married and everyone seemed quite certain they knew her. She was stylish for sure. 'Ish, so stylish,' the older girls said to each other. It meant you looked fine or it meant you were attempting to look fine and could thus be mocked.

A and C were less than ten years old and not yet stylish. Perhaps they'd never be. They could not aspire to stylishness, being skinny, awkward, myopic, and unwealthy. They didn't have what it took. The right clothes were crucial to being stylish but it was not just the right clothes, a worrying mystery was part of it too—something ineffable about the way a sleeve caressed your wrist or a collar enclosed your throat, about how you walked, tossed your head, put your hands in your pockets. Leaning on the garden wall, they looked out for the stylish every evening. Meanwhile, A knitted panties for her dolls and let her hair grow till her waist while her younger sister C's was too long to be short but too short to be long.

She could have entrusted herself to their left-hand neighbour, who'd trained with Shahnaz Husain and even looked a little like her—smooth, plump, and confident. The lady had recently set up a beauty parlour in her front room where a poster of her big-haired, big-eyed heroine hung and on the shelves were jars of pink, black, and green beauty products.

The girls had been in there to shyly confer with her. She could give Lady Di haircuts for fifty rupees. Her husband was out in the compound of their bungalow where his long, big-snouted, copper-coloured antique car was parked, calling out for their Pomeranian, 'Pom-pom!' That was what they called him. They heard him yelling this name so often. 'Pom-pom!' But they didn't have fifty rupees to spare for Shahnaz.

So, one Sunday when A was nine, she took up their grandfather's scissors, the heavy iron ones he used for his tailoring, and said to C, 'Let me give you a haircut.' At this point in her life, she was forever running towards or away from something; every game involved fleeing or hiding under dusty beds, flinging the basketball far and away, climbing a ladder to the roof for the badminton shuttle. She would trip and fall, twist ankle or wrist, then be swathed for weeks in Relaxyl and stretch bandages. But she'd also pick herself up and carry on. She could not turn perfect cartwheels like their right-hand neighbour but she taught her to skip. This neighbour and C were the same age and friends. A taught them skipping, single and doubles, how to twist the rope in mid-air. She was the head skipper. She could outrun everyone and deftly bring down Shillong's tight-skinned tangerines from their garden trees with the clefted bamboo stick, but she was accident-prone. She had a history of crashing into glass doors. At two, she had managed to knock into a pot of bubbling porridge and burn the skin right off the back of one hand. At five, she dropped deep into a forest stream and almost drowned.

That winter morning, she snipped a little of her sister's hair and it came away so easily between her fingers. She was restless, eager to bring some novelty into their lives. Even though they had Lyril soap to bathe with and Cuticura talcum powder, a couple of nice dresses each, made by their grandfather, and new, very shiny sandals, none of this was stylish. In fact, the sandals were downright telu, which in the lexicon was the very opposite of stylish. They were too golden and so they were telu, which was a word they had made up to brand unstylishness, describe those who were pariahs in the house of style, who cared nothing for the oil dripping from their plaits and the missing garters in their school socks. They were telu, others stylish, and these two girls hung on desperately somewhere in between. They put on their sandals reluctantly and perused old copies of *Seventeen* magazine at the right-hand-side neighbour's, brought in by her foreign relatives, agape at the pristine denim and leather jackets, feeling themselves aglow with the possibilities of stylishness.

They were sitting on the front steps—C with a towel around her shoulders, compliant, trusting; A with those big scissors she could barely handle. She cut off C's rattails and cleared her neck. She took up tufts and let them fall away. The hair on the back of her head started to thin out. A combed and snipped, urging her sister to sit still. Then she aimed at her fringe.

Grandfather was not yet missing his scissors. He wasn't tailoring this morning but he was often at it. For birthdays and festivals, he stitched clothes for the girls out of small squares of ordinary cloth and thin air. He would consider an expensive frock worn by the right-hand neighbour and turn out a perfect imitation in a couple of days, down to the ruffled sleeves, smocked front, and lacy frills. He stitched all the clothes he wore—the warm, buttoned, woollen vests, and the sharp-edged trousers. He stitched quilt covers and shopping bags and kurta–pyjamas. It was him and his old, black, hand-cranked Pfaff, well-oiled and singing; the gold-edged pockmarked silver thimble that went onto his forefinger when he took up hemming and putting in the buttons; the faded British-era biscuit tin in which he kept his spools of threads and bobbins.

Grandfather was an artist but he was not stylish. He saw to it that the grandchildren were clothed and to supplement what he made them he'd go to the footbridge in the town's market square where the sellers of second-hand clothes had their stalls and buy them track pants and winter jackets. They had labels from abroad and looked crumpled. Rumour had it that they were meant for the poor in Bangladesh, not for the sellers on the footbridge and certainly not for them. A would listen to George Harrison's song for Bangladesh and feel guilty about those clothes.

Meanwhile, the thrill of taking matters into her own hands. Her first attempt at tidying the fringe was hesitant and led to uneven results. She gave it another go and the lopsided look improved. Strands poked down from one side which she took away. She combed C's hair sideways. 'Show me,' she said and it looked all right. A had given her a haircut in the sense that she had cut her hair. But there was nothing stylish about it. Where were the perfectly set waves that crowned the princess head? Where was the glamour of that golden crop? She pulled down the hair over her sister's forehead and started snipping again.

Careful, said their mother, from somewhere inside the house, but she was distant. A imagined she trusted her because she let her make tea and handle knives, clean out the rice, and broom out the rooms. In any case, A couldn't confide in her about their lack of stylishness because her mother was stylish herself, impossibly so. She wore silk saris in thick colours with matching lipstick, and had her hair done at Jenny's, which was the oldest stylish place in town. She owned fascinating shoes—brown suede and blue leather and a pair of burgundy, crocodile-skin, handcrafted high heels made to order by a Chinese shoemaker. She used only Yardley and Max Factor, and wore pure wool cardigans. So when she said careful, both A and C knew it was to be taken only half-seriously. If A fell off the ladder to the roof and broke her neck, if the open wound on her knee from falling on the tar and chip compound of the right-hand neighbour's turned septic, if a Diwali cracker burst in her face or if Pom-pom escaped from the left-hand neighbour's and bit her, she would rouse herself. For the rest of the time, she merely scolded absent-mindedly.

The hunt for stylish continued despite her. A and C cut out pictures of luxurious clothes and lip-glossed women from the magazines and pasted them at odd angles into old notebooks. They would acquire a TV shortly and watch Shabana Azmi and Zeenat Aman, who were stylish, and the Doordarshan newscasters, who were not.

C's fringe was now shorter but uneven. A cut some more. Now it was straighter. She cut a tiny bit more. Now it was uneven again. And so on till more and more of her forehead was revealed and then the top of her scalp began to show. And still that line of hair wouldn't fall straight. Suddenly C demanded to see a mirror. 'What have you done?' she screamed. She looked like the victim of an illness that had selectively eaten up her hair. Their mother came out and C finally began to cry.

Some moments of mixed emotions followed: their mother's great exasperation at A's stupidity even though she had originally acceded to her do-it-yourself plan. A's own conviction that she had missed stylishness by a whisper, that a few snips more or less would have done it. C's sense of adventure dissolving into a feeling of betrayal. 'Cover up her head and take her to the barber,' said their mother. So, the two of them went, ignominiously, down the street—A disgraced and C with a woollen cap concealing her disfigurement. There was the grocery shop where they bought their atta and soap, the typing school, the pakoriwallah who doubled as an electrician, the mithai shop with basins of syrup-soaked sponges in the window, the panwallah, the gentle man in a dark suit who sold toffees and hard-boiled sweets out of huge glass jars along with pencils and exercise books, and then the barber in his dirty white pyjamas. He was the one who usually dealt with their hair and he had no truck with style and Lady Diana. A had to explain the problem to him, while her sister sat on a wooden plank reserved for children that was balanced on the arms of the barber's chair and scowled.

Was it then, on that shameful morning at the barber's, when this unattainable word started to fall away from them? He did what he could with the mess and in a few weeks C's hair grew out and the accident was forgotten. But the dream of stylish loosened its hold on them. There would be moments in the years to come when they'd be touched by it again—the time their mother took A to town and bought her shoes with the elegant word 'Henry' printed on the soles, for instance, or when her sister went across to the left-hand neighbour and finally got herself that Lady Di haircut. But on the whole, they seemed to have given up the fight. A gradually stopped falling down, lost interest in hide-and-seek, no longer took up the cord of the electric kettle and sang into it like Nazia Hassan.

They remained children for a little longer, still yearning for the sophistications of an adult world, till that too passed and they became, for better or worse, the people they were meant to be, no more those they hoped to become.

NEWS OF A BELOVED FRIEND

SUDHIRANJAN MOIRANGTHEM

Translated from the Manipuri by Soibam Haripriya

One could hear the clanging of the electric post as if bells were ringing. Weary and tired after going to the market, Ema hastily ate dinner and went outside to wait out the night at the beginning of their lane. At the start of their lane, Meira Paibi Ema-Eben—torch-bearing women of the leikai-based women's collective—were likewise waiting out the night. Leikai is a settlement of people belonging to the same clan. It is analogous to a locality albeit with kin ties.

He knew—tonight, the dogs might not bark incessantly. Even if the moonlight was not clear, even if the sky was murky with clouds, even if the glimmer of stars was dulled, even if the breeze did not carry with it the smell of flowers, or even if there was a storm, if the dogs did not bark, all was well.

That day, the dogs barked incessantly. It was sometime after midnight. In the backyard, around the house, the sound of trampling boots was heard. There were knocks at the door. Seconds after that, question after question chased him down.

'Who are your friends?'

'I have a lot of friends and acquaintances. Close friends are Jiten from Kongpal, Manisana from Khurai Thangjam, Tombi from Singjamei Thokchom leikai, and Maisnam Oken, who is from the same leikai as me.'

They brought out and peered into something that looked like an accounts book.

'How long have you known them for? And through whom?'

He was startled. 'What? They are all my college mates.'

'Stop speaking! Tell us who gave them shelter. Where did they keep their weapons?'

'I don't know that. I am just an ordinary person. I don't know anything.'

'Why don't you know?'

Once, there was a rumour that he had died. In a fight with the police. That was after he was arrested by the police. It was around the time they were still perplexed as they didn't know why the police had apprehended him. Everyone was surprised—why did the police arrest him? How did he die?

He too heard the news of his death. Surprising as it was, it was also laughable. Utterly confused, he also laughed. He went to the morgue to see the corpse. The corpse wore combat attire. He saw that other than the bullet wounds, there were many bruises on the body.

On reaching home, even though his mother knew he was not dead, she cried with heart-wrenching lamentations. His elder sister and the younger one also had swollen eyes and faces. Their father had gone to the morgue, they said.

After the incident, there were rumours about him. 'He must have been arrested because of his namesake.'

'Ehh! How?'

'Just recently a person with the same name died, right?'

'Then, is there no consequence to his arrest?'

'No, people say that he was even given an electric shock. If the Meira Paibis had not been in the leikai club that time, he would not have got out alive.'

Believe it or not—that one died only because he shared the same name!

As for names, he had many. How many names does he have? With how much love those names had been given to him. His grandfather called him by one name, his grandmother by another, his aunts by yet another. On top of that, his given name on the birth chart, the leikai, and the name on his certificate were all different. That he was called by so many names by family members and friends, was it not a sign of their love for him? At that time, he used to think—so many loved him dearly.

Today, each of these names had become the name that the dogs barked incessantly every midnight. Numerous such midnights lay before him. How many deaths must he die?

One day, out of nowhere, he met a long lost friend. Since they hadn't met for a while, they asked after each other.

'How are you?'

'I am well, my friend.'

His voice quivering with feelings, the long-lost friend continued, 'I heard the news about you. I was very sad. I got goosebumps as soon as I heard it.'

Hesitating as if he could not express himself entirely, the friend in a guilt-ridden, weakened voice said, 'I don't know what to say. This is all my mistake. One can say that I am the reason all this happened to you.'

He was shocked. In that surprised state, he asked his friend, 'What are you talking about?'

'While we were still unaware of the reason why I was first arrested, they came for me a second time. It was unbearable the second time. Amidst the torture, I mentioned names of some friends. I think your name was one of them. They refused to believe that I was just an ordinary man.'

A shiver ran down his spine—Jiten, Manisana, Tombi....

He was able to show generosity despite the act of his friend. 'It is okay. What is past is past; do not think about it. It's unfortunate. At least they did not dress up our corpses with camouflage attires. Some people were picked up from their homes in their khudei or sarong, but turned up in the morgue in camouflage garments. At least that did not happen to us.'

He went to Jiten's house. He met Jiten. And just like his friend explained the situation to him, he wanted to explain the situation to his friend—'I am responsible for your arrest.' But how could one say this just like that? And Jiten had never been arrested by the police. It was good that he had never been arrested. But still, he wanted to caution him.

'Please be careful in the dark, late hours of the night, or, if you hear the incessant barking of dogs in your leikai at midnight.'

Jiten was surprised. 'Why?'

'Just be careful, the times are different.'

'But why?'

'Can't you see the number of people being picked up without an address memo, like vultures and crows preying upon small chicks?'

Jiten laughed heartily. 'Is that why?' He continued, 'No one can simply be arrested for no reason whatsoever. I am not bothered. I am not mistrustful.'

'Don't brush this aside. Misfortune can befall anyone.'

Jiten mockingly responded, 'You are too fearful, my friend. No one can be arrested and put in custody without a reason.'

With a hint of resentment, he retorted, 'Then there must be a reason behind my arrest too?'

'Yes, there must be. Why not? Something which you must have taken lightly but a fault nevertheless. During college some of you were running around for some students' organization.'

'But you too were a part of that.'

'Yes, that's what I am saying.'

'I am not involved in any of that now.'

'Even though you are not a part of it now, you were a part of it once. That could be a reason too.' With elaborate hand gestures, with no fear of God or men, Jiten spoke a lot that day. He also told his friend, 'It all started small but has now escalated and Manisana cannot even stay at home these days. I tried to stop him but he has run away from home.'

'Haa! Manisana?'

He came to know from Jiten about Manisana leaving his home and being on the run. Manisana had gone underground.

'A few days ago, when I had gone to Manisana's leikai to supply a few things, I met his mother. She was very distressed about him. It was sad to see her like that. I gave her some detergent powder and soap,' Jiten told him.

'What are you doing currently?'

'Nothing. Should I call it a business? A few things I supply, here and there.'

'What things? If it is lucrative I want to join too.'

'It is nothing serious. I buy things like detergent powder, soaps, toothpaste from the police canteen and supply it to the smaller shops in the lanes of leikai. In the canteen, you can get things cheaper.'

After hearing that Manisana had gone underground, he had not given much thought to him. But one day he met Manisana's younger brother who gave him another news. Manisana is in jail.

'We consulted a lawyer to try and get him out on bail but it was of no use. He was caught along with weapons and some documents so the Acts under which he was arrested seem quite stringent,' the younger brother told him.

He was not surprised to hear the news about Manisana. Such things could have happened to him. The distressing part was what he must have been subjected to during the interrogation.

He imagined the whole thing in his head—Manisana must have been meek. Monstrous questions must have pursued him, as if to swallow him whole or eat him up after tearing him apart. Moreover, beatings for questions, beatings for answers, and beatings for no response. Beatings and beatings, his whole body full of marks and bruises. What if he did not answer any question? If he didn't answer any question, he would feel the 'zing' of the coursing electricity. At that, he would let out a soul-shattering cry, 'E-m-a!' He might not see any light in his own eyes. In the midst of the darkness, flickers of light in front of his eyes like fireflies. After that he would feel afloat.

'Manisana is living well in jail. He is healthy. No one did anything to him. Even when he was arrested, he was not beaten up or tortured. The only problem is posed by the Act under which he has been arrested and for which he has to serve time in jail,' Manisana's brother continued.

Did he say this because he did not want to share the news of his brother's misfortune? How could one live happily inside a jail?

In Tombi's case, he went to pay his condolences.

It was immensely sad. He never got the chance to meet Tombi properly after he dropped out of college. He would come by unexpectedly. Always chirpy. And then pretending to be immensely busy, he would leave soon. He narrated stories of travelling to various places, meeting different kinds of people, mediating grievances, and disciplining people. Today, he was no more. One could say it was the fruit of his karma. The punishment for extracting money by impersonating members of the armed groups.

'Have you heard the other news?'

'What news?'

'Jiten was shot....'

'Ehh, why?'

'For passing on news of insurgents to mayang siphai; it is rumoured that he was an informer.' A mayang is an outsider, referring to people from other parts of India. Here, mayang siphai seemed to suggest army men.

The barking of the dogs piercing through the silence of the night made him uneasy. Even when he drifted off to a deep sleep, he woke up with a start. With eyes and ears on alert, he listened intently to the barking of the dogs. The sound of the barks seemed to be drawing near. Was that the sound of a vehicle coming to a stop? As if in a daze he rolled his eyes, looking at every nook and corner; when would it be morning?

The frightening howls of dogs did not make him wary. The howls meant nothing except that they must have seen ghosts or spirits. It is said that dogs can see ghosts and spirits. Sometimes the barking of dogs made him, out of fear, want to defecate so urgently, that there was a risk of soiling his clothes. The barking seemed to him a kind of forewarning from the dogs.

His family members looked at him as if he was an invalid in need of supervision. They were worried about him—would he be dragged around again as a sacrificial goat? Carrying his exact details, would they come knocking at the door again? What was crucial was the hands that would knock on his door. Whose hands would they be? Would it be for befriending Jiten, Manisana, or Tombi?

He still remembered the fragments of lives he had built with his friends. During school, high school, and college. They fought, shouted, got angry at each other. But wasn't that a mark of friendship? After college they each went their different ways. Was that what you call the end of relationships? No. Can human relations break so easily?

He knew that even if not a full moon, the moon nevertheless would be shining in the sky in the small hours of night. The stars would be twinkling. The Milky Way would be there in all its majesty. The breeze would bring the fragrance of flowers. Trees would sway in the intoxicating fragrance of the breeze. The hills, lakes, and rivers would remain unchanged. The beauty of nature would still be there. Love would still exist. The only ones missing would be his friends. The problem was that his imagination was unable to conjure his friends, frolicking freely in the lap of the Earth.

He did not want the clanging of the Emas' bells to announce the news of his friends' disappearances.

As for the weariness of mothers, let it be. They were worried about their children. They should be. Who else should they be worried about if not their children?

Like the good old days, he wanted to hear the news of his beloved friends. He wanted to hear pleasant news. To tell the future generations the cherished news of his beloved friends. If only beloved friends cherished news....

THE SONG

NAMRATA PATHAK

Fhagunore posuwa,
Montu tumar usoroloi uri jai O,
Fagunore posuwa,
Eia juifulor posuwa O.

(The westerly wind of Phagun,
my heart flies away to you O,
the westerly wind of Phagun,
this is Juiful's westerly wind O.)

The night refuses to flow by. It is a block of dark arrogance today, lifeless and still. The voice is gone. The lilt is gone. The song, a bit crimson and a bit azure, hangs placid right there, sometimes ruffled by the familiar wind, sometimes torn to shreds by the pine's probing. Sometimes it turns hopelessly pale like the nonchalant Shillong sky that wants to, but refuses to bleed in a language of love. No, it won't rain today. At last, the song turns into a colourless lump, a mound of flesh and bones. The song limps. It can't stand tall. I wonder if it's still there in my head today. No, it is not. When I covered the vast expanse of the veranda that connected my living room to the kitchen, of my old quarter, the dark corners, with the exception of a few Shillong orchids my colleagues had gifted me, glared at me angrily. Ah! The song! The song? I cannot hear it. Or can I? I search for it, scanning the whimsical abode of mine and an even more whimsical Shillong night opening its mouth wide to eat the last glitters in the northern sky.

The song. There it is, wheezing languidly, perched on the pine tree outside the quarter. Outside, it is cold. I wonder what it is to be outside, to be at the heart of the mysterious pine grove that surrounds my quarter in Mawlai, that, too, at this unearthly hour? Why am I drawn to a desire to be elsewhere? Is it because I want to be that Nitori again who wears air, water, ether, and earth in her hair and on her glistening crown? To be that Nitori who touches the blazing red juiful with the least caution, knowing well that the fire is bound to set her ablaze, engulf her in blue and golden flames, and turn her into a heap of ashes? But Nitori is free. Nitori is the wilderness of the whole Pobitora. Nitori is a juiful that defies all logic of existence, of both life and death. Juifuls dot the otherwise bland, monotonous canvas of Pobitora in rebellious red. They are an obtrusion swaying sometimes from right to left, sometimes left to right, with a gleeful abandon. The flowers that signal a glint of spring, bringing a hint of hope in everyone's eyes, are not meant to bloom eternally. Why do these efficacious beings bend low in a strange pallor? Why do they want to defy life's transience? Why do they want to be immortal like love? Can they not wither away? In someone's hair or someone's palms? Someone's heart, like Nitori's.

Tumi juiful
Fuli thakibane mur hridoyot
Eidore hodai?

(You, juiful, the burning flower,
Would you forever
bloom in my heart like this?)

Love? The song? Him? Where is he now? Nitori has not met him for a decade. On the riverbank, a familiar song wafted through the pungent, sweaty breeze tenderly combing the silvery char-chapori and shaking the only juiful tree. He calls the tree that stands next to the river Brahmaputra his comrade, his ally. Many a times, Nitori has found him in the shadow of the tree in scorching summers, his eyes pivoted on the turbulent, stormy Brahmaputra, as if he was eliciting a meaning out of the foamy, frothy water, the rhythmic gurgle of the river adding to his meditative stance. Its constantly changing course and the wind's communion with the currents and cross-currents of the river created a symphony of loss and longing. He talked to the river in a language unknown to her. She was an alien to their ways of living, to their friendship with the approaching and receding water, their homes vanishing instantaneously as if a sorceress cast a magic spell. That day he smelt of the Brahmaputra. And of sweat. And everything that the river takes away, gorging on in a big mouthful. 'You go, Nitori. I don't have anything to give you. I shall follow my father's footsteps and start selling dry fish on the bank of this river. Those big universities, you know, they teach you to dream big. Change. Rebellion. Rights. Ah! These are big words too! They are not real. But hunger, Nitori, is real, and so is struggle.' That day I saw the river eating away humans. I saw the streak of red at its heart, and the Bor Luit turn into a stinky, rotten carrion. A mass of dead dreams. The look in his eyes made me flinch. Did I even know him? He was a stranger to me. I wanted to run and run, evaporate into nothingness. I wanted to run for my life. I wanted to run and run, cross the river, run and run, cross the forest, run and run, cross my village. I wanted to run away from him, run away from myself. But then, where could I go? Where would I find myself? Which place would shield me from his prying eyes? Is there an escape from his glare? I am found. I will be found. With no gravitational pull to anchor me to the ground, I am a mere figure on the run being thrown up in the air, fleeting and becoming one with the darkness of the universe and endless space. I am still flying and floating in space. And till now, I have not found myself.

Kyo janu
Sokue tumak bisare
Juiful fula botorot!

(Why is it that
My eyes searchingly look for you
in the season of juiful, the fiery flower?)

That day I saw his eyes. His eyes with the luminescence of twenty summers and the brightness of the fireflies fluttering in sinister, unlit places of the canopied forest, and then those eyes being eaten by a voraciously hungry Brahmaputra, becoming two incandescent embers twinkling in the bosom of the river. The river has eyes. Is this what we call a constantly changing relationship, friends metamorphosing into foes, one becoming the other? How synonymous they are, how interchangeable, how fragile! A lover became a stranger. Nothing stays. 'Nitori, Nitori, Nitori.' When he calls her the woods dance in tandem, the cottony clouds fleet in magical alignments rousing a red-blue-purple coloured storm above, the sky becomes a blanket of white loneliness and the earth is thirsty again. 'Nitori, Nitori, Nitori.' When he does not call her, the starry juifuls wither and fade away; they cease to ornament the night sky, those hanging bulbs of red; the pines conspire, rifles in hand, they shoot her with prickly needles of loneliness that winter bestows on them every year. The world stops spinning for her or it's the contrary, her head starts spinning raucously. Eventually, she is caught in a lethargic, sleepy fixity, a sense of immobility; she does not move an inch, does not move at all, just stays fixed to the same spot for years and years. She is frozen in time. That Nitori died with the last gleam of his eyes in the wild Pobitora eleven years ago.

The song smells of moss and grieving pine trees now. The song grows fingers, firm hands. His hands? But it will shed its skin and come back to her again. With a new face. With a new longing. With a new leap. Probably it will sing of love tomorrow.

I look out of the mahogany window of my quarter, my gaze sweeping through the pine trees standing in rows in odd clusters. Some are fluorescent green, some peacock green, some a strange tint of muddy green, and some brownish and yellowing green. Yes, it is a bizarre concoction.

Every day, early in the morning, say, around five, the song wafts through my window. Touched by the first rays of the sun, ripened by the anticipation of the day, it grows plump, carefully caressed by his long, bony fingers. The song carries a strange longing at its heart. Maybe it is the same longing that I have seen in the amber eyes of the fishermen in Bor Luit, sailing through the turbulence of storms. It is the same longing I have seen in his twinkling eyes when, with gusto, hands poised mid-air, he described Ambedkar and told me about the debilitating caste system of our country. I listened to him with animated interest. When the tiny boats floated up and down like wooden corks, abandoned and useless, the body of this man turned gold and azure, perhaps melting away at the fury of the sun. And the longing! It stayed even after the brown man became a tiny dot at the horizon. He became the distant sky, the earth, and then both. At last, he vanished at the point where the sky and the earth met. That was in Pobitora more than a decade ago before I moved to Meghalaya and joined a university in Shillong as a teacher.

But I met him again in the most unpredictable of circumstances. There is this old man, a local from a nearby Khasi village, who takes a winding path through the bountiful Khasi hills to reach our quarter every week. He carries vegetables, fresh and rotund ones, in his hand-woven bamboo baskets. He ties the two baskets on either side of a pole so that his frail body can deftly balance the load of his green harvest. He has everything that I prefer to cook: coriander leaves plucked from the moist bed of his garden; fat juicy gourds; different types of fluorescent herbs—heart-shaped, star-faced, dancing agog on his palms, some so rare that I cannot recall their names; three or four apples that can compete with the red Kashmiri ones usually found in supermarkets, and some sewali that smell of yesterday's leftovers, of frosty, cold nights of Shillong. The coriander lends a familiar aroma to my rohu curry. Prepared with red chillies and herbs, the fish pieces rest in a symposium of spices, in an aromatic curry of finely ground garlic, ginger, and onions. The dewy red apples immediately go to the fruit basket on my dining table. Every morning the old man brings out the food connoisseur in me, a part that I never thought existed. I have started to realize that the food I prepare carries the old man's Midas touch. He is a constant presence in my kitchen. So, when Lily, my house help, told me one fateful day that he was brutally shot in the head by a miscreant in his village, which borders Assam, an ocean of emotions surged within me. Who will look after his granddaughter now? Who will tend to his small jhum cultivation? Who is to nurture the saplings in his garden? His orchard and garden were his only source of sustenance. I remember him once saying that he lived with his granddaughter in the very lane where the village headman lived. He lived in Muipua village located on the slope of a hill right at the border separating Meghalaya from Assam. Nevertheless, I wait. I wait for him to return. I wait for the slanting hills to make way for him on fine mornings so that he can take the zigzag, snaking path to my quarter. I want him to descend, to come down like a gush of wind cutting through the treetops, shaking the blue flags of the sky, heralding a fresh dawn. I want him to sing the song he sang every morning.

The old man is no more. It was a fatal blow to me, to us who got used to his familiar voice, his gait, his Khasi flowing like mellifluous notes from a timeless flute, his gleaming eyes when he spoke of his little granddaughter, the smell of his village that hung on his lanky silhouette like droplets clinging to button flowers after a heavy downpour. Lily knows the kind of loss it is for me. I saw Lily's eyes welling up at each word that escaped her mouth when she described his death to me. How can a stranger whip up so many storms within me? Perhaps Lily would know, but yes, how a stranger can be so familiar, so close to my heart, so known, I don't know. How can a stranger have an iron grip on my heart? Stranger. Strange emotions. Strange stranglehold. Strange affinity. Strange love. Have I not known a strange love before? Have I not known a stranger before?

Yesterday I bought a crisp white shirt for him from Bara Bazaar.

The old man had a fondness for white. When I went to collect grocery for the week from the old shop that most of my colleagues frequent in Bara Bazaar, my eyes fell on this starched, spotless shirt. The brown parcel is now lying on the mahogany table. On its left side, scattered are the sewalis that the old man brought the previous morning. They emit a soft lingering fragrance, not heady or strong any more. Wilted flowers. Remnants of a dark night. Slices of bygone moments. Now, death dances on the orange-and-white flowers, the petals bow low in submission, nudging at the frozen time. As humans, aren't we a mute testimony to the tricks life plays on us? I folded my palms and pressed them together. The flowers now crushed to perfect blobs. I look away. Tears run down my cheeks.

∽

Maipua, the village of the old man, greets me with a dry spell and a grainy veil of dust. On a sombre day like this, it is not a surprise that the village is covered by a thick blanket of yellowness. Even a gust of wind on my face tastes like dust. It enters the creases and crevices of the thatched huts lining the sloping hills, leaving a morbid trace behind. No light. No light in the eyes of the children playing near huge rocks and boulders. No light above in the sky too. A thin, transparent sheet of dust hangs like a concave lens preventing light from entering the village. Maipua is mourning the old man's death. Jolted, I stop in my tracks, unable to move forward, my body paralysed, my limbs suddenly numb, my head going round and round like a spinning top. His eyes, the glaring eyes. I know this pair of eyes. I have known these eyes for more than a decade.

Tumar sokut kyo akura jui?
Jana neki tumiu
Juifulor bhaxa?

(Why are your eyes ablaze?
Are you well versed
in the language of juiful too?)

Piercing notes. Cacophony. Hullabaloo everywhere. People thronging in. People running hither and thither. The police vehicles bleating and blowing ringlets of smoke on the dusty roads. Maipua turns into a hotbed of terror. 'The miscreant is arrested, the miscreant is arrested,' some boys are shouting at the top of their voices. The miscreant who gunned down the old man is arrested. And I am standing in front of him. Him? It is none other than him. Him? The one who wrote poems about changing the world. Him? The one who changed the whole world of the old man's granddaughter.

Him? The one who changed my whole world a decade ago in Pobitora.

BOATS ON LAND

JANICE PARIAT

I can measure our days together by the number of times we went to the river. Ten in fourteen days. Which by most accounts is not long, yet a dragonfly, you told me, may live for only twenty-four hours, and if we were dragonflies, we would have spent ten lifetimes together.

When we went to the river that winter, you said it wasn't half as wide as during the monsoon when the water stretched out vast and splendid as the sea. Instead, we had miles of sandy banks to write on with our footprints, or to sit on and watch the Kaziranga forest on the opposite side darken as the light faded. Those were sun-tempered, smoke-hazy days that lengthened with the evening shadows until the nights seemed endless and intimately ours. You smoked cigarettes in secret. The ones you rolled burned like slender torches, pinpricks of light in a dark and unknown universe. You conjured them quickly, like a magician.

'Years of practice,' you said.

You were nineteen then, three years older than me. We met because my parents and I went on holiday to Chandbari, a tea estate in Assam, one of many sprawling plantations of neatly trimmed bushes that spread for miles like a dense green carpet. I'd only ever driven past them, on family trips to Potasali and Nameri, and they seemed far removed from the countryside's lush wildness—ponds overflowing with hyacinth, thick clusters of swaying bamboo, and gulmohar that burst into a rage of orange and yellow blossoms. I'd always wondered what they were like inside, beyond the gated and guarded entrance. Our fathers, who had been in school together, friends, met at an Old Boys' dinner, and yours invited us over for a fortnight in January. For my parents, it was tempting; Shillong, where we lived, was crippled by winter and cloaked in dull, monotonous grey.

'Is it all right to stay that long?' my mother asked, sounding a little doubtful.

My father laughed. 'They have a battalion of household help at the bungalow. I don't think we'll be much trouble....'

While they looked forward to the break, I wasn't keen to go. All my school friends were in Shillong, and during the winter vacation, we had plans to visit each others' houses and make trips to Police Bazaar to eat momos at Peking Restaurant and cream buns at Flurys. More than the culinary delights though, it was a chance to meet boys, walk past them as though we didn't care they were watching, be approached and asked if we'd like to go to Ward's Lake for a boat ride, or to Udipi Hotel for a coffee. There was a whole world waiting to be explored now that we weren't confined mainly to the grounds of our all-girls convent school. One boy in particular filled my waking hours with lucid daydreams. His name, I'd recently discovered, was Jason; he had longish brown hair that fell over his eyes, and wore a striped flannel scarf with élan. This love affair, of secret smiles and glances, however, would have to wait.

'If your brother were here, you could have stayed behind, but we're not leaving you alone at home,' my mother told me, and no amount of sulking would change her mind. My elder brother was studying law in Pune; my plans, also laid out clear and simple, were to do medicine at Lady Hardinge in Delhi. Our parents gently nudged us towards our choices: these were respectable, lucrative careers.

'And you'll have company there,' she added. 'The Hazarikas have a daughter your age…or maybe a little older.'

So, I packed my dresses, made my friends promise to fill me in when I returned on all that had happened, and said a silent, aching prayer that Jason wouldn't find somebody else to love.

Chandbari was eight hours away, and my father drove there in our trusty grey Ambassador. We soon left the pine-tree slopes and winding roads of Shillong behind, and from about halfway to Jorabad, the highway widened and flattened, flanked by vast stretches of paddy fields lying crisp and harvested in the sun. We passed by dusty hamlets that my father described as 'immigrant Bangladeshi towns' and great sandy lengths of rivers that only came to life in the summer. I drifted in and out of sleep, sometimes catching snatches of conversation—something about my brother's upcoming exams, an ailing distant relative, a neighbour's newly born baby. Halfway through, we stopped by the roadside to eat packed sandwiches for lunch. It was warmer in the plains, and the sunshine was pleasant and welcoming.

When we resumed our journey, my father told us that his friend

Ranjit Hazarika came from an old, wealthy Assamese family which had owned many successful businesses in Shillong, all of which folded during the trouble in the '80s, when the locals turned against the outsiders. The Hazarikas then bought plantations in the Bishwanath district and, with the tea boom in the '90s, had done exceedingly well.

'They're one of those families marked by tragedy though,' he added, dropping his voice. 'First, they had to leave their hometown, then his first wife Mamuni killed herself...'

The loud, dragging roar of the engine drowned out the rest of his words. At that age, though, the fear of death, my own or others', hadn't yet clutched me, and instead I found myself thinking about you and whether we'd get along, and become friends. Perhaps, I dreamed, we'd be like sisters. I awoke much later when we turned into a side road with a gate held open by a uniformed guard. It was late evening and somewhere the sun had set, leaving behind orange gashes in the sky. We were on an avenue of tall birch, whose silver-grey bark glinted in the twilight. The bungalow stood at the end of a long driveway; it was white, open and airy, and our entire house back in Shillong could have probably fit into the veranda. Your parents were there, having tea that had been brought out on a trolley. Your father was tall and well built, dressed in crisp khaki trousers and a spotless white shirt. His skin was evenly tanned, and his hair stylishly grey at the edges. He shook hands with mine, and gave my mother a quick, neat hug. Your mother was a tribal Mising lady, with chic shoulder-length hair and flawless skin. She was dressed in a floral-patterned kurti and dark green pyjamas. I wished my mother was in something more appealing than a crumpled jainsem. Our luggage was deftly handled by two silent liveried bearers, and we were shown to our rooms to freshen up. My parents were given the main guest room, and I had a smaller place in an annexe joined to the bungalow by an open corridor overhung with coils of flowering thunbergia. Your mother had apologized for my room—'It's small but we hope you'll be comfortable'—yet I found it more than spacious and, with its light walls and large, creamy bed, utterly delightful. There was a table with magazines, and a wardrobe large enough for me to hide in. I slipped off my shoes and walked across the carpet, thick and spongy under my feet. There were no signs of you. I thought it extremely rude you hadn't emerged to greet your guests.

∽

Instead, when I entered the bathroom, you were there, in the bathtub, fully clothed, smoking a cigarette. The window above your head was wide open.

'Oh,' I said, 'I'm sorry.'

You laughed. 'For what? I'm not taking a bath.'

It was true; the tub was dry. You hoisted yourself up—'And technically this is your bathroom for now'—and taking a last drag, flung the cigarette out the window. Your T-shirt barely touched the top of your jeans. You were taller than me and thinner, and even though your clothes were crumpled and your hair uncombed, it was I who felt inelegant and scruffy. Your movements were slow and unstartled, as though I wasn't there.

You washed your hands at the basin and rinsed your mouth. 'Don't tell anyone about the smoking. Poor Shambu mali will get into trouble again.'

'Why would that happen?' I asked.

'Because he brings me the local stuff.' When you saw my incomprehension, you added, 'Tobacco. The stuff inside cigarettes.'

Only after you left the room did I realize you hadn't apologized for being in the bathtub. Or asked me my name. Or said hello.

For the next two days you kept out of our way, emerging from your room only at mealtimes. And even then, you sat there, silent, eating small, finicky platefuls. Often, you disappeared for hours on end. Your parents seemed embarrassed by your behaviour but didn't appear to know how to deal with you. In a way, I was relieved you weren't around to watch me clumsily adjust to a way of life I'd hardly been aware of—where morning tea was brought to us on trays; beds were made and rooms cleaned by invisible hands while we were at breakfast; towels were changed twice a day; dirty laundry magically reappeared in a neatly folded, ironed pile; meals and fresh fruit juice were ordered at the touch of a bell. During the day, the bungalow could be cool as a cave, its high ceiling soaring above us, its corridors deep and endless. I waited for the evenings in the veranda outside and watched the countryside darkness close in over the trees and felt the sun-warmed air turn chilly and brittle. Later, we'd emerge from our rooms, showered and changed, and gather in the living room, where the fireplace was lit, the ice bucket filled, and bowls of roasted cashew nuts were placed on the side tables. Your father would bustle around the bar, mixing whiskies and opening bottles of homemade wine, of which I would be given a small glass.

Even though I'd usually sit alone in a corner, looking through picture books on the shelf, it was a life entirely new and enthralling.

Your father and mine talked a lot about Shillong—their escapades at school, and where various classmates had ended up. They spoke of midnight shows at Kelvin Cinema and parties where they danced to The Beatles and The Monkees. The town, they agreed, had changed almost beyond recognition from what it was in the '60s. Or what they referred to nostalgically as 'the good old days' when it was safer, less crowded, and the roads were clean and empty. After a fair number of whiskies were downed, they'd speak of the trouble, and how it changed and took away everything they knew and cherished.

'One evening,' your father said, 'Mamuni was coming back from the market, and this Khasi guy stopped her and slapped her, in the middle of the road.... I remember when she got home and told me, I was so angry, but she only seemed surprised that he'd called her an outsider. She kept saying, "I've lived here all my life." That was it though... I'd tried to put it off for as long as I could, but I knew we had to leave....'

Then a long silence would settle, troubled only by the crackle of firewood and the faraway hoot of an owl.

Your mother and mine would join in their conversation sometimes, or carry on with their own intimate talk. I overheard your mother say you were studying psychology at Loreto College, Calcutta, but there'd been some 'trouble' and you were sent home early. 'We thought it would help to have someone close to her age around,' she said, unaware that I was listening, 'but she can be just like her father...headstrong and difficult.' Mostly, though, they would exchange notes on recipes and gardening. Your mother called it a quiet life here, with not much to do or many people to meet, and said sometimes she'd fall into a restlessness that no amount of painting, cooking, or stitching could dissolve. She tried to visit her family village often, but it was difficult with you around. It was nice, she said, that my mother ran a bakery; she, too, had always wanted to do something on her own.

There were traces of you littered all over the bungalow as though you were a visiting ghost. Occasionally, I'd catch the lingering smell of cigarette smoke even though you were nowhere around. Once, I found your slippers in the veranda, discarded under a chair. Your T-shirt slipped by mistake into my pile of washed and ironed laundry. At times, I had a feeling you watched us from afar, sullen and undecided.

One afternoon, we all went to the planter's club. Even you, though you sat by the window next to my mother, who was in the middle, and stared out without saying a word. When we got there, we headed to the tennis courts, where matches were in progress. You, I noticed, were not with us any more. My parents were introduced to everyone by your father as 'old friends', visitors from his home town, Shillong. The afternoon was filled with chatter, the monosyllabic thud of tennis balls, and shouts of support and laughter. At some point, a chubby girl in shorts, clutching a racquet, dropped herself into the white wicker chair next to mine.

'Hi. I'm Radhika,' she said. 'You're staying at Chandbari?'

I introduced myself and said yes, I was.

'How's the depressed damsel?'

I asked if she meant you.

'Who else?' She laughed. 'She has a soul too tormented to play tennis.'

I wanted to defend you but didn't know how. Radhika was about twenty-five and had the friendly, bossy air of some of my seniors at school. Her black eyes were set within a round, plump-cheeked face that reminded me of an owl I'd seen outside my window the past few nights.

'Be careful of that one,' she said.

Again, I asked if she meant you.

She nodded. 'People say she's….'

Someone beckoned from the courts. 'Coming,' she replied. 'I'll catch you later.'

But that didn't happen. I didn't see Radhika again because, after a while, I wandered off for a walk.

'I won't be long,' I whispered to my mother and made off in the direction of the golf course, the only open space I could find. I soon discovered why no one else was on the grounds—the place was littered with pats of dried and fresh cow dung. Yet I trampled on, aiming for a distant hillock which had a trickling stream curled around its base. To my far left, bordering the course, stood a row of thatch shacks hazily covered in light rising mist. A few children, almost naked, ran after each other, laughing and screaming. Further away, a boy was herding cows and their lowing, along with the chirrup of roosting birds, filled the air. On winter evenings, Assam dissolved into a careful watercolour of flat shimmering horizons and low, languorous clouds. So different from Shillong where the skyline loomed with pine-shielded hills.

You were standing by the water, smoking, watching a pair of dragonflies dance on the surface. You'd rolled up the ends of your trousers and, despite the winter chill, you wore only a light half-sleeved T-shirt. You looked up in alarm.

'Sorry,' I said, 'I didn't mean to startle you.'

'Do you always begin every conversation with an apology?' You laughed at the look on my face. 'No one usually takes the trouble to walk across this golf course—immaculately maintained as it is.'

I scraped off bits of dung from my shoe against a stone. You sat on a spot of dry grassy bank. When I finished, I stood awkward and unsure, undecided whether I should stay or leave. Perhaps you preferred to be alone.

'Do you know,' you said, 'that dragonflies sometimes live only for a day?' The ones you were watching now hovered over a clump of fluff-tipped reeds.

'That's sad.'

'Why?'

I flushed. You made me nervous. More nervous than even being around boys or Jason.

'Why is that sad?' you repeated.

'B-because that's such a short time…to be alive.'

'But the dragonfly doesn't know that.'

I said, that was probably a good thing. I remember how you looked at me then, sharp and searching.

You stubbed out the cigarette. 'Come.'

We walked along the stream until it meandered into a marshy pond choked with blooming water hyacinth; we'd left the golf course far behind.

'Why aren't you playing tennis?' you asked suddenly.

I, too, have a tormented soul, I wanted to joke, but instead admitted that I didn't know how to; I mentioned my brother was the one fond of sports. That he'd wanted to be a football player.

'What does he do?'

I told you.

'And you? What will you do after school?' You stopped, and stood face to face with me. I could smell the cigarette on your breath, and something sweet, like cloves.

Again, I told you.

'Is that your greatest dream? To be a nurse?'

You picked up a stone and tried to skim it on the water, but it hit a lavender blossom instead. I said I'd never really thought about it, that it seemed all right.

'All right.' You turned the word over in your mouth slowly like something precious.

Encouraged by your rare, sudden verbosity, I asked, 'What do you want to do?'

You dusted your hands and stood up. 'I want to follow the rivers.'

~

That night you shook me awake.

'Come with me,' you whispered.

'Where?' In reply you took my hand and led me outside. The lawn was bathed in shadows from tall trees, and even the flower beds disappeared into inky darkness. It was chilly, and I shivered in my nightdress; you didn't give me time to grab a sweater. You were in the same clothes as earlier, but slippers, a few sizes too large, slapped against your feet. We headed to the far right of the garden, behind the annexe, through a gated gap in the bamboo hedge where the path opened onto a wide overgrown air field. Years before, your father had explained, when the Chinese attacked in '62, it was used to drop off food and weapons. Now it lay there benignly as a venue for evening walks, remarkable for its early-morning views of the Himalaya. At night, the field could have been a shimmering body of water, the way the grass rippled silver in the pale moonlight. The countryside silence was pierced only by the steady chirrup of crickets. We lay in the field, undiscovered in our kingdom of weeds.

You asked me to look at the sky. The stars were numberless.

'Don't ask me about constellations,' you added.

'I only know that's Orion's Belt.'

I said I had Orion's Belt on my neck. You pushed yourself up on your elbow; for the first time since we'd arrived, there was a look on your face I hadn't seen before—interest.

'Show me.'

I turned my face away from you and pointed to a mole just below my left earlobe. 'That's one.' Another lower, near the centre of my throat.

'That's two.'

I undid the buttons of my nightdress. The last one was far below the hollow of my neck. 'That's three.'

You traced a line over them all. You were smiling.

The next day, you were thoroughly charming. Not just to me, but even to my parents, whom until now you'd largely ignored. You accompanied my mother and yours on their walk around the large backyard vegetable garden; offered to show my father, since he was a professor of history, a collection of old journals your grandfather had written, and at lunch, which we ate at a table laid out on the lawn under a garden umbrella, you were an impeccable little hostess. You talked about where the cook acquired the freshest fish; how the nearest town, Bishwanath Chariali, was merely a small cluster of shops—'Blink and you'll miss it'; you queried my mother about the bakery and asked if she could make us some lemon tarts. Your parents, I noticed, looked delighted.

'What are you girls up to today?' your father asked.

You looked at me and smiled. 'I was thinking we could go for a walk….'

Everyone said it was a good idea. The plantation was dotted with historical landmarks from the days of the Ahom kings. We could go see the Vishnu temple, your father added, or the water tank that apparently dated back to the fourteenth century.

I waited, impatient and excited, as everyone retired for their afternoon nap—even my parents had given in to this rare indulgence. When you emerged from your room, sulky with sleep, I was sitting on the wooden swing on the veranda, swaying over the cool sea-green floor. I jumped off it quickly, feeling as though you'd caught me doing something childish.

A little while later we set off. By then though, your energy had waned, and you'd retreated back into your brooding, reclusive self. As we walked, rather than making conversation, you rolled cigarettes. On both sides of the dirt road were miles of low-lying tea bushes, interspersed with tall silver oak, grown for protective shade.

I asked where we were going.

'Nearby.'

We didn't go far; in fact, we didn't even leave the borders of Chandbari. You took me to a pukhuri, a large pond bordered on all sides by raised red-soil ground and rows of birch. In one corner stood a gnarled old banyan under which we sat, brushing away stinging red ants and fat black beetles. You lit a cigarette and let it smoulder between your fingers. Your hair clung to your neck in dark, sweaty streaks. Again, I wasn't sure whether you'd prefer to be alone.

'Are you all right?'

You looked at me as though no one had asked you that in a long time.

'Someone I know,' you said, 'tried to kill herself.'

'Oh.' I wasn't sure whether to ask if she'd succeeded.

'It was one in a long line of unfinished projects. The end of life.'

In the stillness of the evening, your words skimmed over the water and then sank without a trace. You told me how she didn't want a decisive relinquishment—a once-and-for-all hanging, or a fatal leap or a bullet through the brain. She only had an inexplicable urge to extinguish herself and flicker back like a trick candle. She wanted, for instance, to throw herself in the path of oncoming buses, or fall down a steep flight of stairs, or constantly push the number of sleeping tablets she could take. Just enough to sink into a deep and dreamless sleep, where she didn't have to be rushed to hospital and stomach-pumped and forced to open her eyes in a nasty little room so blindingly white and sanitized.

'That's what it was,' you finished. 'This duality she wrestled with for months.'

'And how is she now?'

'Still gathering courage.'

'To live or to die?'

'Both.'

You stubbed out your cigarette and stood up, extending your hand. 'Let's go for a swim.' Then you pulled me down the slope, rough and strong, running faster and faster. I could see the edge of the lake, oozing mulch, and the water deep and dark, littered with leaves.

'Stop,' I shouted. 'Stop.'

You gripped my hand tighter, and carried on, your shoes crunching grass and stone.

'Let me go,' I screamed and yanked myself away. 'I don't know how to swim. If you push me in, I'll drown.'

The water lapped at our feet. It seeped into the edges of my sandals. I didn't realize it then, but my eyes were wet with tears. Of fright mainly, and anger. We walked back to the bungalow in silence.

That night you offered a wordless apology.

I was in bed when you walked in and went straight through to the bathroom. I could hear the sound of running water. I thought you'd come to smoke. I didn't ask because I was still angry with you. Then you called me over.

'Why?'

'Please.'

The bathtub was almost full, and steam rose thickly, clouding the mirror, the windows. You stood behind me and started unbuttoning my nightdress. I began to protest but caught a glimpse of our image in the mirror, and in there I was someone else. Held by a stare, by your hands, quick and cold through the fabric. When it dropped to the ground you asked me to step into the tub.

I did. The water was scathing. In a moment you were out of your T-shirt and jeans. We fit snugly, like twins. Then you soaped my back, my shoulders, my hair.

I did the same for you. And despite the steam, I saw how you looked nothing like the woman I thought was your mother. That you came from elsewhere, a life cut unnaturally short, and that even though you were only nineteen you were filled with an old sadness. I noticed the delicate slope of your shoulders; the plane of your back like a smooth river stone; the tiny red beauty spots speckled on your skin; your neck, thin and long, swerving up in a tense line; your fingers pale and white. When you turned around and faced me, your eyes were closed, and drops of water glistened on your cheeks, hollow like emptied lakes. We lay there, perfectly still, until the water cooled.

The next day, the world was washed anew. The flick of a page, a sip from a glass, a leg crossing over the other. Sometimes your hand trailed over mine, your shoulder grazed my arm, or you'd stand close behind me, your breath on my neck. Every gesture, I thought, was significant and added something unforgettable to our lives.

You never took me back to the pukhuri; instead, we walked to the river that bordered Chandbari, that lay beyond a line of railroad tracks at the end of a dusty, lonely road. We strolled down to the water, which spilled endlessly before us, mirroring a vast, empty sky. All along the bank burned small lanterns, and in their golden glow fishermen sat and untangled their nets. Their boats were moored on land, long, narrow vessels that looked like elegant paper cut-outs.

'During the monsoon,' you said, 'the river is as wide as the sea.'

Before I left, we walked there every afternoon, sitting on the bank for hours, doodling on the sand. You told me your mother used to write in journals, filling them out year after year, and that after she died you looked for them. They became the most important thing in the world, except you couldn't find them, and you thought perhaps she had walked here one day and drowned them in the river. Sometimes, we clambered around the bank like lost children, climbing large, rough boulders and dipping our feet into the pools that formed between them, crystal clear mirrors that reflected our faces and the sky. Once, we went much further than usual and came across a temple on a cliff filling up for the evening puja. The worshippers were mostly women from the nearby villages with solemn, earnest faces framed by their cotton saris. We stayed a while and listened to the chanting, watched the offering of lights. Near by stood a large slab of rock, marked with strange lines, squares, and squiggles. A woman from the village, who happened to pass by, told us, 'It's the place where the gods play dice.' Another time, we found a stretch of stones that looked like pale, bleached bones. We tread on them gently; it could have been the graveyard of a herd of prehistoric animals. Close to where the fishermen sat, we climbed a hill from where we could see the dry sandy stretch of an old river.

'Don't you feel,' you asked, 'as though you are elsewhere?'

I knew what you meant; in the midst of Assam's lush landscape, it was a sudden desert hollowed by dips and dunes. When we were close to the dry river, you threw off your slippers and walked in; I followed. The sand was warm and slippery, shaping itself fluidly under our feet. It was hard to imagine that once, where we were standing, a river flowed, swift and spirited. We found perfectly smooth stones that fit the palm of our hands, and strange, contorted driftwood, some large enough to cradle us like boats.

On some evenings, when the light seemed to last longer, we'd hire a boat and a fisherman would row us out on the Brahmaputra. Mostly you'd ask him to go upstream and then allow us to drift, stopping before the current swept us too far out. We'd sit on the plank in the middle; it smelled of fish, and a certain wet-wood dampness, like a forest, I thought, that grew in caves. You looked happiest then, when we floated past the world, gently rocked by lapping water. On some evenings, dusk fell around us, and we were guided only by lanterns and the fisherman's song.

Every night we'd curl around each other in the bathtub, like river reeds, the water deep and warm around us. Sometimes, down my neck, you traced the stars. Sometimes you spoke about your mother.

'Why did she do it?'

You shrugged, the water rippling over your shoulders, the steam quivering off your skin. 'I know why even though I can't explain it.'

Sometimes you tried; you sat up, smoking, feverishly talking. 'Don't you feel that way? This awkwardness with your place in the world. You know, when I put my head underwater, I hear nothing, I see much clearer....' And you'd plunge into the tub, grazing against my stomach, my thighs.

~

The morning we left, you were nowhere to be found.

'I do apologize,' your father said. 'Ever since her mother...you know, ever since it happened, she's been like this, a bit difficult.'

My parents, ever gracious, said they understood, that there was no need for him to be sorry, that they'd had a wonderful time. In turn, they invited your parents to Shillong, and although they promised to come, you and your family have not made a visit.

On our way back I was mostly silent, watching the landscape outside the window flash past. Everything seemed unreal—the low-roofed houses, the swathes of paddy land, the endless stretch of bridges—changing, I felt, on a screen at a distance. Soon, we were climbing, the engine moaned, and the valleys deepened. We passed the sweeping blue waters of Bara Pani, shimmering coldly in the sunlight, and I felt a great sense of emptiness—as though it had been drained and all the world lay hollow like the lake.

The Shillong we drove into was as cold and dispirited as we'd left it. I found it hard to believe we'd been away. Nothing, and everything, had changed. That evening, Sarah, one of my close friends, called, as she'd promised, to fill me in on events I'd missed. She had a crush on twin boys, but couldn't tell one from the other; someone else had been kissed behind the shelter of an umbrella at Ward's Lake. Jason, she giggled, was eagerly awaiting my return.

'And you?' she asked breathlessly. 'How was your holiday?'

I thought of you, your hands, your face. And folded them up, our secret lives.

I went to a lake and drowned.

'Nothing special.'

When I think of you now, it's the feel of wet sand and long grass that comes to me, the smell of cigarettes, and cloves and creatures that live close to water. The stench of your old sadness. I imagine you waiting, like when I first found you, for someone to lead you out to where all rivers end, to the sea.

FOR THE GREATER COMMON GOOD

ARUNI KASHYAP

Neerumoni was the first one in the family to suspect the bark manuscripts. Anil had stared at her in silence. Where on earth had she heard of books being haunted? She said firmly that it wasn't the soul of her dead husband—his father, Horokanto—whom she had first suspected, but the souls trapped in the manuscripts. She stood up and went out to the one-acre pond behind her house, bamboo creel in hand. She would spend some time there. Washing the rice, vegetables, clothes, and vessels from the afternoon's meal wouldn't take long. Chores done, she changed into a petticoat, tied just above her breasts, and swam for at least an hour.

Winters weren't harsh in Teteliguri, not like the villages at the foot of the Jaintia Hills on the Meghalaya border. The wind from the hills entered every nook and cranny there. Meghalaya was the abode of clouds. The white clouds descended as quiet as cats' paws, and soon people would be in the middle of a fog, even before the cat's tongue could scrape their bones. No, here, in Teteliguri village, things were better. There were huge paddy fields. There were many houses and many people in those houses. Here, the climate remained warm and comfortable. Of course, when the trees in the stunted hills that guarded the village started to sway, there was a storm. But the chill reigned only on nights when the winds froze the stones and then carried the bite of it into the houses of the village, an uninvited guest. That was why, when Neerumoni first said she was hearing things, Anil had suggested it was the wind. It was usual for the wind to knock at the door, hover over the straw roof of their thatched hut. They had never finished reinforcing the walls with mud.

Back then, she had been confident that it was the soul of her spiteful husband, Horokanto, who had had many unfulfilled desires before he died in that accident last year. He wanted to return to the mortal world, she thought. In the process, he would rob them of all peace. Eventually, Anil took her seriously, as did most other women in the village. They prayed. They left a meal with Horokanto's favourite dishes on the western side of the house. But the manuscripts still opened and shut in the middle of the night (mainly on Saturdays and Tuesdays) all by themselves. Nor did strange souls stop troubling Neerumoni: they left earthworm mounds on the food she cooked and strange handprints on the bedsheets she washed with khar. And one day, when she had cooked duck meat with banana flower, they dropped a ball of curly hair in the pot.

Gradually, those murmurs, faint songs, the rustle of bark as the manuscripts turned their own pages, invaded the dreams of Neerumoni, and Anil, too. On lonely afternoons, when everything was quiet, those sounds were louder, quicker, more restless. One night, Neerumoni woke up, disturbed by the choric melody of the singing crickets. She saw four lanky men standing over the small wooden box where the manuscripts were kept. They were trying to open the lock with a knife that had a blue plastic handle. When she shouted at them, they turned towards her, grew black wings, and flew off through the ceiling, leaving it undisturbed. Her screams woke up the rest of the family, and she told them one of the figures had worn a long green dress, and the others three white turbans and dhotis. They looked as if they were from a royal family. They didn't wear ornaments, though.

No one believed her. Her suspicions were fortified when she saw one of the manuscripts take the shape of an old man in her dreams. He was crying, asking her to set him free, telling her that he was trapped there by mistake, unlike the other souls who had committed sins. He promised never to disturb her if she freed him from the fetters of the spells in the bark manuscripts. When she said that she hadn't trapped him, she wasn't holding him there, he got angry and screamed, called her a liar. Anil laughed it away. But Anju, who would have said many sarcastic things about her mother's superstitions, who would have fought with her even a month ago, was quiet.

Anil looked at Anju and felt again that, after she had been raped, he required inhuman strength just to look at her face, let alone her eyes. She was sitting in a corner when her brother and mother were speaking about the old man trapped in the manuscripts, fingering the crisscross of welts on her wrists, the result of being tied to a bed with steel threads ordinarily used to tie bamboo. Everyone had been away. It was the death anniversary of the village headman's mother. Neerumoni had asked her to come along, tried to tempt her by saying that she'd get to eat porridge at the function, but Anju said that Biren was coming to leave his baby son with her. His wife was away, and the little one wouldn't sleep until Anju sang him a lullaby. Even that day, Neerumoni reminded Anju that she shouldn't forget that Biren was, after all, a man. Though he was her first cousin, the sudden intimacy between them over the last two years was the talk among certain sections of the village.

But Anju was a popular girl. Everyone loved her. Almost every household in the village was indebted to her in some way or the other. 'Anju, would you please weave this mekhela for me? I won't pay you the full price, but I will give you something as a token of love.' Anju turned into Mother Teresa when phrases such as 'token of love' were mentioned. 'Anju, could you come to our house tomorrow morning? I have asked everyone in the village, but you know how the girls in our village have become after the cinema hall opened in Sonapur; they are afraid their hands will melt away like a leper's if they so much as touch the mix of cow dung and loamy soil. Who else will I ask?' Anju nodded vigorously, agreeing with the old woman. 'Anju, don't you dare forget to come a week before the wedding. You know there is no one else I can trust with keys to the money, the ornaments, with supervising... oh, you are such an angel, what would I do without you!'

So, while some tongues were wagging, others remained quiet. Why should anyone suspect the relationship between first cousins? Those tongue-waggers said 'first cousins' in a dismissive, mocking tone, and suggested that Biren was 'woman-hungry'.

Thus, the day after Neerumoni found an unconscious Anju lying on the bed with bleeding wrists, the whole village blamed Biren and accompanied a near-crazy Anil to the police station to lodge a complaint. Biren was in jail now for raping Anju. And inside that haunted house, where books with souls created strange noises, a new Anju lived with a constantly growing belly. This new Anju didn't speak and often cried silently.

Slopp-slopp-slopp! The sound brought him back to the present. His mother had rushed in and was now standing in front of him, her adult son, in wet clothes that had become translucent. She hadn't brought her bamboo creel back and looked terrified. When he asked what was wrong, she told him that a rough, hairy hand had pulled her down by the leg while she was bathing in the pond. 'I didn't see it, Anil, but it was a man's hand. Hairy. It's the manuscripts, I am telling you.'

∽

Anil's father, Horokanto, learnt sorcery from Neerumoni's father, Doityo Burha, long before the Indian army camp in this village became an integral part of the lives of people here.

As a result of a small disagreement with his own father, Horokanto left home for good. He took shelter in the house of his closest friend, Neerumoni's brother, Nilambor. The next day, when they were having breakfast in the kitchen, Neerumoni's father had asked him what he was interested in. Horokanto replied that he would like to learn the art of sorcery from Doityo Burha. It wasn't an easy art, said the man who was known across seven villages as a great magician, the man who controlled the souls of many rowdy ghosts and forced snakes to come crawling back to suck poison out from the wound of a dying man. Doityo Burha sipped his hot milk and looked at the younger man. But Horokanto was determined to learn. He promised to follow all the rules and regulations. The old man with the long white beard warned him again: if he neglected the rituals for even one day, the bark manuscripts that held the trapped spirits of wild but dead men would strike him dead.

In fact, when he was finally a master of the art, Horokanto managed to imprison a bidaa, a ghost who would be under his command like a genie in a bottle. But the only way to keep the bidaa under control was to give him more and more work. In the next room, Neerumoni, who was a seventeen-year-old girl then, laughed and told her elder sister that it wasn't difficult at all—one could just send the bidaa to a desert and ask him to dig as many wells as possible.

Neerumoni saw Horokanto for the first time three days later. He was swimming in the pond wearing a white gamusa around his waist. It clung to his buttocks. She remembered a long-forgotten feeling. The strange and disturbing pleasure she had felt when her pot-bellied thirty-year-old cousin, who had come to invite them to the rice ceremony for his second son, had pushed up her petticoat, taken out his penis, rubbed it against her inner thighs, asked her to hold it and move her hand slowly up and down. When he started to moan strangely, she got suddenly scared and fled, but not before he had kissed her lips, pushed his tongue inside her mouth, and sucked her upper lip. That was her first time with a man. After a long time, seeing Horokanto, she wanted to lie down beside him.

They had sex for the first time on a rainy winter afternoon, just after the grains were harvested. It wasn't the sort of sudden winter rain that farmers worried would blacken the leaves of the potato. The day had been windy since morning. Clouds gathered little by little in the sky, leisurely, like people trickling into a wedding reception. Her grandmother had advised everyone not to spread out the new grains for drying in the courtyard that day because it might rain. Though it was winter, the sun was strong—you had to drink at least two glasses of water after a half-hour walk. When it finally rained, everyone was ready for it and had taken to their beds or settled down near the hearth with a drink of tea. The cold, the fresh smell of water on earth, the wind: it was ideal. When she reached her house, the quietness of it and the empty veranda seemed to instruct her to go straight to the room that Horokanto shared with Nilambor. Inside, he was lying on his stomach. She latched the door. He looked at her, startled, and tried to smile, but she knew he found her sudden entry odd. She started taking off her clothes. When she was finished, she moved to Horokanto who was staring at her, breathing rapidly. Later, lying naked beside her, he pulled her closer and said he had never seen a more beautiful woman in his life. They smelled like coconut water.

After four months of random, wild lovemaking, behind the house at midnight, beside the pond early in the morning, in the mud of the Tamulidobha River, behind cowsheds, on hay stored to serve as fodder, they eloped. They knew her father would rather kill her than let her marry him. He stole most of the manuscripts. Her father died ten years later; by then, Nilambor had died unmarried, and Neerumoni had given birth to three daughters and a son. Anju was her firstborn. Anil her second. On his deathbed, her father had seen Horokanto finally, given him the rest of the manuscripts, cautioned him to use them carefully and for the good of humanity. Doityo Burha also mentioned that since he had eloped with Neerumoni against her father's wishes, he would not be able to use the spells when he most needed them. 'It's not my curse. I have seen that Fate has decided this punishment for you. These manuscripts are powerful, but they are unforgiving if you disrespect them.' Horokanto died in an accident about thirty years later. That morning, he had fought with Neerumoni and hadn't worshipped the ancient books for the first time in his life.

~

After the army crackdown, everybody in the family began believing Neerumoni's claims about the bark manuscripts. The previous day, rebels had blown up a bridge that connected the village with the National Highway and Guwahati. In the explosion, three Indian soldiers from the battalion stationed in the village were killed. The tall longhaired Punjabi soldier, who always wore a red turban and was respectful towards women (unlike the others), lost his hand in the impact and died of bleeding. The intensity of the explosion caused it to fly and land on the roof of the village fisherman's house. His wife had been sitting in the courtyard having her lunch at the time. A stream of blood fell on her shoulders (some say most of it fell on her rice and face). At first, she thought a bird had shat on her clothes, but the shit was red, and the bird looked like a hand. For a while, she stood staring at her roof where the hand was and then fainted. When her neighbours found her an hour later, sprinkled water on her eyes, and brought her back to her senses, she vomited and started to wail hysterically. Everyone in the village went to see the wailing woman and the clenched fist with five golden rings on its fingers—stones meant to ward off the evil influence of powerful planets. They sucked in sharp breaths through clenched teeth and wished Horokanto was still alive. When Dilipram came, they fell quiet. He was the only sorcerer left in the village now to take care of spirits and snakebites and barrenness in married women. They were convinced that the soul of the Punjabi man was refusing to leave.

The army crackdown happened the next day. Scores of soldiers came in jeeps and surrounded the village. Their boots were loud as they ran towards the hamlets. Someone had started to play the drum in the village prayer hall, and it boomed like the announcement of a war. Neerumoni's neighbour, Bibha, came running to tell her to flee. 'Save yourself and your family members, forget the belongings.' Neerumoni stood frozen for a moment, not knowing how Anju would run with that bulging stomach. Then the two of them hurried along as fast as Anju could manage, hoping it was just a false alarm, hoping that, in the village's central meeting ground, everyone would say, go back, nothing is wrong.

But Neerumoni saw that all the young men were running towards the forests. She saw women, children, girls, and old men running across the fields to get to the next village. They would cross the Tamulidobha River, dry in winter. She, too, ran that way with a heavily pregnant

Anju, thinking how Horokanto and she had made love on the banks of this river, in the mud, like two buffaloes, one morning. It was the monsoon, and the river that ran beside the passionately lovemaking couple flowed with force, creating whirlpools, voluptuous with desire and laughter. Neerumoni heard gunshots. She turned back. Someone said it was Hiren, and someone else said, no, no, no one has been shot. They started to run again.

They returned the next morning, after spending a worried night in Maloybari village across the river. Each and every house had been ransacked. There were boot prints on clothes, white bedsheets were soiled brown and black. Food was strewn around. Beds upturned. Tables broken. Chairs piled up in front of the courtyard and burnt, both plastic and wooden. Mattresses left out in the rain or set on fire and still smoking. Mud walls broken down. Earthen pots shattered in courtyards. As they were putting their houses back together somehow, the village folk could hear the cries of Prodhan Mahatu, the village milkman. He had forgotten to untie his twenty cows, and the army had shot and killed all of them. Their corpses were lying in the cowshed, stinking of blood and the greenish dung that had come out along with their intestines.

In the haunted house, Neerumoni said to Anil, 'Every single object in this house has been thrown around, but look, the bark manuscripts are where we had left them. They have even thrown away the mustard oil lamp that we lit in front of the manuscripts, so why didn't they try to open this locked wooden chest?' All of them believed that the chest would have been broken and the manuscripts removed, but those were haunted manuscripts, they didn't need legs to return to their original place. They imagined that the soldier who had disrespected the manuscripts was now dying slowly of some strange disease. For the first time, Neerumoni and her family felt safe because of the presence of the bark manuscripts. All these weeks after Horokanto's death, they were petrified, unable to solve the mystery of the sounds. That night, Prodhan Mahatu went to the army camp, stabbed one soldier, and set one of the camps on fire. They shot him dead.

∽

Dilipram wasn't a great sorcerer. Now middle-aged, he had learnt most of his charms from Horokanto, even though he was apprenticed to an old sorcerer in Hatimura village, Mayong, for about five years. He lived in the old man's house and worked on his fields in lieu of fees. The sorcerer had given Dilipram the teeth of a male crocodile, the dried hands of a pregnant female monkey, severed legs of mating lizards, snakeskin, and many other indispensable things required in the art of serious sorcery for the greater common good. When Horokanto was alive, Dilipram would occasionally come to him with questions: 'Do we use a pregnant bitch's morning urine to make this potion?' 'I made the potion for cobra bite with khar, but I'm worried about whether the concentration is strong enough.'

The people in the village had thought Dilipram would inherit the bark manuscripts. In fact, Neerumoni had offered him the books, but he refused. She must know, he said, that those manuscripts had a soul, and they always chose their owner, just as her father had once been chosen. So had Horokanto—or why would he have fought with his father and gone to stay in their house to learn sorcery when he belonged to such a rich family? It's all decided 'above', he told her with conviction, pointing to the sky. 'You will get signs.' One day, she would have to let go of the manuscripts so that they reached the rightful owner. That person could even be Anil or one of her future sons-in-law.

Now, when Anil told him about the strange sounds that shook their house and robbed them of their sleep, Dilipram suggested that they take out the manuscripts every Tuesday and Saturday, spread them under the sun (if there was no sun, the veranda would suffice), light a mustard-oil lamp, offer some white or red flowers, and pray to the gods of the ancient books, requesting them not to trouble the family. 'Try it,' he said calmly. When Anil stood up to leave, Dilipram told him that, if it didn't work, he should return on the night of the twenty-second Saturday with a new steel plate. They would go to the cremation ground. Anil started to walk away. The breeze lifted the light cotton cloth that covered Dilipram's flabby body. He turned and told Anil that he had this strange feeling that one of the trapped souls had become very powerful since they hadn't been controlled by spells for nearly a year now, since Horokanto's death; that soul might be trying to take corporeal form to fulfil its worldly wishes.

In the deathly silence that followed, Anil felt he could hear ants moving across the courtyard. He broke out in a cold sweat. Dilipram added that the soul could be trying to take birth through Anju, so they would have to kill the child as soon as it was born if the first remedy didn't work. Anil decided that he wouldn't tell his mother about this last part. She would worry unnecessarily.

On the way home, Anil passed Prodhan's house. A strong stench of rotten animals rose from it. He rushed to get ahead of the smell and vomited. Tearing off some leaves from a eucalyptus tree nearby, he inhaled the scent until he felt better. The village would have to do something as soon as possible, he thought, wiping his face with the cotton handkerchief that Anju had woven on the waist loom before she was raped. After Prodhan was shot dead, his wife and two daughters vanished mysteriously. They must have fled to a relative's home. They didn't even wait to receive the body. But that was wise—the army would have killed them, too, had they gone to ask for his body. It was the villagers who received Prodhan's decomposing body. Before that, young men and women from the city had come with pens and tiny notebooks and cameras that made loud sounds. The army had flown them in a helicopter and taken them on a tour of select localities. They would then report that no villagers had been harmed during the operation. Some of them came by car, and the army helped them cross the river on boats.

Anil stopped by the grocery shop to buy some red lentils that his mother had asked for. The shopkeeper wrapped it in an old newspaper. Anil didn't notice the bloody picture that was printed on it.

On reaching home, he apologized to his mother. They should have believed her. He conveyed what Dilipram had told him, except the part about Anju's unborn baby. Neerumoni said, 'Let's wait and see what happens.' They would worship the manuscripts for twenty-one Saturdays and Tuesdays.

She went in to ask Anju if she needed something. But the girl just wept soundlessly, which she did a lot these days. Neerumoni knew why. After she was raped, for a long time, Neerumoni had blamed her for the incident: didn't I tell you not to roam around with Biren too much? Wasn't I cautioning you for a long time until it finally happened? You destroyed your life and ours, too.

After talking to Anil, Neerumoni shivered. She didn't know if she would raise Anju's child or kill it with the help of other women—as people in the village usually did in such situations. She recalled how Binapani Pehi, an elderly woman in the village who had died in the early nineties, had given birth to a green-eyed, blond-haired baby after she was raped by the British soldiers in the early forties. Neerumoni had been a young girl then. People discussed for years how the village women had shoved fistfuls of salt into that baby's mouth. Two more months left! It was already February. What would happen if she gave birth to twins? No, no, as if one child wasn't enough trouble. Would she be able to stuff a handful of salt into the infant's mouth and take his life? Wouldn't this child be her first grandchild?

When she went to the kitchen and unwrapped the lentils, Neerumoni saw the bloodied face of the slain man printed on the newspaper. She trembled and imagined the blood being mixed with the lentils. Should she wash the lentils again to remove that blood? She felt queasy looking at the blood, the rose-pink lentils. Then she realized it was Prodhan's face: distorted with anger, full of the pain of losing twenty cows that he had reared like his own children—cows that came running to him whenever they saw him, red and brown and white cows that liked to rub their heads on his back, cows that licked their calves' balls and ears, cows that he rebuked if they chewed the clothes hung on the line to dry, cows that had the most beautiful eyes in the world.

She called out to Anil to ask if it was really Prodhan in the photograph. He looked at it and said, yes, that's him. He read the headline out to her.

TOP MILITANT GUNNED DOWN IN TETELIGURI VILLAGE

She threw away the lentils. They didn't have lunch that day.

∽

The day Anju spoke a full sentence in her normal tone, Neerumoni couldn't believe her ears. In the nine months since the assault, she'd only heard her daughter cry in agony and impotent rage. Anju was whispering something. At first Neerumoni thought it was the sigh of the rain-bearing wind from the hills. It had been raining hard for a few weeks, an early monsoon. The previous morning, Neerumoni had noticed that the edges of the veranda had disintegrated. Probably the first wave of floods would arrive soon, too.

Neerumoni went to Anju's room and asked what she was saying. Anju said she had seen a child with eyes that shone like flames in her dreams last night. When her mother heard this, she was sure the manuscripts were now troubling her daughter. She looked worried and promised that she would send Anil to Dilipram's house again as soon as he returned. Neerumoni sat beside her daughter. Anju extended her hands and pressed her mother's, wept, and said she didn't want the child. As soon as it was born, she would shove a handful of salt into his mouth.

It was dark outside, as if the sky had covered itself with a black shawl to keep away the chill. Even though it was still early in the day, a soft blanket of darkness settled on the wet roofs, over the rain-drenched trees, paths, stones, and red soil. Neerumoni held her daughter's hands. Through the window, she looked at their dog who was shivering in the sudden chill, curled up on hay in a corner of the cowshed. She noticed that the small wooden chest shook mildly—was it throbbing? moving?—as if someone was trying to escape. She could feel her breaths become heavy, shallow.

Anil didn't return until late afternoon. After serving him lunch, Neerumoni mentioned Anju's dream, and Anil was too stunned to speak for a while. Then, slowly, he told her what Dilipram had cautioned him about—that one of the souls might have become too powerful and could be trying to attain physical shape by possessing Anju's child. Neerumoni whispered: he must have already taken possession of the unborn.

By the time Anil left for Dilipram's house, it was raining harder. He passed the Tamulidobha, suddenly becoming aware of its noisy waters. The hilly tributaries had given her a new life, youthful blood. It was as if she was mocking the village or perhaps trying to wake people from their stupor, warning them of something. He also crossed Prodhan Mahatu's house. Last month, the villagers had cleaned up the mess. They didn't know what to do with his land and property, and they left everything the way they had found it. Even the clothes. One of the men had entered the house and told the villagers that, on the hearth, there was still a container of cooked rice and huge steel pots of milk that had curdled, grown fungi, turned green and yellow and brown, and were letting out another smell that was difficult to describe. Now, Anil noticed, wild creepers had completely covered the house, the huge cowshed, and even the bamboo gate. There was not a glimpse to be had of the mud walls or the wood in the windows.

When he returned home, it was evening. When he told his mother that Dilipram had advised him to relinquish the manuscripts to the flowing waters of a river, she asked him if he was hiding something from her again. He lit a fire, and as he warmed his hands with it, Anil told her that he wasn't. In fact, he should have told her everything the last time, too. A storm had broken out, running through the village like a madwoman. Their thatched hut started to vibrate.

Neerumoni wondered aloud if they would be able to go out. Anju's abdomen was hurting. Anil said that that was even more reason to go, because Dilipram had told them they had to act immediately, even if lightning were to strike down the whole village and the hills. They would have to do it on their own, before Anju gave birth, otherwise the soul would be born in their own house, and no one could predict what it might do.

As they were leaving the house, Anju's water broke. She screamed, but in the wild roar of the dusk thunderstorm, they didn't hear her cries. Anju crawled down from her bed, breathless, lay on the green mattress on the ground, spread her legs, and waited, wondering if she would be able to do it all alone. She lost consciousness.

Anil looked at the betel nut trees moving like drunken men weaving their way down a village street. He wondered if one of them would fall, killing them both. He held the wooden chest firmly with one hand and the umbrella over his mother's head. But they didn't have the umbrella for long. The wind was strong, like the spring storm Bordoisila. People believed the storm was the soul of a newly married woman rushing back to her mother's house with her long hair open, destroying everything in her way: huts, trees, cowsheds, and crops. The storm that evening was as mighty as the impatient Bordoisila. So when they finally heard the wicked laughter of the youthful river, they were relieved.

The riverbank was slippery, and below, the water flowed furiously. Anil saw a wooden chair being carried away. Would they go, really? The souls? It had to be done by Anil's hand, since he was the heir to his father who had died without choosing the rightful owner of the bark manuscripts, who couldn't train someone, who had not given away the knowledge of those books before dying. After they had emptied the box into the tempestuous waters, Neerumoni told him that someone had breathed on her cheeks, and she had heard a sigh. Anil didn't say anything, but she stressed that it had been warm, as warm as it could be on that chilly evening. Then he said it was just the wind, just the sound of the wind moving across the leaves and over the waters. On their way back, they didn't worry about Anju, but only thought about

Horokanto—the husband, the lover, the father. Before opening the gate to their compound, Neerumoni said, 'You know, even my father found most of those manuscripts in a wooden box. Things just get repeated.'

'What will happen now?'

'They will travel, maybe even to the sea, in search of another owner.'

Inside the house, Anju was lying unconscious, a newborn between her legs, slick with blood. Neerumoni took a sharp knife and cut the cord. There was absolute silence. She waited; she patted the boy's back. It didn't cry.

Anil wanted to say that it'd be too soon, too good to be true, but he kept quiet. He looked at his sister's face, called to her. He wanted to show her the baby before he buried him.

The soil at the back of their house would be soft like mud now. Digging a deep hole would be easy. Neerumoni sniffed. The air smelled of fresh mud. She wondered why the baby's face reminded her of her dead father who had been hurt because she had eloped with Horokanto.

MAKING AMENDS

PRAJWAL PARAJULY

2015 was the year of momos.

He believed he was an expert on South Asian cuisine. She, the twenty-two-year-old Nepalese woman, may have lulled him, the twenty-two-year-old British tourist, into believing that.

He liked determining the ingredients from which a dish had been crafted. He'd never start a meal mixing vegetable with meat, meat with lentil, lentil with rice. First, he wanted to soak in the spices that had gone into the making of individual dishes—the pungency of black pepper in the aloo gobi, the nuttiness of fenugreek in the dal, the earthiness of cumin in the jeera chicken, the piquancy of red pepper in the tomato sauce—and then he would mix the foods up, rice and dal and cauliflower florets and a big, juicy chunk of chicken, skin intact, torn from its tendon, all coming together in an imperfect ball. There would be dalle, just a hint of it, chilli so hot that his nose would water. He would soon abandon fork, spoon, and knife to eat with fingers.

He had first seen her making Tibetan dumplings by the candlelight in her Kathmandu home, which doubled as a guest house. He wanted to experience a place that wasn't a hotel, and this guest house—a homestay, they called it—with its constant power failures was perfect for that authentic experience he craved, different from the palace hotels he had stayed in on his tour of India. She was mincing onions—rap, rap, rap, rap, thump, rap, rap—on a thin chopping board, adding them to the rapidly growing mountain of vegetables by her side as she sniffled, sometimes letting go of the knife so she could brush aside strands of hair that fell on her face.

It was a face he kept casting sidelong glances at. She had a face that became prettier the more familiar you got with it. It glowed, and it turned red when she saw him stare. She avoided his gaze, concentrating instead on getting rid of browned coriander stems, chopping and dicing and slicing. The cabbage, too—fresh from the ground and glistening with dewdrops—demanded her attention. She washed the vegetable, hacked it in two, and shredded each half into thousands of pieces that she mixed with carrots, ginger, onions, and coriander.

Her father, whose accent he was still getting used to, made his presence felt with a cough.

'These are what we call momos,' the father spluttered. 'They could very well be the national dish of Nepal.'

'Brilliant,' he said. He asked her if he could help her knead the dough. She laughed.

'It's not as easy as it looks,' she said.

And then their eyes met, locked.

She made little balls of dough and rolled them into circular wrappings, inside which she stuffed the vegetable mix, closing them in perfect pleats, like those of a sari.

'Do you eat the dumplings by themselves?' he asked, knowing the answer.

'No, there's a sauce.'

'The chutney?' he bragged.

'Yes, the chutney.'

'Watching you cook is like watching someone create art.'

'It is an art,' she said.

The momos went into the steamer.

'When do you know they are ready?' he asked.

'When the momos are shiny,' she said, her face shiny.

He had encountered momos in India but was unprepared for their ubiquity in Nepal.

'I've eaten them before,' he said, as she transferred eight dumplings, plump, white, and glossy, to his plate. The sauce, a concoction of tomatoes and chilli, went on the side.

'I'm sure you have,' she replied, in a manner that could have been dismissive.

He waited for her to join him, but she was busy with another batch of momos—rolling, stuffing, pleating, steaming—that her father helped her with.

'My daughter just returned from medical school for holidays,' the father said, hardly able to disguise his clumsy attempt at closing a momo. 'Stayed away from home for too long.'

At first, he thought the father was warning him to stay away from her, but after he restrung the old man's words, he decided the sentence had nothing to do with him.

'Aren't you going to eat?' he asked her.

'No, I have too many of these to steam,' she replied.

He pierced a momo with a fork and brought it to his mouth. She looked at him to gauge his reaction. It was good but nothing extraordinary. He moved the dumpling around his mouth to make a more informed verdict.

'It's delicious,' he said, exaggerating.

'You aren't eating it right,' she reprimanded.

She slathered a spoonful of chutney on a momo. 'Now, eat this. This is the way.'

He ate eight, then another eight, and then another eight momos. He stopped because he could eat no more.

'These are excellent,' he said, meaning it. 'They are so succulent.'

'Everything is garden-fresh,' she replied.

The father was pleased. 'You like it,' he said. 'We can make momos every day for you.'

'It's too much work to make them every day,' the daughter said.

The father and daughter quarrelled in Nepali. He could make out words like 'guest' and 'honour' until the argument abruptly stopped when the daughter exiled herself from the kitchen.

'She's tired,' the father said.

After excusing himself, he went into his room to lie down. He had overeaten. He couldn't sleep.

The next morning, he asked her to take him out for some meat momos.

'What would you like? Mutton, pork, or chicken?' she asked.

'I can't decide between lamb and pork,' he replied.

Her father was at work, so she took him to her favourite restaurant—a shack, in a cluster of equally decrepit shacks.

'I hope you won't hold this place to Western standards of hygiene,' she said.

Inside the kerosene-lamp-illuminated hovel, he might have seen a cockroach. They were the only customers.

'I'm adventurous,' he said, perching himself on a rickety stool.

'I saw that last night. Given how many pieces you consumed, I'm guessing a plate won't be enough for you here.'

'I was afraid you would mind if I didn't eat three hundred pieces.'

'I'll warn you, the food here takes long to arrive.'

'We could get a few beers then?' he asked, hopeful.

'You can,' she replied. 'I'm not drinking.'

'Don't you drink at all?'

'Oh, like a fish, but in Kathmandu, I behave like a good Nepali girl.'

He laughed. She laughed.

'Why did you choose to go to college in Delhi?' he asked.

'So I could give vent to my wanton ways before I finally succumb to an arranged marriage.'

'Couldn't the giving vent to—you know—those ways be done in Kathmandu?'

'No, here I have to be the dutiful daughter helping her single dad run his failing homestay. What about you?'

'Just finished uni. Training to be a barrister. Taking time off.'

'Backpacking in Nepal? Such a cliché.'

'And your mum?' He wondered if he had gone too far, but he'd been curious since he set foot in the house.

'She left us.'

'Oh, I am terribly sorry. I assumed she was dead.'

'She is to me.'

He reached out to her, but she drew away from his hand.

'I am sorry your father and you had a fight about me last night,' he said. 'I understood something about honouring the guests. You and your father are so hospitable.'

'You misheard,' she replied. 'You misunderstood.'

'Are you sure? I could've sworn.'

'It was the furthest thing from hospitality. A big, fat bill will confront you at checkout. Twenty-four momos don't come cheap.'

He had been so sure he was staying with nice people.

'We're a business, not a charity,' she said, perhaps reading his mind.

To mitigate the awkwardness, he changed the subject. Food was a safe topic.

'I think I've learnt the right way to eat with my fingers, but I still drop some stuff on my shirt,' he said. 'Can you teach me to do it better?'

'It's easy,' she said, exaggeratedly demonstrating how to eat a momo with her hand. 'Like this.'

'No, teach me how to eat rice with my fingers.'

'I can't make promises.'

'That's generous,' he said.

'It's an art,' she replied.

'What is?'

'Eating with one's fingers.'

She would only eat one chicken momo. She said being a cook as good as she was meant facing constant disappointment when eating out.

~

They developed a routine.

Soon after the father headed for work, they would venture out. Often, they walked. Sometimes, they took the safa tempo, a shared taxi where they were packed in with two dozen people. In the cramped vehicle, aided by bumps and turns, their bodies would touch. He would steal glances at her when flesh inadvertently grazed flesh, but she did a good job of pretending she didn't feel any contact. They would mix and match the touristy with the obscure—one minute they were surrounded by guides promising him nubile girls and the next they were in some isolated dirt road from where they caught mountain views. And they went to many restaurants, a mix of middle- and low-brow places in Patan. She was convinced no high-end eatery served authentic Nepalese food. He wondered if she liked his company as much as he did hers. He was good-looking, charming, and funny, yes, but he sometimes suspected that she made these trips so she could escape boredom when Kathmandu underwent daily ten-hour power cuts.

The food education continued. She was never truly happy with restaurant food. She needed north Indian food to taste like north Indian food and Nepalese food to taste like Nepalese food. When one aped the other, she was furious. He had just about begun noticing the distinction between the two cuisines—he still thought they were more alike than different—but would soon know where the similarities ended. 'All that grease and oil in north Indian food—nothing of that you find in Nepalese food,' she would say. She disliked it when one spicy flavour overpowered another—like in the aalooko achaar, the potato salad he was trying to develop a taste for, copious spoonfuls of which she ate to determine where exactly the problem lay.

'Oh, yes, just too many spices—your tongue doesn't know what spice to hold and what spice to release,' she complained.

'Like a man falling for an exasperating woman he knows is wrong for him.'

'Stupid, senseless analogy.'

'No, not so stupid. Hear me out. He doesn't know what feelings to keep and what emotion to let go of.'

'Quite a philosopher you are.'

'I think I made sense.'

'You speak like a lovelorn, jilted lover—it's sad. You're pathetic. We are the same age, but you are so immature. Pathetic.'

No one had called him that before. He was the one who usually thought people were pathetic. He was the most 'solid' person he knew. He knew this without conceit, just as he knew he was handsome without being proud of it. He had grown up surrounded by love and wealth, excelled at sports, and had gone to Harrow and Cambridge. His name was most likely to come up when friends discussed who among them had the perfect life. That's why he was taken aback when this strange Nepalese woman called him the last thing he thought of himself as. It was insulting, but he might have enjoyed the insult; it compounded his desire to be nurtured by her. Now that was definitely pathetic.

She had moved on to more important topics, unaware of the turmoil in him she had just unleashed.

Had this been a movie, he would have leaned in and kissed her. But Nepal was no movie. To kiss her this early in their acquaintance would be wrong here. They hadn't even held hands.

'You look beautiful when you talk about food,' he said.

She must have heard him, but she continued yammering. 'I can't tell you how mad I get when momos get Indianized. When I visited London, every Nepalese restaurant served Indian food. The owners should all be sued. I called a few restaurateurs cheats to their faces. It was strangely satisfying.'

'I said you look beautiful today.'

'Yes, I called them thieves and cheats to their faces. What business does chicken tikka masala have in a Nepalese restaurant?'

'Am I not allowed to say you look beautiful?'

'Indian restaurants masquerading as Nepalese restaurants—terrible, terrible thing. You should do something about it.'

He gave up.

He had to ask her out. He did it in the most matter-of-fact way.

'Would you like to go out with me?' he said.

'No,' she said.

'Why not?'

'Well, for one, you white people think you can waltz in here like you own us.'

'That's unfair.'

'Two, I am already seeing someone. The thought never occurred to you, did it?'

'I thought we were having a good time.'

'You don't even know me.'

'I want to get to know you better.'

'You're a patron at my father's guest house.'

'There's nothing wrong with that. When I saw you chop onions, I....'

'Are you serious?'

'I am.'

'No. Are you serious about the onion bit? You were attracted to the sight of a woman in the kitchen? The subservience was appealing to you, wasn't it?'

He wanted to explain himself to her, to let her know how much the moment had meant to him.

'I mean, you were looking so beautiful by the candlelight.'

'What now? The poverty was romantic? Yes, we have power failures here.'

'You don't get it, I am afraid.'

'Ugh. What you need is a servant.'

'Please...I am trying to explain my feelings.'

'You're only making things worse. Go blabber about how beautiful I look when I sweat over your momos to someone else.'

'I thought we bonded.'

'Are you accusing me of leading you on?'

'No, I didn't mean that.'

'Talking to you about spices for two minutes doesn't mean we bonded.'

'Did I do something wrong?'

'Yes, you don't ask out a woman who's already seeing some other man.'

'Had you told me....'

'Oh, now I need to spell everything out?'

He didn't know what to say.

'I think you should stay elsewhere. I don't feel comfortable sleeping under the same roof as you.'

The father wondered what went wrong. He wouldn't charge money for his meals.

'But I ate twenty-four momos,' he said.

'That was my treat,' the father insisted. 'You're my guest.'

He heard father and daughter arguing when he descended the stairs.

∽

In London, they were all the same. Nepalese restaurants with very Nepalese names—Everest Kitchen, Gurkha Grill, Sherpa Café, Kathmandu Restaurant, Himalayan Foods—that served very Indian dishes. They all sported Tibetan prayer flags, colourful and bearing mantras, statues of the laughing Buddha, fat, fed and incensed, and the Nepalese flag, triangular and tattered. The Gregorian chant would play in a loop, like it did at the Buddha Café right now.

He scanned the menu and proceeded to harass an unsuspecting waitress.

'I thought this was a Nepalese restaurant,' he said.

'It is,' she replied.

'I don't see anything Nepalese here.' It felt oddly satisfying when the person at the other end was a woman his age.

'I came to eat Nepalese food,' he said. 'I don't see anything Nepalese here.'

'But sir, you have chicken mango,' she said. 'It's very good.'

'And how's chicken mango a Nepalese dish?' he asked. 'I'd have gone to an Indian restaurant if I wanted Indian food.'

'But sir, Indian food and Nepalese food are the same.'

'Say that to some other person.'

'And we have momos.'

'Where?'

'Momos, you know, Tibetan dumplings.'

'I know what momos are. Where?'

'At the bottom.'

Yes, there they were, like footnotes, almost embarrassed to be there, two font sizes smaller than the rest of the items on the menu, interlopers in a menu they should have dominated.

'I'd like the lamb momos,' he said.

She returned with an apologetic look.

'Cook says no momos today,' she said.

'Are you serious?' he asked.

'Yes, demand for momos is not high. Why don't you try samosas?'

'I wanted momos. I came here for momos.'

'Sorry,' she said.

'They have nothing,' he said to the other diners. 'No momos, nothing. It's not a Nepalese restaurant.

No one uttered a word.

'You're all cheats,' he said and stormed out. He was loud enough to cause others to stop eating. 'Why say it's a Nepalese restaurant when it's not?' He banged the door shut.

It was the sixth London Nepalese restaurant he had walked out of in the month he'd been back from Kathmandu. He had a trip to Edinburgh planned for New Year's Eve. He wondered if he'd find a Nepalese restaurant there. 2015 needed to end with momos. 2016 would have to start with momos.

DIELIENUO'S CHOICE

AVINUO KIRE

Dielienuo entered my life shortly after my parents announced that I was getting a baby brother. Mother tenderly rubbed her stomach as she sat me down to explain that he was still inside her tummy, just as I had been before I came into the world. My initial reaction to this news was insecurity. I had been the centre of my parents' world for too long, ten glorious years. I wondered whether this new addition would affect my standing in the family and worried that they might love me less. However, as time passed, I became increasingly excited at the prospect of becoming somebody's elder sister. I must admit that there have been times when I experienced envy towards my cousins who had younger siblings. They would act all grown-up and bossy, even towards me, despite us all being the same age. I suppose being older than someone else in the family does tend to make one appear more grown-up somehow.

Mother's stomach steadily grew bigger as the months passed, and she began to pad around the house barefoot a lot, something she never allowed me to do. Mother was a housewife and father, a busy doctor who worked at our local hospital. As Mother's pregnancy advanced, housework became problematic, and she also began to feel unwell quite often. This was when my parents started to discuss the practicality of hiring a live-in maid to help out around the house. They asked around a lot but could not find anyone suitable. Then one afternoon, my father informed me that besides getting a baby brother, I would also be getting a new friend. Father explained that there was a poor family in one of the more remote Naga villages, who was struggling to make ends meet. My parents had therefore, agreed to take in one of the children, who was the same age as me. This girl would help Mother around the house and in return, my parents would send her to school, and also dispatch money to her family every month. Her name was Dielienuo.

The first time I saw Dielienuo, she was timidly sitting on a small moora beside her uncle, who had brought her from the village. I had come home from school to find Mother conversing with Dielienuo's uncle inside our kitchen which always smelled divine, courtesy of the aroma of smoked meat hanging above the fireplace. Dielienuo seemed sad but did not cry when her uncle left. He was her maternal aunt's husband. We learned that both Dielienuo's biological parents had passed away when she was very young, and her aunt and uncle had taken her in thereafter. After her uncle left, Mother showed Dielienuo where she would be sleeping. We did not have extra rooms but there was a small storage space between the kitchen and the corridor which led to the other rooms. Mother cleared the space and Father installed a bed for Dielienuo. I noticed to my immense astonishment that she had not brought any luggage. She only had with her a polythene bag containing two tattered pieces of clothing and an overripe banana, more black than yellow, obviously meant to be consumed much earlier. After inspecting her meagre belongings, Mother gave her some of my hand-me-downs to wear. Although we were the same age, my clothes hung on her painfully emaciated frame. In time, Dielienuo slowly filled out, thanks to my mother's solid meals. My parents were initially a little apprehensive about the language barrier. Hence, they were pleasantly surprised to discover that Dielienuo could speak Nagamese, the common Naga lingua franca. Contrary to what my parents had assumed, Dielienuo was not completely new to the urban areas. Her uncle revealed that she had worked for some time in the household of an elderly lady in Dimapur district. He further explained that Dielienuo had been miserable there and so, he had taken her back to their village. He said this with an air of magnanimity, conscious of his act of compassion towards a little girl under his care. However, poverty had compelled them to send her away a second time, this time to us.

Dielienuo didn't talk much. She would quietly do the chores assigned to her by Mother. Every evening after washing the dishes, she would go to the back of the house and sit outside our bamboo shadze, an extended platform stretching away from the ground. Suspended in mid-air, Dielienuo would watch the starlit Kohima sky. She was always so calm and mature that I wondered whether she ever did such a childish thing like missing her family. Early one morning, as I sleepily walked towards the kitchen for a glass of water, I could smell the stench of urine wafting from the mattress where Dielienuo slept. She had wet her bed. I found out that Dielienuo had been wetting her bed regularly ever since she arrived. My exasperated mother finally had to cover her mattress with a plastic sheet. When Mother learned that I was aware of the situation, she sat me down and warned me not to tease Dielienuo, and suggested that I should try to befriend her instead as she was obviously very lonely and homesick. Mother had read that bed-wetting by older children was commonly due to psychological stress and trauma, possibly caused by sudden transitions in life. My awe of Dielienuo disappeared with this revelation, and I reached out to her that evening. At first, she appeared a little wary of my sudden friendliness but I wore her down fast. We were still little girls after all and soon, we were chatting animatedly. We sat underneath the stars and spoke about inconsequential things, which didn't matter as much as the fact that we were saying them to each other. Finally, Mother called us in as it was time for bed.

Dielienuo and I became grand friends soon. Since she had arrived at an odd time when school admissions were already over, my parents decided to send her to school during the next academic year instead. I enjoyed playing with Dielienuo more than anyone else. She was always so sweet and agreeable, pandering to my every whim as if her very survival depended on my happiness. I looked forward to coming home from school, knowing that Dielienuo would be waiting for me. We would play kitchen, dress-up, and an exhausting series of hand games which involved a lot of synchronized clapping and nonsensical rhymes. Sometimes Mother would complain that I was keeping Dielienuo away from her chores, but I don't think she minded all that much, now that I no longer pestered her by complaining of boredom. Father always came home from work late, and since there were no neighbourhood children my age, it was mostly always just Mother and I alone.

I began to have a sense that my friendship with Dielienuo was different from the usual. There was an underlying unease which quietly grew alongside our budding friendship. It seemed that this perplexing feeling steadily increased the more I grew to love her. There were times I felt terribly guilty, although I could not exactly comprehend why. Such times as when one ordinary night, we would be two little girls playing with my Barbie dolls and the next morning I would wake up, sleepily in my pyjamas, to see her scrubbing the floor on her knees. Perhaps I chose to remain ignorant. Dielienuo always had to wake up at the crack of dawn, even on weekends and other holidays, on the coldest winter mornings too. She loved to watch cartoons on television, and would squeal in delight over kiddie serials, which I myself have outgrown.

Whenever Mother called her midway during such a programme, she would answer very reluctantly with her eyes still glued to the screen. Mother would then storm over and switch off the television herself, bringing the programme to an abrupt end. Dielienuo was also always in awe of my ten-year-old self's possessions. 'Are all these yours?' she had reverently whispered, when she entered my room for the first time, browsing through my playthings and my many clothes in open-mouthed bewilderment. My initial pride over Dielienuo's wonder at my material belongings wore off swiftly. In time, I did not want her inside my room. Her unflagging admiration not only irritated but shamed me as well.

It wasn't mine but Dielienuo's life which changed with the birth of my baby brother. She was the busiest ten-year-old I have ever seen. She would hover over him constantly, looking after him, carrying and mothering him. Seeing Dielienuo slightly hunched to the right with the weight of a large duffel bag stuffed with my brother's baby essentials became a common sight during family outings. But sometimes, while my baby brother was asleep, Dielienuo was free to be my friend again. And in spite of everything that was happening around us, our friendship miraculously seemed to remain intact.

Time went on and soon, my eleventh birthday approached. Turning eleven felt no different from being ten, but my parents obviously thought otherwise, and made quite a fuss over me. They decided to throw a gala birthday bash in my honour. All my cousins from both the paternal and maternal sides of my family as well as a few friends from school were invited. I had been feeling a tad sidelined by my parents ever since the arrival of my baby brother, and this party almost seemed to make up for it. Mother even ordered a special pink birthday cake with candles, and allowed me to choose the sweet treats to give away as party favours. Poor Dielienuo was bewildered. She could not understand the concept of a birthday party. 'So your parents celebrate the day you were born every year? Why?' she asked in a tone that conveyed amazement as well as a little scorn. I realized that Dielienuo had never been wished on her birthday, let alone had a birthday celebrated. I asked her when her birthday was, and she pointed to a number on the wall calendar rather randomly. I was sure she did not know her birthday. In fact, I began to doubt whether she even knew her actual age at all. I was allowed to miss school on my birthday. I watched cartoons on television while Mother and Dielienuo kept busy the entire day, preparing for the evening party.

'Who's that?' a friend whispered in my ear, pointing towards Dielienuo who was serving black tea to the adults in a huge tray. Everyone had already eaten by then. I looked at Dielienuo's dishevelled hair and second-hand dress which was spotted with the scrumptious food she had helped Mother prepare. I knew she had been working the whole day on my account. This knowledge could not prevent me from being ashamed of her. Seeing Dielienuo's pitiable appearance beside my friends in their clean clothes and bright faces mortified me. 'Oh, she's just a servant,' I replied airily. Later, while we were indulging in some party games, Father encouraged me to include Dielienuo as well. I found her inside the kitchen, scraping leftovers off the plates, keeping aside the bones for our pet Alsatian Teizei, just as she had been taught. Dielienuo refused to join us, claiming that she had too much work to do. I knew that Mother would not mind if I took her away but I did not insist. I was, in fact, relieved that she had declined.

Dielienuo reverted to her old reserved self ever since my eleventh birthday. She was always busy, either with my baby brother or some other housework. She never wanted to play any more. It was ironic that my birthday had aged her into a little adult. Dielienuo was never rude to me. She just had other things to attend to. At first, I was convinced that she was ignoring me on purpose. I anxiously worried whether she had possibly heard me dismiss her so nonchalantly that night, and imagined that she had recognized the relief on my face because she had not behaved familiarly as she passed by me and my curious friends. I was so sure she was punishing me. But the weeks turned into months without any sign of outburst from her and finally, I had to accept that Dielienuo was no longer the little girl I still was. After some time, I stopped asking her to play with me.

One late evening, Father came home from work in an extremely disturbed mood. He sat on his usual chair beside the dining table and related his day's experience while Mother warmed his food. A twelve-year-old non-local boy had been brought to the hospital where Father worked. The boy was a domestic help and had been repeatedly subjected to physical abuse by a male relative of his employers. The employer himself had brought the boy to the hospital. He claimed to have no knowledge of what had been transpiring in his own house, and said that he had only just discovered the boy's latest injury and had therefore, immediately brought him to the hospital. Although agreeing to submit the boy under the care of a local NGO, the employer refused to press charges against the perpetrator as he was a close relative. Father said that the young boy had been staying with his employers for years now, and did not remember anything about his biological family or about his past. He only vaguely recalled that a woman known to his parents had brought him to his employer's house a long time ago. He had been working there ever since. Father remarked that the chances of this boy being repatriated to his family were bleak. I found myself asking what 'repatriated' meant. Father swiftly turned around at the sound of my voice, and realized that Dielienuo and I were intently listening to his story. He had been too engrossed to notice our little figures sitting beside the kitchen fireplace. Father scolded Mother for letting us stay up so late even though it was still early. Realizing that he was in a tense mood, Mother quickly shooed us away from the kitchen, telling us that this conversation was not appropriate for our 'little ears'. I followed Dielienuo outside our shadze where she always sat during the evening after finishing her chores. I wanted to discuss what we had heard, but Dielienuo remained very quiet the entire time. After a while, I got bored and left Dielienuo to her nightly stargazing.

Dielienuo's uncle arrived on a lazy Sunday afternoon to take her home for their village's Christmas celebration. He had rung Father from Dimapur district two days before, and informed him that he would be coming to collect her. Dielienuo had been with us for almost two years now, and was also attending the government primary school located near our house. Father took Dielienuo's uncle aside after he arrived, and the two men conversed while Mother helped Dielienuo pack her essentials. Mother included a blanket and some hand-me-down clothes for the rest of Dielienuo's family. She had come to us with nothing, but Mother ensured that she was going home with a lot more material possessions, if nothing else. After some time, Father and Dielienuo's uncle emerged and summoned Dielienuo. The latter looked her over, and merrily commented on her weight gain. Glancing at her conspicuous new luggage, he instructed Dielienuo to say thank you to Mother, and added that he would bring her back soon. Dielienuo obediently thanked Mother in a small voice but remained sullen otherwise. I couldn't make out whether she was excited to be going home at all. Father then answered that as much as we were helped by Dielienuo's services, she should come back only if she wanted to. Her uncle laughed at Father's remark, and asked how any sane person could not want to return to a house with facilities that were non-existent in their village. 'Running water, good food, school, new clothes, aru ki lage—what more can one ask for?' he asked rather crudely. A look of irritation crossed Father's face, but he ignored the man's presumptuous remark and determinedly looked at Dielienuo, encouraging her to speak up for herself. Father then impulsively asked Dielienuo to sit down. He glanced towards Dielienuo's uncle, as if wishing the man away and suggested that Mother prepare another cup of tea for him. Taking the hint, Mother made casual conversation with Dielienuo's uncle while leading him away towards the kitchen. I could hear my mother genially asking the man whether he would like some food packed for himself and Dielienuo to have on the journey. Father kneeled in front of a timid Dielienuo and gently asked whether she was happy, and if she wanted to come back to stay with us. Dielienuo looked stunned. It was apparent that she had never been asked for an opinion about her own life. Dielienuo fidgeted for some time, wringing her hands and looking down her sandalled feet. Finally, she looked up and whispered, 'I'll only be sent somewhere else.'

Dielienuo returned after a month's stay at her village. I found myself a little more indifferent towards her arrival than I would have expected. I was, of course, glad to have her back. But I could no longer greet her arrival like that of a cherished friend's. We were growing up, and with it, our relationship. Nevertheless, I still joined her underneath the stars on the first night of her return. We sat in silence for a while. I asked, without much mulling, 'Do you watch the stars when you're home as well?' She smiled, clearly pleased with my question. 'Yes, every night. And do you know? They're the same everywhere I go.' Dielienuo did not look at me when she replied. She had a faraway look, her tone reassuring no one but herself.

THE PAY RAISE

GANKHU SUMNYAN

Chani baido, as people at the office called her, was in her early fifties. She worked as a contractual staff—impermanent tenure and minimal pay—and her tasks were to open and close the office rooms, run errands, and prepare tea for the rest of the staff. Her husband's earnings as a labourer were inconsistent and couldn't be counted on to run the household. It was a blessing, she often told herself, that through twenty-five years of marriage, they have had no children. How would she have fed them?

So, she considered it extremely cruel of Raj sir to announce in front of everyone that morning, 'Baido, your salary is going to double from next month. That will make you happy, won't it?'

For a few seconds her world spun and she nearly dropped the tray of teacups. As if her happiness was his concern!

'Why make fun of us, sir?' she said and went inside the kitchen.

The laughter behind her felt like a shower of stones. She placed the cups down noisily, so as not to hear what they were talking about, and tried to concentrate on her actions. Nima, her good friend and colleague, came in to ask what they were laughing about. She was shy and consulted Chani on all matters.

'They have gone mad—saying our salary will be doubled from next month!'

'Isn't that a great thing?'

'It's a lie, you idiot! They are mocking us!'

But as she sipped her tea, Chani thought what a blessing it would be if the news were true. There was her nephew's wedding a few months away; she could also buy a heater for the winter, then new dishes, new furniture. The list of things she could buy went through her head, giving her a dim kind of pleasure. She gulped down the remaining tea and went in search of her friend whom she had scared away.

She found Nima standing in the corridor, staring at something far away. Which was but the same stale scene from the last twenty years: tall grasses growing unchecked on empty patches of land interspersed with areca nut and other trees; dull and low-built houses, sunk as if under the weight of the rain and heat the town received. Above the rusted tin roofs of the staff quarters, clouds lurked, threatening a downpour in the evening.

Chani pulled Nima down to the empty yard where they could sit and chat.

'Where did you hear the news? About the raise in our salary?'

'They were discussing something like that yesterday…day before yesterday. The government announced, it seems,' Nima answered in her slow manner.

'Those were the exact words? That's what you heard?'

Nima nodded her head and named Dina sir, Raj sir, and two others.

Chani couldn't help but smile. Nima smiled too, though she looked around immediately, embarrassed.

She would repair her kitchen, Nima said, make it larger. It was a solid idea, and Chani wondered whether she should do something similar—extend the kitchen, lay a concrete floor for it, also lay a concrete path to the toilet, and replace the old sheets on the roof, making her house sounder. It was from the house that her sense of well-being and completeness emanated. Of course, there would be—unavoidably—a small gathering where Jaggu and his friends would drink and chat in the front room, she hoped, without quarrelling, while she and her girlfriends would soak the warmth of the fire inside the new kitchen, rubbing and patting their feet on the new floor. They shouldn't quarrel; that was her only worry. She also would have to decide whom to invite and whom to leave out.

These were her thoughts when two regular staff of the office passed by, shaking their heads and exclaiming, 'No, no, no'—typical election gimmick. They fell silent on seeing the two women and turned the corner. Chani and Nima looked at each other, taken aback by how far they had gone in their dreams. Nima's eyes drooped, a veil of vagueness coming over them, but Chani got up and said she would confirm once again with someone who would properly know. Like Jakap, or Cashier babu. 'You go and wash the cups,' she told her friend.

Jakap—taciturn, unsmiling—was a far cousin, much younger than her. Chani claimed she had played a role in his recruitment at the office—she couldn't exactly say what—and still felt irritated he had left without meeting her when he came for the first time to submit the joining letter. She called him a younger brother whenever the topic came up, although they have never had a proper conversation. Sometimes, she would rebuke him for not respecting her, to which Jakap would lean back, nod his head, and give an inscrutable smile.

'I have seen you running naked—your face black with soot, your nose leaking. Don't give me airs,' she would snarl.

Respect, people had said, what was that about? They had grumbled that she was bullying him, when instead she should be proud of him. To these words, Chani would turn her head away. During situations where she had to ask something of him, she didn't know how to behave, whether to demand or request, and would falter in her voice and action.

She now sat in front of him, at the very edge of the chair. 'You have heard about the raise in our salary, haven't you?'

Jakap barely glanced up.

'Is it true?'

She was mesmerized by the pen moving across the white paper—such surety and confidence—and the same over the computer keyboard when he leaned to check something on the screen. Those long, clean fingers filled up blank forms, undecipherable columns, turned them into something cogent and acceptable, and marked them with a seal which he kept in a deep corner of his drawer. He had style and assurance, doubtless; no wonder a beautiful girl had married him. But in the wedding, Chani had been made to sit in a corner and was told to have her food as early as possible although she hadn't been there for even ten minutes.

He looked up finally. 'I don't much believe it, but it could also be true.'

'Can you speak more clearly?'

'It could happen, or it couldn't.' He smiled at her, without any affirmation. There he was, slipping away again, not meaning anything—cold and pitiless.

Doesn't matter, Chani thought, fuming, I will ask Cashier babu. Never had much hopes from Jakap anyway; she only went because he would feel bad if she asked anyone else first, she told herself.

But the idea of going to the babu, the office accountant, gave her no comfort. It was the reticence, the obliqueness, the banal look he gave to all things, and then the sudden temper and sullenness. She tried hard to think tenderly of him—since she was older—but all such feelings slipped off the man's persona—stout, hands behind his back, and the unsmiling face. He was someone to be placated, worshipped, or flattered with gifts. Nima told her he had taken an early leave for the day, and to meet him she would have to go to his home.

∽

During the lunch break, Chani timidly called at the door, 'Babu, it's me.'

She heard the television go silent, and then the door opened.

It was the maid. 'Bhaiyya is not keeping well.'

'Yes, I heard. I got these for him.' She brought forth the papayas she had plucked from her garden.

The maid turned back and Chani followed her into the house. She had to wait for some time before the babu came out, bleary-eyed. He looked at her once and shouted inside to bring glasses of water. Chani watched the water being gulped down in great glug-glugs. He then smacked his lips and burped.

She put the bag of papayas on the table. 'Babu, I got these. I heard you were not feeling well.'

The man looked at the papayas for some time before picking them up. 'Just a slight headache. Too much work.'

He put them back and looked outside at the veranda. How old would he be? Forty-three? Forty-four? The same age as her cousin back in the village, who had been his classmate during their college days. The light from outside streamed onto his face, highlighting the pockmarks and the stubble, making him appear vulnerable. Not many have seen him like this, Chani thought.

The maid brought tea for her and a glass of what seemed like whisky for the babu.

'Is that a tonic?' Chani smiled.

'This is the only cure sometimes,' the babu said, smiling back.

She let him take a few sips before asking about the raise.

'Some say it will happen but....' He paused. 'We don't know.'

Chani was disappointed. 'You have no idea too?'

He shrugged.

'Then who would know? I asked Jakap and now you.'

The babu snorted. 'Jakap won't know—he lives in his own world. Asked him to process a file a week back—still hasn't done it.'

'Do advise him sometimes,' he added. 'He is your brother, isn't he?'

'Yes, yes.' Chani leaned back on the sofa, contemplating.

'So, who do you think will really know?'

'About what?'

'The pay raise?'

'Maybe…Raj sir. He has the correct information in these matters; comes with being a sneaky character I suppose.'

The babu took a further sip before speaking. 'No one has any idea what they do—Raj sir and his friend Dina. They hide things and take away things without any trace, without any papers. I had told Jakap that such things shouldn't be allowed to happen. At least we ought to get the system right in our own place. But, like you said, and everyone says too, Jakap is strange. Still hasn't done those papers! If those papers were done….' He trailed off, realizing he had been rambling.

Chani didn't understand the details, but she got the part about needing to remind Jakap to finish what the babu had asked of him. This she would do even though Jakap didn't treat her well. And in truth, everyone took something from the office, directly or indirectly—fans, chairs, pens, cups, tea sets—and these were small things. Everyone did it, without doubt. And so, it really wasn't her duty to take sides. But if ever things got bad and she had to pick a side, she would be on the side of Jakap, or would want Jakap to be on her side. Why, she would at times ask herself, and would arrive at the memory of her wedding. It had been scantily attended and quickly got over—like a midday summer rain—leaving her bereft as vapours rose from the leaves and the earth in the empty yard, and all because she was marrying a non-tribal man. But in the morning, as her mother and other female relatives took leave of her, her mother had whispered, 'You are still us.'

'Are you going?' the babu asked as she stood up.

A tenderness had hit her upon the memory of her dead mother. Things always got mixed up once that happened, so she said to him in a choked voice, 'Take care of yourself, Babu.'

Touched, the babu came to the door, his face tender. 'Don't …don't worry, Baido. I will take care of everything. Jakap is my brother too.'

And as she reached the gate, he shouted, 'Tell that Raj I sent you… if he doesn't help, I will deal with him.'

In the past, times like these when the old questions about her life, her decisions, the doubts cast by her own people reared up, she would point to the grand and beautiful things of her life. But through the years, these things changed their nature from being beautiful or ugly into things that just existed. Thus, she would regain her composure. And once she was inside her house, remnants of the putrid thoughts further lost their edge, seeping into the smooth floor she had trodden upon for so many years. This was her reality—the high walls, the sturdy ceiling, the intimate rooms, the broad wooden windows. She liked it; loved it, in fact.

The rest of her noontime routine was performed with pleasure—cooking rice, heating vegetables, and drinking black tea afterwards on the kitchen steps overlooking the backyard.

~

The post-lunch hours at the office were casual, non-threatening. Raj sir hadn't turned up but she was kept busy nonetheless, shifting files from one room to the other, sweeping and dusting, making one more round of tea and then washing the cups. It was quite late when everyone finally left, and she locked up the rooms of the offices with Nima beside her.

The evening was muggy and the sky clouded as she started towards Raj sir's house. She had waited for Jaggu to come home, but it seemed like he would be late. There was a power cut; she had to navigate the narrow road using her phone's torch. She thought of turning back a couple of times.

When she knocked at the door she forgot to say her name. The voice from inside sounded irritated, and it made her shout out her name—it's only me, Raj sir. She heard a chair being pushed back, then footsteps. When the door opened, there was the tall frame of Raj sir occupying the doorway, but without the feeling of familiarity of the office. He peered down at her and then suddenly smiled, inviting her to come in.

Inside the drawing room, she could see pens and papers strewn about on the table. She requested that the main door be kept open, but the low evening light made no impact upon the darkness of the room. Raj sir disappeared into another room, and came out with a glass of water. He then picked up the files, pens, and papers, and disappeared again. When he finally sat down opposite to her, he still fidgeted, adjusting his glasses now and then to look at her. It was about the pay raise, Chani said.

'I have heard something like that,' he said, leaning forward. 'But even I am not sure.'

With a sudden movement, he thwacked his left arm with the right, and cursed the mosquitoes.

'Should I close the door?' he asked, getting up.

'Oh no, sir,' she stuttered. 'I need to see my husband walk back. The house keys are with me. Who can I confirm this with, then?'

Raj sir sat down.

'Let me check on the phone; I think some notice was given to that effect.'

It felt inordinately long, Raj sir scrolling through his phone, the light of which caught in his glasses, so she couldn't be sure whether he looked at her furtively at times or not.

'If you have not found it, I will leave, sir,' she said, getting up.

But he put out a hand and turning back, shouted towards the neighbouring house, 'Sovi sir, please come in for a while. Chani baido is here.'

A door opened, and a man appeared on the doorway of the neighbouring house wearing only a vest and lungi. 'Who?'

'Baido, our Chani baido. She is….' Raj sir trailed away and told him to just come.

The rotund form of a man—so quick, so urgent—came to Raj sir's door, peering down towards her. He sat down next to her and looked at her once again. Chani could not recognize the man in the dark, and thought that she had never seen him in the small town where most residents knew each other.

'Our Baido wants to know whether the contingency staff will get their pay raise.' Raj sir smiled into the phone.

'Oh definitely, definitely you will, Baido. Why not? It's the government order. Show her the notice, sir, show her,' he demanded.

Then turning back to her: 'Arrey! Your salary will be doubled, the government has announced. You will have to give me a treat, at least for the news.'

Raj sir looked up from the phone, grinning from ear to ear. 'I should get the treat first. I told it to her first, didn't I?'

'I will show you the notice, Baido, just wait.'

The man began to demand the phone from Raj sir who couldn't stop laughing. 'Very cunning, sir, very cunning.'

Just then there was a noise from the kitchen. Raj sir jumped up and rushed into the darkness inside, followed by his neighbour. 'It's the damn cat again.'

Chani rushed out from the house. She opened the gate and turned to see the two figures at the door—one tall, one short—calling to her to come back, at least have tea. But she stumbled away, looking back a few times, afraid that she was being followed.

Reaching her house, she pushed the door open, and rushed into the small bedroom. She had huddled down on the floor when someone opened the door—she had forgotten to lock it. A tall figure came into the room and looked down at her. Her throat went dry.

'Why were you running and why are you sitting in the dark?' Jaggu asked, switching on the lights.

Relief washed over her like summer rain.

Then taking in the brightness, the familiar objects of her house, and that hard, warm man, whom she had loved and quarrelled with for twenty-five years, she felt her eyes smarting. 'We are getting a pay raise—can you believe it?'

THE AFTERMATH

MAINU TERONPI

She shuddered. She pressed her ears to the bolted old wooden door and listened closely. There was someone out there; she could hear heavy breathing. She was unsure whether she should open the door or just stand there doing nothing. She caressed her unborn child, and her hands slowly reached out for the door latch. As she opened the door, she could feel the misty air of the night on her face and the wind in her hair. The darkness stared back at her face. Not a single soul to be seen.

'Who could have knocked on the door in the wee hours?' thought Kabon.

She bolted the door, clumsily walked to her bed and reached for the beaten steel jug, which had long lost its lustre, to quench her thirst. Without much thought she placed the pillow more to the right of the bed, leaving room for her husband whom she awaited. Caressing her belly, she kept thinking, 'Was I dreaming or was there really a knock on the door?'

It's not the paranormal or the lost spirits that she feared but the night patrol. She feared the patrol the most. It is said that the people of the village have a way with the lost spirits; they are able to pacify them. According to their beliefs, the spirits are never deemed malevolent or destructive. Rather, they have coexisted with humans for ages without causing any harm. It was the Western world that brought the concept of malevolent and evil spirits into their world. Well, Kabon was a strong woman. Born and raised in the village amidst nature, she was gifted with the ability to endure any kind of pain. But this time, the pain of not seeing her husband for more than a week gnawed at her. The roaring rivers of the hills ran through her veins. She could endure any pain. The unkempt wilderness of the blue hills resided in her heart. She was resilient. She remembered how, with no proper medical facilities in the village, she almost died while giving birth to her fourth child. She had endured with the passage of time. But this time, it was different.

She couldn't sleep. Sleep refused to comfort her in her pain even temporarily, the pain of separation from her husband. She tossed and turned on her bed for hours. She slowly picked herself up and squatted on the floor to light the lantern. Kabon was in her last trimester, eight months to be precise. Longbi, her husband, had never deserted her, no matter how demanding the situation was. He always came back to her. Though he had to attend festivals such as Chojun or Seh Karkli in nearby villages from time to time, as he was the kurusar—village priest—he was always right on time. He might be tipsy on some unfortunate nights but his wobbly legs would help him crawl back home.

He would often brag in front of Kabon. 'Sarpi, old woman. I might be drunk, I might be out making merry, I might be dying, but it's home that I will return to.' Saying this, Longbi would give his sweetest smile to Kabon, showing his betel nut-stained reddish-black teeth. This was their way of expressing love. People of their community believed in actions rather than merely talking about love. Maybe that's why they seldom expressed their love for one another in words. One could see how madly they were in love—Longbi and Kabon were made for each other.

It was in the month of July that Kabon saw Longbi for the first time. It was during the same month that the heavens unleashed torrential rains and the winds howled with a wild fury. The fields, golden with ripened maize, swayed under the tempest's embrace. Young girls with hak, long cylindrical baskets balanced on their heads, made their way to the jhum to harvest the bountiful corn. Among them was Kabon, draped in her mother's pini and wrapped in a piba adorned with intricate motifs and cowrie shells that danced with every step. She was a vision of radiance, her skin shimmering like the soft, golden light of dawn. She was an epitome of beauty, yet it wasn't her looks that captivated Longbi. It was her remarkable display of strength in the jhum fields that made Longbi weak in the knees. Longbi knew that in the rugged hills survival depended on both mental and physical strength, as well as wisdom. And Kabon fit perfectly in the picture, a partner for life. From the beginning, they knew they belonged to each other.

In the hills, the people are simple. They don't go for dates or spend their time wooing each other. They choose their partner. Karbi men would often help their chosen partner and her family in fetching water from the stream, fetching firewood from the forest, and would even stay in the woman's house doing all kinds of household chores until they proved themselves worthy of being her husband. This ritual is called piso kemen. Once they had won the heart of the woman, they would get approval from the parents and the elders of the village.

Longbi, like a true Karbi man, helped Kabon in all possible ways. They would often be seen working together in the field, helping each other with the harvesting of the corn and carefully putting it in the hak. Besides working in the jhum, Longbi was also practising the chants and hymns taught by his grandfather, who was a celebrated kurusar in the vicinity. His grandfather would also travel to places to perform seh karkli and chojun. He would be away from home for days, sometimes for weeks. His grandmother would often be seen taking care of the house and the children by herself during his absence. Kabon knew that she, too, would have to swallow the bitter pill of loneliness shoved down her throat in choosing Longbi as her life partner. Longbi would also one day become a kurusar, which would mean he would no longer be able to help her with the household chores or in the jhum like he always did. But Kabon had already given her heart to him and had accepted him as her husband.

∽

The room that was enveloped in darkness, now saw light coming from the lantern. The dim light accentuated the features of the room. It was a quaint little house. It had a thatched roof with neat mud walls. The house was spacious enough to accommodate four more innocent souls sleeping peacefully in the same room next to their mother. The youngest one, around two years old, was sucking her thumb and waking up from time to time. Kabon, like a good mother, patted her back, pacifying her as she slept. The light from the lantern might have disturbed her sleep. She softly caressed the toddler's little back and lulled her to sleep. But Kabon couldn't find any peace herself because she had no idea about the whereabouts of her husband. Men from her village and from neighbouring villages had been shoved inside a police van like cattle the previous week.

'Have they also taken Longbi?' was the thought that had troubled her all this while.

On her way to the jhum, she overheard some women talking about how these patrol vans were forcefully taking men from villages without any rhyme or reason. And those who confronted them were beaten black and blue. These innocent men knew nothing. They were too petty, too sheepish for any kind of violence. They were too lost in their jhum, in their cattle, in Mother Nature.

Well! It all started on that ill-fated evening. Two innocent young souls were beaten to death. They were mistaken for child traffickers, and their big black vehicle only confirmed the rumours that had been spreading. The youth of this village and other nearby ones became scared of the two strange-looking men. The village was beyond the reach of the law. The village had been neglected by the men in power and many other officers. With no help and cooperation from the law and police for ages, the youth turned to vigilantism and took law into their own hands. Some elders of the village tried to interfere and save the boys but they failed. It was the men of the hills who had to face the consequences. The bond between different communities that had been so painstakingly built with years of trust, faith, and goodwill shattered in seconds.

Kabon remembered Geeta baideo from the weekly market—where she went from time to time to sell her home-grown produce like herbs, tubers, and wild berries. Her sweet nature could melt anyone's heart! How good that woman was to her! She would look after her kids every time she was away to fetch water from the nearby hotel. How she would happily feed her little daughter everything from her shop! And would never ask for a single penny in return. Kabon highly respected her. She was like a sister to her. She always had it in her mind that one day, she would also run a variety store like Geeta baideo did.

But her attitude changed all of a sudden. She refused to recognize her now. Their eyes hardly met, and they barely exchanged any words. The babbling of her little daughter did not warm Geeta baideo's heart any more. The silence between them was choking. It broke her heart into pieces. Kabon did not know of a way back to Geeta baideo's heart. She and her community had been ostracized. Their only mistake was that they belonged to a community who were believed to be a part of the mob.

'Why blame Longbi, my little daughter, or me? What have we done?' were the thoughts that were screaming inside her head in the silence of the night. She was already concerned about Longbi who had been missing for weeks now. Even the homegrown tubers and herbs she had foraged from nearby foothills were rotting in the corner of the kitchen. She could not go to the market, which was some kilometres away from their village, to sell them. She felt an uneasiness in the air, as if all eyes were on her, as if she and her family were to be held accountable for all that happened. And with Geeta baideo turning into a stranger, she felt even more miserable! She had no one to turn to. She hoped against hope that the situation would get better! She prayed to the Almighty that the sins that this virgin land had witnessed be washed away. Praying that the two souls find eternal peace and the pristine land be saved from being cursed. She sobbed silently. Her thoughts came to an abrupt end when she heard the screeching of brakes outside.

Kabon heard a faint sound of an engine screeching somewhere in the paddy fields. A place that had never seen any modernization, now had a road where patrol vehicles sped past frequently. This village, which was once forgotten by the people who lived outside, had witnessed a lot of changes. The commotion woke the baby up. This time, she was crying her lungs out. Kabon held her in her arms. She caressed her soft tiny back, lulling her to sleep. Kabon was not just pacifying her little baby but was trying to find solace in her tiny arms. They reminded her of her Longbi. Helpless and unable to find her husband, she found comfort in singing the lullaby, 'Tu-wa-eh', to her little children. The midnight sky was slowly paving way for the sun to shine on an uncertain tomorrow. The commotion grew louder; it could be heard distinctly. Some more men were picked up from their sleep and shoved into the van. Some more Longbis would be separated from their beloved Kabons. Many more babies would never see their fathers. The commotion grew louder and louder creating fear in the minds of the children who were awakened from their sleep. But Kabon hugged them while singing 'Tu-wa-eh' even louder, as if it would erase all their pain.

THE MADNESS OF TREE GHOSTS

SHALIM M HUSSAIN

This is how it happened. It was the season of dryness and the snakes were ready to hibernate. Late in the evening, before entering the earth, they sat still where they were and shed their skins. Then they let out their last breath and went to sleep. The snakes' breath is a terrible thing. There was this man in the village whose poor wife had breathed it. First, she caught a fever. Then her skin went dry like a snake's. That was when the villagers understood what was happening. They called a meeting and, because the woman was too ill to attend, they called her husband. Your wife has the disease, they said. She must live outside the village, they said. Let's hope that you and your son are not infected, but as long as you don't show any signs of illness, you can remain here with us. We will all help you build your wife a house on the edge of the forest. The husband agreed. He was a reasonable man and didn't want the village to suffer his misfortune. But let me and my son go live with her, he said. We will not return until the illness has taken my woman. If the disease gets to us, we will stay outside the village until it takes us too.

So, man, woman, and son left the village and chose a spot on the forest's edge, where a long row of betel nut trees marked the end of the village and the beginning of the forest. They carried twenty sacks of rice and ten bags of pulses with them—enough to see a small family through six months and more. They built their hut next to an old pond filled with fish and hyacinth, and started living there. As expected, the woman's condition got worse. First water-filled boils grew on her body. Then water turned into pus, the boils burst, and she was in terrible pain. Man and son bathed her with fresh ash and water from the pond, but it was of no use. Every day one set of boils burst only to be replaced with another set on a different part of her body. Clothes began to stick to the open wounds.

What could the two men do? They removed her clothes, washed her again, then wiped a reed mat with mustard oil and laid her naked on it. The woman winced. Mustard oil irritated the wounds, and the reed mat dug into her raw skin. The man told his son that the only way to relieve his mother of her pain was to roll her in tender banana leaves. It's evening and it will soon get dark, said the man. Take care of your mother while I go to the forest and get banana leaves. The son was young and innocent, and always did what his parents asked. So, the man took his dao and left, and the son fanned his mother with a tal leaf to keep the flies away.

Then the sun set, and the father didn't return. The son tied a mosquito net around his mother's bed and whispered in her ear, Mother, please remain asleep. Father has not come home. I should go find him. On the way, he met an old woman who was returning from the ration shop with her monthly allotment of kerosene and salt. Now he was a good boy, so he said to the old woman, Father is in the forest cutting banana leaves, and I must find him before it gets too dark. But I can help you carry your rations home first. The old woman's heart melted. Oh, that's all right, my lovely boy, she said. I have lived long enough to know that no one can carry your burden every time. But, since you have offered, I will sit with your mother until you return. Then you can carry my bags home. The boy thanked her because he had good manners, and left.

In this forest of ours, as in forests everywhere, there were tree ghosts—lovable little invisible things who love human food. Tree ghosts don't travel much. They pick one tree and live on it for all eternity. When travellers come their way, they throw mud patties to scare them and steal their food. This is why when a new bride or a new mother is returning from her parents' with pots of puffed rice and date palm jaggery and it gets dark on the way, she hangs a piece of dried cow dung around the pot's neck. Tree ghosts hate dung, chillies, and iron. I call them ghosts, but in form, they are closer to humans, beings of fire and steam, but without a body. In behaviour they are like animals, only seeking food and self-preservation.

Now, one of our tree ghosts had gone mad. His madness made him more jinn and more animal. Deep in his formless being, steam and fire condensed into a tiny seed. This seed gained weight, a tiny minuscule weight, but enough for him to feel it. Think of it as a loose eyelash in the corner of your eye—light, but very much there. And all of a sudden, for the first time in his existence, the ghost understood the feeling of being held down. With madness came hunger of a different sort—not for sweets or rice but for human flesh. The seed in his body now became a magnet and it pulled the ghost towards the nearest human. And the nearest human just happened to be a man with a dao, cutting banana leaves in the forest.

The mad ghost saw the father from a distance, and his whole being shivered. For a ghost, madness is the path from ethereality to complete existence. The seed in his belly which was condensing the remaining fire and steam into a solid form, combined with an unbearable hunger, did weird things to our ghost. He was still mostly a spirit, and like all spirits he could fit himself into any space, and that body of his, which was not fully formed, was equally liquid. He could mould it into any form.

So, our ghost dragged his new body towards the man and opened his mouth wide to swallow him. This is when he saw, hidden under the mass of banana leaves on the man's shoulder, the large iron dao. That's it. He couldn't touch the man any more. He was a clever ghost though, and he knew that if there was one man in the forest, there must be more where he came from. So, he hid behind a gamhar tree and waited for the man to pass. While he waited, he observed him closely and began to acquire the man's features—his wide shoulders, chest hair spread out like a peacock's wings, and the slight stoop of his shoulders. He grew hands and feet, too, but because he had never been on the ground, his feet were rather heavy. The father went into the forest for more banana leaves, completely oblivious of the ghost, and the ghost dragged his feet in the opposite direction, towards the village in search of humans.

Suddenly he heard rustling in the leaves and a boy came rushing towards him. Father, the boy said, I have been looking for you. Let's go home. We can pluck leaves in the morning. The ghost stood still, burning with hunger. This was his moment. Open your mouth and eat this child, his head told him, but something was holding him back. That something was his new form. Old people say that the body is everything—in flesh is memory, in flesh is soul. Once a soul wears a body, even if it's a ghost wearing a pretend-body, the body infects the soul. This had happened with other ghosts many times over and this happened with our ghost too. What should have happened—his mouth on the boy's back, the blades on his inner cheek digging through the boy's skin, tearing muscles and embedding in the ribs—flashed through his newly forming mind. What did happen instead was that the ghost felt a fleeting sense of tenderness for the boy, desperation, and an intense desire to shoo him away. A moment passed and the feeling, too, passed.

The boy turned around and began walking towards the village. The ghost followed, dragging his heavy feet. The boy's mind filled with doubt. Why was his father not talking? Where were the banana leaves? Why did his father suddenly smell of fish and slime? He turned around to check, but the ghost had lifted his arms over his head, his mouth wide open and ready to strike. The boy screamed and ran. The ghost again felt an unfamiliar feeling of love, sadness at what was about to happen, and some of the boy's fear. He paused for a minute, and this allowed the boy to run towards the forest opening. Fuelled by fear, the boy tore through the dense forest undergrowth with the ghost close behind.

Now the boy could see the last big trees, now he could see the row of betel nuts, now he could see the pond near their hut. A few more yards and he would be in the village where there were fire and iron. The ghost opened his mouth again, spiral blades in his mouth gleaming in the moonlight, and threw himself at the boy. The boy, unable to decide what to do, jumped on the first betel nut tree and started climbing. The ghost wrapped his body around the tree and tried to climb but his feet were heavy and his body was slimy and he slid down. He tried again and, again he failed. Desperate, he bit into the bark of the betel nut tree. The blades in his mouth were sharp and created a deep gash. He was happy. Chew the bark to shreds and the boy will fall, his newly forming mind told him. The boy climbed to the top of the tree, and now there was nowhere for him to go. So, he joined his hands and prayed as hard and as loudly as he could. My God, my keeper, my protector, help me, he shouted. His voice was loud and clear, and even his father, deep in the forest, heard him and started running towards the clearing. The old woman heard him too. She left the sick woman's side and ran to the forest's edge to see what was happening.

Because he was a good boy and his heart was clean, God sent the wind to help him. The wind was strong and the wind was clever. It brought the tops of the betel nut trees together and created a pathway of leaves in the sky. This pathway stretched from the forest's edge to the hut where the boy's mother was sleeping. The ghost saw what was happening and dropped his disguise. Now he looked nothing like the boy's father. With the shedding of his human form, all sadness and sympathy for the boy's fate disappeared. With one blow of his claws, he tore the betel nut tree from its roots. The wind saw the strike coming and whispered in the boy's ear—jump! The boy closed his eyes, jumped and landed on top of the next tree. The ghost also moved to the next tree and snapped it in half. Meanwhile, the wind blew steadily and continued lining the treetops side by side. The boy was so clever that he jumped from one tree to the next quickly, as if he was running on a straight path in the sky.

Soon the betel nut trees started getting less dense; the boy was nearing the village. The ghost opened his eyes wide and saw the old woman standing all alone at the edge of the forest. He left the boy and changed tracks, moving towards the woman because she looked weak. He crouched, gathering all his powers and pounced on the old woman with his jaws wide open. The woman took one step back and drew something from the folds of her sari. Even as the ghost fell on her, she flung a handful of white powder in the air and said, I curse you.

The powerful ghost, driven to violence, felt the powder hit his skin and was struck by an agony far stronger than hunger. He fell on the ground, twisting and turning, because his skin had cracked and his soul was pouring out. He reached out for the old woman's feet, pleading, Mother, please stop. Instead, the woman held another handful of powder over his head and whispered, 'I curse you with salt. I curse you and all your future generations to crawl on the ground. The weight of your feet will now be all over your body, and every step you and your children take will be taken in pain. You will thirst for human blood and only get it once in your life and the salt will kill you.'

The ghost shrivelled into a worm the size of the woman's little finger. His skin was burnt black with salt, and his mouth, filled with razor blades, became so tiny that although it could attach itself to a body, it would never be able to eat flesh. The ghost became the world's first leech. The boy climbed down the betel nut tree and thanked the old woman. The father came running from the forest with his mighty dao, but there was nothing for him to do. The old woman lived many years and created many beings: some with love, some with regret.

As is the nature of things, the pox eventually took the boy's mother. They buried her where the hut was and burnt the hut. Neither father nor son was infected, so thirty days after the mother's death they rubbed their body with ash and bathed in the pond. The leech followed them into the pond and lived there. His new body took over his soul, and in time he forgot that he was once air, fire, and steam.

HOME

RAMZAUVA CHHAKCHHUAK

During the first COVID-19 lockdown in March and April 2020, Aldrin Lyngdoh, a migrant worker from Shillong employed at a hotel in Agra, tragically died by suicide. According to multiple media reports, Aldrin took this drastic action after his employers refused to provide him with support during this critical time. Before his death, he posted a heart-wrenching status on Facebook addressed to the then Delhi ADGP, Robin Hibu, where he recounted his experiences of harassment and pleaded for help. Many workers and labourers, like Aldrin, from unorganized sectors were similarly left to fend for themselves, with lakhs resorting to walking back home without any assistance from the authorities. 'Home' *is a story that reimagines Aldrin's journey as one of survival.*

Andrew Syngkon trudged on the bituminous road. The searing temperature bore down on him and radiated back from below. He wiped sweat from his face and neck with his shirt sleeves. The transparent polythene bag that hung from his wrist rustled as it brushed against his side. He had been walking for hours, and every step felt like pinpricks all over his body.

While he was working at the eatery, he heard people talk about a disease that was spreading fast. He wasn't worried, not until he was suddenly forced to leave. His boss hadn't paid him or the other workers—a cook and a waiter—for months. The owner cited losses due to a financial dispute with his brother. He had promised to pay them the following month, but when payday arrived, he repeated the same excuse.

Located outside Kolar, the eatery served filter coffee, idlis, and dosas. Every night, after the last customer left, they put the standing steel tables in a corner, poured buckets of water and scrubbed every inch and crevice of the shop. But no matter the effort, the place looked the same—smudges of mud and muck sticking to the white tiles of the floor and the walls.

Then, they cut the vegetables to make the sambar and rice batter for the morning snacks. This way, they could sleep an extra hour. Satisfied that everything was ready for the next day, they spread out their thin thatch mats and lay down, falling asleep almost immediately. They started at 6 a.m. and got no days off.

Another month without pay riled up the workers. Talks escalated into a full-scale physical altercation with the workers, barring Andrew, turning everything in the eatery upside down. Their owner called a group of local goons who thrashed the workers and chased them away. And with that, they bid their money goodbye. Andrew was allowed to stay on, a reward for his non-participation. He didn't get his money, but he knew he could not afford to anger his boss. His home was thousands of miles away in Shillong, a place no one had heard of around these parts. He would be on the streets if not for this place and, unlike his former co-workers, he didn't know anyone he could bank on. A contact from his hometown had worked in Bengaluru and gotten him the job. But they had only spoken over the phone. When he had first arrived at the Majestic railway station after an idle three-day journey, he had hoped to meet his benefactor. But the other person didn't seem too keen, and Andrew didn't press him. So, he left it at that. He had walked aimlessly around the markets near the station and did not stay too long in the city. He took a bus to Kolar to his employers as instructed.

Now, at the eatery, Andrew had to do the work of three people. He hoped the effort would get him his dues. Once he got his money, he would leave and head to Bengaluru.

The number of people coming to the eatery dwindled. Then, one morning, as Andrew was preparing for the day, his boss ordered him to pack his things and leave. He didn't mention a word about his payment. For a second, Andrew went quiet, contemplating his next course of action. As his boss waited for him to react, Andrew jumped forward, grabbed his collar, and threw him to the ground.

Andrew kept repeating, 'Mera paisa do! Paisa do!' in his broken Hindi as he punched his boss.

Shrieks of pain, screams, and cusses, clangs of the steel table falling, brought people from the neighbourhood into the eatery. The two were on the floor, Andrew over his boss, pulling his hair. A few men plucked Andrew away and threw him outside. Dazed and bleeding, his boss stayed on the floor for a while before gathering himself and getting up. He went around the eatery and returned with a log of wood, charging towards Andrew, who was down.

Andrew got up and tried to run away but was caught by the same ruffians who had beaten up his co-workers. Someone had phoned them. They descended on him, pummelling him mercilessly along with the other men from the locality. Before losing consciousness, he thought about his mother.

Andrew woke up inside a bush next to a pile of rotting garbage. His face hurt. He winced as he tried to sit, adjusting his legs and torso. He crawled out of the bush, towards the road, getting up slowly, and buttoning what remained of his shirt. After dusting himself off, he limped towards the eatery, not caring about the consequences. It wasn't too far off from where he was thrown, but it took him a while. He felt his pocket for his phone. He took it out and examined it for any damage. There was none. Two bars of battery remained, enough to last him for days. He felt his pockets again for his wallet, but it wasn't there. It had stamp-sized photographs of him and his mother, and an ATM card.

Already afternoon, the streets were sparse, and most shops, including the eatery, were shut. Andrew scanned the drain in front of the eatery for his wallet and looked in and around a wall on the side of the road. He searched further and reached another shop's front, one of the few that was open. Here, he bought bidis or cheap cigarettes and paan to have as kwai during his breaks.

Andrew looked inside and saw the familiar face of the shopkeeper's wife. He often chatted with her and her husband. He knew he looked bedraggled but still gave her a smile and explained what he was doing. She nodded. Some minutes passed. He was ready to give up and go when he noticed the woman holding out a polythene bag towards him. Andrew stared at the transparent bag and its contents: two small bottles of water, another with juice, some biscuit packets, and a hundred-rupee note. Overwhelmed, he got teary-eyed, but a sharp pain on his face prevented him from crying. He took the bag and joined his palms near the centre of his face as a thank you. The woman waved her hand as if saying, 'It's nothing', smiled, and disappeared back inside her shop.

Andrew considered breaking into the eatery to retrieve his possessions, but there was no way in through the metal-grilled windows. He decided it was best to forget about it and went to a nearby lake, spending the rest of the day thinking about what to do next.

It was time to head to Bengaluru.

While hesitating at first, he called his contact in the city, who was sympathetic and promised to make arrangements. Andrew thought about starting immediately, but he was too bruised and battered, putting off the journey until the next day. He drank stingily from the bottle and opened a biscuit packet. Then he lay on a bench under a tree and drifted to sleep, waking up just before dusk. His body still ached, but he felt better. He limped towards the bus station.

There, he found people lined up in every corner, bag and baggage, but no one seemed to be going anywhere. The ticket counters and offices were shut. He waited for an hour. A group of cops arrived and commanded everyone to vacate the place immediately. Tempers flared. The men in uniform tried to calm people down initially but some from the crowd got too close and raised their voices. The cops then caned the ones in the front while others began to run away. Andrew tried to make sense of the situation and realized it was futile to wait any longer. No one was coming to help them. He walked out of the bus station, and more people followed behind.

As he walked towards the highway, the enormity of what lay ahead hit him. The roads, buildings, and houses—everything looked empty. A group of people he recognized from the bus station were catching up. They carried humongous rucksacks on their backs and aluminium boxes on their heads. Andrew wondered how they'd get to the city carrying all that weight, but they soon passed him by and went ahead. One turned and stared without saying a word and then looked ahead, continuing on his way.

The thought of sleeping on his thin mat made him dizzy with delight and delirium. A cheap cigarette with a tiny plastic cup of tea, no matter how burnt and sugary, would be great right now. He imagined being back home and walking below the tall pine trees with the smell of wax everywhere in the woods. But all he could do was rest under a rock's shade near the road. Andrew didn't know what was in store for him in the city. His contact hadn't called him yet.

He came near a stretch with restaurants made of glass, concrete, and polished wood. Some had lush lawns, while a few had palm trees and creepers. No one was inside. In the background, rocky hillocks and sparse vegetation stretched everywhere. The afternoon sun was blazing when he reached a water reservoir. Houses dotted the outline, and beyond them, the rocky topography continued. A path that led down to the water had shrunk. He washed himself and sat down. Unable to resist, he took a large gulp from his bottle and put it back in the plastic bag. He stayed at the spot for a while. A memory of swimming in pristine rivers with his friends back in his village came to him, and he soon dozed off in the mud.

Awoken by the sound of splashing water, he rubbed his eyes and saw two kids playing in the water nearby. The sun was getting weaker. He climbed back up towards the road and continued his journey. Written next to 'Bengaluru' on the green signboards that hung above the road was the distance: 55 kilometres. It was a miracle he had made it this far, and he felt proud and encouraged to continue.

His phone rang as he walked, and he quickly took it out of his pocket, almost dropping it, and answered within the first two rings. His contact told him about trains being arranged from the city to take many like him back to their homes. He was to head to the nearest train station once he reached Bengaluru. It was a short call, but he was glad someone was looking out for him.

He saw some figures up ahead in the darkness. In front of a shop with its shutters pulled down, he decided to retire for the night. He felt weary at the thought of eating the biscuits again, but his stomach growled and he ate a few.

There were days at the eatery when he was severely homesick. Eating the same sour-tasting dal that he served customers made him more miserable. But at the moment, some sambar on white rice would mean the world. He lay down on the shop's steps and was out within moments.

The nip in the air woke him up early the next morning. He sat up and tried to enjoy the cool temperature before the day started to swelter. It was still dark with hues of orange in the distant sky. He sipped juice from the bottle and decided to begin early. His muscles stiffened and resisted the movement, but after walking a few steps, he felt better and went on.

A white van with a beacon zoomed past him. It had been a while since he saw a vehicle. Inside a lane next to a house on the road was a mobile cart with cycle wheels. Near it, an old woman poured water from an old plastic bottle into an aluminium dish kept atop a gas burner. She flinched upon seeing Andrew appear from behind. His swollen face and untidy clothes gave him the appearance of a beggar, a drunk. Andrew took the hundred rupees note from his bag and said,

'Chai!' She nodded and started the flame with a matchstick. Andrew cupped the tiny plastic cup and took slow sips. He didn't mind its burnt taste and handed her the folded money when he finished. She promptly returned the change. He asked whether he could fill some water from the jerrycans kept underneath the cart. She agreed. Andrew thanked her and moved on.

He reached the outskirts of a settlement and an hour later, he was walking across it. Everything was shut, but some people walked along the road. A vegetable vendor sold his supplies from a mobile cart. The mercury was rising again, and he needed a place to rest. At a distance, he saw an old, abandoned building nestled between some trees. It was cooler inside. Empty liquor bottles and old, worn-out, mouldy mattresses were on the cement floor. He sat near the door with his back against the wall.

At his current pace, it would take him a day or two more to reach the city. Another ambulance and then a truck passed. He felt hopeful about hitching a ride. He tried flagging a vehicle as he walked further. Some hours later, he spotted another van, but its driver asked him a ludicrous sum for the ride to the city. Andrew showed him all the money he had and begged for a ride. But the driver drove away.

It was a while till he saw another vehicle. He took out his money, clutched it, and kept walking. He saw a truck driving towards him and stopped in his tracks. When it got nearer, he waved his arms frantically. It worked. The vehicle stopped. Its driver looked out the window, and Andrew shouted, 'Bangalore! Bangalore!' as he showed him the change in his hand. The driver stared at him without speaking and went back inside to consult with his assistant. They decided to let him in and told him to take the back seat.

They didn't seem interested in the fare or conversing with him or even among themselves. Their attention was on the road. Andrew's eyes grew heavy. The sound of the vehicle's engine became distant until he heard nothing. Andrew slumped in his seat. He was woken in less than an hour.

The driver told him they were heading in another direction and asked him to get down. Andrew rubbed his eyes and took out the money to give the driver. The driver shook his head and gestured for him to keep it back. Andrew didn't know what to do or say. This time, his eyes welled up and he began sobbing, wiping away the tears with his palms and arm. The driver and his assistant patted him on his back and mumbled something to comfort him. After a few minutes, he thanked them and asked about any nearby railway station.

'KR Pura station,' said the driver, pointing to the other side. Andrew went under the flyover and walked to the station. When he arrived, throngs of people were waiting for their train home.

SACRED POOL

RISHAV KUMAR THAKUR

I am inside the sanctum sanctorum under the conical dome of the Ugratara temple. I sit cross-legged in front of the eponymous deity. I do not see her directly. I only perceive a figure under layers of red cloth, various flowers, vermilion, and silver jewellery with a greenish tint. At her feet is a small round pool of murky water. The still air is heady with the smell of burnt wood, ghee, and dhuna—the fragrant resin from sal trees.

A tingle runs up my right thigh. It seems that I have been sitting in this position for some time. I get up slowly but my right leg almost gives way under me. Gingerly, I start walking towards the pool.

Countless earthen lamps are strewn in patterns with no particular order around the pool. Mustard oil feeds the lamps, lending the flame a pungent yet comforting smell, and collects in spills here and there.

Thickets of incense sticks on brass holders or impaling small, yellow, prostrate bananas remind me of those who came before me. The skin between my big toe and little toe tingles. Many years ago, when I didn't really know what being burnt felt like, I had stepped on an incense stick and had my first blister right there.

The stone floor seems to have absorbed the oil and ash over the centuries. Its texture is now sticky velvet as I make my way carefully, trying not to slip and fall headlong into the pool.

I increase my pace, disturbing the white ribbons of fragrant smoke. The upright multitude of flames continues to flicker.

The water in the pool has almost reached the floor level. In the dim light, it seems as if stone extends into the pool of water, or the pool has mixed with stone. I am not fooled, almost.

I stop where my toes reach the very edge of solid ground and gaze downwards into the murky waters.

I sit down there with my knees folded up to touch my chin and continue gazing intently at the pool.

The water is so still.

I extend my toes tentatively and touch the surface. A pang of coolness upon contact. A ripple escapes from that point, echoing my transgression. The circles hit the stone shores and become invisible, dying and giving birth to fainter reverberations. I wonder if there is a way to capture the music produced when water ends and stones begin.

I look in the direction of the Goddess. I adjust my angle so that she is towards my left, for our feet must never point her way.

I breathe and let my toes slide into the pool. I continue this descent until the water is right up to my knees.

It is a curious feeling like I am neither here, nor there. Slowly, I start swinging my feet in the pool like that Bollywood heroine I once saw swinging her feet in a babbling stream somewhere pretty, somewhere under the sun, as the hero serenaded her.

I look up.

I follow the ribs and veins of the dome but as my vision climbs, light itself is sucked out of my eyes. I am rendered blind. Where is that point where the conical dome of the sanctum sanctorum peaks?

Who knows what lies up there—maybe a colony of bats?

I hear a loud scream.

The old priest, his face a wrinkled, crumpled white, is making his way towards me. His face contorts as he shouts at me to get out of the pool. He is making his way with one arm holding onto the wall for support while his other hand clutches his white dhoti lest it come undone in the wake of this unusually paced pursuit.

He grabs me by my shoulders while continuing to shout. Someone else walks in then—it is Aita, my grandmother. Maybe she was praying in the adjoining chamber?

The priest yanks my four-year-old self out of the pool.

Aita looks at my dripping wet feet with a bewildered look. She claims me as her grandson and the priest directs his ire at her for letting a child wander on his own. He cannot utter what exactly I have done.

'I was just playing in the water like in that movie....'

Aita doesn't let me say anything else. She simply drags me out of the temple while apologizing to the priest.

As we hastily walk on Lamb Road, I am annoyed. Because she didn't dry my legs, the flip-flops are slapping mud on my calves. I hate that feeling, don't you?

I was only swinging my legs like in the movie....

Perspiration clings onto her back. I can see her light brown cotton blouse become damp as we make our way home.

The midday summer sun shines above us.

Frangipani trees with impossibly twisted trunks and white flowers with buttery centres do not provide much respite, only fragrance.

We reach Aita–Koka's house in Ambari soon.

I wash my hands and feet and make my way to the dining table. It's the usual masor tenga—sour-fish curry—with rice.

We eat without a word and don't talk about what happened.

∽

'Please open your window shades for landing.'

Aita had just finished deboning the piece of fish on my plate, and I was ready to eat it with rice when a cool disembodied voice intruded.

I tried to go back to sleep but failed. My right leg had gone uncomfortably numb. In any case, soon they would start requesting passengers to sit upright.

It wasn't that I was dreaming about anything new or exciting. I had these dreams often, but then they stopped when I left Guwahati for university in Delhi. I had been living in the metro for a decade now but the dreams began to appear again recently.

The dream centred on an incident from my childhood when I was thrown out of the sanctum sanctorum of the Ugratara temple in Guwahati after being found with my feet in the sacred pool. And it usually ended as Aita and I reach home escaping the—perhaps legitimate—fury of the priest in the wake of this discovery.

There was some variation to the dream each time. This time, it involved lunch. I wanted to go back to taste that exquisite simple meal, which I did appreciate as a child, but now crave from time to time with an obstinate zeal. I haven't had it in all these years since Aita's passing.

Aita's tenga was a mildly flavoured clear soup-like curry made from slices of tomatoes and potatoes. It could be prepared with lentil fritters or ferns and other indigenous greens. But the best version always involved pieces of rou fish freshly caught from the Brahmaputra which Koka had bought every week for rupees thirty a kilo, a price that remained fixed for him even after Liberalization.

To make Aita's masor tenga, you first had to rub turmeric powder onto the rou pieces and then half-fry the fish in mustard oil. In the same oil, you put fenugreek seeds and black cumin till they sizzled.

Right before they started to burn, you added the chopped tomatoes and fried till slightly mushy. Subsequently, you would pour in water along with a thinly sliced potato or two. You would then add the fish pieces in this watery concoction and cover up to let it cook. At some point you would also add a pinch of asafoetida, a few hot green chillies, and some salt and sugar.

It was difficult to replicate the exact taste of Aita's tenga. Somewhere along the way, the end product always ended up being 'my' tenga. Even Aita's rice was unique. My mother suspected that it was because she always used the same pressure cooker to cook the full meal, or would surreptitiously add some sugar in anything she made. She first used the pressure cooker as a wok to fry the fish and make tenga. Once this was done, she would rinse the utensil with water and make rice in it without really scrubbing off the turmeric-stained fishy mustard oil from the aluminium interiors. So, the rice always ended up with a yellow hue, which was a source of embarrassment for my mother whenever guests would be invited for meals.

Aita's pressure cooker was also faulty. I sometimes heard her argue with Koka about it. But even after replacing the rubber gasket, the thing that made it airtight, the lid would just not fit well. This meant that the steam would leak out while the food cooked.

Being diabetic, Aita was easily tired. So, after cooking fish and putting the rice and water in her cooker, she would run off for a quick nap. Knowing that steam would escape inevitably—which meant that the first whistle would come only after some delay—she would put more water than the usual half-a-finger-above-the-rice measurement. It was indeed a complex task to negate the impact of escaping steam by adding the right amount of extra water while estimating cooking time. So it wasn't surprising that Aita's equilibrium between cooking rice and nap time was always off. By the time she came running back to the kitchen to switch off the heat, the bottom layer of rice would be burnt caramel brown. But the layer on top was this jorjoriya chewy white multitude of rice such that each grain of cooked rice was separate, a star unto itself. To be sure, for some it was too dry. But her jorjoriya rice went so well with the watery tenga on languid summer Guwahati afternoons.

'Please open your window shades for landing, sir,' a male voice spoke loudly, forcing me out of the wandering thoughts that sometimes afflict us when half asleep.

Assam may not have ornate forts of North India or anything of note architecturally, but as I glimpsed the sheer green lushness of the land, there was something satisfying about it. Perhaps such a feeling is evoked only when you start to think of a piece of land as home.

Sometimes, clouds would fly by, disturbing my view. Soon we would cross the low, rounded hills and see the patchwork of paddy fields in varying shades of green and yellow, after which we would glide over the seemingly endless stretch of silver, the Brahmaputra, that would be tinted pink as the sun would start setting over the hills by the time the airplane landed. These sights endured as a perk of taking the late afternoon Friday flight from Delhi to Guwahati.

∽

Two decades ago, one day in April, Aita had made lunch like she always did. As was her habit, she went to take a nap while the rice steamed inside her faulty cooker.

That afternoon, I wasn't with her. Since I was in middle school, I directly went home after school with my sister instead of going over to our grandparents' who lived a few streets away. We would eat lunch alone, watch TV, and wait for Ma and Deuta—Father—to come back from work.

That afternoon, as Aita got up from her nap based on her estimation of the time taken for the rice to cook—assuming the rate of escaping steam, evaporation of extra water, and intensity of heat from the stove—she slumped back on her bed.

Koka was in the other room, perhaps fuming after another one of their unreasonable fights. But my aunt who was temporarily staying with them, recovering from her surgery, was sleeping next to Aita. The sudden thud of Aita falling back on the bed woke her and she found her mother lying unconscious next to her. She screamed, which brought Koka to the room.

Being a physician, Aunty was in her element. She instructed Koka to pump Aita's chest while she breathed air into her mouth. In the meantime, Koka called an ambulance.

Aita had died almost instantly of a massive heart attack. So the frantic effort in trying to revive her was driven by the irrational force that grips us when we rebel against letting go of things or accepting the wishy-washy fate.

All this while the rice kept on cooking in the kitchen, and because of the faulty lid the whistle went off only after a long delay. This alerted Koka, who ran to the kitchen to switch off the stove lest a fire in the kitchen append to the unfolding tragedy.

Most of the rice had burnt to a crisp. But no one would have had food that afternoon anyway.

'गुवाहाटी के बाहर का तापमान 36 है और आर्द्रता 98 है।'

'The temperature in Guwahati is 36°C with humidity at 98 per cent.'

Goo-haatti.... I hated how they pronounced our words in the Hindi tongue.

'हमें यह बताते हुए खुशी हो रही है कि हम निर्धारित समय से 20 मिनट पहले ही लोकप्रिय गोपीनाथ बोरदोलोई एयरपोर्ट पहुँच चुके हैं। हम आपको फिर से सेवा देने के लिए तत्पर हैं और हमें उम्मीद है कि आपका गुवाहाटी में सुखद प्रवास हो!'

'We are glad to inform you that we have reached Lokpriya Gopinath Bordoloi Airport twenty minutes before scheduled arrival. We look forward to serving you again and we hope you have a pleasant stay in Guwahati!'

Bore-the-loii.

∽

I still couldn't believe that I had decided to come to this humid city in the middle of the summer after cancelling a mountain getaway to Manali with my friends in Delhi. When I was told last month that Aita–Koka's old house was getting demolished, I didn't think much about it. But when Ma told me that my uncle had found some old journals hidden among mekhela sadors in Aita's almirah, something told me to come home.

My grandparents lived a few streets away from our house in Ambari, which is one of the older settled areas in Guwahati. Growing up in this area in the 1990s, I remembered it as a neighbourhood of predominantly Assam-type houses. The construction of most of these buildings—including my grandparents' house—dated back to the early 1900s. The key features of Assam-type houses were their slanting tin roofs which ensured that rainwater trickled down and walls made of light reed covered with sandy cement. This was especially well-suited given that the city sat on a seismic fault line even though the recent houses had brick walls. But in all Assam-types, a criss-cross of wooden beams cured with a black paint made from some petroleum derivative to ward off termites, held the walls in place.

Today, Ambari has mutated. Most old Assam-types, like Aita–Koka's house, with their back and front yards make for excellent plots to erect tall reinforced concrete apartment blocks.

I remembered watching, as a kid, Aita making me scrambled eggs after one of her fights with Koka. She pointed at the ceiling to show me the three teak beams that held up the roof. Those were her father's gift to her after her marriage when as a young couple, after having their children in rented houses, Aita and Koka had bought a dilapidated house in Ambari. They had to entirely rebuild the kitchen. I wondered what would happen to those beams when the old house would give way to another apartment complex. Would the beams be smashed and sold as firewood for bonfires during Magh Bihu next year?

Of the couple, it was Koka who outlived his wife by several long, productive years, and wrote feverishly till dementia took away language. But I did remember Ma telling me that while Koka wrote texts on temples, Aita used to write poetry. Ma also told me that in fits of rage Aita would end up burning everything.

I did not ask why Aita decided to burn her poems. How many were there? And how much fire did it require to consume words? I could imagine her tearing up reams and reams of old yellowed paper from exercise copies, even as silver fish fell off the pages like dandruff, where line after line was written with blue ballpoint pens one could buy cheap from the nearby paan shop. I could imagine her not even waiting for the fire to eat up the art-turned-fuel. She must have started to take off the clothes from the drying lines that spread like a web in that little backyard. Or perhaps she moved the buckets of water collected at different intervals from the old Onida washing machine, rationing out the buckets with the dirtiest water first, to be reused by the cleaning lady to clean the floor.

Aita burning her own writings made sense to me. They were hers, after all. But maybe it was also another one of her volatile outbursts. One day, I had arrived at my grandparents' thirsty after playing with neighbourhood friends. But the old ceramic chalk filter wasn't there in its usual corner. I asked Aita where it was and she told me that it had broken. Koka looked the other way and simply walked out of the room. Only later when the cleaning lady came, she told me, 'Baba, your Aita smashed it to pieces that morning after fighting with Koka.'

I had heard her complain for years about how slowly water percolated through its outdated mechanism. Recently, it had started leaking incessantly, adding to her chores. No matter how many times she would wipe the floor dry, that corner of the house had developed an endemic dampness. Maybe she had had enough, and who can deny the fun in a good smash?

One afternoon, when my sister and I were alone at home after school, Aita turned up at our door unannounced. I had been raring to play badminton but because no adult was present, I had stayed indoors. So once Aita arrived, I grabbed the racquets and shuttle and went outside to play with my sister. Initially, Aita just sat on the porch watching us play. But then something crossed her mind and a sense of urgency gripped her. She asked us to drop our game and come indoors immediately. Being little and obedient, my sister ran back in without a word. But I refused to budge. This led to my first fight with Aita. The situation escalated to the point where Aita tried to pull away the racquet that I held to my chest. My strength waning, I let go while Aita kept pulling at the racquet. The sudden release meant that the steel frame of the racquet hit her over the eyebrow.

As blood started trickling down from her skin, I felt I would die from emotions. I was angry, sad, guilty, and fearful. I turned red, broke into tears, and ran to my room. My sister went out with some Dettol and cotton and sat next to Aita quietly.

From the folds of the curtains in my room, I checked on Aita, who, with my sister by her side, just sat on the porch sullenly, gazing at passers-by on the road, as the blood congealed on the wound. Soon, I spied Ma opening the gates of our yard and walking up to the veranda. My heart started racing as she stopped to speak to Aita. I am sure she asked Aita what happened, but Aita was silent and continued staring at the road. Then my sister seemed to be animatedly explaining something to Ma, her little hands flying up once or twice as she finished her account. That obliging pest, I thought.

In a minute or so, I could hear Ma marching towards my room, so I jumped away from the window and composed myself on the bed. But instead of slapping me—for I deserved a good thrashing—she sat next to me and told me that long ago before Uncle—who was the youngest of my mother's siblings—was born, Aita used to wear high heels. One day, she twisted her ankle and fell down. She was in a coma for many months. After that, she just wasn't the same.

'Baba, you have to be more compassionate with Aita. You may not understand why she asked you to stop playing, but you have to just listen to her when she is like that. Okay?'

I nodded as tears welled up again in my eyes. I had many questions but decided not to ask them.

~

In the following week, my sister and I resumed playing in the afternoon with no adults around.

My sister hit the shuttlecock in the bushes that flanked the rusty iron gate.

I fished for it by plunging my hands deep into the wildness of the mix of holy basil, creepers, and sharp grass. I felt for the smooth texture of the shuttlecock and pulled it out. But this was some kind of a shiny smooth black thing, pointed, with a base of rounded velvet. I was fascinated by what I had discovered and I ran to show this to my sister. But even as I put it in front of her, I realized that it was the severed head of a crow, dried and desiccated.

~

It is an act of severing the Goddess' corpse that anoints the pool around which the Ugratara temple grew. Ugra Tara, the angry Tara.

Tara was the name of my grandmother.

Tara Devi Bhattacharyya, or Abu aita, which later became Mamoni aita.

The navel is a piece of the divine body that connects a mother to child, remembered in pools, or as a lack in our body, in the land of the Goddess.

~

I had that dream again. That dream of the temple. But this time, once we reached Aita–Koka's house, there was a surprise party, like a soirée of sorts. To be sure, I only started partying as a young professional—with a beer or like a wannabe with a wine glass in hand, little finger out—in a big city like Delhi. There was something very weird in this dream, like multiverses crossing, as I didn't have the concept of a soirée when I was a kid. That dream was weird also because after walking back from the temple, as we opened the door to the house, I was no longer a child but a grown-up.

The party seemed to have been thrown in honour of Aita coming back to this world. Only I seemed to know that she didn't leave the city on some extended sabbatical but that she had, in fact, died of a heart attack twenty years back. But again, how could I not have believed my own eyes as she stood among us, family and friends, older than I remembered, a bit faded and stooped like an old Assamese granny, but unquestionably, irreverently, alive?

Just like she had woken up from her coma when she was a young mother, she had successfully staged another comeback. I remembered inching close to the woman of the hour and whispering, in an intimate moment amidst all the jubilant socializing, a single question:

'How was your break?'

She turned to me with her smile, that could never quite cover her two bunny-teeth.

~

It doesn't take a dream analyst to know that there is something significant in having an image or event repeated in dreams. So, in the hope that by understanding the reason behind the recurring dream, I would unravel some psychological knot, I had often wondered why I was visited by that incident—when I found myself with my feet dipped in Ugratara's pool—with its various improvisations.

I say I found myself, because I really did not have any recollection of how I arrived at the temple in the first place. I remembered making my way to the Devi's pool, I remembered my motivations clearly—that it would be fun, it would be like the movie, cinematic, that it just felt right or that I was supposed to do it even though I knew this was something that one shouldn't—but on how I arrived from my grandparents' house to the sanctum sanctorum, I was blank.

Certainly, one doesn't remember everything that transpired in one's childhood.

But the fact that I couldn't remember how I arrived at the temple made me think that perhaps something happened during that time that would shed light on my actions in the temple. Let me recount to you what I did remember from what transpired that morning. It was probably a Saturday as I had no school but my parents still had work, so I was dropped off at my grandparents'. I do not remember my sister being around at the time. Maybe she wasn't born as yet. Also, Koka had gone out to one of his meetings, so he wasn't home that morning. Aita was doing chores around the house, so she switched on the TV for me and I started watching the first movie I could find on Zee Cinema.

At that age, I didn't really know Hindi. But I was an avid film-watcher and a budding singer of Bollywood songs. I would mimic the tunes and rhythms more or less accurately while peppering my renditions of classic songs with words which sounded like Hindi to an Assamese speaker, but were, in fact, gibberish. Even the names of my favourite actresses—there were two queens who ruled my heart—Madhuri Dixit and Karishma Kapoor turned into Madhuri Dek-sii and Kaa-riss-maa.

I vaguely remember that the movie I was watching was set in a beautiful mountainous region. Maybe it was Kashmir. It was an old film, so maybe Bollywood had little access to the Swiss Alps then.

While I sat in front of the TV, Aita would come now and then to give me fruits and snacks or to catch bits of the movie in between cleaning and cooking. I remember her telling me that we would have lunch a bit later than usual as we were to go to the temple.

The hero and the heroine were walking in a beautiful forest. The time was ripe for them to break into a song–dance sequence as they do in Bollywood movies. I remembered the hero had pranced around, twirling his hands in the air theatrically with enhanced joy, while the actress, playing coy, went right up to edge of a gurgling stream and upon finding a boulder, perched on it. She then dipped her feet in the stream and started swinging them, sprinkling water playfully all around her. As the sun shone, it was as if the drops of water became like uncut gems. They showered all around her.

Something in me clicked at that time. I was so enamoured by it all. I enacted this scene with whatever prop I got, be it a sacred pool in a dark sanctum of a temple of the mother goddess.

Recently, I tried to find that movie in the hope that it would bring me closer to understanding how I came to the temple that morning. This meant watching many old Hindi films with song–dance sequences involving a female swinging her feet in a mountain stream. But no matter how many such movies I devoured, I still didn't have that revelation, which, I understood by reading some psychology, would play out in a manner where a vivid new world would emerge to sight—if only just for a moment—as thunder would light up everything in the shadowed interiors of a dense forest at night.

∽

The moment I got the journals home after having lunch at Uncle's place on Saturday, I started flipping through them. Their pages consisted mostly of random lists of things to do or grocery lists that Aita perhaps forgot to give Koka on his trips to Uzan Bazaar. Sometimes I would find pages and pages of additions and subtractions which—from the modest numbers—seemed to be the calculations of daily household expenses.

But sometimes there would be bits of text that read like poems hastily written in the dark. The writing was different here—narrow, less deliberate, as if the words wrote themselves. The sentences would start sloping at odd angles midway and would sometimes stop abruptly mid-thought, as they do when mosquitoes start biting. Sometimes sentences stretched the whole breadth of the page. At other times, they would consistently maintain an imaginary margin leaving a neat strip to the right eerily blank as if keeping room for future roots to grow.

Since my Assamese reading skills were rusty at best, Ma joined me that evening as I pored over the journals. This was especially helpful when we found substantial bits of writing. This continued through the weekend and into the following Monday, my last night in Guwahati as I was due to fly back the next day.

Everyone was interested to learn what we found. So, Deuta would ask what we had read and sometimes my sister, who had recently moved to Bengaluru for her first job, would call to find out if we had come across some salacious titbit. Once or twice Uncle called too.

I guess all of us were driven to know what these few thin volumes held. But most of the pages had inscriptions that probably made sense only in a particular context. Aita almost never wrote about us.

There was one long entry in her most recent journal which seemed to have been written as if she stopped to breathe between sentences separated by the calligraphic vertical dashes representing a full stop in the Assamese script.

This was an entry about a weekend when she had planned to go to the temple with me. She wrote that she decided to take me to the temple because it was the only outing she could think of for the both of us. She mentioned some other options only to dismiss them immediately. We couldn't go to the zoo, which, though cheap, was too far. It would have also involved changing city buses which never really came to a standstill when picking up or dropping passengers, so people had to jog to get on them, or run while hopping off.

It was almost comical to imagine Aita breaking into a trot in her mekhela sador beside a decelerating bus while I ran behind her holding her hand. She would have stretched her other hand so that another passenger or the ticket collector—whose bodies would be hanging half-outside the bus doors—could grab and pull us onto the bus. Maybe we could have gone out to have papdi chat in Fasi Bazaar, but then I realized that she didn't really have cash on her as she had never worked for an income.

Aita's prose had a matter-of-fact quality to it, something I hadn't expected of someone who, I was told, wrote poetry. It lent her words an exactness that gave them a strange authority which seemed at odds with her quiet demeanour. She wrote that she wasn't sure if I had wanted to go to the temple instead of watching TV or playing with Agarwal's son who lived opposite to the temple.

My heart started beating in apprehension.

She wrote that when it was time to leave for Ugratara she couldn't find me in the house. She simply assumed—given my stubbornness as a child—that I had run off to Agarwal's house to avoid going to the temple. So, she decided to go by herself and pick me up on her way back so that at least we could have lunch together at home.

She described how she picked some red flowers from the chilli hibiscus bush on the boundary wall between Mahanta aunty's and Ali uncle's house. She also complained about how the price of mustard oil had risen again but that she managed to get a good deal from the seller as she also bought earthen lamps, a matchbox, and incense sticks.

She then mentioned that while praying right outside the sanctum sanctorum to a lesser deity, she heard a scream from inside. Curiosity was stronger than devotion; she chided herself matter-of-factly, then jumped up mid-prayer and rushed to the sanctorum hoping to catch some action. She described the scene that I know all too well: the priest shouting at me while I played about with my feet dipping in the sacred pool.

My mother shot me a quizzical look as if to confirm if this was true, for neither I nor Aita—presumably—had told her about this incident. But I continued reading.

Aita described in detail her horror at this scene and why this was something that no one should do. But she wrote that something about it seemed right. She described the way I was waving my hands, swinging my feet, and smiling. And so, when she heard me say that I was imitating the heroine from the movie, it felt like things had fallen together. But then the priest started screaming at her, so she apologized to that old wretch whom she admitted to have never liked in the first place. She was always the one to keep quiet but hold burning grudges.

My heart was aflutter by now as she continued to describe the scene where we walked back, which I have reproduced below in translation.

'I was so hot but I made sure to walk fast. The sooner we leave that priest's unpleasant voice behind the better. We were nearly home when I asked him, Why did you do it—and he just smiled and said, I liked what I saw in the movie....I want to be like the heroine.

All children are divine. There is God in them. It is only when we become older that God leaves us. I just smiled and told him that yes, that movie is nice. And that actress was one of the great beauties of Indian cinema. Once I heard her interview in the All India Radio where she shared how she came from a poor family and struggled to make it big in Bombay.'

My ears burnt hot as I read these words out loud. I had tried so hard to hide these things from Ma who must be wondering why I, a boy, had imitated an actress.

A surge of memories came back from my childhood, of playing dress up in hiding, being called maiki—girl—and of the shame that followed. I stopped reading to take a deep breath. As if on cue, Ma took over.

'When we had taken your mother to Delhi for college, your koka and I watched this movie in Batra cinema—I wanted to tell the child. But the day wasn't done with its share of revelations—as I was about to speak about my memories of watching the movie in Delhi, just for a moment, the world around me rippled like it wasn't fully real, but it changed back almost immediately.'

Ma started reading rapidly, her voice almost down to a whisper now, as I strained to follow her.

'I remember how things were before I had slipped and fallen down in Dibrugarh. Once I came back, it was like I had arrived split. I am unsure at times whether I am dreaming or awake. When I do dream, I dream about unknown people, things, and places. In those months when I was sleeping, maybe I had lived another life with another family, had other dreams.

The doctor had said that these visions would stop with treatment. I was scared but then everyone insisted that I should do everything to be better. But it hurt so much, this treatment—and the shocks made it worse to live. Now, I continue thinking about other places while living my life here with my husband, children, and their children. But neither here nor there in those other places, do I feel real.

In children I see what fullness could look like. I cannot put in words, but it is something I have forgotten as it has been taken from me. His antics at the temple also reminded me of the movie, and for a moment I remembered that sometimes even I have felt whole.'

My mother ended the above lines in a broken whisper. Tears started trickling down her cheeks, as she muttered. 'Ma suffered so much in her life. We were told she had schizophrenia.... Did I ever tell you?'

My eyes started watering. I realized that I didn't need to understand what I didn't remember. I just needed to work with what I had so well hidden from myself.

'It's okay.'

Ma sighed as she rubbed my back.

THE LOVER OF STORIES

LEDE E MIKI POHSHNA

I

Good Friday.

The Lover of Stories. That's his name. That's what I call him. Two times my lips touch when I say his name. Meye Perom. The Lover of Stories. He doesn't want to read them himself.

'Reading is too difficult, too monotonous,' he says.

It takes away his concentration, his energy, and his will. It drains him much faster than the hard labour he performs every day, like hauling limestones from a platform into the back of a truck. He returns home. His mother sits by the fireplace, and he hands her his wages. He hands her ninety per cent of it and keeps ten for himself. Like God, or a loving dutiful son. She cooks for him and for his brothers. One is a driver; the other is a fireman. Each of them gives everything to their mother. The only thing he never gives her is time. He gives that part to me entirely. He is mine from six in the evening till midnight. And then, early in the morning, before he leaves for the quarry, he comes to see me.

'Be good,' he says.

I smile and give him a kiss in secret. Some things can only be done in secret. Especially our kind of kiss.

'Read me something,' he says.

I don't have to ask any further. I know he enjoys everything I pick. I know it's not because I have good taste but because my taste in books has stuck with him and become his. He claims me even in this little act of reading, something I consider my own. He claims me in bed, and he claims me during those dark hours at night.

'I will tell you the story of Echo,' I say. I utter the name 'Echo' in English without him realizing it is about what we call 'Ka Chap Chang'.

He lowers his head, rests it on my damp belly, and stares at the ceiling. He closes his eyes and reaches for my hand—the expectant longing that can only be satiated by the touch of my hot, damp skin.

I open my mouth, and words tumble out of it about how Echo helped Zeus, how Hera punished her by making it impossible for her to say anything except the last word spoken to her. He listens with the attention of a bewildered child. He hates it when I tell him ancient Greek stories. For him, a storyteller must tell something that is close, something that one can identify with. For him, a story should be homely, something that belongs to him. That's why he likes me; I am a story to him—something his mouth utters in sadness, in happiness, in boredom, and in a long hour of him toiling in a quarry. It comes naturally, without pretension and effort.

'I like it,' he says after I finish.

This is the first time he appreciates a story that's not set in our time and space. I am surprised and happy.

'I'm glad you like it.'

'I like the fact that Narcissus chose not to be with Echo. I like the fact that she can only exist as a voice. He can destroy her body, like mutilate her or kill her. But her voice will remain. It speaks freely and without fear.'

'You are right.'

He has a perceptive way of seeing the story. I am proud of him and his ability to see through the veneer of a story the way a trained mind in literary criticism does.

'Imagine if we could say what we want without fear or embarrassment,' I say.

'We can say just as much, at least when we are together,' he says, assuring me by holding my hand.

I am jealous. Isn't he the one who tells me that a story should be homely? And yet he finds a tinge of salvation in this story. Am I to read that as a sign that one day he will leave as he finds his home elsewhere, and not somewhere close to me? I smile at him because that's the only way I can express my emotions without giving away too much of my mind. A smile can be deceptive. Here, I am using it as a stratagem of withholding, a remarked absence.

The church bell rings in the distance, summoning the faithful to the evening service. His mother wraps herself in a black merina cloth. Black is the colour of sadness because it is the day the Lord died for our sins. In the room, his mouth runs across my midrib, biting me as he seeks to redeem me from my pent-up desire. Both he and the Lord try to redeem the one they love. Only one chose death over life. His mother closes the door, complaining that he never attends the service.

'It's boring,' he says. 'Full of lifeless, boring people. Not my taste.'

My phone rings as I laugh at his remark. Mother is on the line. She is angry because she cannot find the hymn book that she needs for the service. She has ransacked the house in search of the book.

'Where does he keep it?' she shouts from the other end.

'Search for it on my bookshelf. It must be there.'

'It better be,' she says as she cuts the line. Mothers can't let their sons rest easy or give them privacy.

Mothers go to service to thank the Lord for his sacrifice and to cry as they pray for their sons and all their vices. They couldn't pray for us because they know nothing about what we do while they pray.

These are the stories that he hates. Of salvation, repentance, sins, miracles, and everything in which mothers find joy or a reason to hope for death. He hates the stories that make his home unhomely. He loves my stories because they bring him closer to himself.

The night ends with him finishing inside me. It has become our routine now. He takes a bath after work to clean himself of the smell that differentiates his life from mine; he comes to my house, or I go to his; I tell him a story or two, and then we have sex. But tonight doesn't feel like our usual night of storytelling and fucking. Something about his newfound taste of 'other' stories makes me worried.

'Don't be so jealous,' he says to me when I complain about the guys who talk to him.

'It's my line of work,' he emphasizes, without trying to sound as if he is defending himself. He doesn't want to be defensive about what he does for a living.

II

Saturday.

For the first time in six years, it rains during the holy weekend. He is not religious, but he keeps a count of all the little obscure events, happenings, and gossip that are casually revealed during the holy week. He doesn't go to work and his boss gets angry at him.

'You son of a whore,' his boss calls him because everyone in town knows that he is not his father's son.

His father had been suffering from a debilitating stroke for two years when his mother conceived him. Everyone knows who his father is, including me, except him, probably because he doesn't want to. Whatever the situation is, he always says he never really had a father.

'You're gonna cost me a lot of money, and you will repay that one way or another,' shouted his boss. 'He is as lazy as his kind. I should have known better before hiring him.'

His boss is a chubby middle-aged man. A devoted father. A loving husband. A penny-pinching boss. And a bad neighbour. He would complain excessively about the smell emanating from a neighbouring house or their crying babies. One time, three dogs were found dead, oozing blood out of their orifices. He tells me it was his boss who poisoned them. He knows him like one would know how to cross an empty street. Natural, easy to read, and open.

He calls me.

'I just want to hear your voice.'

'We just saw each other seven hours ago,' I remind him.

'Yet, I want to hear your voice. I want it to linger on in my ears like an echo.'

I smile at his words. There is a poem that churns inside him. A bit of Dante, a bit of Petrarch, and a bit of Neruda. He doesn't know it. He isn't familiar with those names. For him, poetry is something that sounds like 'Twinkle Twinkle Little Star'. If I ask him to explain poetry to me, he would only be able to describe the sound. But little does he know that he is a poem in himself.

Once, he said to me, 'You are a sunset—a sight I love to behold. A scene that I always look up to, and it keeps me going.'

How could I ever argue with him? How could I ever argue with his poetry?

'Why did you choose someone like me?' he asks as he covers his half-naked body with a blanket. Now that we are five months into this, he has the audacity to ask me such a question. 'Is it out of desperation? That there's no one here, and I'm the only available option?'

He throws this question to release the pent-up pressure caused by the desire to know why we chose each other. He has the courage now to ask this because he is certain that what we have now is the truth, because he is deeply aware that we have peeled away every layer that we had wrapped ourselves in till our souls became bare. Like Echo, who was torn into pieces by Pan, leaving nothing but her voice, love shreds all our layers, our pretence, our fear, our reticence, our stigma and shame, and we are left with nothing but the truth. So, he asks me, and I have to answer: 'Because you never cared about my imperfections, and you cherish the one thing that I'm really good at. And that makes you the most special person in my life.'

We have learned how to listen to stories but we rarely cherish the storyteller. That's why we only remember stories and not people who told them first. Stories belong to everyone. In that sense, there is nothing special in what I am doing for him. But he is the only person who grants me a sense of authorship. He is the only one who listens to me. There is something unique about the stories that I tell when I tell them to him. They become ours—he is the reader and I, the author. He is the first person to make me feel this way.

Saturday afternoon passes by. The sky rumbles as the wind blows the top of the trees into meaningless hours. He asks if he should come over, and I say no.

'Papa is here,' I say.

He knows that is not a good sign. There is something about his presence that unsettles Pa. He thinks he is weird, but not because his family is different from mine or the fact that his mother had four more children after his father was paralysed. There is just something about the way he talks, or walks, or the way he looks at me that discomforts Papa. He hates it when he and I disappear into my room. Papa knows about us.

Mama prays in the afternoon.

My elder brother will get married in December, and she is extremely proud of him. She prays for his future family. She prays for my sisters and her children. She prays for me so that I'll finish college with good grades. She prays for him too.

Mama loves him. I wonder if she would still love him if she knew that he has claimed me both in stories and in bed.

Mama loves to pray during the holy weekend.

'A Week of Passion,' she would say and fast from Friday night till Sunday morning.

Ravaged by hunger and satiated by prayer, her lips travel throughout the fabric of our lives, asking for forgiveness for our sins and for the Lord's blessing.

His mother prays too.

Everyone in this village prays. It's like a plague that keeps on infecting people with expectations. Many prayers go unheard and unanswered.

He visits my house because that's what a dutiful son does when his mother needs privacy. But he also visits me because he has things to tell me.

He does not say anything when he sees me. His arms wrap themselves around my chest as we stand in front of the mirror, taking a selfie. Saturday evening is as tedious as the day Christ died. But we are not dead; we have to bear with the monotony of waiting. Christ slept the entire day and woke up the next day to redeem the world. The power that only sleep can confer or as Nietzsche said, 'Blessed are these sleepy ones: for they shall soon nod off.'

'He wasn't sleeping,' he says as he throws himself onto my bed.

'Of course,' I say. 'He was dead.'

He sighs, disappointed by my ignorance.

'For a storyteller, you know so little about the stories from the Bible. The Lord went to the underworld to preach to those who were dead before him,' he says as he calmly cites from the Epistle of Peter.

'At least he had something to do then.'

I don't want to argue with him about the veracity of such a claim. I know it's a theological concept used to explain salvation and grace; it's not necessarily a fact.

'Don't make fun of such a thing,' he rebuffs my joke and sits up.

I sit down by his side and gently rest my head on his thighs.

'Do you know what's the best thing about boredom?'

'Is there anything even good about it?' he asks.

'It's something that ancient people understand intimately. Well, look at the Sabbath. After God created everything, he must have been bored. So, he sanctified it. Same thing with Jesus in the underworld story. We are not allowed to be bored. Some God cannot just sit around, and if he does, it's only because that day is sacred. Jesus cannot sleep in peace for one day. Even when he is dead, he has to work. No one is allowed to be bored in this life. To be bored is to be against society. Just like our love. That's the best thing about it.'

'Of course, everything is about being productive. That's why we aren't accepted.'

'And just like that, the best thing about boredom is that it is about rebelling.'

I should have noticed that something was holding him up. He used to be so relaxed when we were together. But this afternoon he looks preoccupied with something else. I know this because I have learnt how to read him. Like a story.

He waves goodbye after a few hours.

'I need to get home and finish some work,' he says.

I nod. I can only bide my time. I know he will open up to me. He loves a new story. He is absent from work. He is holding back something from me. I wonder whose stories he has fallen in love with.

III

Easter Sunday.

The stone of the grave where he keeps his secret is rolled aside to reveal something. His mother doesn't go to church. His uncle arrives by eleven in the morning. His father doesn't care about him. He keeps saying he isn't 'his' and that he won't have anything to do with him. He lies there pretending not to see or hear anything. On that Sunday morning, a sudden sense of peace descends upon him when he discovers that he has a boyfriend.

'That whore gave birth to u hynthea.'

He is proud because his seed isn't like my lover. He is proud because his wife is punished for her sins by having given birth to a gay son. His mother doesn't care about whom he makes love to, which was why he chose to tell her on Saturday morning. Out of boredom. Like the ancients before him, he has also learnt how to solemnize boredom into something much more important than it is. He has learnt how to tell his story in a confession to his mother.

'Once upon a time,' he starts.

That's how he started telling her about him, exactly in the same style that our forefathers would tell a story.

'Not a very long time ago,' he continues, 'there was a boy.'

And then he continues with the story: of how this boy came across another boy; he had dared to swim the mighty Umngot River to retrieve the other boy's drowning body, and how he gave him mouth-to-mouth CPR. And how the drowning boy has longed for those lips ever since.

'Those are the lips of life,' he says. 'And one of the boys is me as you might be aware.'

His mother spits out the tobacco, which she had tucked inside her cheek, onto her palm and throws it out of the window. He expects her to tell him that she loves him, an expectation that he got after watching many Western films. He had told me how he wanted to have a mother like Nick Nelson's mother. His mother, instead, says, 'Cunt! So how do you even fuck one another? Through which hole?'

'Is that all you can say?' he asks her, clearly hurt, embarrassed, and shocked by her question.

'So, what do you want me to say? If you want to fuck boys, then by all means, please do. It's not my fucking business. But you have to marry a woman someday. That's the only life I can find respectable.'

'But that's the problem. I cannot. I'm just not attracted to them'.

'And how is that related to anything? I married your dad for many reasons, but not because of attraction and love.'

'Well, I'm not him.'

'Don't tell me you want to marry this boy. What would the world think of him if you do that? I mean, I can't even imagine how it would work.'

He leaves because he has said enough. He doesn't want to hear his mother's line of questioning any more. Now that the tomb is open, he feels free just as the Lord does when he rises.

He makes up his mind to call me.

'Come away,' he says. 'Come away where we can dream and be bored and tell each other stories without anyone bothering us.'

The church bells have stopped ringing and Mama has merged herself with the hymns she sings. I stand at the window and look in the direction of his house. I picture him standing by his window, trying to see me through that distance. How much he owns me, how much he has claimed possession of me, and how many more stories are left in me to tell him; this is all I can think of as I look in his direction. Papa is playing the piano in the living room. 'Up from the grave he arose' reverberates through the walls of our house.

'Come away,' he says. 'I still need your stories in order to complete mine.'

Riang Khangnoh

SAWEINI LALOO

I am here again. From the trees and the shops lined in a row to the pond on the left side of the street, everything is shrouded in a dull hue of orange and red. People around me are blurry smudges of grey and black, and the street is less crowded than usual. The noises of the day become softer and are pushed to the corners like the garbage heaps lining the street.

The pond is the only thing that is alive, shining with a dirty yellow glow. Nan Kashari is her name and underneath her are the bones and muffled cries of people who go to her to weep and drown their sorrows. Like an eye that watches this town silently, she does not stir. She never does.

I am here again. I can see my house on the hill and the narrow road that gradually disappears from view behind the big old tree. Someone grabs me by the shoulder. Startled, I turn around and see a man wearing a white turban, dark grey vest, white shirt, and a white loincloth.

Move aside, girl. They are coming.

The ground beneath me shakes and I hear a rumbling sound in the distance. Is it the rain clouds? The rumbling grows louder and I realize that it is not the rain clouds nor thunder but the sound of beating drums.

Dhum dhum dhum. The sound grows louder and louder.

Behind me are men similarly dressed. They all gradually make way for something.

You better run on home, girl, another man tells me. *You better run on home before the procession ends. You know she is coming soon.*

I pick up my pace, which soon turns into a sprint. But somehow, I cannot outrun the procession. The people and the music drown me.

She's coming. She's coming, they chant.

My mind screams, urging me to run faster but my feet are like stones under water.

The procession is about to reach the bend on the road that leads down to the river. The people and the music will disappear soon.

I can see my house.

Dhum dhum, dhum dhum. The beating of drums encases the sky like a glass container.

The procession moves ahead and disappears from view. The street is empty again. I am alone.

Dhum dhum dhum in the distance again.

Behind me, I hear another procession but the music is a strange one this time. It is eerie and sounds as though it is coming from the trees, the pond, and the sky.

It is her! She is coming. She is coming.

I try to run faster this time but my body is numb. I cannot move. I try to scream for help but no sound comes out.

Dhum, dhum, dhum, along with the sound of feet marching closer towards me.

Run! I tell myself.

∽

I wake up with a start. I cannot see anything. My eyes take time to adjust to the darkness, and I soon begin to notice the faint rays of blue and yellow light emanating from our veranda and the neighbour's. My shirt is damp and my hair sticks to my forehead. I clear the strands away with my cold hand and wipe my face with the blanket.

It was just a dream.

Tick-tock tick-tock.

Outside, it is quiet. There are no drums; even the trucks are absent tonight. The junction in front of my house, leading towards the Dawki road, is like a whirlpool that sucks in all things until they eventually disappear. It is also a Sunday, I realize. I look to my left; Bei and Diah are sound asleep. I stare at the ceiling and watch the dance of shadows cast by the trees as they bend to the will of the wind. It had rained earlier, and I had gone to bed content. The warmth of the blanket and the sound of rain provided comfort. Now, the night is pervaded with an eerie stillness. I wonder what time it is but soon decide that it is better to not know. I wish I was not the only one wide awake because of a nightmare. I should not have begged Papun to tell me that story before I went to bed.

Tick-tock tick-tock.

The darkness erases all notions of time. How much time has passed?

For how long have I been awake?

I feel the panic rise, and my hands become clammy.

Dhum dhum dhum.

Is that the sound of drums?

I need to fall asleep now. What if she comes and senses that a little girl is still awake?

Happy thoughts. Happy thoughts. I try to think of happy thoughts but none come to mind.

On the roof, the sound of raindrops falling from the branches of trees.

One, two, three...I count them instead. There is such comfort in the last few drops of rainwater.

∽

'No. I think you should not listen to horror stories before you go to bed,' says Papun for the second time without looking up from his newspaper.

We had just finished dinner and were sitting around the diñnar—the brazier where the charcoal was burning a bright red against the black metal encasing it—when the rain started to pour down heavily. It is the beginning of the monsoon season and even at this time of the year, the coal heater burns and crackles, the wind howls and the rain lashes the treetops. Everyone fights for a place next to the only source of warmth. I fight for a seat next to Papun. I rest my arm on his leg and coax him into telling me one of my favourite stories. The story of Ka Riang Khangnoh.

Papun is a treasure trove of stories. His stories are always the best ones. Perhaps because he is old and the stories he tells always begin with 'Once upon a time...'. There is always a sense of realness to the stories, as though they happened yesterday, as though he dug them up from his own experience. On particularly cold days, he would dig up a story or two while the rest of us huddled around him. I am not especially fond of anything horror-related but when we are together around the hearth, the stories beckon to be told.

The fermented scent of tungtap and dai—fermented fish and lentil—still hovers in the kitchen. This scent, mixed with the fumes from the charcoal and tinder made from pine, is familiar to all who reside in these parts.

I beg Papun for the third time to tell me the story. Knowing that I will go to bed upset, Papun finally gives in.

All right, but just that one story.

Ishish, Bei retorts. *Don't tell her any horror stories before bed. She will get a nightmare and wake me up later.*

Papun looks at me and winks.

I will tell you the story if you promise you will not wake up your mother later.

All right! I shout in glee before my mother gets the chance to protest.

∽

Once upon a time when animals conversed with humans and trees and rivers imparted wisdom to people, there was a woman called Riang. This is her time. A time when the rain drowns everything, from the trees and the fields, to the people, in a veil of grey and green. It is also a time when the nan—the lake—swells. It is the season of drums and rituals. After the festivities are over, she, too, comes to dance, leaving behind only the echo of the din of the day. She emerges at night with her servants leading the way, beating their drums and announcing her arrival. They emulate the dance of the humans.

The path from Pohskur to a place called Tre iong Riang, which is located on the Myntdu River, is her favourite path. Riang is described as having long, flowing hair, and she is usually dressed in ordinary clothes. On special occasions, however, she dons the most exquisite attire with ornate jewellery. It is said that having an encounter with her is better than having one with her servants as she is more reasonable and forgiving but it is always best to avoid both.

Her servants are malevolent spirits or nymphs who cause all kinds of mischief. When one hears their drums or their song, it is best to hide or run away because one never knows what they will do. They are scary-looking creatures. Some say they look like boits or dwarf-like creatures with long, unruly hair; sharp nails, and feet that are turned backwards and not towards the front. Their eyes are blood-red and their teeth, sharp and yellow. Her servants also comprise river spirits who are of the malevolent type, and it is believed that these spirits lure people to their deaths in the river. They are not fond of people and often create mischief for most and cause great injury to those they particularly dislike.

Have you had such encounters, Papun? I interrupt.

No, he responds, *but there have been accounts of people who had close encounters with her servants.*

What happened to them? I enquire further.

Well, they ran away of course! But those who were unfortunate to meet her—no, her servants, they never returned home the same. Some don't return at all.

What happens to them? I ask, more curious than ever.

Those who encounter Riang's servants either fall under their spell and lose their minds, or they follow them into the river and are never heard of again.

Before I could interrupt, Bei Heh, busy with her knitting, chimes in. *Do you want Papun to finish the story or not?*

I nod at Papun, and he continues with the story. I make a mental note to ask him for details another time. A shiver runs down my spine as I recall a faint memory of an old man who once visited Papun to report a particularly disturbing story about a person who had lost his mind and was seen wandering the streets. I only heard snippets of the story as I was sent away by Papun when he caught me eavesdropping by the door.

Ehem, he clears his throat and resumes the story.

There are many stories about Riang strolling the streets of the town on ordinary days. Woh Chem, who lives in Pohskur, told a story once about how she would visit the grey house near the church and converse normally with the people there, only to disappear, leaving the family dumbstruck. Only then would they realize that it was Riang whom they had just offered kwai, betel leaf, and nut to.

Was she a real person? This time, Diah, my younger brother, raised the question.

I believe she was, replied Papun.

Really? All the young ones chimed in.

Yes. Papun smirks, sensing how the atmosphere in the room suddenly changed to a more sombre one.

Some say that she was a young woman who went by the name of Riang Nikhla, who suddenly disappeared one day. It is not clear what happened to her. Some say that she got lost, while others speculate that she perhaps drowned in the river, or worse, willingly plunged into the abyss.

Is she a bad person, Papun? Our youngest cousin, Diah Khian, asks.

Not really. We have not heard stories of her harming anyone. In fact, when she meets people, she often converses with them, enquiring if they had kwai or where they were going before leaving them with a warning to walk in the opposite direction of her servants.

Be careful of meeting my servants, she would often warn the passer-by, they are not as kind.

Perhaps her untimely death is the reason why she still lingers around. Perhaps, she has turned into a river nymph like Ka Lidakha who can transform into a human whenever she likes.

The legend of Ka Riang Khangnoh still holds sway over the hearts of many people in this town even to this day. This is the reason why no one wanders about at night here. They are all afraid of seeing her ghost and encountering her servants.

A moment of silence fills the room after Papun concludes the story.

All right. That's the end of the story.

Bei, who noticed it was already nine o'clock, begins putting out the fire. Beiheh helps her rearrange the muras and the chukis. Beikhian tries to carry Naki without waking her up. Five-year-old Naki had dozed off halfway into the story. The rest of us cling to our mothers and fathers or each other as we wait for them to lead us to bed.

Bei, can I sleep in the middle tonight? I ask hesitatingly.

I did not want to show her that I was scared but the thought of sleeping on the far end of the bed was unappealing. I wanted to be tucked in the middle where it was safer.

Are you scared? I told you not to listen to ghost stories before bed. Besides, where will Diah sleep if you take his place?

Diah protests that he will not sleep anywhere except beside Bei.

Before a fight ensues, Bei promises to wrap her arms around the both of us.

The rain starts to pour heavily outside and I think about boits and nymphs and a long-haired woman.

THE BLEEDING FLOWERS

LINTHOI CHANU

Before the violence, our village was what you would call a sleepy and sequestered village. A place beyond the touch of modernization is now revered as a thing of splendour. But back then, that was our existence. That place is no more. A past. Almost unreachable in our memory; with no hope of seeing it again. Those gleeful winds of our memories exist only as phantom shadows, flickering behind the disquietude.

All that we can see and feel are fire and smoke from the place we escaped with only our souls packed in our bodies. Some even left their slippers behind. They must have been like our Mam Boinao, who never failed to tell us to remove our shoes or slippers while stepping inside his house. He was known to be 'the cleanest man in the village', a badge of ridicule given by men who said their wives were his only unsuccessful competitors, but he wore it with pride.

For miles we ran; our destination was to run away from the debris. The sound of gunfire mimicked the crackers we burst during festivals. The crackers threw up sparks and laughter, but the bullets were meant for our flesh. Some got wounded; they yelled. No one stopped to look their way. Doing so would make one dead body two.

I wish I had the privilege to think tranquilly and then present all the events accurately so that readers could feel the horrors of that night. But I realize now that such accuracy needs far more than just the privilege of tranquillity. Bear with me; all I can remember is that after running the whole night, we were told to form a haphazard line, begging the army trucks to pick us up and drop us anywhere away from the village.

By then, I was alone. I had lost my family and friends in the crowd. Nobody who was fit enough to run had the time to mind anyone else. I was sure that my parents were with my grandmother. My brother had yelled at me to run without turning back. He was right behind me but when I turned around, the person after me in the queue was a pregnant woman, poking my back with her protruding belly every time the crowd pulsated in protest, voices yelling to be picked up.

In other circumstances, I know I would have offered her the place in front of me or made way for her, sending her ahead of anybody else. That day, it didn't happen. She stood behind me, her belly poking me. People yelling and crying. The baby churning inside the mother's belly. I climbed onto a truck at last.

I do not recall how I reached the camp in the middle of nowhere. The army cadets put us in a tent with more than a hundred people. I can't recall how we managed to sleep that night. I am sure none of us slept. What I can distinctly remember is the smell of sweat and earth inside the tent. I remember frantically searching for a clean teak leaf to take rations that the cadets were providing. I don't even know what I ate that night. It went straight into the burbling acid. At least it calmed the grumbling.

We were asked to go to the nearest town. I left with a group of some forty people. By the time we reached the town, it was noon. A large gathering of volunteers welcomed us. For the first time, I got a thin bedding to sleep on. Inside a giant community hall, ironically curtained with the kind of screens used during weddings and festivities, I hid my weeping.

We stayed there for days. There we heard news about the shortage of water and food and also of riots breaking out in several other places. We barely complained. How could we? We hardly had anything left to complain about. Where to begin? Our houses were burned in a night. All I could think of was to find a way to reunite with my family. As a person who rarely makes friends easily, I curled up in the farthest corner of the hall, listening to people speak of things that had happened in other villages. Just a few days earlier, there were no specific people that we strongly disliked. It seems absurd that people like us, who had little more than a bit of food and a few warm clothes, had so little to complain about. We had our squabbles and disagreements, but nothing foreshadowed the loss of everything we ever had.

But things are different now. Our enemy burned our houses, they say. Our enemy attacked us, they say. I couldn't stand up and say that I never had an enemy in my life. But I decided to agree with them instead.

We did nothing to earn the animosity, but we do have enemies now. Those who let our houses burn and those who burned our houses. Those who chased us away from our homes. Those who had been brewing hatred in their hidden cauldrons won, pouring the poison of divide over all of us. I just wished I did not feel so lost and numb, so numb that I could not even bring myself to hate them at that moment. The reality of my loss, our village's destruction, hadn't yet settled in my mind.

I don't remember how long I spent in that camp. Appreciation for the volunteers who took care of us, despite the shortages, grew stronger. There was the grim news of a malaria outbreak in some other camp. We were told not to avoid getting bitten by mosquitoes but there were many people who slept without nets. I prayed that the mosquitoes that bit me were not part of the infected gang carrying the parasite.

Then came another piece of news—we could go towards the city if we wanted. They said there were better camps there. I jumped onto the first vehicle I saw. I shifted from one camp to another. Nothing they said about the city camps being better was true. By now, I was dogged by the sickening worry that I would never reunite with my family after coming all the way to the capital. Something told me that my brother was still out there defending our village from the attackers. The way he yelled at me to not turn back was suspicious. He must have decided to stay behind.

Finally, I was taken to a camp at a college. These were well-maintained institutions in the city so the amenities were sufficient for 140 of us staying there. The riot marked its second month while I was at that camp. I became accustomed to greeting people who came to donate whatever they could. There were also those who came to celebrate how much they could donate and shower us with things. I am glad we humans have this vice, pride, which sometimes makes us do good. Except for the effort it took to hide from their cameras or their aggressive requests to stand in lines, I was glad they came. They brought me things I needed; things I desperately required to survive. Nothing about returning home or reuniting with family was discussed with us. I, too, had not spoken to anyone about it.

A few elders made sure that I never missed any meals at the camp. 'Have you eaten?' they would always ask. In our culture, this question is a form of greeting; only lately have I realized that this simple question is an encouragement to move on with life.

It was another normal day at the camp. We were commanded to prepare the vegetables for our meal. We all had our duties, and we did them diligently. It was the least we could do. Some felt bad about how, after our houses were burnt, we became a burden on people and we were staying for free in a camp that was supposed to be their place of education. I was not one of them—that was not my burden to carry—but still, I did my part. I sat with the others and began cutting the chives.

A group of people came as usual. They were no longer visitors for us. Some people in the camp had forged strong friendships with them. If not for the bloodshed, they would never have crossed paths. One lived in the spectral world of urban dwelling, while the other tilled the earth, eyes fixed on the soil and the sky. My shyness limited my interactions. They, too, were careful when they talked to us. Once I conveyed my unwillingness to respond, they let me be. And so, I lived in that camp, a person who rarely talked or interacted.

When the riot turned three months old, I received news of my parents. I asked to be reunited with them and capable people arranged for it. I went to a nearby village; there I was reunited with my family. They were all safe and sound except for my brother. I asked where he was, and my mother said that he went to answer the call from the other side of the river. In riddles and proverbs do our elders speak. I asked no more. Away from the capital, my mind tricked me into thinking that I was closer to my home and things would improve in a few days.

Like little droplets of dew on winter mornings, memories of my village began to shimmer. I began to miss home.

We did not have much but at least we always had charcoal for the winter. There was no charcoal to light a fire in the camp. My mind wandered back to the last moments in my village. Up the hill we went for our lunar new year supplies. The reverse happened during Christmas. Hordes of our neighbours in the hills would come down to our tiny market to feast and shop for gifts. The chatter and the banter would ring out during those holiday mornings. I repeatedly poked the memories of happy times, worried that they now only lived in my head.

The fires and the smoke, the bullets and dead bodies went on for many nights. Those who could have protected our right to survive were not to be found. Whom were we supposed to hate and kill? I sat by the riverside when the sun blessed us. I wondered if my brother was still alive. If he was dead, who would bring that news to us? I heard that even innocent women and children were not spared. I heard that our neighbour, Mam Boinao, was also missing—dead, his few family members staying with us in the same camp assumed. I heard a lot of things every day.

There was a visitor who wrote stories as a profession. I knew who she was; I had just never spoken to her. She knew I rarely talked or paid attention to anything other than food and camp chores, but she never gave up trying to sit with me. Her awkward giggles and strange way of asking questions drew me in. For some reason, I accepted her acquaintance.

One day, we sat by the river, gazing at the hills, painfully tall, hopelessly far. She had come with her aunt, who pointed out, 'Look at that line of engellei blooming across the foothills. It is as if the juncture between the hill and the plain is bleeding. The flowers are blooming uncontrollably. Painting everything as red as our blood….'

I waited for the writer's response. She sat quietly. She looked down, as if too overwhelmed.

'My brother is out there defending our village. He is yet to be found….' I began.

She turned, surprised. I rarely spoke unless pestered with a question.

I knew she wanted to feel things, everything in detail. It was a painful passion she nurtured.

She told me about her other aunt who had gone out onto the streets at night to guard the village. Her husband, who would earlier get drunk and then beat her, had been transformed by her bravery and now made meals and tea for her.

'Who would have thought? We always learn something different.' She chewed the words as if it meant more than just an event narrated.

What she learnt from the bleeding engellei I was not sure, but her face told me that she needed me as much as I needed her.

I began to tell her my story. Many a story will come, and for us, even one of them being heard counts, she said at the end of our little exchange on the riverbank.

BLACK MOON

AISU MINAM YIRANG

Like a herd of cows approaching a tub of water after long hours of grazing, a crowd of villagers swarmed in disorder through the narrow muddy path, now made slippery with the moss from the rain. The path led to the house where the group had collected itself. They walked with quick, curious strides and with an uncommon agility, never fumbling or uncertain in their steps, the bare skin of their feet so comfortable against the wet ground.

Appun sneaked through a crowd of murmurs to find out what the huge commotion was about. Her heart was beating fast. She had never seen a gathering of such scale before, not since her nephew's first birthday, which the entire village had attended. As she surfaced at the front, her gaze met an object standing lowly in a corner next to Uge, her ayo—aunt, who stood facing the crowd as if she wanted to address it. It appeared like a giant mushroom, pitch-black. It struck her that she had seen something similar elsewhere, but where could it have been? Appun dug into her memory. She wasn't sure if it was the same thing that she had once seen on TV. Oh! But what if it was?! Her heart leapt at that thought.

Earlier that morning, Appun had awakened, next to her sister, to a sudden spell of rain and not the usual crowing of the family rooster. There was nothing unusual about an unsolicited and untimely downpour in her village. The rains loved her village and came with vigour whenever they visited. The rains poured with a grandness, cutting through trees and thick foliage. It trickled faster than the tap water in Appun's house.

The loud pouring continued for hours, draining all the sounds around her. A layer of dampness engulfed her entire house, and she looked outside, knowing that her playing hours were slipping away behind the thick sheet of rain. She noticed the water rising a little above the ground. Appun sprang up and pleaded to her mother if she could make paper boats and set them sailing in the rainwater.

'I will take shelter under the house and play,' she assured her mother before she could say anything.

'I promise I won't get wet! And I will take the botok with me to protect myself from the rain. Please.'

With that, she darted towards the wall in the kitchen where all the botok and botari, the cone-shaped bamboo hat worn by women and men, were hung on nails along with old plastic bags containing plastic sheets and rusted nails. All of these assortments were collected diligently by Appun's grandmother who preached that everything could be reused and nothing should be thrown away. Appun picked up a dried bamboo from the corner to pluck the botok from the wall. Once she managed to pluck it, she picked it up and propped it on her head. Appun's tiny body disappeared inside the cone. And when she ran downstairs, the tail of the cone flapped behind her and trailed on the steps. Her six-year-old body did not have to bend in order to stand under the house. She stood next to one of the posts that held the house and moved her little hands above a landing where she hid her paper boats.

The rain had calmed down a little by then, and Appun wondered if she could go and find out what it was that propelled the villagers to leave all their work in the middle of the day and come together in such large numbers. She called out to her mother to tell her that she was going out and ran without even waiting for a response.

As Appun hopped away, humming a melody, her mother sang while working in the house, and her mother's shrill voice trailed behind her. Appun almost tripped on the slippery ground as she turned to check if her mother was looking in her direction or not. Her eyes caught her mother's and she giggled, embarrassed, as if she was being punished for running away like that.

Once Uge had beckoned everyone to settle, she flashed a toothy smile at the villagers. Appun noticed how funny she looked; the eyes looked like a single arc drawn on the face. Appun slapped herself on her thigh to focus, in case she missed the important revelation that was to come. Her ayo bent down and raised the object from where it was sitting on the ground and held it in front of her like a trophy. Suddenly, the entire room burst into chatter and everybody kept looking at each other, and then at the object, repeatedly.

Appun looked around to search for someone who could confirm that she had seen this somewhere before. A shaky voice chimed in through the whispers that were getting louder, 'Thandi hawa...kaali ghata (Cold wind…black clouds).'

All of them turned to look at the young woman who had spoken and after a brief pause, as if on cue, clapped in unison. They had heard the song at the cinema hall. The young woman glanced nervously at everyone when someone interrupted, crying, 'Sati, aying sati (Umbrella, the foreigner's Umbrella)!'

There was a fresh excitement in the air now.

It was an umbrella and this was the first time anybody in the village had seen one. They immediately turned their attention back on Appun's ayo, wondering what she had to say, what she'd like to do with it, and where did she find it?

Having the villagers' attention back on herself, the mother of the umbrella spoke with a glint of pride spread all over her face. The umbrella kept blocking her face as its handle was broken in half and she had to hold it close to her face. She had found the umbrella on the main road the other evening, and she had waited a long time for someone to come and claim it before she brought it back home. Realizing the enormous expectation hanging upon her, of what to do next, Appun's ayo announced with pride, 'Each one of you is welcome to borrow this umbrella for a certain period of time during summers and monsoons alike.'

Appun wanted to grab it first, but she stopped herself and thought that going first would mean a very rushed moment with the umbrella. So, she calmed her bouncing heart and stayed glued to the floor awaiting her turn. When her turn arrived, it was late in the afternoon. Appun quickly pounced on it and took it outside so that it would just be the two of them, the umbrella and her.

Appun rushed out to the courtyard, still glistening with wetness. She held the broken handle of the umbrella, and now almost invisible under it, twirled it, first upright, then on her shoulder, and then freeing it out in the air. She hummed a tune, and pretended to be in a movie, attempting a peek-a-boo and blushing behind the black moon. And while Appun played around some more with her new companion, her botok watched her in silence from a corner like a good spectator.

As if sensing a looming degradation of their friendship with the arrival of the umbrella in Appun's life, the botok wanted to call out to Appun. That evening, when Appun came back home, she was alone.

But she was too excited to realize that.

A week had passed, and all Appun wished for was the rain to not stop, scared that the Rain God would dismiss her plea against the wishes of the elders in the house. Appun prayed late every night before she went to bed because she wanted to be the last person to talk to the Rain God before the night slipped into a new day. The rest of the day, until bedtime, she watched her mother crying, complaining about the excessive rains that made working in the fields impossible. Appun's only wish was that the rain should not stop until it was her turn to hold the umbrella.

But the rain seemed to have gotten tired now. As its pace slowed down, Appun grew worried. She thought to herself, 'It's only the elders that God listens to, because God is also a grown-up and God doesn't understand us.'

Appun stopped talking to her mother and her mother's God. Instead, she started wishing for a child God who would truly understand and listen to her.

The next few days when it didn't rain, Appun refused to go and help her mother in the fields. The umbrella was in Appun's house now, collapsed in a corner, like a lifeless black chicken waiting to be cooked. And still no rain. The everyday sight of the umbrella in her home, showing no urgency of going over to the next person's hand, suddenly planted a feeling of doubt in Appun's heart. She found the initial excitement slowly dying and instead started wondering if this was all for nothing, when suddenly one morning, Appun was greeted by the sound of rain; it was the best sound she had ever heard. Her heart leapt and started dancing.

'I am accompanying you to the fields today, Mother!'

'But no getting wet! And no playing around,' her mother announced without any argument because she knew how long Appun had been waiting for this.

That day, Appun changed into her old clothes, ate breakfast with the umbrella next to her, and set out, leaving behind her botok. She ran here and there in the fields, taking the piles of saplings to her mother and the helpers, and showing off her new companion every single opportunity she got.

But after a while, when she wanted to help sow the saplings, she realized that the umbrella would not stay upright or sit comfortably over her shoulder. It kept slipping, and she struggled as everybody with their botoks left her far behind. She tried other methods: holding the umbrella under her jaw, holding it with one hand, inserting the handle inside the cloth behind her head, but she kept failing. Frustrated, she threw the umbrella away and lamented aloud, 'Mother! Don't these people go to the fields?'

Her mother gestured to her fellow helpers and they all smiled together. After so many weeks, Appun missed her botok!

The umbrella now stood outside on the veranda—dried mud caked inside it. Appun did not even look at it through the corner of her eyes. She wanted it out of her sight. She hated the umbrella for coming between her and her botok. Appun decided that it was best that it was sent back to its original owner, her ayo.

But there was a shock waiting for Appun, as news arrived that her ayo was gone. No one had seen her. It was as if she had just vanished into thin air without a trace. The villagers looked for her for days, even as Appun could hardly bear to glance at the umbrella and was so desperate to get rid of it. Every time she saw the umbrella, something boiled inside her. She would feel it slowly rise inside her and then override her entire being, and she would feel like breaking out of it by tearing her heart open.

Appun wanted nothing more than for these emotions to be tangible, to see it with her eyes and not only feel it. But in the end all Appun could do was weep, weep, and weep as if she were mourning. And when she was done, she felt so much better, like it was all that she needed. Appun could not understand why this was happening to her, but a glance at the umbrella would again make her crumble. Gradually, she became more and more aloof from her mother, her home, her own life, and all she thought about was how to find her ayo and give the umbrella back to her. Where had she gone? What was taking her so long? Was she lost somewhere? As time went by, these thoughts repeatedly played inside her head until one night, she decided that she herself would go find her.

It was after three in the morning when Appun jolted her sister into consciousness. They each took a battery-powered torch, and were made more awake as cold water touched their skin. It was now summer so they decided not to take any warm covers. Appun knew that this was the time when everyone was in deep sleep and no one would hear them. She just felt like she should go find her ayo.

They were walking in silence, when Appun's sister spoke. 'Do we know where we are going?'

Appun shuddered. Her sister threw her a look.

'I don't know, let's just keep walking,' Appun replied.

'Puna, I am doing this because you asked. Are you sure you want to go? I don't know why you are doing this but I trust you, you know. I just want to know you are sure,' her sister said.

'Oh, yes, yes, Aami, elder sister. We'll go east towards the main road.'

It was an open road and as they walked further, strange things started happening. Appun felt as if she saw someone lying on the edge of the road, but when she pointed it out to her sister, she saw nothing. Sometimes her sister would see something similar but Appun wouldn't. It was strange, not because they saw bodies lying on the edge of the road but because it didn't scare them at all. They just kept on walking.

As the day broke, the forest lining the road grew thicker and the road became narrower. It felt as if they were ascending into darkness, the air cold and bare. Not a word was spoken by Appun or her sister or by the spirits of the forest. Appun had no idea for how long they had been walking or how deep into the forest they were. But neither of them suggested that they stop and turn back. It felt right to keep walking.

The canopy of the trees blocked out the light. Appun and her sister were in a world where the sky was green and the air smelled of fresh dew, heady and damp like the inside of a bamboo shoot. Appun had never seen so much greenery. It was never-ending. Silence washed over the air, save for the faint footsteps of Appun and her sister. Appun almost felt knocked out of her senses when she heard a distant bird call. Then there was another, and another, and it felt like they were in their farm. The birdsong tugged at Appun's heart and she felt that everything would be okay.

They walked close to the left side, scanning every spot, careful not to miss anything. But the path was endless, and Appun was weary. After a few dozen miles, Appun thought that she saw a clearing to her left. She beckoned her sister and this time her sister saw it, too. Surprised that they could have missed something so obvious, they walked towards it. That was when Appun saw it. The body.

Ayo was wearing a shimmering, long, flowing, black ankle-length wraparound that outlined her bony legs. A little white top hugged her body tightly. She looked fresh, as if dressed for an occasion. She did not look hurt or tortured. There was not a single bruise or cut that marked her skin, but her eyes looked like they had seen something. Her face appeared spotless and normal. But the eyes had been somewhere and had seen something. They were scared, vacant, and rolled back. She lay there lifeless and broken like the umbrella in Appun's house. There was no trace of her breathing but she looked as if she would just turn and talk to the sisters at any moment.

Soon, a group of elders from the village found them, and they carried the lifeless body back. It was then, while they were walking back, that Appun realized that the day was drawing to an end. It didn't really seem like they had spent the whole day in the forest. Appun shuddered, expecting her mother to be furious back home. All the cane beatings her mother gave her came rushing back to her and she clasped her sister's hand.

But all her worries faded against the commotion that welcomed them. No one took any notice of Appun and her sister. It was like they had never gone. Everyone was talking about the body—where it was for so many days, what had happened to it, and how it ended up in the forest. A wind blew through the entire village carrying the news of the mayhem caused by the return of the lifeless body of the lost person.

It was a small village, so everything happened quickly. Appun and her sister were dragged away for a bath. Their mother washed them with her own hands. Appun understood that her mother was worried. At night, after the family had finished dinner and were sitting around the fire, Appun's mother prompted her to come and sit on her lap. The occupants of the house stayed awake for a long time that night, talking about what might have happened to Appun's ayo, Uge. Appun couldn't understand a thing but she knew that she would never forget a word of it. Seriousness washed over their faces, as Appun's grandmother narrated her clear speculation.

'In the land of the Adi, a lot of children were abducted and taken captive by the eepom, the forest-dwelling ghosts. Sometimes even the young women, men, and elders weren't spared. It is said that the eepom look just like ordinary, normal humans and often come to people in disguise of their close relatives. They are said to be heavily built and tall. These creatures live deep in the forests, on top of tall trees called the sirot rotnee. They also keep their captives there.

'It is believed that in order to bring back the captives, the eepom need to be appeased with offerings of meats, wild birds, and animals. The offering can be made by only one particular family member of the abducted person—their mother's brother. Search groups are led by him carrying machetes, daggers, axes, and they threaten to cut down or burn down the dwelling of the eepom if they are unable to find and free the victim. In many cases, after days of hunting through the forest in search of the victims, they have found them at random spots in the forest. They sometimes found the victims sitting casually or walking around normally, and other times, dead. I have heard all these stories about eepom abductions but never closely witnessed the return of the captives, whether dead or alive, so the whole truth will never be discovered. It must have been some foreign, outside person who would have brought the umbrella and left it there. It must have been a bait, a disguise. Uge didn't look normal. It looked like her soul had been robbed.'

After a brief pause, she added, 'The eepom took your jing, grandfather, too, when he was a young boy.'

Appun stirred uncomfortably on hearing Ojo's final revelation. A feeling of fear, curiosity, and amazement washed over her and ensnared her completely. In that moment, she turned as if to meet a stare. Sure enough, in the far-right corner where the wood was stacked, stood the night-black umbrella. It appeared so distant and foreign against the quaint, dirt-consumed, yellowed wall of Appun's house.

In that moment, Appun longed to hold her botok.

WE ALL KNOW SOMETHING ABOUT CHINA

MAYOOKH BARUA

Spring was a great time to handle a knife. It was not humid yet, so it wouldn't slip out of the fingers. It was not cold, so the fingers wouldn't freeze around the grip. There was free will in spring. So my mother took the knife and pointed it at me, then my father, and then at my brother. That was the way we were seated across the oval wooden table. She didn't point a butter knife, but a big Santoku knife. It was her favourite for it sliced through any fruits, even those with a hard shell. It gave her comfort. So, when she saw it lying next to the condiments on the rajma-brown dining table, she picked it up.

'One more discussion on China, and I will cut through all of you,' she threatened, moving the knife up and down.

The men around the table, arranged in a triangle, looked at the woman with the knife. Silence followed for a few seconds. At last, my father slurped on the rice and curry from the brass plate. My brother took a piece of mutton from the pot. I looked at my plate, the greens, yellows, and oranges somersaulting around my fingers. My mother slowly put the knife beside her, expecting to pull it back up again.

'Well, China's GDP is twenty times more than ours. There is no way we will be a superpower by 2050,' I blurted before taking in a mouthful of rice and other colours.

'There we go again,' my mother said, sighing. She looked at the knife beside her. There was an expectant raising of the shoulder, perhaps to pick up the knife again. But then those shoulders suffered an unexpected slump. She knew that for us the dining room did not serve food, and did not have a portrait of Lakshmi on the wall; instead there were microphones and military maps. We were wearing forest-green camouflage uniforms and not our Hanes boxers and Lux Cozi vests. And with every movement on the dinner plate, we were manoeuvring different pieces on the diorama of a conflict zone.

'It is not twenty times more than us. It is probably three times more,' my brother argued.

'That is not possible,' I said.

'I will check Wikipedia.' He fished the phone out from under the table.

'Why is there a phone at the dinner table?' my mother shouted.

'How much is it?' I asked, feeling happy that he was looking perplexed.

'Fourteen. We are two trillion dollars,' he whispered.

'Ha! Seven times then!'

'What are you ha-ing about? You said twenty times.' He shook his head from left to right. 'No, no, no, you always make up facts.' Then, as if to ridicule me, he laughed and howled.

'Overall, I am correct. We won't be able to beat China.'

'Anti-national. That is what you are. Anti-national. Your left-leaning university has taught you nothing but how to be a Maoist. What next? JNU?' My father tried to keep his gaze on his plate. The sentiment around Jawaharlal Nehru University has gone from being prestigious to insulting. It had become a party joke for adults. For boomers who voted for godmen, devil came in the form of students who threw a shawl over their shoulders, fashioned an unruly beard, and had one too many opinions about class inequality.

'What's so bad about being a leftist?' I asked.

'We will have World War III and it will be between India and China,' my father claimed, ignoring me. Since May 2020, the television went around talking about the great tussle between India and China. It was about the conquest of Aksai Chin, a disputed plot of land between the Asian neighbours. The infraction had flared up like a herpes sore since the 1950s, coming out of the blue, and with no solution but to see it through. Some say it began because of China's expansionist foreign policy, others say it is a consequence of a virulent India, all depending on the geopolitical orbits one wanted to satisfy. But like most things, the colonizers had not been able to make up their minds when it came to the borders between India and China. The region of Aksai Chin has been a source of conflict since the 1950s when a road that was being built by China, connecting Xinjiang and western Tibet, caused a stir within the Indian cabinet. And, instead of bombing Great Britian and saying, 'Short live the Queen', people just began fighting over where the border was drawn.

'That would be so great! I will go and fight!' my brother said. He had always wanted to be in the army. I marvelled at his unequivocal enthusiasm to fight. I wish I had something to be that committed to. But he had borrowed this energy from my father. Both had once aspired to be a part of the army, and had printed out the form to fill it. Both were discouraged by my mother's crying. They both excelled in their preferred contact sport, and moved their shoulders up and down when they laughed at their jokes. Their love language was maniacally hooting over good news, and they believed in integrity and their right to hold their ground.

'Even I will draft myself,' my father said, raising his fist.

'Who will you draft? You are fifty,' my mother reminded him.

'It is because of you he is like this,' he said, directing his voice from my mother to me. I laughed with my mouth open and a grain of rice fell onto the table. I didn't pick it up. My favourite contact sport was denial and speaking the wrong things at the right time, just like my mother. And my love language was disbanding myself into the abyss. I couldn't meet the men in my family somewhere in the middle. If there was a middle to begin with.

'We lost the last time. What do you want? Another loss?' I asked. My mother always told me that loss came in unexpected ways, and if one kept the door open, one day or the other, loss would walk in. A war was that open door. Perhaps my father forgot that when we lost the war, we had also lost a lot of people. But how could he remember? My parents were born in the decade when the Sino–Indian war broke out in 1962. The borders along the eastern side of the Himalayas were also rife with friction. The jagged lines along the mountains on the map denoted areas that belonged to either India or China. If these tall rocks could speak, would they have chosen a side? 'Hey! I am here for China', 'Don't disturb this Bhutanese beauty', 'India has already taken me folks!' I gravely doubted that any mountain would assertively suggest they belonged to anyone. Why should something so mammoth belong to one country? What would they gain? The sky, mountains, rivers, and trees don't choose. Instead, we choose them because they make us feel less of the speck that we are.

'Imbecile! You are a traitor! You should be ashamed!' My father slapped the wooden table for added auditory effect, which, for the most part, worked, but we were so used to it that after a few seconds of hesitation, we continued with our meal. 'Do you know how many young men have given up their lives to make this country safe?' he asked and looked right at me, perhaps for an answer.

'Well, why is this a general knowledge question? Who even knows that number? And why do we want more of these young people gone? Half of them fly abroad after engineering, and the rest are dead. Who will make the country a superpower, Dad? Some crinkly people in saffron dhotis?' I returned the jab, precisely because I didn't have an answer to his question. I doubted if he knew the answer himself. When did anyone at the dinner table know the number of lives lost in wars? I could've put a number; there may have been a few thousand. But that seems less. Maybe a lakh? A few lakhs? Even guessing felt like some kind of disrespect to the dead. And I can't have the dead against me during a heated argument.

'When we go to war and when we win—' he began.

'If we win, that is,' I corrected.

'When we win,' he slowly repeated, tilting his head towards me, 'we will become the superpower that we were predicted to become.' He opened his palms into the air. If not for the sheer militaristic force of his delivery, they could've made for perfect jazz hands.

'Indeed. Indeed. Indeed. We must become a superpower. After all, we'll get to do anything once we become that. Nobody can tell us anything. Look at the US. You need some optimism, brother. Cheer up. Imagine all the power we will have,' my brother said and elbowed the air with his free arm and winked.

'Superpower...sheesh.' My mother rolled her eyes. 'I think all three of you need to worry more about washing your underwear out of embarrassment instead of thinking about super or power.'

'Exactly! By the time we become a superpower, we will all be ashes. The world will fall apart into the oceans. And, even before that happens, who will compete with China? The ghosts of your lost priests?' I declared with my haughty nose pointed upwards.

'Oh Lord, imagine there could be aliens by then, and we could fight them as well. Dad, isn't that exciting? We'll be a superpower that will save the world,' said my brother, grains of rice falling out of his mouth with equal frantic enthusiasm.

'Hey! Can you chew your food inside your mouth, idiot?'

'You're an idiot,' he shouted back. 'Well, you wait and watch. With all these things that China has been doing—all their games, all this hiding information and getting into other people's houses—eventually,

eventually, you see, the world will take notice. And right then we will knock them off their high horse.'

'What do you mean by "their games"?' I asked, employing my debating skills. Whenever someone could not be argued with, ask for clarifications.

'This game of getting into other people's business. What are you even trying to argue here, Kakun? Do you think this world is made up of just people who live by the moral rulebook? Do you really think so? Do you think that we will get what we want by waiting for our turn?' My father's moustache touched his nose with anger.

I was left perplexed. I didn't know what to say. 'I am trying to argue that we don't need war in order to figure things out.'

'Well, brother, we don't live in that world. There is always someone dying. We just don't want to die.' My brother gave the final blow.

It was an eerie feeling to have a younger brother tell me about the need for death. I had always imagined it was my responsibility to tell him that the world was cruel, and yet, every day we needed to make a case for being alive. Instead, I turned to my father and asked, 'And who even predicted this thing for India? Some weird guy on the evening news?' I thought it was sensible of me to distract the other person with the machinations of logic, leading my opponent to a different topic since I did not have anything more to add.

'You're wrong. The great British philosopher Nostradamus predicted that India will be a superpower by 2030.'

'Wait, isn't he French, Dad?' my brother asked as he sucked the marrow from the bone. It was his favourite part of the meal.

'How does that matter, Jeet? British people, French people, they all look the same to me. They all have done the same thing. They all cry about the same thing without putting in any thought.' He took the last bite of the food, and having finished eating, flicked his fingers inside the circumference of the brass plate.

'Why do we have to do this again and again? What even is the point of such a discussion at the dinner table? Do you guys actually think this will bring about any resolution? What is the point of eating together when all you do is fight and argue?' my mother asked. She had barely eaten the rice on her plate.

'There is a lot to it that you won't understand, woman. Children need to know that letting go of the identity they were born with is not rewarding. We cannot escape our inheritance,' my father said. 'We will become a superpower.'

'That is logistically impossible. The numbers tell us everything. We can't take over China just like that,' I said, infuriated because I had lost my appetite even though I had barely eaten anything. My body needed nourishment, and I did not know how to provide that.

'What numbers do you want?' my brother asked.

'China has the largest manufacturing industry in the world. How do you even compete with something like that?' I told the table.

'That's a lie that the foreign media crafted to scare us. They want to make us weak. They want us to lose,' my father countered.

'India has the largest growing workforce in the world,' my brother said, placing his card on the table.

'China has more Olympic medals,' I said, as if that helped with winning the war.

'No, the US has more Olympic medals,' my brother contested.

'That's not true.'

'Check Wikipedia!' I challenged. On the first search, Michael Phelps came in. Then, we typed the country.

'Well, China has more than us, at least,' I said, resigning to the loss.

'Why do you like China so much?' my brother asked.

I looked at my brother. For a brief moment, I wanted to wish for him a stay in Delhi where people would call him 'Chinki'. I wanted him to be hooted at as though he were performing in a circus. I wanted to tell him that during some introduction he would claim to be from a tribe called Ahom, which he was proud of but it had its roots somewhere close to the border of present-day China. I perhaps lacked empathy. There was no reason for me to care for China or those who were Chinese and living in India, or for those who looked Chinese but had only known one national anthem. A nation, unlike other things, moves into intimate territories of the dinner table and breaks things. As it had done for a long time. But I did not want to wish these things on my brother. I was against the kind of understanding that came only from torment.

'Exactly! Ask your brother. What is he even talking about? The Chinese have pushed along the agreed lines. You don't understand that if we don't resist now, they will take things away from us.'

'Why do you want to go to war so badly?' I pleaded, wanting to know why people fought at all. I could not understand how people could choose to eliminate others only to make space for themselves. How did anyone's death help anybody? Perhaps it did. Death, after all, comes with certain gifts like new life. But to want it? How could we want something that gave us nothing but sadness for a long time?

'All right, enough is enough. This is not a conversation we have at the dinner table. You go kill other people in wars but don't kill people on the dinner table,' my mother said. She picked up her now-empty plate and left the table.

'Well, there is no point in continuing this conversation,' my father declared. He washed his hand, pouring water from his glass, and stood up.

And I was left with the cold curry that darkened the half-broken hill of rice. I tried to eat it again but couldn't. Everyone held their ground for their own reasons. Some for the stories they believed in, some for the truths they held onto, and some for the narratives of their own selfhood.

'Relax brother, you can write about us in glory after the war,' my brother said and winked as he took the plate to the kitchen.

My plate was empty. That's all I had.

ACKNOWLEDGEMENTS

I would like to thank the people who have been instrumental in bringing this anthology to light. First, to the writers and translators, without whom these stories would not exist. Second, to the people at Aleph who first reached out to me with ideas for this book: to David Davidar, Aienla Ozukum, and Shatakshi Singh, who were with me every step of the way. Aienla and Shatakshi, thank you for stilling my nerves in my maiden voyage through anthology-making. I have learned so much from you. Third, to my friends and family who give me the time and space to pursue my dreams: Vivek and Mehdi, Pa, Mei, Kong Meetu and Miw Maw, Reuben and Meba, Amma, Achhan, and Vandana. To Avinash, Tessa, Lanette, Elouza, Leki, Lapdiang, Bhogtoram, Lima, Alex, Feba, Mohib, and Ramesh for being there for me through calm and troubled seas. This would not have happened without you. Fourth, to my academic mentors, Professors Anna Kurian and Pramod K. Nayar who, in asking me to write about the Northeast, made me realize how rich and valuable the literature from that region is. To Professor K. Narayana Chandran, who was the first to encourage my interest in anthologies. Fifth, to my colleagues at Vidyashilp University: Priyambada, Tania, and Kavya, for giving me room to breathe and exist just as I am. For being fierce, independent women and making me realize that I could be one too.

~

Grateful acknowledgement is made to the following copyright holders for permission to reprint copyrighted material in this volume.

'Rats' by Bhabendra Nath Saikia, translated by Gayatri Bhattacharyya, is reprinted by permission of Preeti Saikia.

'Intermission' by Saurav Kumar Chaliha, translated by Stuti Goswami, is reprinted by permission of the translator.

'Values' by Mamoni Raisom Goswami, translated by Gayatri Bhattacharyya, is reprinted by permission of South East Asia Ramayana Research Centre.

'Laburnum for My Head' by Temsula Ao is reprinted by permission of Penguin Random House India. The story was first published in *Laburnum for My Head: Stories*, in 2009.

'Child of Fortune' by Nini Lungalang is reprinted by permission of Tamara. The story was first published in *India International Centre Quarterly*, in 2005.

'The Smell of Bamboo Blossoms' by Yeshe Dorjee Thongchi, translated by Aruni Kashyap, is reprinted by permission of the author and the translator.

'Brothers' by Mamang Dai is reprinted by the permission of the author.

'Ka Diangtimai' by Desmond L. Kharmawphlang, translated by Ellerine Diengdoh, is reprinted by the permission of the author and the translator.

'His Mother's Pork and Why He Is Not a Christian' by Kynpham Sing Nongkynrih is reprinted by permission of the author. The story was previously published in the *Indian Quarterly*.

'The Cost of Hunger' by Abdus Samad, translated by Aruni Kashyap is reprinted by permission of the author and the translator.

'The Question of Style' by Anjum Hasan is reprinted by permission of Penguin Random House India. The story was first published in *A Day in the Life*, in 2018.

'News of a Beloved Friend' by Sudhiranjan Moirangthem, translated by Soibam Haripriya, is reprinted by permission of the author and the translator.

'The Song' by Namrata Pathak is reprinted by permission of the author.

'Boats on Land' by Janice Pariat is reprinted by permission of Penguin Random House India. The story was first published in *Boats on Land: A Collection of Short* Stories, in 2012.

'For the Greater Common Good' by Aruni Kashyap is reprinted by permission of the author.

'Making Amends' by Prajwal Parajuly is reprinted by permission of the author. The story was first published on *Mint*, in 2015.

'Dielienuo's Choice' by Avinuo Kire is reprinted by permission of Zubaan Books. The story was first published in *The Power to Forgive: And Other Stories*, in 2015.

'The Pay Raise' by Gankhu Sumnyan is reprinted by permission of the author. The story was first published in *Out of Print* in September 2022.

'The Aftermath' by Mainu Teronpi is reprinted by permission of the author.

'The Madness of Tree Ghosts' by Shalim M Hussain is reprinted by permission of the author.

'Home' by Ramzauva Chhakchhuak is reprinted by permission of the author.

'Sacred Pool' by Rishav Kumar Thakur is reprinted by permission of the author.

'The Lover of Stories' by Lede E Miki Pohshna is reprinted by permission of the author.

'Riang Khangnoh' by Saweini Laloo is reprinted by permission of the author.

'The Bleeding Flowers' by Linthoi Chanu is reprinted by permission of the author. The story was first published on *Mint Lounge*, in 2024.

'Black Moon' by Aisu Minam Yirang is reprinted by permission of the author.

'We All Know Something About China' by Mayookh Barua is reprinted by permission of the author.

NOTES ON THE AUTHORS

Abdus Samad is the author of six novels and two fiction collections, including *Boi Jai Chompaboti, Kurukhetrar Akhora*, and *Bonkukurar Daak*. Widely loved and read in Assam, his subversive fiction critiques Assamese nationalism and religious divides and often depicts the life of the immigrant Muslim community of Bengal origin in Assam. He is the winner of some of the highest literary awards in Assam, such as the Munin Borkotoky Award (2006) and the President's Centenary Literary Award (2017) from Asom Sahitya Sabha.

Aisu Minam Yirang is an Arunachal Pradesh-based writer. She is a postgraduate in English Literature and writes both fiction and creative non-fiction. Her personal essays are published in *Globally Rooted* and *The Blahcksheep*. She is working on a historical memoir about her grandfather.

Anjum Hasan is a novelist, short story writer, poet, and editor. Her works have been shortlisted for the Indian Academy of Letters Prize, the Sahiya Akademi Award, the Hindu Best Fiction Award, and the Crossword Fiction Award, as well as being longlisted for the Man Asia Literary Prize and the DSC Prize for South Asian Literature. Her short fiction and essays have appeared in *Granta, Paris Review, Los Angeles Review of Books*, among many others.

Aruni Kashyap is the author of the novels *How to Date a Fanatic, The House With a Thousand Stories, Noikhon Etia Duroit*, and the story collection *His Father's Disease*. Along with editing a collection of stories called *How to Tell the Story of an Insurgency*, he has translated three novels from Assamese to English. Recipient of a Harvard Radcliffe Fellowship, the National Endowment for the Arts Fellowship, the Faculty Research Grant in the Humanities and Arts Program, the Arts Lab Faculty Fellowship, and the Charles Wallace India Trust Scholarship for Creative Writing to the University of Edinburgh, his poetry collection, *There is No Good Time for Bad News*, was nominated for several prestigious awards. He is an associate professor of English & Creative Writing and the director of the Creative Writing program at the University of Georgia, Athens.

Avinuo Kire is a writer and teacher. She is the author of *The Power to Forgive and Other Stories*, *The Last Light of Glory Days and Other Stories*, *Where the Cobbled Path Leads*, and a collection of poetry, *Where Wildflowers Grow*, and has co-authored an anthology of oral narratives entitled *Naga Heritage Centre, People Stories: Volume One*. Kire lives in Kohima where she teaches English at Kohima College.

Bhabendra Nath Saikia (1932–2003), filmmaker, playwright, and writer, was a recipient of the Sahitya Akademi Award for fiction. He was also a Padma Shri awardee, as well as a recipient of seven Rajat Kamal awards for his films, several of which are based on his own stories. He was also a recipient of the Srimanta Sankardeva Award and the Assam Valley Literary Award. A teacher of Physics at Gauhati University, he was also a member of the Sangeet Natak Akademi, New Delhi. Among his works are three novels, eleven short story collections, twenty-eight plays, several books for children, and collections of essays. His short stories are known for their delineation of character and their psychological motivations, as well as their powers of observation and plotting.

Desmond L. Kharmawphlang is a poet, folklorist and short story writer. He has published collections of poetry and books on folklore and folkloristics. He has collected, compiled, and edited folk narratives and folk songs of Northeast India. An Associate Member of the Folk Fellows instituted by the Finnish Academy of Science and Letters, Helsinki, he has held teaching positions as visiting fellow and professor at various universities in India and abroad. He teaches folkloristics at North-Eastern Hill University, Shillong. He is principal investigator of 'Protecting Endangered Heritage in the Abode of Clouds', a project undertaken in collaboration with Melbourne University and sponsored by the British Library. He is also principal investigator of the project 'Folklore, Wildlife and Nature:A Study on their Inter-relationships', sponsored by the North Eastern Council, Government of India.

Gankhu Sumnyan teaches English at W. R. Govt. College, Deomali, Arunachal Pradesh. His short stories have appeared in magazines like *Out of Print, Gulmohur Quarterly, East India Story, Cafe Dissensus*, as well as in the anthology *The Best Asian Short Stories,* 2021 (Kitaab, Singapore). He also has a poetry book titled *Old Friends' Parade* with Writers Workshop,

Kolkata. His poems have appeared in the magazines *Muse India, Indian Literature, The Little Journal of Northeast India*, and others.

Janice Pariat is the author of *Boats on Land: A Collection of Short Stories*, the novels *Seahorse*, *Everything the Light Touches*, and *The Nine Chambered-Heart*, bestselling in India, and translated into ten languages including Italian, Spanish, French, and German. She was awarded the Young Writer Award from the Sahitya Akademi and the Crossword Book Award for Fiction in 2013.

Kynpham Sing Nongkynrih writes poetry, drama, and fiction in Khasi and English. He is the winner of the Shakti Bhatt Prize 2024. His latest works are *The Distaste of the Earth, Funeral Nights, Late-Blooming Cherries: Haiku Poetry from India* (co-edited) and *Lapbah: Stories from the North-east* (co-edited). His other recent works include *Dancing Earth: An Anthology of Poetry from the Northeast* (co-edited), *The Yearning of Seeds* and *Time's Barter: Haiku and Senryu*. He teaches literature at North-Eastern Hill University, Shillong.

Lede E Miki Pohshna is a writer based in Sohkha Mission, Meghalaya. He has a doctorate in queer literature and actively engages in research on queerness. His works, both academic and creative, have been published in *Rupkatha Journal of Interdisciplinary Studies, Dialog, The Criterion, Society and Culture of South Asia,* the *Bangalore Review, Gulmohur Quarterly, Café Dissensus,* and others.

Mainu Teronpi is an assistant professor in the department of English at Chandra Kamal Bezbaruah College, Teok, Jorhat. She hails from the town of Diphu, Karbi Anglong, Assam. A poet and storyteller, her work often explores the themes of women and nature, reflecting a deep sensitivity to personal and environmental narratives.

Mamang Dai is a poet, novelist, and journalist based in Itanagar, Arunachal Pradesh. Her poetry, fiction, and articles have appeared in numerous journals and anthologies. Her published works include a poetry collection, *River Poems*; a book of interlinked stories, *The Legends of Pensam,* and a novella, *Stupid Cupid*. She received the Verrier Elwin Award in 2003 for her book *Arunachal Pradesh: The Hidden Land* and was awarded the Padma Shri in

2011 in recognition of her contributions in the fields of literature and education.

Mamoni Raisom Goswami (1942–2011), also known as Indira Goswami, is a Jnanpith awardee, a Sahitya Akademi awardee, and a noted Ramayan scholar whose work was recognized and lauded worldwide. Though awarded a Padma Shri, she declined the award. She was also the recipient of the Principal Prince Claus Laureate Award of the Netherlands, the monetary component of which she donated to charitable causes. Among the numerous other awards she received were the Kamal Kumari Award, the Mahiyoshi Joymoti Award, the Katha National Award, a honorary DLitt degree from Rabindra Bharati University, West Bengal, The International Tulsi Award, and the highest civilian award of the government of Assam, the Assam Ratna. Her popular novels are *Chenabor Srot, Neelkanthi Braja, Mamore Dhora Torowal, Dontal Hatir Uiyey Khowa Howdah, Tej aru Dhulirey Dhuxorito Prishtha, Thengphakhri Tehsildaror Tamor Tarowal* as also several collections of short stories and autobiographical works.

Mayookh Barua is a Los Angeles-based writer from Northeast India. He is currently a PhD candidate in USC's Creative Writing and Literature Department. His work explores sexuality, art, mythology, education, and family through a queer South Asian voice. He is a 2025 Anthony Veasna So Scholar, 2025 Lambda Emerging Writer Fellow, and 2023 Roots. Wounds.Words Fellow and his work appears or is forthcoming in *Michigan Quarterly Review, The Adroit Journal, LunchTicket, The Pedestal Magazine, The Audacity* by Roxane Gay, and elsewhere.

Namrata Pathak is an academic, critic, and writer. She is a recipient of FCT Library Fellowship and UGC-Associateship by IIAS, Shimla. She has six books to her credit, and her latest books are *Indira Goswami: Margins and Beyond* (Routledge, 2022) and *A Reader on Arun Sarma* (Sahitya Akademi, 2024). She was a Charles Wallace India Trust Fellow at SOAS University of London, 2022–2023. She is featured in *Riverside Stories: Writings from Assam* (2024), the anthology from Assam published by Zubaan; *Mukoli* magazine (2023) housed in the School of Conflict Management, Peacebuilding and Development in Kennesaw State University; *Muse India* (2024) special issue on Literature from the Northeast curated by Bibhash Choudhury; the *Sangam House Monsoon Issue: A Special on Poetry from North East*, July, 2019, curated by Nitoo Das.

Nini Lungalang (1948–2019) was a poet, writer, teacher, and musician. She was known for her works in English and her contribution to the Naga literature. She attended Loreto Convent in Shillong, St. Edmund's College, and then Delhi University. She taught literature and classical music at Baptist College in Kohima during its early years and later served as Vice-Principal at Northfield School in Kohima till 2019. In 2020, her complete collection of poetry was published posthumously in a reprinted edition of *The Morning Years* by PenThrill.

Prajwal Parajuly is an Indian writer whose works include the short-story collection *The Gurkha's Daughter*, which was shortlisted for the 2013 Dylan Thomas Prize and longlisted for The Story Prize that same year, and the novel *Land Where I Flee.* His works have also been nominated for the Mogford Prize in the UK, and the Emile Guimet Prize and the First Novel Prize in France. He was a judge for the Dylan Thomas Prize in 2018 and 2023. His writing focuses on Nepali-speaking people and their culture.

Potsangbam Linthoingambi Chanu, known as Linthoi Chanu, is an award-winning writer hailing from Imphal, Manipur. She has established herself as a prominent voice in contemporary literature with a diverse portfolio spanning children's literature, speculative fiction, and mytho-historical narratives. Her notable works include The Child Who Played with Spirits (2023), a poignant children's book; *Wayel Kati* (2023), a speculative fiction piece; *The Tales of Kanglei Throne* (2017), a mytho-historical novel, and *The Bleeding Flower* (2024), a distinguished short fiction piece featured on *Mint Lounge* and more.

Ramzauva Chhakchhuak is a writer and social media manager based in Bengaluru. His short stories, creative nonfiction, and travelogues have appeared in the *New Indian Express, Himal Southasian, Helter Skelter Anthology, Loft Books, NatGeo India, The Hindu Businessline, Deccan Herald,* and various journals and webzines. Ramzauva is currently working on a novel-in-stories set in his hometown in Shillong, Meghalaya.

Rishav Kumar Thakur is a New York-based writer from Northeast India. They are a PhD candidate in Columbia University's ISSG and Anthropology department. Their work explores belonging, play, pedagogy and pleasure through a study of nightlife in Assam. They are an Elaine Combs-Shillings Memorial Fellow (2022) and the curator of Queer Objects, a community incubator in Assam, which they launched with a Zubaan–Sasakawa Grant (2023). Their work appears or is forthcoming in *Insurgent Domesticities Anthology*, *Queer & Trans Life: Anthropological Futures*, *Borderlines*, *Allegra Lab*, *TheChinkyHomoProject,* and elsewhere.

Saurav Kumar Chaliha (1930–2011) was the pen name of academic and writer Surendra Nath Medhi. A teacher of Physics at the Assam Engineering College, Guwahati, his works are credited with giving a new direction to Assamese fiction, especially short stories. A Sahitya Akademi awardee, he was also a recipient of the Assam Valley Literary Award. The story 'Oxanto Electron', written in 1950 when he was very young, created waves when it first appeared, and has influenced many writers. He wrote for literary journals and periodicals such as *Banhi, Ramdhenu, Dainik Asom,* and so on. His stories were compiled into several collections, some of which are *Ehat Daba* and *Oxanto Electron.*

Saweini Laloo is a research scholar and assistant professor based in Shillong, India. Her writing has appeared in *The Bombay Literary Magazine, Muse India, Zubaan, Teesta Review: A Journal of Poetry, Induswomanwriting,* and *Caesurae Magazine.* In addition to her academic and literary pursuits, she is also an illustrator.

Shalim M Hussain is a writer based in Assam. His books include *Betel Nut City* (2019), a poetry collection that won the RL Poetry Award 2017; *Post-Colonial Poems* (2019), a translation of Kamal Kumar Tanti's Sahitya Akademi winning poetry anthology; *Again I Hear These Waters* (2024), a collection of translated Miyah poems, and *Asimot Jar Heral Sima* (2025), a translation of Kanchan Baruah's classic Assamese novel of the same name. His poetry, short stories, essays, and translations have been anthologized in *The Penguin Book of Indian Poets* (2022), *Sahitya Akademi Modern English Poetry by Younger Indians* (2019), and *Penguin Complete Short Stories of Premchand* (2018) among others. He has held the Charles Wallace India Trust Creative Writing and Translation Fellowship (2019-20) and been awarded the PEN Translates Award (2021) by English PEN.

Sudhiranjan Moirangthem is an associate professor at Jiri College, Jiribam. He has a doctorate in chemistry. While a scholar of science, he is an avid lover of literature and popular short story writer. His collection of short stories, *Nungshiraba Marupki Mapao,* published in 2004, won the Thokchom Yogendra Memorial Gold Medal (2005), an award for young writers instituted by Naharol Sahitya Premi Samiti.

Temsula Ao (1945–2022) was a celebrated poet, short story writer, and ethnographer from Nagaland. She was a key figure in the literature of Northeast India, often highlighting themes of tribal identity, displacement, and the resilience of the Naga people. Her works, such as the short story collection *These Hills Called Home* and the poetry collection *Songs That Tell*, deeply reflect the oral traditions and folklore of her Ao Naga community. Beyond literature, she was an advocate for indigenous cultures and women's rights, contributing significantly to preserving Naga heritage. Ao was awarded the Padma Shri and the Sahitya Akademi Award for her contributions to literature and advocacy.

Yeshe Dorjee Thongchi is an acclaimed writer from Arunachal Pradesh, known for his contributions to Assamese literature. Born in a Serdukpen tribal family, he began his literary journey by writing poetry, later shifting to short stories and novels. Thongchi's works vividly depict the customs and traditions of various tribal communities in Arunachal Pradesh, reflecting their struggles with modernity. A retired civil servant, Thongchi has been honoured with prestigious awards like the Padma Shri and the Sahitya Akademi Award.

NOTES ON THE TRANSLATORS

Aruni Kashyap is the author of the novels *How to Date a Fanatic, The House With a Thousand Stories, Noikhon Etia Duroit*, and the story collection *His Father's Disease*. Along with editing a collection of stories called *How to Tell the Story of an Insurgency*, he has translated three novels from Assamese to English. Recipient of a Harvard Radcliffe Fellowship, the National Endowment for the Arts Fellowship, the Faculty Research Grant in the Humanities and Arts Program, the Arts Lab Faculty Fellowship, and the Charles Wallace India Trust Scholarship for Creative Writing to the University of Edinburgh, his poetry collection, *There is No Good Time for Bad News*, was nominated for several prestigious awards. He is an Associate Professor of English & Creative Writing and the Director of the Creative Writing Program at the University of Georgia, Athens.

Ellerine Diengdoh teaches English at Saint Mary's College, Shillong, where she has been on the faculty since 2002. She is also the college choir director and founded her own choir in the same year, reflecting her deep engagement with music and cultural expression. Her academic interests include Romanticism, Irish bardic poetry, Khasi folklore, and popular music studies. Her research spans topics from African American women's music to Shillong's traditional Iewduh market. A trained soprano, she was part of the acclaimed Aroha Choir and the Shillong Chamber Choir and served as the general secretary of the Aroha Music and Cultural Society. As a composer and translator, Diengdoh brings an interdisciplinary voice to both literary and musical landscapes. She is a regular contributor to the *Shillong Times*, where her satirical and humorous opinion pieces explore pressing contemporary issues in Meghalaya.

Gayatri Bhattacharyya worked in St. Edmund's College, Shillong, before joining Gauhati University. After retirement, she took up translation as a hobby, and has since translated many anthologies of short stories and novels written by eminent Assamese writers, into English, including works by Sarat Chandra Goswami, Bhabendra Nath Saikia, Mamoni Raisom Goswami, Anuradha Sarma Pujari, Dipak Barkakati, and Birinchi Kumar Barua. She has written fifteen books, and has published short stories and articles in anthologies and newspapers.

Soibam Haripriya is an assistant professor of Sociology and a member of the Ethnography Lab at the Indraprastha Institute of Information Technology-Delhi. She has edited the multi-genre anthology *Homeward* (2022) published by Zubaan. Her key areas of interest are gender, violence, Northeast India, and poetry and/in ethnography. She is also a poet and translator. Her poems have appeared in anthologies such as *Witness: The Red River Book of Poetry of Dissent* (2021), *A Map Called Home* (2018), *Centrepiece* (2017), *40 Under 40: An Anthology Of Post-Globalization Poetry* (2016). Some of her poems have been included in the issues of *Muse India* (May–June 2019), *Poetry at Sangam* (July 2019), and the bi-monthly journal of Sahitya Akademi—Indian Literature. Her translations have appeared in *Crafting the Word* (2019).

Stuti Goswami is a bilingual author, translator, and editor. Her writing has appeared in regional, national, and a few international publications including the *Times of India, Assam Tribune, Sentinel, MuseIndia, Silhouette, English Language Notes, Quest, Café Dissensus, Nezine, Satsari, Prakash*. She shares editing credits in books published by Gauhati University Press (2015), National Book Trust of India (2018), Red River, New Delhi (2022), Asam Sahitya Sabha (2022). She is currently translating Manipuri poet Thangjam Ibopishak's poetry collection into Assamese. She has been invited to speak at seminars, workshops, and literary festivals at Sahitya Akademi, Tezpur University, Cotton University, Indira Gandhi National Centre for the Arts (IGNCA). She has digitized all issues of *Jonaki* (for the years 1901,1902,1903) and is in the initial stage of documentation of plant-based folk tales from Northeast India. Her areas of interest and specialization are Translation studies, British Assam, plant studies, traditional knowledge systems, and Northeast India studies.

www.ingramcontent.com/pod-product-compliance
Lightning Source LLC
Chambersburg PA
CBHW020912310726
48980CB00011B/849/J

* 9 7 8 9 3 6 5 2 3 6 7 8 1 *